Dedalus European
General Editor: Mike

En Route

J. K. Huysmans

En Route

Translated by W. Fleming
and with an introduction by David Blow

Dedalus

eastengland|arts

Published in the UK by Dedalus Ltd,
Langford Lodge, St Judith's Lane, Sawtry, Cambs, PE28 5XE
email: DedalusLimited@compuserve.com
web site: www.dedalusbooks.com

ISBN 1 873982 14 3

Dedalus is distributed in the United States by SCB Distributors,
15608 South New Century Drive, Gardena, California 90248
email: info@scbdistributors.com   web site: www.scbdistributors.com

Dedalus is distributed in Australia & New Zealand by Peribo Pty Ltd,
58 Beaumont Road, Mount Kuring-gai N.S.W. 2080
email: peribo@bigpond.com

Dedalus is distributed in Canada by Marginal Distribution,
Unit 102, 277 George Street North, Peterborough, Ontario, KJ9 3G9
email: marginal@marginalbook.com   web site: www.marginal.com

Dedalus is distributed in Italy by Apeiron Editoria & Distribuzione,
Localita Pantano, 00060 Sant'Oreste (Roma)
email: grt@apeironbookservice.com   web site: apeironbookservice.com

Publishing History
First published in France in 1895
First Dedalus edition 1989
New Dedalus edition 2002

Introduction copyright © Dedalus 1989

Printed in Finland by WS Bookwell

A C.I.P. listing for this book is available on request.

INTRODUCTION

Some writers relentlessly explore obsessions which
may, at first sight, appear strange and
uncompromisingly esoteric. Are their obsessions ours ?
To comprehend them, you have to know something
about their life and times. Joris-Karl Huysmans is one
such monomaniac. His preoccupations were distinctly
his own, but by pouring them into his fiction he gave
them a wide currency. Huysmans more or less
invented the modern anti-hero, the solitary, agonised
and alienated individual.

     Huysmans spent most of his professional life as
a clerk in the Ministry of the Interior. But his career
as a writer unwound against a more inspiring
background. Edmond de Goncourt inspired *Marthe*
(1876), Huysmans' first novel, and his next, *Les Soeurs
Vatard* (1879), was dedicated to Zola. Huysmans early
novels associated his name with the naturalism of Guy
de Maupassant, Paul Alexis and Zola himself. But *A
Rebours* (1884) marked a new departure, both for
Huysmans and, eventually, for the European novel in
general. Zola called the book 'a terrible blow to
naturalism.' It flaunted Baudelaire's influence and
contained references to Mallarme and Verlaine.
Moreover, *A Rebours* was transparently
autobiographical. The main character, Des Esseintes,
was the very embodiment of late-nineteenth-century
decadence, a role model for twilight people, but little
more than a thinly disguised version of the author.
In his subsequent novels, of which *En Route* (1895) is
one, Huysmans continued the journey of self-discovery
that he had initiated in *A Rebours*. And it is a sign of
the success of his enterprise that so many of his
obsessions and worries should now sound so
familiar.Decadence, its colours, smells and textures
(mauve, incense and velvet), pervade his writing. It

was a moral predicament, an artistic posture, and the natural outcome of his loss of religious faith.

Huysmans' later novels tell of how he was consumed by decadence, but also describe how he emerged from it. Three novels in particular lead us into decadence and out again. *La Bas* (1891), *En Route* (1895), and *La Cathedrale* (1898) form an autobiographical trilogy.

La Bas is a dark tale of Satanism and brutal impiety. Relieved of his religion by the pressures of modern life, by science, technology and the encroachments of American culture, Huysmans, in the form of a character named Durtal, finds himself adrift in a sea of doubt. Durtal dabbles in black magic and weird travesties of scientific investigation. In *En Route*, Durtal is morally mended and spiritually healed, led back to God by art and aesthetic inspiration. Architecture and music rekindle his belief and by the end of the novel Durtal has retired to a Trappist monastery.

In *La Cathedrale*, Durtal finds himself in Chartres cathedral, amazed by the architectural virtues of the place and, again, led to God by art and music. A gothic gloom and density pervades all three novels, and Huysmans is constantly preoccupied with the vestiges of medievalism, and with pre-scientific modes of thought. The modern world, we gather, is too much with him. He shrinks from the future and finds spiritual comfort in the past. He recoils from the prospect of modernity, and finds refuge in old art and older religion.

His anti-modernism, paradoxically, makes Durtal sound like a distinctly modern character. And it is no small part of Huysmans' achievement to have invented him. Like the alienated individuals of twentieth-century fiction, he is at odds with his surroundings, a victim of history, unsure of himself, dragged down by unhealthy living, and on the look-out for something valuable in a worthless world. He is wary of the brevity of life and his ennui and neuroses have a contemporary ring.

Huysmans' late-nineteenth-century decadence has something in common with our late-twentieth-century condition, and begins to look like the shadow of post-modernism. In common with Huysmans, some of our deepest and most persistent worries appear to mock nineteenth-century certainties. For example, a hundred years ago it was easy to be sure about the future, to have settled, stable thoughts about what the future would look like. It was easy to be confident that science and the march of progress would see to that. But the decadents, and many of us, are not so sure. A hundred years ago people dreamed of the coming of the modern age. Now we are tempted to look back and put modernity behind us. Huysmans sought refuge in a more distant past, while his contemporaries looked to a future made clean and safe by science. They were sure that the future would come and that it would be a better place. We wonder about tomorrow and entertain the idea that whatever the future holds in store for us, it is most likely to be a run-down version of the way things are now.

Perhaps our feeling that modernity has failed stems from our doubts about science, from our suspicion that science is an unreliable engine of progress. If the rise of science made the world a disenchanted place, then we are growing tired and disenchanted with science. Our hopes are changing colour and gradually turning green. People who were blinded by science are now searching for something more substantial. The contemporary recoil from science has all the trappings of a crisis of faith and we are prone to viewing that great nineteenth-century promise, the promise that science will promote progress, with irony and detachment. And that detachment, that suspension of belief, is fostering a second wave of decadence.

Huysmans' fiction has gained a new lease of life because our concerns are drifting closer to his. Now we are beginning to lose our faith in science and modernity, and science is beginning to look like just one more way of thinking dogmatically. So there is a fresh sense of freedom in the air; but also an odour of danger. It is a danger which lies at the disillusioned heart of Huysmans' later novels. A hundred years ago the rise of science provoked a flight from religion. Those who lost their faith either embraced the new materialism of the sciences or drifted into an unspecified zone of doubt. Huysmans tells the story of faith lost and found. His later novels tell a success story. But what if that quest had failed? What would have become of Durtal? God's death, for Huysmans, was a temporary demise. The objects which surround the business of worship, the art and institutions of prayer, pointed the way to Rome. But that recursive journey took Huysmans along a road that is less easy to navigate now the millenium is on the horizon. That is part of the fascination of the literature of decadence. It describes a familiar point of departure. Where we will end up is hard to say.

David Blow

EN ROUTE.

CHAPTER I.

DURING the first week in November, the week within the Octave of All Souls, Durtal entered St. Sulpice, at eight o'clock in the evening. He often chose to turn into that church, because there was a trained choir, and because he could there examine himself at peace, apart from the crowd. The ugliness of the nave, with its heavy vaulting, vanished at night, the aisles were often empty, it was ill-lighted by a few lamps—it was possible for a man to chide his soul in secret, as if at home.

Durtal sat down behind the high altar, on the left, in the aisle along the Rue de St. Sulpice ; the lamps of the choir organ were lighted. Far off, in the almost empty nave, an ecclesiastic was preaching. He recognized, by the unctuousness of his delivery, and his oily accent, a well-fed priest who poured on his audience, according to his wont, his best known commonplaces.

" Why are they so devoid of eloquence ? " thought Durtal. " I have had the curiosity to listen to many of them, and they are much the same. They only vary in the tones of their voice. According to their temperament, some are bruised down in vinegar, others steeped in oil. There is no such thing as a clever combination." And he called to mind orators petted like tenors, Monsabré, Didon, those Coquelins of the Church, and lower yet than those products of the Catholic training school, that bellicose booby the Abbé d'Hulst.

" Afterwards," he continued, " come the mediocrities, each puffed by the handful of devotees who listen to them. If those cooks of the soul had any skill, if they served their clients with delicate meats, theological essences, gravies of prayer, concentrated sauces of ideas, they would vegetate misunderstood by their flocks. So, on the whole, it is all for the best. The low-water mark of the clergy must conform to the level of the faithful, and indeed Providence has provided carefully for this."

A stamping of shoes, then the movement of chairs grinding on the flags interrupted him. The sermon was over.

Then a great stillness was broken by a prelude from the organ, which dropped to a low tone, a mere accompaniment to the voices.

A slow and mournful chant arose, the " De Profundis." The blended voices sounded under the arches, intermingling with the somewhat raw sounds of the harmonicas, like the sharp tones of breaking glass.

Resting on the low accompaniment of the organ, aided by basses so hollow that they seemed to have descended into themselves, as it were underground, they sprang out, chanting the verse " De profundis ad te clamavi, Do—" and then stopped in fatigue, letting the last syllables " mine " fall like a heavy tear ; then these voices of children, near breaking, took up the second verse of the psalm, " Domine exaudi vocem meam," and the second half of the last word again remained in suspense, but instead of separating, and falling to the ground, there to be crushed out like a drop, it seemed to gather itself together with a supreme effort, and fling to heaven the anguished cry of the disincarnate soul, cast naked, and in tears before God.

And after a pause, the organ, aided by two double-basses, bellowed out, carrying all the voices in its torrent—baritones, tenors, basses, not now serving only as sheaths to the sharp blades of the urchin voices, but openly with full throated sound—yet the dash of the little soprani pierced them through all at once like a crystal arrow.

Then a fresh pause, and in the silence of the church, the verses mourned out anew, thrown up by the organ, as by a spring board. As he listened with attention endeavouring to resolve the sounds, closing his eyes, Durtal saw them at first almost horizontal, then rising little by little, then raising themselves upright, then quivering in tears, before their final breaking.

Suddenly at the end of the psalm, when the response of the antiphon came—"Et lux perpetua luceat eis"—the children's voices broke into a sad, silken cry, a sharp sob, trembling on the word " eis," which remained suspended in the void.

These children's voices stretched to breaking, these clear sharp voices threw into the darkness of the chant some whiteness of the dawn, joining their pure, soft sounds to the resonant tones of the basses, piercing as with a jet of living silver the sombre cataract of the deeper singers ; they sharpened the wailing, strengthened and embittered the burning salt of tears, but they insinuated also a sort of protecting caress, balsamic freshness, lustral help ; they lighted in the darkness those brief gleams which tinkle in the Angelus at dawn of day ; they called up, anticipating the prophecies of the text, the compassionate image of the Virgin, passing, in the pale light of their tones, into the darkness of that sequence.

The " De Profundis " so chanted was incomparably beautiful. That sublime prayer ending in sobs, at the moment when the soul of the voices was about to overpass human limits, gave a wrench to Durtal's nerves, and made his heart beat. Then he wished to abstract himself, and cling especially to the meaning of that sorrowful plaint, in which the fallen being calls upon its God with groans and lamentations. Those cries of the third verse came back to him, wherein calling on his Saviour in despair from the bottom of the abyss, man, now that he knows he is heard, hesitates ashamed, knowing not what to say. The excuses he has prepared appear to him vain, the arguments he has arranged seem to him of no effect, and he stammers forth ; " If Thou, O Lord, shalt observe iniquities, Lord, who shall endure it ? "

"It is a pity," said Durtal to himself, " that this psalm, which in its first verses chants so magnificently the despair of humanity, becomes in those which follow more personal to King David. I know well," he went on, " that we must accept the symbolic sense of this pleading, admit that the despot confounds his own cause with that of God, that his adversaries are the unbelievers and the wicked, that he himself, according to the doctors of the Church, prefigures the person of Christ ; but yet the memory of his fleshly desires, and the presumptuous praise he gives to his

incorrigible people, contracts the scope of the poem. Happily
the melody has a life apart from the text, a life of its own, not
arising out of mere tribal dissensions, but extending to all the
earth, chanting the anguish of the time to be born, as well
as of the present day, and of the ages which are no more."

The " De Profundis " had ceased ; after a silence, the choir
intoned a motet of the eighteenth century, but Durtal was
only moderately interested in human music in churches.
What seemed to him superior to the most vaunted works of
theatrical or worldly music, was the old plain chant, that
even and naked melody, at once ethereal and of the tomb,
the solemn cry of sadness and lofty shout of joy, those
grandiose hymns of human faith, which seem to well up in
the cathedrals, like irresistible geysers, at the very foot of
the Romanesque columns. What music, however ample,
sorrowful or tender, is worth the " De Profundis " chanted
in unison, the solemnity of the " Magnificat," the splendid
warmth of the " Lauda Sion," the enthusiasm of the " Salve
Regina," the sorrow of the " Miserere," and the " Stabat
Mater," the majestic omnipotence of the " Te Deum " ?
Artists of genius have set themselves to translate the sacred
texts : Vittoria, Josquin de Près, Palestrina, Orlando Lasso,
Handel, Bach, Haydn, have written wonderful pages ; often
indeed they have been uplifted by the mystic effluence, the
very emanation of the Middle Ages, for ever lost ; and yet
their works have retained a certain pomp, and in spite of all
are pretentious, as opposed to the humble magnificence, the
sober splendour of the Gregorian chant—with them the
whole thing came to an end, for composers no longer
believed.

Yet in modern times some religious pieces may be cited
of Lesueur, Wagner, Berlioz, and Cæsar Franck, and in these
again we are conscious of the artist underlying his work, the
artist determined to show his skill, thinking to exalt his
own glory, and therefore leaving God out. We feel ourselves in the presence of superior men, but men with their
weaknesses, their inseparable vanity, and even the vice or
their senses. In the liturgical chant, created almost always
anonymously in the depth of the cloisters, was an extra-
terrestrial well, without taint of sin or trace of art. It was
an uprising of souls already freed from the slavery of the
flesh, an explosion of elevated tenderness and pure joy, it

was also the idiom of the Church, a musical gospel appealing like the Gospel itself at once to the most refined and
the most humble.

Ah ! the true proof of Catholicism was that art which it
had founded, an art which has never been surpassed ; in
painting and sculpture the Early Masters, mystics in poetry
and in prose, in music plain chant, in architecture the
Romanesque and Gothic styles. And all this held together
and blazed in one sheaf, on one and the same altar ; all was
reconciled in one unique cluster of thoughts : to revere,
adore and serve the Dispenser, showing to Him reflected in
the soul of His creature, as in a faithful mirror, the still
immaculate treasure of His gifts.

Then in those marvellous Middle Ages, wherein Art,
foster-child of the Church, encroached on death and advanced
to the threshold of Eternity, and to God, the divine concept
and the heavenly form were guessed and half-perceived, for
the first and perhaps for the last time by man. They
answered and echoed each other—art calling to art.

The Virgins had faces almond-shaped, elongated like those
ogives which the Gothic style contrived in order to distribute
an ascetic light, a virginal dawn in the mysterious shrine of
its naves. In the pictures of the Early Masters the
complexion of holy women becomes transparent as Paschal
wax, and their hair is pale as golden grains of frankincense,
their childlike bosoms scarcely swell, their brows are
rounded like the glass of the pyx, their fingers taper,
their bodies shoot upwards like delicate columns. Their
beauty becomes, as it were, liturgical. They seem to live in
the fire of stained glass, borrowing from the flaming whirlwind of the rose-windows the circles of their aureoles. The
ardent blue of their eyes, the dying embers of their lips,
keeping for their garments the colours they disdain for their
flesh, stripping them of their light, changing them, when
they transfer them to stuffs, into opaque tones which aid still
more by their contrast to declare the seraphic clearness of
their look, the grievous paleness of the mouth, to which,
according to the Proper of the season, the scent of the
lily of the Canticles or the penitential fragrance of myrrh
in the Psalms lend their perfume.

Then among artists was a coalition of brains, a welding
together of souls. Painters associated themselves in the

same ideal of beauty with architects, they united in a:
indestructible relation cathedrals and saints, only reversing
the usual process—they framed the jewel according to the
shrine, and modelled the relics for the reliquary.

On their side the sequences chanted by the Church had
subtle affinities with the canvases of the Early Painters.

Vittoria's responses for Tenebræ are of a like inspiration
and an equal loftiness with those of Quentin Matsys' great
work, the Entombment of Christ. The " Regina Cœli "
of the Flemish musician Lasso has the same good faith,
the same simple and strange attraction, as certain statues of
a reredos, or religious pictures of the elder Breughel.
Lastly, the Miserere of Josquin de Près, choir-master of
Louis XII., has, like the panels of the Early Masters of
Burgundy and Flanders, a patient intention, a stiff, threadlike simplicity, but also it exhales like them a truly mystical
savour, and its awkwardness of outline is very touching.

The ideal of all these works is the same and attained by
different means.

As for plain chant, the agreement of its melody with
architecture is also certain ; it also bends from time to
time like the sombre Romanesque arcades, and rises,
shadowy and pensive, like complete vaulting. The " De
Profundis," for instance, curves in on itself like those great
groins which form the smoky skeleton of the bays ; it is like
them slow and dark, extends itself only in obscurity and
moves only in the shadow of the crypts.

Sometimes, on the other hand, the Gregorian chant
seems to borrow from Gothic its flowery tendrils, its
scattered pinnacles, its gauzy rolls, its tremulous lace, its
trimmings light and thin as the voices of children. Then it
passes from one extreme to another, from the amplitude of
sorrow to an infinite joy ; at other times again, the plain
music, and the Christian music to which it gave birth,
lend themselves, like sculpture, to the gaiety of the
people, associate themselves with simple gladness, and the
sculptured merriment of the ancient porches; they take the
popular rhythm of the crowd, as in the Christmas carol
" Adeste Fideles " and in the Paschal hymn " O Filii et
Filiæ ; " they become trivial and familiar like the Gospels,
submitting themselves to the humble wishes of the poor,
lending them a holiday tune easy to catch, a running

melody which carries them into pure regions where these simple souls can cast themselves at the indulgent feet of Christ.

Born of the Church, and bred up by her in the choir-schools of the Middle Ages, plain chant is the aerial and mobile paraphrase of the immovable structure of the cathedrals; it is the immaterial and fluid interpretation of the canvases of the Early Painters ; it is a winged translation, but also the strict and unbending stole of those Latin sequences, which the monks built up or hewed out in the cloisters in the far-off olden time.

Now it is changed and disconnected, foolishly over-whelmed by the crash of organs, and is chanted, God knows how !

Most choirs when they intone it, like to imitate the rumbling and gurgling of water-pipes, others the grating of rattles, the creaking of pullies, the grinding of a crane, but, in spite of all, its beauty remains, unextinguished, dulled though it be, by the wild bellowing of the singers.

The sudden silence in the church roused Durtal. He rose and looked about him ; in his corner was no one save two poor women, asleep, their feet on the bars of chairs, their heads on their knees. Leaning forward a little, he saw, hanging above him in a dark chapel, the light of a lamp, like a ruby in its red glass ; no sound save the military tread of the Suisse, making his round in the distance.

Durtal sat down again ; the sweetness of his solitude was enhanced by the aromatic perfume of wax, and the memories, now faint, of incense, but it was suddenly broken. As the first chords crashed on the organ Durtal recognized the "Dies iræ," that despairing hymn of the Middle Ages ; instinctively he bowed his head and listened.

This was no more as in the "De Profundis" an humble supplication, a suffering which believes it has been heard, and discerns a path of light to guide it in the darkness, no longer the prayer which has hope enough not to tremble ; it was the cry of absolute desolation and of terror.

And, indeed, the wrath divine breathed tempestuously through these stanzas. They seemed addressed less to the God of mercy, to the Son who listens to prayer, than to the inflexible Father, to Him whom the Old Testament shows us, overcome with anger, scarcely appeased by the smoke of the pyres, the inconceivable attractions of burnt-offerings. In this chant it asserted itself still more savagely, for it threatened to strike the waters, and break in pieces the mountains, and to rend asunder the depths of heaven by thunder-bolts. And the earth, alarmed, cried out in fear.

A crystalline voice, a clear child's voice, proclaimed in the nave the tidings of these cataclysms, and after this the choir chanted new strophes wherein the implacable judge came with shattering blare of trumpet, to purify by fire the rotten-ness of the world.

Then, in its turn, a bass, deep as a vault, as though issuing from the crypt, accentuated the horror of these prophecies, made these threats more overwhelming, and after a short strain by the choir, an alto repeated them in yet more detail. Then, so soon as the awful poem had exhausted the enumeration of chastisement and suffering, in shrill tones— the falsetto of a little boy—the name of Jesus went by, and a light broke in on the thunder-cloud, the panting universe cried for pardon, recalling, by all the voices of the choir, the infinite mercies of the Saviour, and His pardon, pleading with Him for absolution, as formerly He had spared the penitent thief and the Magdalen.

But in the same despairing and headstrong melody the tempest raged again, drowned with its waves the half-seen shores of heaven, and the solos continued, discouraged, interrupted by the recurrent weeping of the choir, giving, with the diversity of voices, a body to the special conditions of shame, the particular states of fear, the different ages of tears.

At last, when still mixed and blended, these voices had borne away on the great waters of the organ all the wreckage of human sorrows, all the buoys of prayers and tears, they fell exhausted, paralyzed by terror, wailing and sighing like a child who hides its face, stammering " Dona eis requiem," they ended, worn out, in an Amen so plaintive, that it died away in a breath above the sobbing of the organ.

What man could have imagined such despair, dreamed of such disasters ? And Durtal made answer to himself : " No man."

In fact the attempt has been vain to discover the author both of the music and of the sequence. They have been attributed to Frangipani, Thomas of Celano, St. Bernard and a crowd of others, and they have remained anonymous, simply formed by the sad alluvial deposits of the age. The "Dies iræ" seemed to have, at first, fallen, like a seed of desolation, among the distracted souls of the eleventh century; it germinated there and grew slowly, nurtured by the sap of anguish, watered by the rain of tears. It was at last pruned when it seemed ripe, and had, perhaps, thrown out too many branches, for in one of the earliest known texts, a stanza, which has since disappeared, called up the magnificent and barbarous image of an earth revolving as it belched forth flames, while the constellations burst into shards, and heaven shrivelled like a parched scroll.

"All this," concluded Durtal, "does not prevent these triple stanzas woven of shadow and cold, full of reverberating rhymes, and hard echoes, this music of rude stuff which wraps the phrases like a shroud, and masks the rigid outlines of the work, from being admirable! Yet that chant which constrains, and renders with such energy the breadth of the sequence, that melodic period, which without variation, remaining always the same, succeeds in expressing by turns prayer and terror, moves me less than the 'De Profundis,' which yet has not its grandiose spaciousness nor that artistic cry of despair.

But chanted to the organ the psalm is earthy and suffocating. It comes from out the very depths of the sepulchre, while the 'Dies iræ' has its source only on the sill of the tomb. The first is the very voice of the dead, the second that of the living who inter him, and the dead man weeps, but takes courage a little, when those that bury him despair.

"To sum up," Durtal concluded, "I prefer the text of the "Dies iræ" to that of the 'De Profundis,' and the melody of the 'De Profundis' to that of the 'Dies iræ.' It is true also that this last sequence is modernized, and chanted theatrically here, without the imposing and needful march of unison.

"This time, for instance, it is devoid of interest," he continued, ceasing his thoughts for a moment, to listen to the piece of modern music which the choir was just then rendering. "Ah, who will take on himself to proscribe that pert mysticism, those fonts of toilet-water which Gounod invented! . . . There ought indeed to be astonishing

penalties for choir masters who allow such musical
effeminacy in church. This is, as it was this morning at the
Madeleine, when I happened to be present at the interminable funeral of an old banker ; they played a military
march with violin and violoncello accompaniments, with
trumpets and timbrels, a heroic and worldly march to
celebrate the departure and the decomposition of a financier !
. . . It is too absurd." And listening no more to the
music in St. Sulpice, Durtal transferred himself in thought
to the Madeleine, and went off at full speed in his
dreams.

"Indeed," he said to himself, "the clergy make Jesus like a
tourist, when they invite Him daily to come down into that
church whose exterior is surmounted by no cross, and
whose interior is like the grand reception-room at an hotel.
But how can you make those priests understand that
ugliness is sacrilege, and that nothing is equal to the
frightful sin of this confusion of Romanesque and Greek,
these pictures of aged men, that flat ceiling studded with
skylights, from which filter in all weathers the spoiled
gleams of a rainy day, to that futile altar surmounted by a
circle of angels who, in discreet abandonment, dance
in honour of our Lady, a motionless marble rigadoon ? "

Yet in the Madeleine, at a funeral, when the door opens,
and the corpse advances in a gap of daylight, all is
changed. Like a superterrestrial antiseptic, an extrahuman
disinfectant, the liturgy purifies and cleanses the impious
ugliness of the place.

And thinking over his memories of the morning, Durtal
saw again, as he closed his eyes, at the end of the semi-
circular apse, the procession of red and black robes, white
surplices, joining in front of the altar, descending the steps
together, making their way together to the catafalque,
dividing again on each aide, joining to mix afresh in the
great gangway between the chairs.

This slow and silent procession, led by incomparable
Suisses, in mourning, their swords horizontal, and a
general's epaulets in jet, advanced, preceded by a cross, in
front of the corpse laid on tressels, and far-off in all that
confusion of lights falling from the roof, and lighted
flambeaux round the catafalque and on the altar, the white
of the tapers disappeared, and the priests who bore them

seemed to march with empty hands uplifted as though to
point out the stars which accompanied them, twinkling
above their heads.

Then when the bier was surrounded by the clergy, the
" De Profundis " burst forth from the depths of the
sanctuary, intoned by invisible singers.

" That was good," said Durtal to himself. At the
Madeleine the voices of the children are sharp and feeble,
and the basses are badly trained and failing ; we are evidently
far from the choir of St. Sulpice, but all the same it was
superb ; then what a moment was that of the priests' communion, when suddenly arising from the murmuring of the
choir, the voice of the tenor threw above the corpse the
magnificent plain chant antiphon—

> " Requiem æternam dona eis Domine
> Et lux perpetua luceat eis."

It seems that after all the lamentations of the " De
Profundis " and the " Dies iræ," the presence of God, who
comes then upon the altar, brings consolation, and sanctions
the confident and solemn pride of that melodious phrase,
which then invokes Christ, without dread and without tears.

The mass ended, the celebrant disappeared, and, as at the
moment when the corpse entered, the clergy, preceded by
the Suisses, advanced towards the body, and in the blazing
circle of the tapers, a priest, in his cope, said the mighty
prayers of the general absolution.

Then the liturgy took a higher tone, and became still
more admirable. Mediative between the sinner and the
judge, the Church, by the mouth of her priest, implores
the Lord to pardon the poor soul :   " Non intres in judicium
cum servo tuo Domine "—then after the amen given by
the organ and all the choir, a voice arose in the silence,
and spoke in the name of the dead :—

" Libera me ! "

and the choir continued the old chant of the tenth century.
Just as in the " Dies iræ," which appropriates to itself
fragments of these plaints, the Last Judgment flamed out,
and pitiless responses declare to the dead the reality of his
alarms, declare to him that at the end of Time the Judge
will come with the crash of thunder to chastise the world.

The priest marched round the catafalque, sprinkling it

with beads of holy water, incensed it, gave shelter to the poor weeping soul, consoled it, took it to himself, covered it, as it were, with his cope, and again, intervened to pray that, after so much weariness and sorrow, the Lord will permit the unhappy one to sleep the sleep that knows no waking, far from earth's noises.

Never, in any religion, has a more charitable part, a more august mission been assigned to man. Lifted, by his consecration, wholly above humanity, almost deified by the sacerdotal office, the priest, while earth laments or is silent, can advance to the brink of the abyss, and intercede for the being whom the Church has baptized as an infant, who has no doubt forgotten her since that day, and may even have persecuted her up to the hour of his death.

Nor does the Church shrink from the task. Before that fleshly dust heaped in a chest, she thinks of that sewage of the soul, and cries : " From the gates of hell deliver him, O Lord ! " but at the end of the general absolution, at the moment when the procession, turning its back, is on the way to the sacristy, she too seems disquieted. Perhaps recalling in an instant, the ill deeds done by that body while it was alive, she seemed to doubt if her supplications were heard, and the doubt her words would not frame, passed into the intonation of the last amen, murmured at the Madeleine, by children's voices.

Timid and distant, plaintive and sweet, this amen said : " We have done what we could, but . . . but . . ." And in the funereal silence which followed the clergy leaving the nave, there remained only the ignoble reality of the empty husk, lifted in the arms of men, thrust into a carriage, like the refuse of the shambles carted off each morning to be made into soap at the factories.

" If," continued Durtal, " in opposition to these sad prayers, these eloquent absolutions, we call up before us a marriage mass, all is changed. There the Church is disarmed and her musical liturgy is as nought. Then she may well play Mendelssohn's Wedding March, and borrow from profane authors the gaiety of their songs to celebrate the brief and empty joy of the body. Imagine, and indeed it happens, the canticle of the Virgin used to magnify the glad impatience of a bride. Fancy the Te Deum, to hymn the blessedness of a bridegroom ! "

Far away from this infamous barter of the flesh, plain chant remains shut up in the antiphonaries, like a monk in the cloister, and when it goes forth, it is to cast up before Christ his garnered pains and sorrows. It gathers and sums them up in admirable supplications, and if, fatigued with pleading it adores, its impulse is to glorify eternal events, Palm Sunday and Easter, Pentecost and the Ascension, Epiphany and Christmas, then its joy bursts forth so magnificently, that it springs beyond the world to show its ecstatic joy at the feet of God.

As to the very ceremonies of the funeral, they are now only the regular way of getting money, an official routine, a prayer-wheel which is turned mechanically without thought of it.

The organist while he plays thinks of his family, and considers how wearied he is ; the bellows-blower thinks, as he fills the pipes, of the half-pint which will dry his sweat ; the tenors and basses are careful of their effects, and admire themselves in the more or less rippled water of their voices ; the choir boys dream of their scampers after mass ; and, moreover, not one of them at all understands a word of the Latin they sing and abridge, as for instance the " Dies iræ," of which they suppress a part of the stanzas.

In its turn beadledom calculates the sum the dead man brings in, and even the priest, wearied with the prayers of which he has read so many, and needing his breakfast, prays mechanically from the lips outward, while the assistants are in a hurry that the mass to which they have not listened should come to an end, that they may shake hands with the relations, and leave the dead.

There is absolute inattention, profound weariness. Yet how terrible is that thing on the tressels that is waiting there in the church, that empty dwelling-place, that body which is already breaking up. Liquid manure that stinks, gases which evaporate, flesh that rots is all that remains !

And the soul, now that life is over, and all begins ? No one thinks of it, not even the family worn out by the length of the service, absorbed in their own sorrow ; who in fact regret only the visible presence of the being they have lost ; no one except myself, thought Durtal, and a few curious people, who associate themselves in their alarm with the

" Dies iræ " and the " Libera," of which they understand
both the language and the meaning.

Then by the external sound of the words, without the aid
of contemplation, without even the help of thought, the
Church acts.

There it is, the miracle of her liturgy, the power of her
word, the constantly renewed prodigy of phrases created by
revolving time, of prayers arranged by ages which are dead.
All has passed, nothing exists that was raised up in those
bygone times. Yet those sequences remain intact, cried
aloud by indifferent voices and cast out from empty hearts,
plead, groan, and implore even with efficacy, by their
virtual power, their talismanic might, their inalienable beauty
by the almighty confidence of their faith. The Middle Ages
have left us these to help us to save, if it may be, the soul of
the modern and dead fine gentleman.

At the present time, concluded Durtal, there is nothing
left peculiar to Paris, but the ceremonies, very like each
other, of taking the veil and of funerals. It is unfortunate
that when we have to do with a sumptuous corpse, under-
takers have their way.

They then bring out their terrible upholstery, plated
statues of our Lady in atrocious taste, zinc basins in which
blaze bowls of green punch, tin candelabra at the end of
a branch, like a cannon on end with its mouth upwards,
supporting spiders on their backs, with burning candles
set about their legs, all the funeral ironmongery of the
First Empire, with curtain rods in relief, acanthus leaves,
winged hour-glasses, lozenges and Greek frets.   It is
unfortunate, too, that to touch up the miserable furniture
of these ceremonies they play Massenet and Dubois,
Benjamin Godard and Widor, or, worse still, the sacristy
orchestra, mystical bellowing, such as the women sing,
who are affiliated to the confraternities of the month of
May.

And alas, we hear no longer the tempests of the great
organs and the majestic dolours of plain chant, save at the
funerals of the monied classes ; for the poor, nothing—no
choir, no organ, just a handful of prayers, then a few dips
of the brush in the holy water stoup, and there is a dead
man the more on whom the rain falls, who is carried away.
But the Church knows that the carrion of the rich rots as

much as that of the poor, while his soul stinks more, but she jobs indulgences and haggles about masses ; she, even she, is consumed by the lust of gold.

"Yet I must not think too ill of these wealthy fools," said Durtal, after silent thought, "for after all it is thanks to them that I can hear the admirable liturgy of the burial service, these people who perhaps have done no good action in their life, do at least this kindness to a few, without knowing it, after their death."

A noise recalled him to St. Sulpice ; the choir was going, the church was about to close. "I might as well have tried to pray," he said to himself, " it would have been better than to dream in the empty church on a chair. Pray indeed ? I have no desire for it. I am haunted by Catholicism, intoxicated by its atmosphere of incense and wax, I prowl about it, moved even to tears by its prayers, touched even to the marrow by its psalms and chants. I am thoroughly disgusted with my life, very tired of myself, but it is a far cry from that to leading a different existence ! And yet—and yet . . . If I am perturbed in these chapels, I become unmoved and dry again, as soon as I leave them. After all," he said to himself, getting up, and following the few persons who were moving towards a door, driven out by the Suisse, " after all, my heart is hardened and smoke-dried by dissipation, I am good for nothing."

CHAPTER II.

How had he again become a Catholic, and got to this point ?

Durtal answered himself : " I cannot tell, all that I know is that, having been for years an unbeliever, I suddenly believe.

" Let us see," he said to himself, " let us try at least to consider if, however great the obscurity of such a subject, there be not common sense in it.

" After all, my surprise depends on preconceived ideas of conversions. I have heard of sudden and violent crises of the soul, of a thunderbolt, or even of faith exploding at last in ground slowly and cleverly mined. It is quite evident that conversions may happen in one or other of these two ways, for God acts as may seem good to Him, but there must be also a third means, and this no doubt the most usual, which the Saviour has used in my case. And I know not in what this consists ; it is something analogous to digestion in a stomach, which works though we do not feel it. There has been no road to Damascus, no events to bring about a crisis ; nothing has happened, we awake some fine morning, and, without knowing how or why, the thing is done.

" Yes, but in fact this manœuvre is very like that of the mine which only explodes after it has been deeply dug. Yet not so, for in that case the operations are material, the objections in the way are resolved ; I might have reasoned, followed the course of the spark along the thread, but in this case, no ! I sprang unexpectedly, without warning, without even having suspected that I was so carefully sapped. Nor was it a clap of thunder, unless I admit that a clap of thunder can be occult and silent, strange and gentle. And this again would be untrue, for sudden disorder of the soul almost always follows a misfortune or a crime, an act of which we are aware.

"No, the one thing which seems certain, in my case, is that there has been divine impulse, grace.

"But," said he, "in that case the psychology of conversion is worthless," and he made answer to himself,—

"That seems to be so, for I seek in vain to retrace the stages through which I have passed; no doubt I can distinguish here and there some landmarks on the road I have travelled : love of art, heredity, weariness of life; I can even recall some of the forgotten sensations of childhood, the subterranean workings of ideas excited by my visits to the churches; but I am unable to gather these threads together, and group them in a skein, I cannot understand the sudden and silent explosion of light which took place in me. When I seek to explain to myself how one evening an unbeliever, I became without knowing it, on one night a believer, I can discover nothing, for the divine action has vanished, and left no trace.

"It is certain," he continued, after silent thought, "that in these cases the Virgin acts upon us, it is she who moulds and places us in the hands of her Son, but her fingers are so light, so supple, so caressing, that the soul they have handled has felt nothing.

"On the other hand, if I ignore the course and stages of my conversion, I can at least guess the motives which, after a life of indifference, have brought me into the harbours of the Church, made me wander round about her borders, and finally gave me a shove from behind to bring me in."

And he said to himself, without more ado, there are three causes :—

"First, the atavism of an old and pious family, scattered among the monasteries;" and the memories of childhood returned to him, of cousins, of aunts, seen in convent parlours; gentle women and grave, white as wafers, who alarmed him by their low voices, who troubled him by their looks, and asked if he were a good boy.

He felt a sort of terror, and hid himself in his mother's skirts, trembling when he went away, and was obliged to bend his brow to those colourless lips, and undergo the touch of a chilly kiss.

Now that he thought of them at a distance, the interviews which had wearied him so much in his childhood, seemed to him charming. He put into them all the poetry of the cloister, clothed those bare parlours with a faded scent of wainscotting and of wax, and he saw again the convent gardens through which he had passed, impregnated with the bitter salt scent of box, planted with clipped hedges, intermingled with trellises, whose green grapes never ripened, divided by benches whose mouldering stone kept the traces worn by water ; and a thousand details came back to him of those silent lime alleys, of the paths where he ran in the interlaced shade which branches threw upon the ground. These gardens had seemed to him to become larger as he grew older, and he retained a somewhat confused memory of them, amid which was the vague recollection of an old stately park, and of a presbytery orchard in the north, always somewhat damp, even when the sun shone.

It was not surprising that these sensations, transformed by time, had left in him some traces of pious thought, which grew deeper as his mind embellished them ; all this might have fermented indistinctly for thirty years, and now began to work.

But the two other causes which he knew, must have been still more active.

These were his disgust for his life, and his passion for art ; and the disgust was certainly aggravated by his solitude and his idleness.

After having, in old days, made friends by chance, and having taken the impression of souls which had nothing in common with his own, he had at last chosen after much useless vagabondage ; he had become the intimate friend of a certain Doctor des Hermies, a physician, who devoted much attention to demoniac possession and to mysticism, and of a Breton, named Carhaix, the bell-ringer at St. Sulpice.

These friendships were not like those he had formerly made, entirely superficial and external, they were wide and deep, based on similarity of thought, and the indissoluble ties of soul, and these had been roughly broken ; within two months of each other Des Hermies and Carhaix died, the former of typhoid fever, the latter of a chill that prostrated him in his tower, after he had rung the evening Angelus.

These were frightful blows for Durtal. His life, now without an anchor, drifted ; he wandered all astray, declaring to himself that this desolation was final, since he had reached an age at which new friends are not made.

So he lived alone, apart among his books, but the solitude which he bore bravely, when he was occupied, when he was writing a book, became intolerable to him now that he was idle. He lounged in an armchair in the afternoons, and abandoned himself to his dreams : then, especially, fixed ideas took hold on him, and these ended by playing panto-mimes of which the scenes never varied behind the lowered curtain of his eyes. Nude figures danced in his brain to the tune of psalms, and he woke from these dreams weak and panting, ready, if a priest had been there, to throw himself at his feet with tears, just as he would have abandoned him-self to the basest pleasures, had the temptation suddenly come to him.

" Let me chase away these phantoms by work," he cried. But at what should he work ? He had just published the " Life of Gilles de Rais," which might interest a few artists, and he now remained without a subject, on the hunt for a book. As, in art, he was a man of extremes, he always went from one excess to the other, and after having dived into the Satanism of the Middle Ages, in his account of " Marshal de Rais," he saw nothing so interesting to investigate as the life of a saint. Some lines which he had discovered in Görres' and Ribet's "Studies in Mysticism " had put him on the trace of a certain Blessed Lidwine in search of new documents.

But admitting that he could unearth anything about her, could he write the life of a saint ? He did not believe it, and the arguments on which he based his opinion seemed plausible.

Hagiography was now a lost branch of art, as completely lost as wood carving, and the miniatures of the old missals. Nowadays it is only treated by church officers and priests, by those stylistic agents who seem when they write to put the embryos of their ideas on ballast trucks, and in their hands it has become a commonplace of goody-goody, a translation into a book of the statuettes of Froc Robert, and the coloured images of Bouasse.

The way then was free, and it seemed at first easy enough
to plan it out, but to extract the charm of the legends
needed the simple language of bygone centuries, the
ingenuous phrases of the days that are dead. Who in our
time can express the melancholy essence, the pale perfume
of the ancient translations of the Golden Legend of
Voragine, how bind in one bright posy the plaintive
flowers, which the monks cultivated in their cloistered
enclosures, when hagiography was the sister of the barbaric
and delightful art of the illuminators and glass stainers, of
the ardent and chaste paintings of the Early Masters ?

Yet we may not think of giving ourselves over to
studious imitations, nor coldly attempt to ape such works as
these. The question remains, whether we can with the
present artistic resources, succeed in setting up the humble
yet lofty figure of a saint ; and this is at least doubtful, for
the lack of real simplicity, the over-ingenious art of style,
the tricks of careful design and the false craft of colour
would probably transform the elect lady into a strolling
player. She would be no longer a saint, but an actress
who rendered the part more or less adroitly ; and then the
charm would be destroyed, the miracles would seem
mechanical, the episodes would be absurd, then . . . then . . .
one must have a lively faith, and believe in the sanctity of
one's heroine, if one would try to exhume her, and put her
alive again in a book.

This is so true that we may examine Gustave Flaubert's
admirable pages on the legend of St. Julian the Hospitaller.
Their development is like a dazzling yet regulated tumult,
evolved in superb language whose apparent simplicity is
only due to the complicated ingenuity of consummate skill.
All is there, all except the accent which would have made
this work a true masterpiece. Given the subject, the fire
which should course through these magnificent phrases is
absent, there lacks the cry of the love that faints, the gift
of the superhuman exile, the mystical soul.

On the other hand, Hello's " Physionomies de Saints "
are worth reading. Faith flashes out in each of his
portraits, enthusiasm runs over in each chapter, unexpected
allusions form deep reservoirs of thought between the lines ;
but after all Hello was so little of an artist that the fairest
legends fade when his fingers touch them ; the meanness

of his style impoverishes the miracles and renders them ineffectual. The art is lacking which would rescue the book from the category of pale and dead publications.

The example of these two men, in complete opposition as ever writers were, neither of whom attained perfection, one in the legend of St. Julian because faith was wanting, the other because his art was poor and narrow, thoroughly discouraged Durtal. He ought to be both at once, and yet remain himself, if not, there was no good in buckling to for such a task, it were better to be silent ; and he threw himself back in his chair sullen and hopeless. Then the contempt of his desolate life grew upon him, and once more he wondered what interest Providence could have in thus tormenting the descendants of the first convicts. If there were no answer, he was obliged to admit that the Church in these disasters gathered up the waifs, sheltered the shipwrecked, brought them home again, and assured them a resting-place.

No more than Schopenhauer, whom he had once admired, but whose plan of labelling every one before death and whose herbarium of dry sorrows had wearied him, has the Church deceived man, nor sought to decoy him, by boasting the mercy of a life which she knew to be ignoble.

In all her inspired books she proclaims the horror of fate, and mourns over the enforced task of living. Ecclesiasticus, Ecclesiastes, the book of Job, the Lamentations of Jeremias manifest this sorrow in their every line, and the Middle Ages too in the " Imitation of Jesus Christ " cursed existence, and cried out loudly for death.

More plainly than Schopenhauer the Church declared that there is nothing to wish for here below, nothing to expect, but where the mere catalogues of the philosopher stop, the Church went on, overpassing the limits of the senses, declared the end of man, and defined his limitations.

" Then," he said to himself, " if it be well considered, the vaunted argument of Schopenhauer against the Creator, drawn from the misery and injustice of the world, is not irrefutable, for the world is not as God made it, but as man has refashioned it."

Before accusing heaven for our ills, it is, no doubt, fitting to examine through what phases of consent, through what voluntary falls the creature has passed, before ending in the gloomy disaster it deplores. We may well curse the vices of our ancestors and our own passions which beget the greater part of the woes from which we suffer ; we may well loathe the civilization which has rendered life intolerable to cleanly souls, and not the Lord, who, perhaps, did not create us to be shot down by cannon in time of war, to be cheated, robbed, and stripped in time of peace, by the slave drivers of commerce and the brigands of the money market.

But that which remains for ever incomprehensible is the initial horror, the horror imposed on each of us, of having to live, and that is a mystery no philosophy can explain.

"Ah !" he went on, "when I think of that horror, that disgust of existence which has for years and years increased in me, I understand how I am forced to make for the Church, the only port where I can find shelter.

"Once I despised her, because I had a staff on which to lean when the great winds of weariness blew ; I believed in my novels, I worked at my history, I had my art. I have come to recognize its absolute inadequacy, its complete incapacity to afford happiness. Then I understood that Pessimism was, at most, good to console those who had no real need of comfort ; I understood that its theories, alluring when we are young, and rich, and well, become singularly weak and lamentably false, when age advances, when infirmities declare themselves, when all around is crumbling.

"I went to the church, that hospital for souls. There, at least, they take you in, put you to bed and nurse you, they do not merely turn their backs on you as in the wards of Pessimism and tell you the name of your disease."

Finally Durtal had been brought back to religion by art. More even than his disgust for life, art had been the irresistible magnet which drew him to God. The day, when out of curiosity and to kill time, he had entered a church, and after so many years of forgetfulness, had heard the Vespers for the dead fall heavily, psalm after psalm, in antiphonal chant, as the singers threw up, like ditchers, their shovelsful of verses, his soul had been shaken to its depths. The evenings when he had listened at St. Sulpice to the admirable chanting during the Octave of All Souls, he had felt himself caught once for all ; but that which had put most pressure on him, and brought him yet more completely into bondage were the ceremonies and music of Holy Week.

He had visited the churches during that week ; and they had opened to him like palaces ruined, like cemeteries laid waste by God. They were forbidding with their veiled images, their crucifixes wrapped lozenge-wise in purple, their organs dumb, their bells silent. The crowd flowed in, busy, but noiseless, along the floor over the immense cross formed by the nave and the two transepts, and entering by the wounds of which the doors were figures, they went up to the altar, where the blood-stained head of Christ would lie, and there on their knees eagerly kissed the crucifix which marked the place of the chin below the steps.

And the crowd itself, as it ran in the cruciform mould of the church, became itself an enormous cross, living and crawling, silent and sombre.

At St. Sulpice, where the whole assembled seminary lamented the ignominy of human justice and the fore-ordained death of a God, Durtal had followed the incomparable offices of those mournful days, through all their black minutes, had listened to the infinite sadness of the Passion, so nobly and profoundly expressed at Tenebræ by the slow chanting of the Lamentations and the Psalms, but when he thought it over, that which above all made him shudder was the thought of the Virgin coming on the scene on the Thursday at night-fall.

The Church, till then absorbed in her sorrow, and prostrate before the Cross, raised herself and fell a-weeping on beholding the Mother.

By all the voices of the choir, it pressed round Mary, endeavouring to console her, mixing the tears of the "Stabat Mater" with her own, sighing out that music of plaintive weeping, pressing the wound of that sequence, which gave forth water and blood like the wound of Christ Himself.

Durtal left the church, worn out with these long services, but his temptations to unbelief were gone ; he had no further doubt ; it seemed to him that at St. Sulpice, grace mixed with the eloquent splendours of the liturgies, and that in the dim sorrow of the voices there had been appeals to him ; and he therefore felt filial gratitude to that church where he had lived through hours so sweet and sad,

Yet, in ordinary weeks he did not go there ; it seemed to him too great and too cold, and it was so ugly. He preferred warmer and smaller sanctuaries, in which there were still traces of the Middle Ages.

Thus on idle days when he came out of the Louvre, where he had strayed for a long time before the canvases of the Early Painters, he was wont to take refuge in the old church of St. Severin, hidden away in a corner of the poorer part of Paris.

He carried with him the visions of the canvases he had admired at the Louvre, and contemplated them again, in this surrounding where they were thoroughly at home.

Then he spent delightful moments, in which he was carried away in the clouds of harmony, divided by the white splendour of a child's voice flashing out from the rolling thunder of the organ.

There, without even praying, he felt a plaintive languor, a vague uneasiness steal over him ; St. Severin delighted him, aided him more than other churches on some days to gain an indescribable impression of joy and pity, sometimes even, when he thought of the filth of his senses, to weave together the regret and the terror of his soul.

He often went there, especially on Sunday mornings to High Mass at ten o'clock.

He was wont to place himself behind the high altar, in that melancholy and delicate apse, planted like a winter garden with rare and somewhat fantastic trees. It might have been called a petrified arbour of very old trunks in flower, but stripped of leaf, forests of pillars, squared or cut in broad panels, carved with regular notches near the base, hollowed through their whole length like rhubarb stalks, channelled like celery.

No vegetation expanded at the summit of those trunks which bent their naked boughs along the vaulting, joined and met and gathered at their junction, and thin, engrafted knots, extravagant bunches of heraldic roses, armorial flowers with open tracery ; and for more than four hundred years no sap had run, no bud had formed in these trees. The shafts bent for ever remained untouched, the white bark of these pillars was scarcely worn, but the greater part of the flowers were withered, the heraldic petals were wanting, some keystones of the arches had only stratified calices, open like nests, with holes like sponges, in rags like handfuls of russet lace.

And among this mystic flora, amid these petrified trees, there was one, strange and charming, which suggested the fanciful idea, that the blue smoke of the rolling incense had condensed, and, as it coagulated, had grown pale with age, to form, in twisting, the spiral of a column which was inverted on itself, and ended broadening out into a sheaf, whereof the broken stems fell from above the arches.

The corner where Durtal took refuge was faintly lighted by pointed stained windows, with black diamond-shaped divisions set with minute panes darkened by the accumulated dust of years, rendered still more obscure by the woodwork of the chapels, which cut off half their surface.

This apse might have been called a frozen grove of skeleton trees, a conservatory of dead specimens belonging to the palm family, calling up the memory of an impossible phœnix and unlikely palms ; but it also recalled by its half-moon shape and doubtful light, the image of a ship's prow below water. In fact it allowed to filter through its bars, to its windows trellised with all black network, the murmur, suggested by the rolling of the carriages which shook the street, of a river which sifted the golden light of day through the briny course of its waters.

On Sundays, at the time of High Mass, the apse was empty. The public filled the nave before the high altar, or spread themselves somewhat further into a chapel dedicated to Our Lady. Durtal was therefore almost alone, and even the people who crossed his refuge were neither stupid nor hostile, like the faithful in other churches. In this district were beggars, the very poor, hucksters, Sisters of Charity, rag pickers, street arabs ; above all, there were women in tatters walking on tiptoe, who knelt without looking round, poor creatures overwhelmed by the piteous splendour of the altars, looking out of the corner of their eyes, and bending low when the Suisse passed them.

Touched by the timidity of this silent misery, Durtal listened to the mass chanted by a scanty choir, but one patiently taught. The choir of St. Severin intoned the Credo, that marvel of plain chant, better than it was done at St. Sulpice, where, however, the offices were as a rule solemn and correct. It bore it, as it were, to the top of the choir, and let it spread with its great wings open and almost without motion, above the prostrate flock, when the verse " Et homo factus est " took its slow and reverent flight in the low voice of the singer. It was at once monumental and fluid, indestructible like the articles of the Creed itself, inspired like the text, which the Holy Spirit dictated, in their last meeting, to the united apostles of Christ.

At St. Severin a powerful voice declaimed a verse as a solo, then all the children, sustained by the rest of the singers, delivered the others, and the unchangeable truths declared themselves in their order, more attentive, more grave, more accentuated, even a little plaintive in the solo voice of a man, more timid perhaps, but also more familiar and more joyous, in the dash, however restrained, of the boys.

At such a moment Durtal was roused, and exclaimed within himself : " It is impossible that the alluvial deposits of Faith which have created this musical certainty are false. The accent of these declarations is such as to be super-human, and far from profane music, which has never attained to the solid grandeur of this naked chant."

The whole mass, moreover, at St. Severin was perfect. The " Kyrie eleison," solemn and sumptuous, the " Gloria in excelsis," shared by the grand and the choir organs, the one taking the solos, the other guiding and sustaining the singers, was full of exultant joy; the " Sanctus," concentrated, almost haggard, resounded through the arches when the choir shouted the " Hosanna in excelsis," and the " Agnus Dei " was sung low to a clear, suppliant melody, so humble that it dared not become loud.

Indeed, except for a contraband " O Salutaris," intro-duced there as in other churches, St. Severin maintained, on ordinary Sundays, the musical liturgy, sang it almost reverentially with the fragile but well-toned voices of the boys, the solidly built basses bringing vigorous sounds from the deep.

It was a joy to Durtal to linger in the delightful sur-roundings of the Middle Ages, in that shadowy loneliness, amid the chants which rose behind him, without being annoyed by tricks of the mouths which he could not see.

He ended by being moved to the very marrow, choked by nervous tears, and all the bitterness of his life came up

before him ; full of vague fears, of confused prayers which
stifled him, and found no words, he cursed the ignominy
of his life and swore to master his carnal affections.

When the mass was over, he wandered in the church itself,
and was delighted with the spring of the nave, which four
centuries built and sealed with their arms, placing on it those
strange impressions, those wonderful seals which expand
in relief under the reversed groining of the arches. These
centuries combined to bring to the feet of Christ the superhuman effort of their art, and the gifts of each are still visible.
The thirteenth century shaped those low and stunted pillars,
whose capitals are crowned with water-lilies, water-parsley,
foliage with large leaves, voluted with crochets and turned
in the form of a crosier. The fourteenth century raised
the columns of the neighbouring bays on the sides of
which prophets, monks and saints uphold the spring of the
arches. The fifteenth and sixteenth created the apse, the
sanctuary, some windows pierced above the choir, and
though they have been restored by incompetent builders,
they have still retained a barbaric grace, and a really
touching simplicity.

They seem to have been designed by ancestors of the
Epinal foundries, and stained by them with crude colours.
The donors and the saints who pass through these bright,
stone-framed pictures are all awkward and pensive, dressed
in robes of gamboge, bottle-green, prussian-blue, gooseberry-
red, pumpkin-purple and wine lees, and these are made still
deeper by contact with the flesh tints, either omitted or destroyed, which have at any rate remained uncoloured like a
thin skin of glass. In one of these windows Christ on His cross
seems limpid, all in light, between blue splashes of sky, and the
red and green patches, formed by the wings of the two
angels whose faces also seem cut in crystal and full of light.

These windows differ from those of other churches, in
that they absorb the rays of the sun, without refracting
them. No doubt they have been deliberately divested of
reflection that they may not by the insolent joyousness of
stones on fire insult the melancholy sorrow of this church
which rises in the squalid haunts of a quarter inhabited by
beggars and thieves.

Then these thoughts assailed Durtal. In Paris the
modern churches are useless, they remain deaf to the

prayers which break against the icy indifference of
their walls. No man recollects himself in those naves
where souls have left nothing of themselves, or where they
have perhaps given themselves away, have had to turn and
fall back on themselves, rebuffed by the insolence of a
photographic glare, darkened by the neglect of those altars
at which no saint has ever said mass. It seemed that God
had always gone out, and would only come home to keep
His promise to appear at the moment of consecration, and
that He would retire immediately afterwards, despising
these edifices which have not been built expressly for Him,
since by the baseness of their form they might be put to
any profane use, since above all they do not bring Him, in
default of sanctity, the only gift which might please Him,
the gift of art which He has lent to man, and which allows
Him to see Himself in the abridged restitution of His work,
and to rejoice in the development of that flower of which
He has sowed the seed in souls which He has carefully
chosen, in souls which are truly the elect, second only to
those of His Saints.

Ah, those charitable churches of the Middle Ages, those
chapels damp and smoky, full of ancient song, of exquisite
paintings, of the odour of extinguished tapers, of the
perfume of burning incense !

In Paris there remain now only a few specimens of this
art of other years, a few sanctuaries whose stones really
exude the Faith ; among these St. Severin seemed to
Durtal the most exquisite and the most certain. He only
felt at home there, he believed that if he could ever pray in
earnest he could do it in that church ; and he said to
himself that there lived the spirit of the fabric. It is impossible but that the burning prayers, the hopeless sobs of
the Middle Ages, have not for ever impregnated the pillars
and stained the walls ; it is impossible but that the vine of
sorrows whence of old the Saints gathered warm clusters
of tears, has not preserved from those wonderful times
emanations which sustain, a breath which still awakes a
shame for sin, and the gift of tears.

As Saint Agnes remained immaculate in the brothels,
this church remained intact amid infamous surroundings,
when all near it in the streets from the Château Rouge to
the Cremerie Alexandre, only two paces off, the modern

rabble of rascality combine their misdeeds, mingling with prostitutes their brewage of crime, their adulterated absinthe and spirits.

In this especial territory of Satanism, the church rises, delicate and little, closely enveloped in the rags of taverns and hovels, and seen far off, raises above the roofs its light spire, like a netting needle, its point below, and lifting its eye into the light and air, through which can be seen a minute bell surmounting a sort of anvil. Such it appears, at least, from the Place Saint André des Arts. Symbolically it might be called a piteous appeal, always rejected by souls hardened and hammered by vice, of that anvil which was only an optical illusion, and that very real bell.

"They say," thought Durtal, "they say that ignorant architects and unskilled archæologists wish to free St. Severin from its rags, and surround it with trees in an enclosed square. But it has always lived in its network of black streets, and is voluntarily humble, in accordance with the miserable district it aids. In the Middle Ages the church was a monument seen only within, and not one of those impetuous basilicas which are put up as a show in open spaces.

"Then it was an oratory for the poor, a church on its knees, and not standing ; it would, therefore, be the most absolute nonsense to free it from its surroundings, to take it out of the day of an eternal twilight, out of those hours of shadow which brighten the melancholy beauty of a servant in prayer behind the impious hedge of hovels.

"Ah, were it possible to steep the church in the glowing atmosphere of Notre Dame des Victoires, and join to its meagre psalmody the powerful choir of St. Sulpice, that would be complete," said Durtal, "but alas, here below, nothing whole, nothing perfect exists ! "

Indeed from an artistic point of view, it was the only church which satisfied him, for Notre Dame de Paris was too grand, and too much overrun by tourists ; there were few ceremonies there, just the necessary amount of prayers were weighed out, and the greater part of the chapels remained closed ; and lastly the voices of the choir boys always wanted mending ; they broke, while the advanced age of the basses made them hoarse. At St. Etienne du Mont it was worse still ; the shell of the church was charming, but the choir was an offshoot of the school of Sanfourche, you might think yourself in a kennel, where a medley pack of sick beasts were growling ; as for the other sanctuaries on the right bank of the river, they were worthless, plain chant was as far as possible suppressed, and the poverty of the voices was everywhere ornamented with promiscuous tunes.

Yet on the right bank were the more self-respecting churches, for religious Paris stops on that side of the Seine, and comes to an end as you pass the bridges.

In fact, to sum up all, he might believe that St. Severin by its scent, and the delightful art of its old nave, St. Sulpice by its ceremonies and its chanting, had brought him back towards Christian art, which in its turn had directed him to God.

Then when once urged on this way, he had pursued it, had left architecture and music, to wander in the mystic territories of the other arts, and his long visits to the Louvre, his researches into the breviaries, into the books of Ruysbröck, Angela da Foligno, Saint Teresa, Saint Catherine of Genoa, Saint Magdalen of Pazzi, had confirmed him in his belief.

But the upheaval of all his ideas which he had undergone was too recent for his soul at once to regain its equilibrium. From time to time it seemed to wish to go back, and he discussed with himself in order to set it at rest. He spent himself in disputation, came to doubt the reality of his con version, and said : " After all I am united to the church only on the side of art. I only go there to see or hear and not to pray ; I do not seek the Lord, but my own pleasure. This is not business. Just as in a warm bath I do not feel the cold if I am motionless, but if I move I freeze, so in the church my impulses are upset when I move, I am almost on fire in the nave, less warm in the porch, and I become perfectly icy outside. These are literary postulates, vibrations of the nerves, skirmishes of thought, spiritual brawls, whatever you please, except Faith."

But what disquieted him still more than the need of helps to feeling, was that his shameless senses rebelled at the contact of religious ideas. He floated like wreckage between Licentiousness and the Church, they each threw him back in turn, obliging him as he approached one to return at once to that which he had left, and he was inclined to ask if he were not a victim to some mystification of his lower instincts, seeking to revive themselves, without his consciousness, by the cordial of a false piety.

In fact he had often seen realized in himself that unclean miracle, when he had left St. Severin, almost in tears. Insensibly, without connection of ideas, without any welding together of sensations, without the explosion of a spark, his senses took fire, and he was powerless to let them burn themselves out, to resist them.

He loathed himself afterwards, and it was high time. Then came the reverse movement ; he longed to run to some chapel, there to wash and be clean, and he was so disgusted with himself that now and then he went as far as the door and dared not enter.

At other times, on the contrary, he rebelled against himself, and cried in fury : " It is monstrous, I have in fact spoiled for myself the only pleasure that remained to me— the flesh. Once I amused myself without blame, now I pay for my poor debauches with torments. I have added one more weariness to existence—would that I could undo it."

He lied to himself in vain, trying to justify himself by suggesting doubts.

" Suppose all this were not true, if there were nothing in it, if I were deceiving myself, what if the freethinkers were right ? "

But he was obliged to be sorry for himself, for he felt distinctly to the bottom of his soul, that he held unshaken the certitude of true Faith.

" These discussions are miserable, and the excuses I make for my filthinesses are odious," he said to himself, and a flame of enthusiasm sprang up within him.

How doubt the truth of dogmas, how deny the divine power of the Church, for she commands assent ?

First she has her superhuman art and her mysticism, then she is most wonderful in the persistent folly of conquered heresies. All since the world began have had the flesh as their springboard. Logically and humanly speaking they should have triumphed, for they allowed man and woman to satisfy their passions, saying to themselves there was no sin in these, even sanctifying them as the Gnostics, rendering homage to God by the foulest uncleanness.

All have suffered shipwreck. The Church, unbending in this matter, has remained upright and entire. She orders the body to be silent, and the soul to suffer, and contrary to all probability, humanity listens to her, and sweeps away like a dung-heap the seductive joys proposed to her.

Again, the vitality of the Church is decision, which preserves her in spite of the unfathomable stupidity of her sons. She has resisted the disquieting folly of the clergy, and has not even been broken up by the awkwardness and lack of ability in her defenders, a very strong point.

"No, the more I think of her," he cried, "the more I think her prodigious, unique, the more I am convinced that she alone holds the truth, that outside her are only weaknesses of mind, impostures, scandals. The Church is the divine breeding ground, the heavenly dispensary of souls ; she gives them suck, nourishes them, and heals them ; she bids them understand, when the hour of sorrow comes, that true life begins, not at birth, but at death. The Church is indefectible, before all things admirable, she is great—

"Yes, but then we must follow her directions and practise the sacraments she orders ! "

And Durtal, shaking his head, gave himself no further answer.

CHAPTER III.

BEFORE his conversion he had said like all unbelievers:
" If I believed that Jesus Christ is God, and that eternal
life is not a decoy, I would not hesitate to change all my
habits, to follow as far as possible the rules of religion, and,
in any case, to live chaste." And he was surprised that people
he knew, who were in these conditions, did not maintain an
attitude higher than his own. He who had so long
indulgently forgiven himself became singularly intolerant,
so soon as he had to do with a Catholic.

He now understood the injustice of his judgments, and
confessed that between faith and practice was a gulf difficult
to overpass.

He did not like to discuss this question with himself, but
it returned and took possession of him all the same, and he
was obliged to admit the meanness of his arguments, the
despicable reasons for his resistance.

He was still honest enough to say: " I am no longer a
child ; if I have Faith, if I admit Catholicism, I cannot
conceive it as lukewarm and unfixed, warmed up again
and again in the saucepan of a false zeal. I will have no
compromise or truce, no alternations of debauch and
communions, no stages of licentiousness and piety, no, all
or nothing ; to change from top to bottom, or not change
at all."

Then he drew back in alarm, endeavoured to escape
the part he was about to take, endeavoured to exculpate
himself, cavilling for hours, invoking the most wretched
motives for remaining as he was, and not budging a jot.

" What am I to do ? If I do not obey orders, which I feel
with increasing force, I am preparing for myself a life of
uneasiness and remorse, for I know well I ought not to

remain for ever on the threshold, but to penetrate into the
sanctuary and stay there. And if I make up my mind—
no indeed—for then I must bind myself to a heap of
observances, bend to a series of rules, assist at mass on
Sunday, abstain on Friday, live like a bigot, and look like a
fool."

And then to help his revolt, he thought of the air, the
look of people who frequented the churches ; for two men
who looked intelligent and clean, how many were without
doubt rascals and impostors !

Almost all had a side-long look, an oily voice, downcast
eyes, immovable spectacles, clothes like sacristans as if
of black wood, almost all told thin beads ostentatiously,
and with more strategy and more knavery than the wicked,
took toll from their neighbours on leaving God.

The devout women were still less reassuring, they
invaded the church, walking about as if quite at home,
disturbing everybody, upsetting chairs, knocking against
you without begging pardon ; then they knelt down
with much ado, in the attitude of contrite angels, murmured interminable paternosters, and left the church more
arrogant and sour than before.

"It is not encouraging to have to mix with this flock of
pious geese," he exclaimed.

But soon, against his will, he made answer to himself :
"You have nothing to do with others, were you more
humble, these people would certainly seem less offensive ;
at any rate they have the courage you lack, they are not
ashamed of their faith, and are not afraid to kneel to God
in public."

And Durtal remained dumfounded, for he had to admit
that the riposte struck home. It was clear his humility
was at fault, but what was worse, he could not free himself from human respect.

He was afraid of being taken for a fool ; the prospect of
being seen on his knees, in church, made his hair stand on
end ; the idea, that, if he ever had to communicate, he
would have to rise and go to the altar in the sight of all,
was intolerable to him.

"If that moment ever come it will be hard to bear," said
he ; " and yet I am an idiot, for what have I to do with the
opinion of people I do not know ? " but much as he might

repeat that his alarms were absurd, he could not get over them, or free himself from the fear of ridicule.

"After all," he said, "even if I decide to jump the ditch, to confess and communicate, that terrible question of the senses would always have to be resolved. I must determine to fly the lusts of the flesh, and accept perpetual abstinence. I could never attain to that.

"Without counting that in any case, the time would be ill-chosen were I now to make such an effort, for never have I been so tormented as since my conversion; Catholicism unfortunately excites unclean suggestions when I prowl about it, without entering."

And to this exclamation another answered at once: "Yes, but you must enter."

He was irritated at this change of front without change of place, and he tried to turn the conversation, as though it had been held with another, whose questions perplexed him; but he came back to it all the same, and, in his annoyance, summoned all his reasoning powers to his aid.

"Come, let us try to take stock at any rate! It is plain that as I have drawn near the Church, my unclean desires have become more frequent and more persistent; and yet another fact is certain that I have been so used up by twenty years of debauchery that I ought not to have any further carnal appetites. In fact, if I chose it, I could perfectly well remain chaste; but then I must bid my miserable brain be silent, and I have no power to do so! It is frightful all the same that I am more excited than in youth, for now my desires go a-travelling, and since they have not their ordinary shelter they go off in search of evil haunts. How may this be explained? It is a sort of dyspepsia of the soul, which cannot digest ordinary meats, and tries to feed on spiced dreams, highly seasoned thoughts; it is then want of appetite for wholesome meals which has begotten this greediness for strange dishes, this trouble of the mind, this wish to escape from myself, and jump were it but for a moment over the permitted limits of the senses.

"In that case Catholicism would play a part at once repellent and depressing. It would stimulate these sick desires, and weaken me at the same time, would give

me over to nervous emotions without strength to resist
them."

Wandering thus in self-examination, he came to a dead
stand where was no issue, arriving at this conclusion : " I
do not practise my religion, because I yield to my baser
instincts, and I yield to these instincts because I do not
practise my religion."

Brought up thus by a dead wall, he resisted, asking if this
last observation were indeed true ; for, after all, nothing
proved that if he approached the Sacraments he would not
be attacked with even greater violence. It was even
probable he would be, for the devil makes a dead set at pious
people.

Then he rebelled against the cowardice of these remarks,
and cried : " I lie, for I know well, that if I made the least
sign of resistance, I should be powerfully aided from on
high."

Clever at self-torture, he continued to harass his soul,
always on the same line. " Suppose," he said, " for the sake
of argument, that I have tamed my pride, and subdued my
body, suppose that at present there were nothing to do, but
to go forward, I am still brought up, for the final obstacle
terrifies me.

" Up to now I have been able to walk alone, without
earthly assistance, without advice ; I have been converted
without the help of anyone, but now I cannot make a step
without a guide, I cannot approach the altar without the
aid of an interpreter, and the bulwark of a priest."

And once more, he drew back, for in former times he had
been intimate with a certain number of ecclesiastics, and
had found them so mediocre, so lukewarm, above all so
hostile to Mysticism, that he was revolted at the very notion of laying before them the schedule of his requirements
and his regrets.

" They will not understand me," he thought ; " they will
answer that Mysticism was interesting in the Middle Ages,
but has now become disused and is in any case quite out of
touch with the modern spirit. They will think me mad,
will assure me, moreover, that God does not want so much, will
advise me with a smile, not to make myself singular, to do
as others, and to think like them.

" I have indeed no intention of entering on the way of

Mysticism, but they may at least allow me to envy it and not inflict on me their middle-class ideal of a God.

" For, not to deceive oneself, Catholicism is not only that moderate religion that they offer us ; it is not composed only of petty cases and formulas ; it is not wholly confined to rigid observances, and the toys of old maids, to all that goody-goody business, which spreads itself abroad in the Rue Saint Sulpice ; it is far more exalted, far purer, but then we must penetrate its burning zone, and seek in Mysticism, the art, the essence, and the very soul of the Church.

" Using the powerful means at her disposal, we then have to empty ourselves, and strip the soul, so that Christ if He will may enter it ; we have to purify the house, to cleanse it with the disinfectant of prayer and the sublimate of Sacraments ; in a word, to be ready when the Guest shall come and bid us to empty ourselves wholly into Him, as He will pour Himself into us.

" I know thoroughly well, that this divine alchemy, this transmutation of the human creature into God, is generally impossible, for the Saviour, as a rule, keeps His singular favours for His elect ; but after all, every one, however unworthy, is presumably able to attain that majestic end, since God only decides, and not man, whose humble acquiescence alone is requisite.

" I see myself saying that to the priests ! They will tell me I have no business with mystical ideas, and will give me in exchange the petty religion of rich women ; they will wish to mix themselves up with my life, to inquire about the state of my soul, to insinuate their own tastes ; they will try to convince me that art is dangerous, will sermonize me with imbecile talk, and pour over me their flowing bowls of pious veal broth.

" I know what I am ; at the end of a couple of interviews I shall rebel, and become wicked."

Durtal shook his head, remained in thought, and began again,—

" Yet one must be just ; perhaps the secular clergy are only the leavings, for the contemplative orders and the missionary army carry away every year the pick of the spiritual basket ; the mystics, priests athirst for sorrows, drunk with sacrifice, bury themselves in cloisters or exile themselves among savages whom they teach. So when the cream is off, the rest of the clergy are plainly but skim milk, the scourings of the seminaries.

"Yes, but after all," he continued, "the question is not whether they are intelligent or narrow, it is not my business to take the priest to pieces to discover under the consecrated rind the nothingness of the man ; not my business to abuse his inadequacy since it is thoroughly suited to the understanding of the crowd. Would it not be, after all, more courageous and more humble to kneel before a being of whose brains you know the weakness ?

"And then . . . then . . . I am not reduced to that, for indeed I know one in Paris, a true mystic. Suppose I go and see him ! "

And he thought of a certain Abbé Gévresin, with whom he had formerly some acquaintance ; he had often met him at a bookseller's in the Rue Servandoni, old Tocane, who had rare books on liturgy and the lives of the saints.

Learning that Durtal was looking for works on Blessed Lidwine, the priest was at once interested in him, and on leaving the shop they had a long conversation. The abbé was very old and walked with difficulty, therefore he willingly took Durtal's arm, who saw him home.

"The life of that victim of the sins of her time is a magnificent subject," he said ; "you remember it, do you not ? " and as they walked he sketched its lines, broadly.

"Lidwine was born towards the end of the fourteenth century, at Schiedam, in Holland. Her beauty was extraordinary, but she lost it through illness at the age of fifteen. She recovered, but while skating one day with her companions on the frozen canals, she fell and broke a rib. From the time of that accident to her death she was bed-ridden. She was afflicted with most frightful ailments, her wounds festered, and worms bred in her putrefying flesh. Erysipelas, that terrible malady of the Middle Ages, consumed her. Her right arm was eaten away, a single muscle held it to the body, her brow was cleft in two, one of her eyes became blind, and the other so weak that it could not bear the light.

"While she was in this condition, the plague ravaged Holland, and decimated the town in which she lived ; she was the first attacked. Two boils formed, one under her arm, the other above the heart. ' Two boils, it is well,' she said to the Lord, 'but three would be better in honour of the Holy Trinity,' and immediately a third pustule broke out on her face.

" For thirty-five years she lived in a cellar, taking no solid food, praying and weeping, so chilly in winter, that each morning her tears formed two frozen streams down her cheeks.

" She thought herself still too fortunate, and entreated the Lord not to spare her, and obtained from Him the grace that by her sufferings she might expiate the sins of others. Christ heard her prayers, visited her with His angels, communicated her with His own hand, gave her the delight of heavenly ecstasies, and caused her festering wounds to exhale delicious perfumes.

" At the moment of her death He stood by her, and restored her poor body to its former soundness. Her beauty, so long vanished, shone out again, the town was moved, the sick came in crowds, and all who drew near were healed.

" She is the true patroness of the sick," concluded the abbé, and, after a silence, he added,—

" From the point of view of the higher mysticism, Lidwine is wonderful, for in her we can verify that plan of substitution which was, and is, the glorious reason for the existence of convents."

And as, without answering, Durtal questioned him with a look, he went on,—

" You are aware, sir, that in all ages, nuns have offered themselves to heaven as expiatory victims. The lives of saints, both men and women, who desired these sacrifices abound, of those who atoned for the sins of others by sufferings eagerly demanded and patiently borne. But there is a task still more arduous and more painful than was desired by these admirable souls. It is not now that of purging the faults of others, but of preventing them, hindering their commission, by taking the place of those who are too weak to bear the shock.

" Read Saint Teresa on this subject ; you will see that she gained permission to take on herself, and without flinching, the temptations of a priest who could not endure them. This substitution of a strong soul freeing one who is not strong from perils and fears is one of the great rules of mysticism.

" Sometimes this exchange is purely spiritual, sometimes on the contrary it has to do only with the ills of the body. Saint Teresa was the surrogate of souls in torment, Sister Catherine Emmerich took the place of the sick, relieved, at least, those who were most suffering ; thus, for instance, she was able to undergo the agony of a woman suffering from consumption and dropsy, in order to permit her to prepare for death in peace.

" Well, Lidwine took on herself all bodily ills, she lusted for physical suffering, and was greedy for wounds ; she was, as it were, the reaper of punishments, and she was also the piteous vessel in which everyone discharged the overflowings of his malady. If you would speak of her in other fashion than the poor hagiographies of our day, study first that law of substitution, that miracle of perfect charity, that super-human triumph of Mysticism ; that will be the stem of your book, and naturally, without effort, all Lidwine's acts graft themselves on it."

" But," asked Durtal, " does this law still take effect ? "

" Yes : I know convents which apply it. Moreover, Orders like the Carmelites and the Poor Clares willingly accept the transfer to them of temptations we suffer ; then these convents take on their backs, so to speak, the diabolical expiations of those insolvent souls whose debts they pay to the full."

" All the same," said Durtal, shaking his head, " if you consent to take on yourself the assaults intended for your neighbour, you must make pretty sure not to sink."

" The nuns chosen by our Lord," replied the abbé, " as victims of expiation, as whole burnt-offerings, are in fact few, and they are generally, especially in this age, obliged to unite and coalesce in order to bear without failing the weight of misdeeds which try them, for in order that a soul may bear alone the assaults of Satan, which are often terrible, it must be indeed assisted by the angels and elect of God." And after a silence the old priest added,—

" I believe I may speak with some experience in these matters, for I am one of the directors of those nuns who make reparation in their convents."

" And yet," cried Durtal, " the world asks what is the good of the contemplative Orders."

" They are the lightning conductors of society," said the

abbé, with great energy. " They draw on themselves the demoniacal fluid, they absorb temptations to vice, preserve by their prayers those who live, like ourselves, in sin ; they appease, in fact, the wrath of the Most High that He may not place the earth under an interdict. Ah ! while the sisters who devote themselves to nursing the sick and infirm are indeed admirable, their task is easy in comparison with that undertaken by the cloistered Orders, the Orders where penance never ceases, and the very nights spent in bed are broken by sobs."

" This priest is far more interesting than his brethren," said Durtal to himself as they parted ; and, as the abbé invited his visits, he had often called on him.

He had always been cordially welcomed. On several occasions he had warily sounded the old man on several questions. He had answered evasively in regard to other priests. But he did not seem to think much of them, if Durtal might judge by what he said one day in regard to Lidwine, that magnet of sorrows.

" Notice," he said, " that a weak and honest soul has every advantage in choosing a confessor, not from the clergy who have lost the sense of Mysticism, but from the monks. They alone know the effects of the law of substitution, and if they see that in spite of their efforts the penitent succumbs, they end by freeing him by taking his trials on themselves, or by sending them off to some convent in the country where resolute people can use them."

Another time the question of nationalities was discussed in a newspaper which Durtal showed him. The abbé shrugged his shoulders, putting aside the patriotic twaddle. " For me," he said calmly, " for me my country is that where I can best pray."

Durtal could not make out what this priest was. He understood from the bookseller, that the Abbé Gévresin on account of his great age and infirmity was incapacitated for the regular duties of the priesthood. " I know that, when he can, he still says his mass each morning in a convent ; I believe also he receives a few of his brethren for confession in his own house ; " and Tocane added with disdain, " He has barely enough to live on, and they do not look on him with favour at the archbishop's because of his mystical notions."

There ended all he knew about him.   "He is evidently a
very good priest," repeated Durtal; "his physiognomy
declares it, and his mouth and eyes contradict each other ;
his eyes certainly declare his entire goodness, his lips,
somewhat thick, purple and always moist, have on them
an affectionate but somewhat sad smile, and to this his
blue eyes give the lie—blue, childlike eyes which laugh out
astonished under white eyebrows in a rather red face,
touched on the cheeks like a ripe apricot, with little points
of blood.

"In any case," said Durtal, waking from his meditations, "I am very wrong not to continue the relations
into which I have entered with him.

"Yes, but then nothing is so difficult as to become really
intimate with a priest ; first by the very education he
receives at the seminary the ecclesiastic thinks himself
obliged to disperse his affections and not concentrate himself on particular friendships ; then, like a doctor, he is a man
harassed with business, who is never to be found.   You
can catch them now and then between two confessions or
two sick calls.   Nor even then are you quite certain that
the eager welcome of the priest rings true, for he is just the
same to all who come to him, and indeed, since I do not
call on the Abbé Gévresin for his help or advice, I am afraid
of being in his way, and of taking up his time, hence I am
acting with discretion in not going to see him.

"Yet I am sorry ; suppose I write, or go to him one morning, but what have I to say to him ?   I ought to know what
I want before I allow myself to trouble him.   If I go only
to complain, he will answer I am wrong not to be a com-
municant, and I have nothing to answer.   No : the better
plan is to meet him as by chance, on the quays, where no
doubt he sometimes looks over the book-stalls, or at
Tocane's, for then I can talk to him more intimately, at least
less officially, about my vacillations and regrets."

So Durtal searched the quays, and never once met the
abbé.   He went to the bookseller's, and pretended to look
over his stock, but as soon as he pronounced the name
Gévresin, Tocane exclaimed, "I have heard nothing of
him, he has not been here for the last two months."

"I will not turn back, but just disturb him in his own
house," said Durtal, "but he will wonder why I came back

after so long an absence. Besides the awkwardness I feel in calling on people whom I have neglected, I am also troubled by thinking the abbé may suspect some interested object in my visit. That is not convenient ; if I had but a good pretext ; there is certainly that life of Lidwine which interests him, I might consult him on various points. Yes, but which ? I have not concerned myself with that saint for a long time, and must read over again the meagre old books on her biography. After all, it will be simpler and better to be frank, and say, ' This is why I have come ; I want to ask advice, which I have not determined to follow, but I have so much need of speaking, of giving the reins to my soul, that I beg you to be so kind as to lose an hour for my sake.'

"He will do it certainly and willingly.

" Then that is agreed on ; suppose I go to-morrow ? " But he checked himself at once. " There was nothing pressing ; there was plenty of time ; better take time and think ; ah, yes, here is Christmas close upon us, I cannot decently trouble a priest who has his penitents to confess, for there are many communicants on that day. Let him get his hard work over, and then we will see."

He was at first pleased at having invented that excuse, then he had to admit in his heart that, after all, there was not much in it, for there was nothing to show that this priest, who was not attached to a parish, was busy in hearing confessions.

It was hardly probable, but he tried to convince himself that it might be so after all, and his hesitation began again. Angry at last with the discussion, he adopted a middle course. For greater certainty, he would not call on the abbé till after Christmas, but he would not be later than a given time ; he took an almanack, and swore to keep his promise—three days after that feast.

CHAPTER IV.

Oh! that midnight mass! He had had the unfortunate idea of going to it at Christmas. He went to St. Severin, and found a young ladies' day school installed there, instead of the choir, who, with sharp voices like needles, knitted the worn-out skeins of the canticles. He had fled to St. Sulpice, and plunged into a crowd which walked and talked as if in the open air; had heard there choral-society marches, tea-garden waltzes, firework tunes, and had come away in a rage.

It had seemed to him superfluous to try St. Germain-des-Près, for he held that church in horror. Besides the weariness inspired by its heavy, ill-restored shell, and the miserable paintings with which Flandrin loaded it, the clergy there were specially, almost alarmingly, ugly, and the choir was truly infamous. They were like a set of bad cooks, boys who spat vinegar, and elderly choir-men, who cooked in the furnace of their throats a sort of vocal broth, a thin gruel of sound.

Nor did he think of taking refuge in St. Thomas Aquinas, where he dreaded the barking and the choruses; there was indeed St. Clotilde, where the psalmody, at least, is upright, and has not, like that of St. Thomas, lost all shame. He went there, but again encountered dance music and profane tunes, a worldly orgie.

At last he went to bed in a rage, saying to himself, "In Paris, at any rate, a singular baptism of music is reserved for the New-Born."

Next day, when he woke, he felt he had no courage to face the churches; the sacrileges of last night would, he thought, continue; and as the weather was almost fine, he went out, wandered in the Luxembourg, gained the square of the Observatoire, and the Boulevard de Port Royal, and mechanically made his way along the interminable Rue de la Santé.

He knew that street of old, and had taken melancholy walks in it, attracted by its poor houses, like those of a provincial town ; then it was fit for a dreamer, for it was bounded on the right by the Prison de la Santé and Sainte Anne's madhouse, and on the left by convents. Light and air circulated in the street, but, behind it, all was black ; it was a kind of prison corridor, with cells on either side, where some were condemned to temporary sentences, and others, of their own free will, suffered lasting sorrows.

" I can imagine," thought Durtal, " how it would have been painted by an Early Flemish master ; the long street paved by patient pencils, the stories open from top to bottom, and the cupboards the same ; and on one side massive cells with iron bedsteads, a stoneware jug ; little peepholes in the doors secured by strong bolts, inside, scoundrels and thieves, gnashing their teeth, turning round and round, their hair on end, howling like caged animals ; on the other side little rooms, furnished with a pallet-bed, a stoneware jug, a crucifix, these also closed by doors iron-banded, and within nuns or monks, kneeling on the flags, their faces clean cut against the light of a halo, their eyes lifted to heaven, their hands joined, raised from the ground in ecstasy, a pot of lilies at their side.

Then at the back of the canvas, between these two rows of houses, rises a great avenue, at the end of which in a dappled sky sits God the Father with Christ on His right, choirs of Seraphim playing on guitar and viol ; God the Father immovable under his lofty tiara, His breast covered by His long beard, holds scales which balance exactly, the holy captives expiating precisely by their penances and prayers the blasphemies of the rascals and the insane.

" It must be admitted," thought Durtal, " that this street is very peculiar, that there is probably none like it in Paris, for it unites in its course virtues and vices, which in other quarters, in spite of the efforts of the Church, trend apart as far as possible from each other."

Thus thinking he had come as far as St. Anne's, where the street grows lighter and the houses are lower, with only one or two stories, then, gradually, there is greater space

between them, and they are only joined to each other by
blank ends of walls.

"At any rate," thought Durtal, "if this street has no
distinction, it is very private ; here at least one need not
admire the impertinent decoration of those modern shops
which expose in their windows as precious commodities,
chosen piles of firewood, and in glass sweetmeat jars, coal
drops and coke lollipops."

And here is an odd lane, and he looked at an alley which
led down a sharp decline into a main street, where was to
be seen the tricolor flag in zinc on a washhouse ; he read
the name : Rue de l'Ebre.

He entered it, it was but a few yards long ; the whole of
one side was occupied by a wall, behind which were half
seen some stunted buildings, surmounted by a bell. An
entrance-gate with a square wicket was placed in the wall,
which was raised higher as it sloped downwards, and at the
end was pierced by round windows, and rose into a little
building, surmounted by a clock-tower so low that its point
did not even reach the height of the two-storied house
opposite.

On the other side three hovels sloped down, closely
packed together ; zinc pipes ran everywhere, growing like
vines, ramifying like the stalks of a hollow vine along the
walls, windows gaped on rusty leaden hinges. Dim courts of
wretched hovels could be seen ; in one was a shed where
some cows were reposing ; in two others were coach-houses
for wheel-chairs, and a rack behind the bars of which
appeared the capsuled necks of bottles.

"But this must be a church," thought Durtal, looking at
the little clock tower, and the three or four round bays, which
seemed cut out in emery paper to look like the black rough
mortar of the wall ; "where is the entrance ? "

He found it on turning out of the alley into the Rue de
la Glacière. A tiny porch gave access to the building.

He opened the door, and entered a large room, a sort of
closed shed, painted yellow, with a flat ceiling, with small
iron beams coloured grey, picked out with blue, and ornamented with gas-jets like a wine shop. At the end was a
marble a ltar, six lighted tapers, and gilt ornaments, candelabra full of tapers, and under the tabernacle, a very
small monstrance, which sparkled in the light of the tapers.

It was almost dark, the panes of the windows having been crudely daubed with bands of indigo and yellowish green ; it was freezing, the stove was not alight, and the church, paved like a kitchen floor, had no matting or carpet.

Durtal wrapped himself up as best he could and sat down. His eyes gradually grew accustomed to the obscurity of the room, and what he saw was strange ; in front of the choir on rows of chairs were seated human forms, drowned in floods of white muslin. No one stirred.

Suddenly there entered by a side door a nun equally wrapped from head to foot in a large veil. She passed along the altar, stopped in the middle, threw herself on the ground, kissed the floor, and by a sudden effort, without helping herself by her arms, stood upright, advanced silently into the church, and brushed by Durtal, who saw under the muslin a magnificent robe of creamy white, an ivory cross at her neck, at her girdle a white cord and beads.

She went to the entrance-door, and there ascended a little staircase into a gallery which commanded the church.

He asked himself what could be this Order so sumptuously arrayed, in this miserable chapel, in such a district ?

Little by little the room filled, choir-boys in red with capes trimmed with rabbit's skin lighted the candelabra, went out, and ushered in a priest, vested in a grand cope, with large flowers, a priest tall and young, who sat down, and in a sonorous tone chanted the first antiphon of vespers.

Suddenly Durtal turned round. In the gallery an harmonium accompanied the responses of voices never to be forgotten. It was not a woman's voice, but one having in it something of a child's voice, sweetened, purified, sharpened, and something of a man's, but less harsh, finer and more sustained, an unsexed voice, filtered through litanies, bolted by prayers, passed through the sieves of adoration and tears.

The priest, still sitting, chanted the first verse of the unchanging psalm, " Dixit Dominus Domino meo."

And Durtal saw in the air, in the gallery, tall white statues, holding black books in their hands, chanting slowly with eyes raised to heaven. A lamp cast its light on one of these figures, which for a second leant forward a little, and he saw under the lifted veil a face attentive and sorrowful, and very pale.

The verses of the vesper psalms were now sung alter-
nately, by the nuns above and by the congregation below.
The chapel was almost full ; a school of girls in white veils
filled one side ; little girls of the middle-class, poorly dressed
brats who played with their dolls occupied the other.
There were a few poor women in *sabots*, and no men.

The atmosphere became extraordinary. The warmth of
the souls thawed the ice of the room ; here were not the
vespers of the rich, such as were celebrated on Sundays at
St. Sulpice, but the vespers of the poor, domestic vespers,
in the plain chant of the country side, followed by the
faithful with mighty fervour in silent and singular devotion.

Durtal could fancy himself transported beyond the city,
to the depths of some village cloister ; he felt himself
softened, his soul rocked by the monotonous amplitude of
these chants, only recognizing the end of the psalms by
the return of the doxology, the " Gloria Patri et Filio,"
which separated them from each other.

He had a real impulse, a dim need of praying to the
Unknowable, penetrated to the very marrow by this
environment of aspiration, it seemed to him that he thawed
a little, and took a far-off part in the united tenderness of
these bright spirits. He sought for a prayer, and recalled
what St. Paphnutius taught Thais, when he cried, " Thou
art not worthy to name the name of God, thou wilt
pray only thus : ' Qui plasmasti me miserere mei ; ' Thou
who hast formed me have mercy on me." He stammered
out the humble phrase, prayed not out of love or of
contrition, but out of disgust with himself, unable to let
himself go, regretting that he could not love. Then he
thought of saying the Lord's Prayer, but stopped at the
notion that this is the hardest of all prayers to pronounce,
when the phrases are weighed in the balance. For in it
we declare to God that we forgive our neighbours' trespasses.
Now how many who use these words forgive others ? How
many Catholics do not lie when they tell the All-knowing
that they hate no one ?

He was roused from these reflections by sudden silence ;
vespers were over. Then the organ played again, and all
the voices of the nuns joined, those in the choir below and
in the gallery above, singing the old carol " Unto us a child
is born."

He listened, moved by the simplicity of the strain, and suddenly, in a minute, brutally, without understanding why, infamous thoughts filled his mind.

He resisted in disgust, wished to repulse the assault of these shameful feelings, and they were persistent. He seemed to see before him a woman whose perverse ways had long maddened him.

All at once this hallucination ceased ; his eye was mechanically attracted towards the priest, who was looking at him, while speaking in a low voice to a beadle.

He lost his head, imagining that the priest guessed his thoughts and was turning him out, but this notion was so foolish, that he shrugged his shoulders, and more sensibly thought that men were not admitted to this convent of women, and that the abbé who had seen him was sending the beadle to beg him to leave.

The beadle came straight to him ; Durtal was ready to take his hat, when in persuasive and gentle tones that functionary said that the procession was about to begin, that it was the custom for the gentlemen to follow the Blessed Sacrament, and that although he was the only man there, the abbé thought he would not refuse to follow the procession about to start.

Overwhelmed by this request, Durtal made a vague gesture, in which the beadle seemed to see assent.

" No," he thought as soon as he was left alone ; " I will not meddle with the ceremony ; first I know nothing about it, and I should spoil it all, and again I will not make a fool of myself." He prepared to slip away quietly, but he had no time to carry out his intention ; the usher brought him a lighted candle and asked him to accompany him. He put the best face he could on the matter, and while thinking that he was blushing all over, he followed the beadle to the altar.

There the beadle stopped him and bid him not to move. The whole congregation was now standing, the girls' school divided into two files, preceded by a woman carrying a banner. Durtal came in front of the first rank of nuns.

Their veils lowered before the profane, even in church, were raised before the Blessed Sacrament, before God. Durtal was able to look at these sisters for a moment ; at

first his disillusion was complete. He had supposed them
pale and grave like the nun he had seen in the gallery, and
almost all of them were red, freckled, crossing their poor
hands swelled and wounded by chilblains. Their faces
were puffy and all seemed at the beginning or end of a cold ;
they were evidently country girls, and the novices, known
by their grey robes under the white veil, were still more
common looking ; they had certainly been accustomed to
farm labour, and yet on seeing them all turned to the altar,
the poverty of their faces, the ugliness of their hands blue
with cold, their broken nails, injured in the wash, disappeared ; their eyes, modest and humble under their long
lashes, changed their coarse features into pious simplicity.
Lost in prayer, they did not even see his curious looks, and
did not even suspect a man was there examining them.

Durtal envied the admirable wisdom of these poor girls
who alone understood it was mad to wish to live. He
thought : " Ignorance leads to the same result as knowledge.
Among the Carmelites are rich and pretty women who
have lived in the world and left it, wholly convinced of
the vainness of its joys ; and these nuns, who evidently
know nothing, have had an intuition of that vacuity which
it has needed years of experience for the others to gain.
By different ways they have arrived at the same meeting-
place. Then what clearness of thought is revealed by their
entrance into an Order ! for if indeed they had not been
gathered by Christ, what would have become of these
unhappy girls ? Married to drunkards and hammered by
beatings ; or perhaps maids in taverns, ill-treated by their
masters, brutalized by the other servants, destined to the
scorn of the streets and the dangers of ill-usage. And
without knowing anything they have avoided it all, have
remained innocent, far from these perils, and far from this
defilement, under an obedience which is not ignoble,
disposed by their very way of life to experience, should they
be worthy, the most powerful joys which the soul of a
human creature can feel. They remain, perhaps, beasts of
burthen, but at any rate God's beasts of burthen."

He had got so far in his reflections when the beadle
beckoned to him. The priest, who had descended from the
altar, held the little monstrance ; the girls' procession was
moving before him. Durtal passed in front of the line of

nuns who did not take part in the ceremony, and torch in
hand he followed the beadle, who carried behind the priest
an open white silk parasol.

Then the harmonium in the gallery filled the church
with its drawling tones, like an enlarged accordion, and the
nuns standing beside it intoned the old chant, rhythmical
as a march, the " Adeste Fideles," while below the novices
and the faithful repeated after each stanza the sweet chorus
of invitation, " Venite adoremus."

The procession went several times round the chapel,
above the heads bowed in the smoke from the censers,
which the choir boys swung, turning at each pause to face
the priest.

" Well, after all, I have not come so badly out of it," said
Durtal to himself, when they had returned to the altar. He
thought his part was finished, but, this time without asking
his permission, the beadle asked him to kneel at the communion rail in front of the altar.

He was ill at ease and annoyed, at knowing that the
whole school and the whole convent was behind him, nor
was he accustomed to kneel ; it seemed as if wedges were
thrust into his limbs, as if he were subjected to the tortures
of the Middle Ages. Embarrassed by his taper, which was
guttering, and threatened to cover him with spots, he shifted
his position quietly, trying to make himself more comfortable by slipping the skirts of his great coat between his
knees and the steps ; but in moving he only increased the
evil, his flesh was folded back between the bones, and his
skin was chafed and burning. He sweated at last with the
pain, and feared to distract the fervour of the community
by falling ; while the ceremony went on for ever, the nuns
sang in the gallery, but he listened no more and deplored the
length of the service.

At last the moment of Benediction approached.

Then in spite of himself, seeing himself there, so near to
God, Durtal forgot his sufferings, and bowed his head,
ashamed to be so placed, like a captain at the head of his
company, in the first rank of this maiden troop ; and when
in a great silence, the bell tinkled, and the priest turning,
lightly cut the air in the form of a cross, and, with the Blessed
Sacrament, blessed the congregation kneeling at his feet,
Durtal remained, his body bent, his eyes closed, seeking to

hide himself, to make himself small, and not be seen there
in front amid that pious crowd.

The psalm " Laudate Dominum, omnes gentes," rang out
when the beadle came to take his taper. Durtal could
hardly resist a cry, when he had to stand up ; his
benumbed knees cracked, and their joints would hardly
work.

Yet he regained his place somehow ; let the crowd pass,
and approaching the beadle, asked him the name of the
convent, and the order to which the nuns belonged.

" They are the Franciscan missionaries of Mary,"
answered the man, " but the chapel is not theirs as you
seem to think ; it is a chapel of ease for the parish of St.
Marcel de la Maison Blanche : it is only joined by a corridor
to the house those sisters occupy behind us there in the
Rue de l'Ebre. They join in the offices, in fact, just as you
and I may do, and they keep a school for the children of the
district."

" It is a touching little chapel," thought Durtal, when he
was alone. " It is well matched with the neighbourhood
it shelters, with the gloomy brook of the tanners, which
runs through the yards below the Rue de la Glacière. It
gives me the effect of being to Notre Dame de Paris what
its neighbour the Bièvre is to the Seine. It is the streamlet
of the church, the pious pavement, the miserable suburb
of worship.

" How poor and yet how exquisite are those nuns'
voices, which seem non-sexual and mellow ! God knows
how I hate the voice of a woman in the holy place, for
it still remains unclean. I think woman always brings
with her the lasting miasma of her indispositions and she
turns the psalms sour. Then, all the same, vanity and
concupiscence rise from the worldly voice, and its cries
of adoration accompanied by the organ are only cries of
carnal desire, its very pleadings in the most sombre
liturgical hymns are only addressed to God from the lips
outward, for at bottom a woman only mourns the mediocre
ideal of earthly pleasure to which she cannot attain. Thus
I thoroughly understand that the Church has rejected
woman from her offices, and that the musical robe of her
sequences may not be contaminated she employs the voices
of the boy and the man.

"Yet in convents of women, that is changed ; it is certain that prayer, communion, abstinence and vows purify the body and the soul, as well as the vocal odour which proceeds from them. The emanations from them give to the voices of the nuns, however crude, however ill-trained they may be, their chaste inflexions, their simple caresses of pure love, they recall to it the ingenuous sounds of childhood.

"In certain orders, they seem even to prune it of the greater part of its branches, and concentrate the threads of sap which remain in a few twigs ; " and he thought of a Carmelite convent to which he had gone from time to time, remembered their failing, almost expiring voices, where the little health that remained to them was concentrated in three notes, voices which had lost the musical colours of life, the tints of open air, keeping only in the cloister those of the costumes they seemed to reflect, white and brown, chaste and sombre tones.

Ah ! those Carmelites, he thought of them now, as he descended the Rue de la Glacière, and he called up the memory of a profession, the thought of which took entire possession of him every time he meditated on convents. He saw again in memory a morning in the little chapel in the Avenue de Saxe, a chapel, Spanish Gothic in style, with narrow windows glazed with panes so dark that the light which remained in their colours did not pass through them.

At the end rose the high altar in shade, raised on six steps ; on the left a large iron grating in an arch was covered with a black curtain, and on the same side, but almost at the base of the altar, a little arch traced on the plain wall, like a lancet window, with an aperture in the middle, a sort of square, a frame, without a panel, empty.

That morning the chapel, cold and dark, sparkled, lighted by groves of candles ; and the odour of incense, not adulterated as in other churches by spices and gums, filled it with a dull smoke ; it was crammed with people. Crouched in a corner, Durtal had turned round, and like his neighbours looked at the backs of the thurifers and priests, who were going towards the entrance. The door opened suddenly, and he saw, in a burst of daylight, a red vision of the Cardinal Archbishop of Paris, passing up the

nave, turning from side to side a horse-like head, in front
of it a big spectacled nose, bending his tall form all on one
side, blessing the congregation with a long twisted hand,
like a crab's claw.

He and his suite ascended the altar steps, and knelt at a
prie-Dieu, then they took off his tippet, and vested him in
a silk chasuble with a white cross embroidered in silver,
and the mass began.   Shortly before the communion, the
black veil was gently withdrawn ; behind the high grating,
and in a blueish light like that of the moon, Durtal faintly
saw white phantoms gliding and stars twinking in the air,
and close to the grating a woman's form, kneeling motionless on the ground, she too holding a star at the end of a
taper.   The woman did not move but the star shook ;
then when the moment of communion was at hand, the
woman rose, then disappeared, and her head, as if de-
capitated, filled the square of the wicket opened in the
arch.

Then as he leant forward he saw, for a second, a dead
face, with closed lids, white, eyeless, like ancient marble
statues.   And all passed away, as the Cardinal bent above
the grating, with the ciborium in his hand.

All was so rapid that he asked himself if he were not
dreaming ; the mass was over.   Behind the iron grating
resounded mournful psalms, slow chants drawn out, weeping, always on the same notes, wandering lights and white
forms passed in the azure fluid of the incense.   Monseigneur
Richard was sitting, mitre on head, interrogating the
postulant who had returned to her place, and was kneeling before him behind the grating.

He spoke in a low voice, and could not be heard.   The
whole congregation bent to listen to the novice as she pronounced her vows, but only a long murmur was heard.
Durtal remembered that he had elbowed his way, and got
near the choir, where, through the crossed bars of the
grating, he saw the woman clad in white, prostrate on her
face, in a square of flowers, while the whole convent filed
past, bending over her, intoning the psalms for the dead,
and sprinkling her with holy water, like a corpse.

" It is admirable," he cried, moved in the street by the
memory of the scene, and he thought of what a life was that
of these women !   To lie on an hair matress without pillow

or sheets, to fast seven months out of the twelve, except on Sundays and feasts ; always to eat, standing, vegetables and abstinence fare ; to have no fire in winter, to chant for hours on ice-cold tiles, to scourge the body, to become so humble as, however tenderly nurtured, to wash up dishes with joy, and attend to the meanest tasks, to pray from morning to midnight even to fainting, to pray there till death. They must indeed pity us, and set themselves to expiate the imbecility of a world which treats them as hysterical fools, for it cannot even understand the joy in suffering of souls like these.

" We cannot be proud of ourselves, in thinking of the Carmelites, or even of those humble Franciscan Tertiaries, who are after all more vulgar. It is true they do not belong to a contemplative order, but all the same their rules are very strict, their existence is so hard that they too can atone by their prayers and good works for the crimes of the city they protect."

He grew enthusiastic in thinking of the convents. Ah ! to be earthed up among them, sheltered from the herd, not to know what books appear, what newspapers are printed, never to know what goes on outside one's cell, among men —to complete the beneficent silence of this cloistered life, nourishing ourselves with good actions, refreshing ourselves with plain song, saturating ourselves with the inexhaustible joys of the liturgies.

Then, who knows ? By force of good will, and by ardent prayer, to succeed in coming to Him, in entertaining Him, feeling Him near us, perhaps almost satisfied with His creature. And he called up before him the joys of those abbeys in which Jesus abode. He remembered that astonishing convent of Unterlinden, near Colmar, where in the thirteenth century not only one or two nuns, but the whole convent, rose distractedly before Christ with cries of joy, nuns were lifted above the ground, others heard the songs of seraphim, and their emaciated bodies secreted balm ; others became transparent or were crowned with stars ; all these phenomena of the contemplative life were visible in that cloister, a high school of Mysticism.

Thus wrapped in thought, he found himself at his own door, without remembering the road he had taken, and as soon as he was in his room, his whole soul dilated and burst forth. He desired to thank, to call for mercy, to appeal to someone, he knew not whom, to complain of he knew not what. All at once the need of pouring himself forth, of going out of himself, took shape, and he fell on his knees saying to Our Lady,

"Have pity on me, and hear me ; I would rather anything than continue this shaken existence, these idle stages without an aim. Pardon me, Holy Virgin, unclean as I am, for I have no courage for the battle. Ah, wouldest thou grant my prayer ! I know well that I am over bold in daring to ask, since I am not even resolved to turn out my soul, to empty it like a bucket of filth, to strike it on the bottom, that the lees may trickle out and the scales fall off, but . . . but . . . thou knowest I am so weak, so little sure of myself, that in truth I shrink.

"Oh, all the same I would desire to flee away, a thousand miles from Paris, I know not where, into a cloister. My God ! yet this is very madness that I speak, for I could not stay two days in a convent ; nor indeed would they take me in."

Then he thought,—

"Though this once I am less dry, less unclean than is my wont, I can find nothing to say to Our Lady but insanities and follies, when it would be so simple to ask her pardon, to beg her to have pity on my desolate life, to aid me to resist the demands of my vices, not to pay as I do the royalties on my nerves, the tax on my senses.

"All the same," he said, rising, " enough of this, I will at least do what little I can ; without more delay I will go to the abbé to-morrow. I will explain the struggle of my soul, and we will see what happens afterwards."

CHAPTER V.

He was really comforted when the servant said that Monsieur l'Abbé was at home. He entered a little drawing-room, and waited till the priest, whom he heard speaking to someone in the next chamber, was alone.

He looked at the little room, and marked that nothing was changed since his last visit. It was still furnished with a velvet sofa, of which the red, once crimson, had become the faded rose colour of raspberry jam on bread. There were also two tall arm-chairs on either side of the chimney, which was ornamented by an Empire clock, and some china vases filled with sand, in which were stuck some dry stalks of reed. In a corner against the wall, under an old wooden crucifix, was a prie-dieu, marked by the knees, an oval table in the centre, some sacred engravings on the walls ; and that was all.

"It is like an hotel, or an old maid's lodging," thought Durtal. The commonness of the furniture, the curtains in faded damask, the panels hung with a paper covered with bouquets of poppies and field-flowers in false colours, were like lodgings by the month, but certain details, above all the scrupulous cleanliness of the room, the worked cushions on the sofa, the grass mats under the chairs, an hortensia like a painted cauliflower placed in a flower-pot covered with lace, looked on the other hand like the futile and icy room of a devout woman.

"Nothing was wanting but a cage of canaries, photographs in plush frames, shell-work and crochet mats."

Durtal had got so far in his reflections when the abbé came in with extended hand, gently finding fault with his long absence.

Durtal made what excuses he could, unusual occupations, long weariness.

"And our Blessed Lidwine, how do you get on with her ?"

"Ah, I have not even begun her life ; I am not in a state of mind which allows me to engage in it."

Durtal's accent of discouragement surprised the priest.

"Come, what is the matter? Can I be of any use to you?"

"I do not know, Monsieur l'Abbé. I am almost ashamed to talk to you about such troubles," and suddenly he burst out, telling his sorrows in any chance words, declaring the unreality of his conversion, his struggles with the flesh, his human respect, his neglect of religious practices, his aversion from the rites demanded of him, in fact from all yokes.

The abbé listened without moving, his chin on his hand.

"You are more than forty," he said, when Durtal was silent; "you have passed the age when without any impulse from thought, the awakening of the flesh excites temptations, you are now in that period when indecent thoughts first present themselves to the imagination, before the senses are agitated. We have then to fight less against your sleeping body than your mind, which stimulates and vexes it. On the other hand, you have arrears and prizes of affection to put out, you have no wife or children to receive them, so that your affections being driven back by celibacy, you will end by taking them there where at first they should have been placed; you try to appease your soul's hunger in chapels, and as you hesitate, as you have not the courage to come to a decision, to break once for all with your vices, you have arrived at this strange compromise; to reserve your tender feeling for the church and the manifestations of that feeling for women. That, if I do not mistake, is your correct balance-sheet. But, good heavens, you have not too much to complain of, for do you not see that the important thing is to care for woman only with your bodily senses? When Heaven has given you grace to be no longer taken captive by thought, all may be arrànged with a little effort of will."

"This is an indulgent priest," thought Durtal.

"But," continued the abbé, "you cannot always sit between two stools, the moment will come when you must stick to the one, and push the other away."

And looking at Durtal, who looked down without answering,—

"Do you pray? I do not ask if you say your morning prayers, for not all those, who end by entering on the divine way, after wandering for years where chance might take them, call on the Lord so soon as they awake. At break of day the soul thinks itself well, thinks itself firmer, and at once takes occasion of this fleeting energy to forget God. It is with the soul as with the body when it is sick. When night comes our sensations are stronger, pain which was quieted awakes, the fever which slept blazes up again, filth revives and wounds bleed anew, and then it thinks of the divine Miracle-worker, it thinks of Christ. Do you pray in the evening ? "

" Sometimes—and yet it is very difficult ; the after-noon is tolerable, but you say truly when the daylight goes, evils spring up. A whole cavalcade of obscene ideas then pass through my brain ; how can any one be recollected at such moments ? "

" If you do not feel able to resist in the street or at home, why do you not take refuge in the churches ? "

" But they are closed when one has most need of them ; the clergy put Jesus to bed at nightfall."

" I know it, but if most churches are closed, there are a few which remain partly open very late. Ah, St. Sulpice is among the number, and there is one which remains open every evening, and where those who visit it are always sure of prayers and Benediction : Notre Dame des Victoires, I think you know it."

" Yes, Monsieur l'Abbé. It is ugly enough to cause tears, it is pretentious, it is in bad taste, and the singers churn up a margarine of rancid tones. I do not go there then as I go to St. Severin and St. Sulpice, to admire there the art of the old ' Praisers of God,' to listen, even if they are incorrectly given, to the broad, familiar melodies of plain chant. Notre Dame des Victoires is worthless from the æsthetic point of view, and yet I go there from time to time, because alone in Paris it has the irresistible attraction of true piety, it alone preserves intact the lost soul of the Time. At whatever hour one goes there people are pray-ing there, prostrate in absolute silence ; it is full as soon as it is open, and full at its closing, there is a constant coming and going of pilgrims from all parts of Paris, arriving from the depths of the provinces, and it seems that each one, by the prayers that he brings, adds fuel to the immense brazier of Faith whose flames break out again under the smoky arches like the thousands of tapers which constantly burn, and are renewed from morning till evening, before Our Lady.

" Well, I who seek the most deserted corners and the darkest places in the chapels, I who hate mobs, mix almost willingly with those I find there ; because there everyone is isolated, no one is concerned with his neighbour, you do not see the human bodies which throng you, but you feel the breath of souls around. However refractory, however damp you may be, you end by taking fire at this contact, and are astonished to find yourself all at once, less vile ; it seems to me that the prayers which elsewhere when they leave my lips fall back to the ground exhausted and chilled, spring upwards in that place, are borne on by others, grow warm and soar and live.

" At St. Severin I have indeed experienced the sensation of a help spreading from the pillars and running through the arches, but, as I think, the aid is less strong. Perhaps since the Middle Ages that church makes use of, but cannot renew the celestial effluvia with which it is charged ; while at Notre Dame the help which springs up from the very pavement is for ever vivified by the uninterrupted presence of an ardent crowd. In the one it is the impregnate stone, the church itself which brings consolation, in the other it is above all things the fervour of the crowds which fill it.

" And then I have the strange impression that the Virgin, attracted and retained by so great faith, only spends a little while in other churches, goes there as a visitor, but has made her home, and really resides in Notre Dame."

The abbé smiled.

" Come, I see that you know and love it ; and yet the church is not on our left bank, beyond which, you said to me one day, there is no sanctuary worth having."

" Yes, and I am surprised at it, especially as it is placed in a thoroughly commercial quarter, two paces from the Exchange, whose ignoble shouts can be heard in it."

" It was itself an Exchange," said the abbé.

" In what way ? "

" After having been baptized by the monks, and having served as a chapel for the discalced Augustinians, it was horribly desecrated in the Revolution, and the Exchange was set up within its walls."

" I was not aware of that detail," said Durtal.

" But," continued the abbé, " it was with it, as with those

holy women, who, if we believe their biographers, recovered by a life of prayer the virginity they had formerly lost. Our Lady washed it from its violation, and though it is comparatively modern, it is at the present day saturated with emanations, infused by effluences of angels, penetrated with divine drugs, it is for sick souls what certain thermal springs are for the body. People keep their season there, make their novenas, and obtain their cure.

"Now to come back to our point ; I tell you you will do wisely, if on your bad evenings you will attend Benediction in that church. I shall be surprised if you do not come out cleansed and at peace."

"If he have only that to offer me, it is little enough," thought Durtal. And after a disappointed silence ·he rejoined,

"But, Monsieur l'Abbé, even were I to visit that sanctuary, and follow the offices in other churches, when temptations assail me, even were I to confess and draw near the Sacraments, how would that advantage me ? I should meet as I came out the woman whose very sight inflames my senses, and it would be with me as after my leaving St. Severin all unnerved ; the very feeling of tenderness which I had in the chapel would destroy me, and I should fall back into sin."

"What do you know about it ? " and the priest suddenly rose, and took long strides through the room.

"You have no right to speak thus, for the virtue of the Sacrament is formal, the man who has communicated is no longer alone. He is armed against others and defended against himself," and crossing his arms before Durtal he exclaimed,—

"To lose one's soul for the pleasure of momentary gratification ! what madness. And since the time of your conversion, does not that disgust you ? "

"Yes, I am disgusted with myself, but only after my swinish desires are satisfied. If only I could gain true repentance."

"Rest assured," said the abbé, who sat down again, "you will find it."

And, seeing that Durtal shook his head,

"Remember what Saint Teresa said : 'One trouble of those who are beginning is, that they cannot recognize whether they have true repentance for their faults ; but

they have it, and the proof is their sincere resolution to
serve God.' Think of that sentence, for it applies to you ;
that repugnance to your sins which wearies you is witness
to your regret, and you have a desire to serve the Lord,
since you are in fact struggling to go to Him."

There was a moment of silence.

" Well, then, Monsieur l'Abbé, what is your advice ? "

" I advise you to pray in your own house, in church,
everywhere, as much as you can. I do not prescribe any
religious remedy, I simply invite you to profit by some
precepts of pious hygiene, afterwards we will see."

Durtal remained undecided, discontented, like those sick
persons who find fault with doctors, who, to satisfy them,
prescribe only colourless drugs.

The priest laughed.

" Confess," he said, looking him in the face, " confess that
you are saying to yourself, ' It was not worth while to put
myself out, for I am no further advanced, this good fellow,
the priest, practises expectant medicine ; instead of cutting
short my crises with energetic remedies, he palters, advises
me to go to bed early, not to catch cold—' "

" Oh, Monsieur l'Abbé," protested Durtal.

" Yet I do not wish to treat you like a child, or talk to
you like a woman ; now attend to me !

" The way in which your conversion has worked leaves
me in no doubt whatever. There has been what Mysticism
calls the divin touch, only—note this—God has dispensed
with human intervention, even with the interference of
a priest, to bring you back into the road you have left for
more than twenty years.

" Now we cannot reasonably suppose that the Lord has
acted lightly, and that He will now leave His work unaccom-
plished. He will carry it through if you put no obstacle in
His way.

" In fact you are at this moment like a block in His
hands ; what will He do with it ? I do not know, but since
He has kept to Himself the conduct of your soul, let Him
act ; be patient, He will explain His action ; trust in Him,
He will help you ; be content to protest with the Psalmist :
' Doce me facere voluntatem tuam, quia Deus meus es tu.'

" I tell you again I believe in the preventive virtue, the
formal power of the Sacraments. I quite understand the
system of Père Milleriot, who obliged those persons to com-

municate whom he thought would afterwards fall again into sin. For their only penance he obliged them to communicate again and again, and he ended by purifying them with the Sacred Species, taken in large doses. It is a doctrine at once realistic and exalted.

" But reassure yourself," continued the abbé, looking at Durtal, who seemed wearied, " I do not intend to experiment on you in this way ; on the contrary, my advice is that in the state of ignorance in which we are of God's will, you abstain from the Sacraments.

" For you should desire them, and it should come from you rather than from Him ; be sure that sooner or later you will thirst for Penance, hunger for the Eucharist. Well, when unable to restrain yourself longer, you ask for pardon and entreat to be allowed to approach the Holy Table, we shall see, we will ask Him what way He will choose to take, in order to save you."

" But there are not, I presume, several ways of confessing and communicating ? "

" Certainly not, that is just what I meant to say . . . but . . ."

And the priest hesitated, at a loss for words.

" It is quite certain," he began again, " that art has been the principal means which the Saviour has used to make you absorb the Faith. He has taken you on your weak side —or strong side, if you like that better. He has infused into your nature the chief mystical works ; he has persuaded and converted you, less by the way of reason than the way of the senses ; and indeed those are the special conditions you have to take into account.

" On the other hand your soul is not humble and simple, you are a sort of ' sensitive,' whom the least imprudence, the least stupidity of a confessor would at once repel.

" Therefore that you may not be at the mercy of a troublesome impression, certain precautions must be taken. In the state of weakness and feebleness in which you are, a disagreeable face, an unlucky word, antipathetic surroundings, a mere nothing would be enough to rout you—is it not so ? "

" Alas ! " sighed Durtal, " I am obliged to answer that you are right ; but, Monsieur l'Abbé, I do not think I shall have to fear such disillusions if when the moment you predict has come you will allow me to make my confession to you."

The priest was silent for a while ; then said,

" No doubt, since I have met you, I may probably be

useful to you, but I have an idea that my part will be confined to pointing out the road to you; I shall be a connecting link, and nothing more, you will end as you have begun, without help, alone." The abbé remained in thought, then shook his head, and went on : " Let us leave the subject, however, for we cannot anticipate the designs of God ; to sum up, try to stifle in prayer your attacks of the flesh, it is a less matter not to be overcome at the moment, than to direct all your efforts not to be so."

Then the priest added gently to rouse the spirits of Durtal, whom he saw to be depressed,

" If you fall do not despair, and throw the handle after the hatchet. Say to yourself, that, after all Lust is not the most unpardonable of faults, that it is one of two sins for which the human being pays cash, and which are consequently expiated in part at least before death. Say to yourself that wantonness and avarice refuse all credit and will not wait ; and in fact, whoever unlawfully commits a fleshly act is almost always punished in his lifetime. For some there are bastards to provide for, sickly wives, low connections, broken careers, abominable deceptions on the part of those they have loved. On whichever side we turn when women are concerned we have to suffer, for she is the most powerful instrument of sorrow which God has given to man.

" It is the same with the passion for gain. Every being who allows himself to be overcome by that hateful sin, pays for it as a rule before his death. Look at the Panama business. Cooks, housekeepers, small proprietors who till then had lived in peace, seeking no inordinate gains, no illicit profit, threw themselves like madmen into that business. They had one only thought, to gain money ; the chastisement of their cupidity was, as you know, sudden."

" Yes," said Durtal, laughing, " the de Lesseps were the agents of providence, when they stole the savings of fools, who had moreover got them probably by thieving."

" In a word," said the abbé, " I repeat my last advice : do not be at all discouraged if you sink. Do not despise yourself too much ; have the courage to enter a church afterwards ; for the devil catches you by cowardice, the false shame, the false humility he suggests, nourish, maintain, solidify your wantonness in some measure.

" Well ! no good-bye ; come and see me soon again."

Durtal found himself in the street a little confused. " It is evident," he murmured, as he stalked along, " that the Abbé Gévresin is a clever spiritual watchmaker. He has dexterously taken to pieces the movement of my passions, and made the hours of idleness and weariness strike, but, after all, his advice comes only to this : stew in your own juice and wait.

" Indeed he is right ; if I had come to the point I should not have gone to him to chatter, but really to confess. What is strange is that he does not at all seem to think he will have to put me through the wash-tub ; and to whom does he mean me to go—to the first comer who will wind about me his spool of commonplaces, and stroke me with his big hands without seeing clearly ?

" Well, well. . . what is the time ? " He looked at his watch. " Six o'clock, and I do not care to go home. What shall I do till dinner ? "

He was near St. Sulpice. He went in and sat down, to clear his thoughts a little, taking a place in the Chapel of Our Lady, which at that hour was almost empty.

He felt no wish to pray, and rested there, looking at the great arch of marble and gold, like a scene in a theatre, where the Virgin, the only figure in the light, advances towards the faithful, as from a decorated grotto, on plaster clouds.

Meanwhile two Little Sisters of the Poor came and knelt not far from him, and meditated, their heads between their hands.

He thought as he looked at them,—

" Those souls are to be envied who can thus be abstracted in prayer. How do they manage it ? For, in fact, it is not easy, if one thinks of the sorrows of the world, to praise the vaunted mercy of God. It is all very fine to believe that He exists, to be certain that He is good ; in fact, we do not know Him—we are ignorant of Him. He is, and, in fact, He can only be, immanent, permanent, and inaccessible. He is we know not what, and at most we know what He is not. Try to imagine Him, and the senses fail, for He is above, about, and in each one of us. He is three and He is one ; He is each and He is all ; He is without beginning, and He will be without end ; He is above all and for ever incomprehensible. If we try to picture Him to ourselves and give Him a human wrappage, we come back to the simple conception of the early times, we represent Him under the features of an ancestor. Some old Italian model, some old Father Tourgéneff, with a long beard, and we cannot but smile, so childish is the likeness of God the Father.

" He is, in fact, so absolutely above the imagination and the senses, that He comes only nominally into prayer, and the impulses of humanity ascend especially to the Son, Who only can be addressed, because He became man, and is to us somewhat of an elder brother, because, having wept in human form, we think He will hear us more readily, and be more compassionate to our sorrows.

" As to the third Person, He is even more disconcerting than the first. He is especially the unknowable. How can we imagine this God formless and bodiless, this Substance equal to the two others, who, as it were, breathe Him forth ? We think of Him as a brightness, a fluid, a breath ; we cannot even lend to Him as to the Father the face of a man, since on the two occasions that He took to Himself a body, He showed Himself under the likenesses of a dove and of tongues of fire, and these two different aspects do not help to a suggestion of the new appearance He might assume.

" Certainly the Trinity is terrible, and makes the brain reel. Ruysbröck has moreover said admirably, 'Let those who would know and study what God is, know that it is forbidden ; they will go mad.'

" So," he continued, looking at the two Little Sisters, who were now telling their beads, " these good women are right not to try to understand, and to confine themselves to praying with all their heart to the Mother and the Son.

" Moreover, in all the lives of the saints which they have read, they have made certain that Jesus and Mary always appeared to the elect to console and strengthen them.

" In fact, how stupid I am. To pray to the Son is to pray to the two others, for in praying to one among them I pray at the same time to the three, since the three make but one. And the Substances are, however, special, because if the divine Essence is one and simple, it is so in the threefold distinction of the Persons ; but, again, what is the use of fathoming the Impenetrable ?

" Yet," he continued, remembering the interview he had just had with the priest, " how will all this end ? If the abbé be right, I no longer belong to myself ; I am about to enter the unknown, which frightens me. If only the sound of my vices consents to be silent, but I feel that they rise furiously within me. Ah, that Florence"—and he thought of a woman to whose vagaries he was riveted—" continues to walk about in my brain. I see her behind the lowered curtain of my eyes, and when I think of her I am a terrible coward."

He endeavoured once more to put her away, but his will was overcome at the sight of her.

He hated, despised, and even cursed her, but the madness of his illusions excited him ; he left her disgusted with her and with himself ; he swore he would never see her again, but did not keep his resolve.

He saw her now in vision extend her hand to him.

He recoiled, struggling to free himself ; but his dream continued mingling her with the form of one of the sisters whose gentle profile he saw.

Suddenly he started, returned to the real world, and saw that he was at St. Sulpice, in the chapel. " It is disgusting that I should come here to soil the church with my horrible dreams ; I had better go."

He went out in confusion, thinking, " Perhaps if I visit Florence once again, I may perhaps put an end to this haunting sense of her presence, seeing and knowing the reality."

And he was obliged to answer himself that he was becoming idiotic, for he knew by experience that past desire grows in proportion as it is nourished. " No, the abbé was right ; I have to become and to remain penitent. But how ? Pray ? How can I pray, when evil imaginations pursue me even in church ? Evil dreams followed me to La Glacière ; here they appear again, and smite me to the ground. How can I defend myself ? for indeed it is frightful to be thus alone, to know nothing and have no proof, to feel the prayers which one tears out of oneself fall into the silence and the void without a gesture to answer, without a word of encouragement, without a sign. I do not even know if He be there, and if He listens. The abbé tells me to wait an indication, an order from on high ; but, alas ! they come to me from below."

CHAPTER VI.

MANY months passed. Durtal continued his alternation of wanton and pious ideas. Without power to resist, he saw himself slipping. "All this is far from clear," he cried, one day, in a rage, when, less apathetic than usual, he forced himself to take stock. "Now, Monsieur l'Abbé, what does this mean? Whenever my sensual obsessions are weaker, so also are my religious impressions."

"That means," said the priest, "that your adversary is holding out to you the most treacherous of his baits. He seeks to persuade you that you will never attain to anything unless you will give yourself up to the most repugnant excesses. He tries to convince you that satiety and disgust of these acts alone will bring you back to God; he incites you to commit them that they may, so to speak, bring about your deliverance; he leads you into sin under pretext of delivering you from it. Have a little energy, despise these sophistries and resist him."

He went to see the Abbé Gévresin every week. He liked the patient discretion of the old priest, who let him talk when he was in a confidential humour, listened to him carefully, manifested no surprise at his frequent temptations and his falls. Only the abbé always returned to his first advice, insisted on regular prayer, and that Durtal should each day, if possible, visit a church. He also now said, "The hour is important for the success of these practices. If you wish that the chapels should be favourable to you, get up in time to be present at daybreak at the first mass, the servants' mass, and also be very often in the sanctuaries at nightfall."

The priest had evidently formed a plan; Durtal did not yet wholly understand it, but he was bound to admit that this discipline of temporizing, this constant call to thought always directed to God, by his daily visits to the churches, acted upon him at last, and little by little softened his soul. One fact proved it : that he who for so long a time had been unable to meditate in the morning, now prayed as soon as he awoke. Even in the afternoon he found himself on some days seized with the need of speaking humbly with God, with an irresistible desire to ask His pardon and implore His help.

It seemed then that the Lord knocked at his door with gentle touches, wishing so to recall his attention, and draw him to Him ; but when, softened and troubled, Durtal would enter into himself to seek God, he wandered vaguely, not knowing what he said, and thinking of other things while speaking to Him.

He complained of these wanderings and distractions to the priest, who answered,—

"You are on the threshold of the probationary life ; you cannot yet experience the sweet and familiar friendship of prayer. Do not sadden yourself because you cannot close behind you the gate of your senses. Watch and wait ; pray badly if you can do nothing else, but pray all the same.

"Be very sure too that every one has experienced the troubles which distress you ; above all, believe that we do not walk blindfold, that Mysticism is an absolutely exact science. It can foretell the greater part of the phenomena which occur in that soul which the Lord intends for a perfect life ; it follows also spiritual operations with the same clearness as physiology observes the different states of the body. For ages and ages it has disclosed the progress of grace and its effects, now impetuous and now slow ; it has even pointed out the modifications of material organs which are transformed when the soul entirely loses itself in God.

"Saint Denys the Areopagite, Saint Bonaventure, Hugh and Richard of Saint Victor, Saint Thomas Aquinas, Saint Bernard, Ruysbröck, Angela of Foligno, the two Eckharts, Tauler, Suso, Denys the Carthusian, Saint Hildegarde, Saint Catherine of Genoa, Saint Catherine of Siena, Saint Magdalen of Pazzi, Saint Gertrude, and others have set forth in a masterly way the principles and theories of Mysticism, and it has found at last an admirable psychologist to sum up its rules and their exceptions ; a Saint who has verified in her own person the supernatural phases she has described—

a woman whose lucidity was more than human—Saint
Teresa. You have read her life, and her 'Castles of the
Soul'!"

Durtal nodded assent.

"Then you have your information ; you ought to know
that before reaching the shores of Blessedness, before
arriving at the fifth dwelling of the interior castle, at that
prayer of union wherein the soul is awakened in regard to
God, and completely asleep to all things of earth and to
herself, she must pass through lamentable states of dryness,
and the most painful strainings. Take heart therefore ; say
to yourself that this dryness should be a source of humility,
and not a cause of disquietude ; do, in fact, as Saint Teresa
would have you : carry your cross, and not drag it after
you."

" That magnificent and terrible Saint frightens me," sighed
Durtal. " I have read her works, and, do you know, she gives
me the idea of a stainless lily, but a metallic lily, forged of
wrought iron ; you will admit that those who suffer have
scant consolations to expect from her."

"Yes ; in the sense that she does not think of the creature
except in the way of Mysticism. She supposes the fields
already ploughed, the soul already freed from its more
vehement temptations, and sheltered from crises ; her
starting-point is as yet too high and too distant for you, for,
in fact, she is addressing nuns, women of the cloister, beings
who live apart from the world, and who are consequently
already advanced on those ascetic ways wherein God is
leading them.

" But make an effort in the spirit to free yourself from this
mud, cast away for a few moments the memory of your im-
perfections and your troubles, and follow her. See then how
experienced she is in the domain of the supernatural, how,
in spite of her repetitions and tediousness, she explains wisely
and clearly the mechanism of the soul unfolding when God
touches it. In subjects where words fail and phrases
crumble away, she succeeds in making herself understood,
in showing, making felt, almost making visible, the inconceivable sight of God buried in the soul, and taking His
pleasure there.

" And she goes still further into the mystery, even to the
end ; bounds with a final spring to the very gates of heaven,

but then she faints on adoration, and being unable to express
herself further, she soars, describing circles like a frightened
bird, wandering beyond herself, in cries of love."

"Yes, Monsieur l'Abbé, I recognize that Saint Teresa has
explored deeper than any other the unknown regions of the
soul ; she is in some measure its geographer, has drawn the
map of its poles, marked the latitudes of contemplation, the
interior lands of the human sky. Other Saints have explored
them before her, but they have not left us so methodical nor
so exact a topography.

"But in spite of this I prefer those mystical writers who
have less self-analysis, and discuss less, who always do
throughout their works what Saint Teresa did at the end of
hers—that is, who are all on fire from the first page to the last,
and are consumed and lost at the feet of Christ. Ruysbröck
is among these. The little volume which Hello has translated
is a very furnace ; and, again, to quote a woman, take Saint
Angela of Foligno, not so much in the book of her visions
which may not be always effectual, as in the wonderful life
which she dictated to Brother Armand, her confessor. She
too explains, and much earlier than Saint Teresa, the principles and effects of Mysticism ; but if she is less profound, less
clever in defining shades, on the other hand she is wonderfully effusive and tender. She caresses the soul ; she is a
Bacchante of divine love, a Mænad of purity. Christ loves
her, holds long conversations with her ; the words she has
retained surpass all literature, and are manifestly the most
beautiful ever written. This is no longer the rough Christ,
the Spanish Christ who begins by trampling on His
creature to make him more supple ; He is the merciful Christ
of the Gospels, the gentle Christ of Saint Francis, and I like
the Christ of the Franciscans better than the Christ of the
Carmelites."

"What will you say, then," said the abbé, with a smile, "of
St. John of the Cross ? You compared Saint Teresa just now
to a flower in wrought iron ; he too is such, but he is the lily of
tortures, the royal flower which the executioners were wont of
old time to stamp on the heraldic flesh of convicts. Like red-
hot iron, he is at the same time burning and sombre. As you
turn over the pages, Saint Teresa now and then bends over
and sorrows and compassionates us ; he remains impenetrable,
buried in his internal abyss, occupied, above all things, in

describing the sufferings of the soul which, after having crucified its desires, passes through the ' Night obscure,' that is to say, through the renunciation of all which comes from the sensible and the created.

"He wills that we should extinguish our imagination—so lethargize it that it can no longer form images—imprison our senses, annihilate our faculties. He wills that he who desires to unite himself to God should place himself under an exhausted receiver, and make a vacuum within, so that, if he choose, the Pilgrim should descend therein, and purify himself, tearing out the remains of sins, extirpating the last relics of vice.

" Then the sufferings which the soul endures overpass the bounds of the possible, it lies lost in utter darkness, falls under discouragement and fatigue, believes itself for ever abandoned by Him to whom it cries, who now hides Himself and answers not again, happy still when in that agony, the pangs of the flesh are not added, and that abominable spirit which Isaias calls the spirit of confusion, and which is none other than the disease of scrupulousness pushed to its extreme.

"Saint John makes you shudder when he cries out that this night of the soul is bitter and terrible, and that the being who suffers it is plunged alive into hell. But when the old man is purged out, when he is scraped at every seam, raked over every face, light springs out, and God appears. Then the soul casts itself like a child into His arms, and the incomprehensible fusion takes place.

" You see Saint John penetrates more deeply than others into the depths of mystical initiation. He also, like Saint Teresa and Ruysbröck, treats of the spiritual marriage, of the influx of grace, and its gifts ; but he first dared to describe minutely the dolorous phases which till then had been but hinted at with trembling.

"Then if he is an admirable theologian, he is also a rigorous and clear-sighted saint. He has not those weaknesses which are natural to a woman ; he does not lose himself in digressions, nor return continually on his own steps ; he walks straight forward, but you often see him at the end of the road, blood-stained and terrible, with dry eyes."

" But, but," said Durtal, " surely not all souls whom Christ will lead in the ways of mysticism are tried thus ? "

" Yes, almost always, more or less."

" I will confess that I thought the spiritual life was less arid and less complex. I imagined that by leading a pure life, praying one's best, and communicating, one would attain without much trouble, not indeed to taste the infinite joys reserved for the saints, but at last to possess the Lord, and live, at least, near Him, at rest.

" And I should be quite content with this middle class joy. The price paid in advance for the exaltation described by Saint John disconcerts me."

The abbé smiled, but made no answer.

" But do you know that if it be so," replied Durtal, " we are very far from the Catholicism that is taught us ? It is so practical, so benign, so gentle, in comparison with Mysticism."

" It is made for lukewarm souls—that is to say, for almost all the pious souls which are about us ; it lives in a moderate atmosphere, without too great suffering or too much joy ; it only can be assimilated by the masses, and the priests are right to present it thus, since otherwise the faithful would cease to understand it, or would take flight in alarm."

" But if God judge that a moderate religion is amply sufficient—for the masses believe that he demands the most painful efforts on the part of those whom he deigns to initiate into the supremely adorable mysteries of His Person—it is necessary and just that he should mortify them before allowing them to taste the essential intoxication of union with Him."

" In fact, the end of Mysticism is to render visible, sensible, almost palpable, the God who remains silent and hid den from all."

" And to throw us into His deep, into the silent abyss of joy ! But in order to speak correctly, we must forget the ordinary use of expressions which have been degraded. In order to describe this mysterious love, we are obliged to draw our comparisons from human acts, and to inflict on the Lord the shame of our words. We have to employ such terms as ' union,' ' marriage,' ' wedding feast ' ; but it is impossible to speak of the inexpressible, and with the baseness of our language declare the ineffable immersion of the soul in God."

" The fact is," murmured Durtal . . . " but to return to Saint Teresa. . . ."

"She too," interrupted the abbé, "has treated of this 'Night obscure' which terrifies you ; but she only speaks of it in a few lines. She calls it the soul's agony—a sadness so bitter that she strove in vain to depict it."

"No doubt, but I prefer her to Saint John of the Cross, for she is not so discouraging as that inflexible saint. Admit that he belongs too much to the land of those large Christs who bleed in caverns."

"Of what nationality then was Saint Teresa ? "

"Yes, I know she was a Spaniard, but so complex, so strange, that race seems obliterated in her, less clearly defined.

"It is clear she was an admirable psychologist, but also how strange is in her the mixture of an ardent mystic and a cool woman of business. For, in fact, she has a double nature ; she is a contemplative outside the world, and at the same time a statesman, a female Colbert of the cloister. In fact, never was woman so consummate a skilled artisan and so powerful an organizer. When we consider that, in spite of incredible difficulties, she founded thirty-two nunneries, that she put them all under obedience to a rule which is a model of wisdom, a rule which foresees and rectifies the most ignored mistakes of the heart, it is astonishing to hear her treated by strong-minded people as an hysterical madwoman."

"One of the distinctive marks of the mystics," answered the abbé, with a smile, "is just their absolute balance, their entire common sense."

These conversations cheered Durtal ; they planted on him seeds of reflection which sprang up when he was alone ; they encouraged him to trust to the advice of this priest, and follow his counsels. He found himself all the better for this conduct, in that his visits to the churches, his prayers and readings occupied his objectless life, and he was no longer wearied.

"I have at least gained peaceable evenings and quiet nights," he said to himself.

He knew the soothing help of a pious evening.

He visited St. Sulpice at those times when, under the dull gleam of the lamps, the pillars opened out and threw long panels of darkness on the ground. The chapels which remained open were in shade, and in the nave before the high altar a single cluster of lamps, above in the darkness, shone out like a luminous bunch of red roses.

In the stillness no sounds were heard but the dull thud of a door, the creaking of a chair, the short paces of a woman, the hurried stride of a man.

Durtal was almost isolated in the obscure chapel which he had chosen ; he kept himself there so far from all, so far from the city whose full pulse was beating only two paces from him. He knelt down and remained still, he prepared to speak, and had nothing to say, felt himself carried away by an impulse, but no words came. He ended by falling into a vague languor, experiencing that indolent ease, that dim sense of comfort, which the body feels in a medicated bath.

He fell a-dreaming of the lot of the women who were round about him here and there, in chairs. Ah ! those poor little black shawls, those miserable pleated caps, those wretched tippets, those doleful seed rosaries they fingered in the shade.

Some in mourning, sobbed still inconsolable ; others, over-whelmed, bent their backs and hung their heads on one side ; others prayed, their shoulders shaking, their head in their hands.

The task of the day was over ; those wearied of their life came to ask for mercy. Everywhere misfortune was kneel-ing, for the rich, the healthy, the happy hardly pray ; all around in the church were women, widowed or old, without love, women deserted, women whose home was a torture, praying that existence might become more merciful, that the dissoluteness of their husbands might cease, the vices of their sons amend, the health of those they loved grow stronger.

A lamentable perfume went up like incense to Our Lady from a very sheaf of woes.

Few men came to this hidden meeting-place of trouble ; still fewer young people, for these have not yet suffered enough ; there were only a few old men, and a few sick who dragged themselves along by the backs of the chairs, and a little hunchback, whom Durtal saw coming there every evening, an outcast who could only be loved by Her who does not even see the body.

A burning pity seized on Durtal at the sight of those unhappy ones who came to beg from Heaven a little of the love refused them by men ; and he who could not pray on his own account ended by joining himself to their pleadings, and praying for them.

So indifferent in the afternoon, the churches were truly persuasive, truly sweet, in the evening ; they seemed to bestir themselves at nightfall, and to compassionate in their solitude the sufferings of those sick creatures whose complaints they heard.

And their first mass in the morning, the mass of working women and servant maids was no less touching ; there were there no bigots nor curious persons, but poor women who came to seek in communion strength to live their hours of onerous tasks and servile needs. They knew as they left the church that they were the living custodians of a God, of Him who was ever while on earth the Poor Man, who took pleasure only in souls who had scarce where to lay their head ; they knew themselves His chosen, and did not doubt that when He entrusted to them under the form of bread the memorial of His suffering, He demanded of them in exchange that they should live in sorrow and humility. And what harm then could do to them the cares of a day spent in the salutary shame of base occupations ?

"I now understand," thought Durtal, "why the abbé made such a point of my seeing the churches early or late ; those are, in fact, the only times in which the soul expands."

But he was too idle to be often present at early mass ; he was content to take his relaxation after dinner in the chapels. He came out with a feeling of peace, even if he had prayed badly or not prayed at all. On other evenings, on the contrary, he felt tired of solitude, tired of silence, tired of darkness, and then he abandoned St. Sulpice and went to Notre Dame des Victoires.

In this well-lighted sanctuary there was no longer that depression, that despair of poor wretches who dragged themselves to the nearest church and sat down in the shade. The pilgrims to Notre Dame des Victoires brought a surer confidence, and that faith softened their sorrows, whose bitterness was dissipated in the explosions of hope, the stammering adoration, which spouted up all around. There were two currents in that refuge, that of people who asked for favours, and that of those who, having gained them, were profuse in thankfulness

and in acts of gratitude.   Therefore, that church had its
especial physiognony, more joyous than sad, less melancholy,
more ardent under all circumstances than that of other
churches.

It had, moreover, the peculiarity of being much
frequented by men, but less by hypocrites, who will not look
you in the face, or with upturned eyes, than by men of all
classes whose features were not degraded by false piety.
There alone were to be seen clear expressions and clean
faces ; there, above all, was not that horrible grimace of the
working man of the catholic clubs—that hideous creature in
a blouse, whose breath belies the ill-defined unction of his
features.

In that church, covered with *ex votos*, plastered even
above the arches with inscriptions on marble celebrating
the joy for prayers granted and benefits received, before that
altar of Our Lady where hundreds of tapers pierced the air
blue with incense with the gilded blades of their lances,
there were public prayers every evening at eight.   A priest
in the pulpit said the rosary, sometimes the Litany of Our
Lady was sung to a singular air, a sort of musical cento, but
it was impossible to say whence it was constructed, very
rhythmical, and continually changing its tone, now fast,
now slow, bringing with it, for a moment, a vague recollection of seventeenth-century airs, then turning sharply at a
tangent, to a barrel-organ tune, a modern, almost vulgar,
melody.

Yet, after all, there was something taking in this singular
confusion of sounds after the " Kyrie eleison " and the opening invocations. The Virgin came upon the scene to a dance
measure like a ballet girl ; but when certain of her attributes
were paraded, and certain of her symbolical names declared,
the music became singularly respectful ; it became lower, halting and solemn, thrice repeating, on the same motive, some
of her attributes, the "Refugium Peccatorum" among others ;
then it went on again, and began her graces again with a skip.

When by chance there was no sermon, the Benediction
took place immediately afterwards.

Then with raspings of the choir, a bass with a cold, and
two boys who snivelled began their liturgical chants :
" Inviolata," that languishing and plaintive Sequence, with
its clear and drawling tune so weak, so frail, that it would

seem as if it should only be sung by voices in a hospital ;
then the 'Parce Domine," that antiphon so suppliant and so
sad ; lastly, that scrap, detached from the " Panga Lingua,"
the " Tantum ergo," humble and thoughtful, attentive and
slow.

When the organ sounded out the first chords, and that
plain chant melody began, the choir had only to cross
their arms and hold their tongues. As tapers which are
lighted by threads of fulminate attached one to the other,
the faithful caught fire, and, accompanied by the organs,
struck up for themselves the humble and glorious strains.
They were then kneeling on the chairs, prostrate on the
pavement, and when, after the exchange of antiphons and
responses, after the " oremus," the priest ascended to
the altar, his shoulders and hands enfolded in the white
silk scarf, to take the monstrance, then, at the shrill and
hurried sounds of the bells, a wind passed which at once
bent every head like the mowing of grass.

In these groups of souls on fire there was a fulness of
devotion, a complete and absolute silence, till the bells again
rang out, and invited human life which had been interrupted to wrap itself in a great sign of the Cross and
resume its course.

The " Laudate " was not ended when Durtal left the
church, before the crowd began to move.

" Verily," he said, as he entered his lodgings, " the
fervour of that congregation, who do not come as in other
churches from the districts, but are pilgrims from everywhere and one knows not where, is out of tune with the
blackguardism of this foolish age."

Then at Notre Dame at least one hears curious singing,
and he bethought him of those strange litanies which he
had heard nowhere else, and yet he had experienced all
kinds, in churches. At St. Sulpice, for example, it was
recited to two tunes. When the choir sang it was set to a
plain chant melody, bellowed by the gong of a bass to
which the sharp fife of the boys made answer ; but during
Rosary month, on every day except Thursday the task of
singing it was entrusted to young ladies ; then in the
evening round a wheezy old harmonium, a troup of young
and old geese, made Our Lady run round on her litanies as
on hobby horses to the music of a fair.

In other churches, at St. Thomas Aquinas, for example, where they were also dropped out by women, the litanies were sprinkled with powder and perfumed by bergamot and ambergris. They were, in fact, adapted to a minuet tune, and therefore did not disagree with the operatic architecture of the church, where they presented a Virgin walking with mincing steps, pinching her petticoat with two fingers, bending in beautiful curtseys, and recovering herself with a fine bow. This has evidently nothing to do with church music, but it was none the less disagreeable to hear. It would have made the whole performance complete if the harpsichord had been substituted for the organ.

Far more interesting than this lay quavering was the plain chant, given more or less badly, as it was moreover given, but yet given, when there was no special ceremony at Notre Dame.

It was not arranged there as at St. Sulpice and the other churches where the " Tantum ergo " is almost always dressed up in foolish flourishes, tunes for military ceremonials or public dinners.

The Church has not allowed the actual text of Saint Thomas Aquinas to be altered, but she has let any and every choirmaster suppress the plain chant in which it has been wrapped from its birth, which has penetrated to its marrow, has clung to each of its phrases, and become with it one body and one soul.

It was monstrous, and it must really be that these curés have lost, not the sense of art, for that they never had, but the most elementary sense of the liturgy, to accept such heresies, and tolerate such outrages in their churches.

These thoughts enraged Durtal, but he returned little by little to Notre Dame des Victoires and grew calmer. It was well he should examine it under all aspects, but it remained none the less mysterious nor the less unique in Paris.

At La Salette, at Lourdes, there have been apparitions. " Whether these have been authentic or controverted matters little," he thought. " For even supposing Our Lady were not there at the moment her coming was announced, she was attracted there, and dwells there now, retained there by the tide of prayer and the emanations cast up by the faith

of crowds.   Miracles have happened there ; it is therefore
not astonishing that pious crowds flock thither.   But here
at Notre Dame des Victoires has been no apparition ; no
Mélanie, no Bernadette, have seen and described the
luminous appearance of a ' beautiful Lady.'   There are
no piscinas, no medical staff, no public cures, no mountain
top, no grotto, nothing.   One fine day in 1836 the curé of
the parish, the Abbé Dufriche Des Genettes, declared that
while he was celebrating mass Our Lady manifested to him
her desire that the sanctuary should be specially consecrated to her, and that alone was enough.   The church,
then a desert, has never since been empty, and thousands
of *ex votos* declare the graces which since that day the
Madonna has accorded to the visitors."

"Yes, but in fact," concluded Durtal, "all these sup-
pliants are not specially extraordinary souls, for indeed the
most part of them are like me, they come in their own
interests, for themselves and not for Her."

And he remembered the answer of the Abbé Gévresin, to
whom he had already made the observation.

"You must be singularly far advanced on the road to
perfection if you go there for Her only. "

Suddenly, after so many hours spent in the chapels, there
was a reaction ; the flesh extinguished under the cinders of
prayers took fire, and the conflagration, springing up from
below, became terrible.

Florence seemed present, to Durtal's imagination, at his
lodgings, in the churches, in the street, everywhere, and
he was constantly on the watch against her recurrent
attractions.

The weather was mixed up with it all ; the heaven broke
up, a stormy summer raged, shattering the nerves,
enfeebling the will, letting the awakened troop of vices
loose in their gloomy moisture.   Durtal blenched before
the dread of long evenings and the abominable melancholy
of days that never ended.   At eight o'clock in the evening
the sun had not set, and at three in the morning it seemed
to wake again ; the week was only one uninterrupted
day, and life was never arrested.

Oppressed by the ignominy of this angry sunshine and
these blue skies, disgusted at bathing in Niles of sweat,
and feeling Niagaras run from his hat, he did not stir

from home, and then, in his solitude, foul thoughts
assailed him.

It was an obsession by thought, by vision, in all ways, and
the haunting was all the more terrible that it was so special,
that it never turned aside, but concentrated itself always on
the same point, the face and figure of Florence.

Durtal resisted, then in distraction, took to flight, tried
to tire himself out by long walks, and to divert his mind
by excursions, but the ignoble desire followed him in his
course, sat before him in the Café, came between his eyes
and the newspaper he strove to read, becoming ever more
definite. He ended, after hours of struggle, by giving
way and going to see this woman ; he left her overwhelmed, half dead with disgust and shame, almost in
tears.

Nor did he thus find any solace in his struggle, but the
contrary ; far from escaping it, the hateful charm took more
violent and tenacious possession of him. Then Durtal
thought of and accepted a strange compromise, to visit
another woman he knew, and in her society to break this
nervous state, to put an end to this possession, this weariness
and remorse ; and in doing so he strove to persuade himself
that in thus acting he would be more pardonable, less sinful.

The clearest result of this attempt was to bring back the
memory of Florence, and her vicious charm.

He continued therefore his intimacy with her, and then
he had, during a few days, such a revolt from his slavery,
that he extricated himself from the sewer, and stood on firm
ground.

He succeeded in recovering and pulling himself together, and he loathed himself. During this crisis he had
somewhat neglected the Abbé Gévresin, to whom he dared
not avow his foulness, but since certain indications warned
him of new attacks, he took fright, and went to see him.

He explained his crises in veiled words, and he felt so
unnerved, so sad, that tears stood in his eyes.

" Well, are you now certain that you have that repentance which you assure me you have not experienced up to
this time ? "

" Yes, but what is the good of it, if one is so weak, that in
spite of all efforts one is certain to be overthrown at the first
assault ? "

"That is another question. Come, I see that at present you are in fact in a state of fatigue requiring help."

"Comfort yourself therefore ; go in peace and sin less, the greater part of your temptations will be remitted you ; you can, if you choose, bear the remainder, only take care, if you fall henceforward, you will be without excuse, and I do not answer for it, that instead of mending, your condition will not be aggravated."

And as Durtal, stupefied, stammered out : "You believe—"

"I believe," said the priest, "in the mystical substitution of which I spoke to you ; you will moreover experience it in yourself ; the saints will enter into the lists to help you ; they will take the overplus of the assaults which you cannot conquer ; without even knowing your name, from their secluded province, nunneries of Carmelites and Poor Clares will pray for you, on receiving a letter from me."

And in fact, from that very day the most acute attacks ceased. Did he owe that cessation, that truce, to the intercession of the cloistered Orders, or to a change in the weather, which then took place, to the less heat of the sun, which gave way to floods of rain ? He could not tell, but one thing was certain, his temptations were less frequent, and he could bear them with impunity.

This idea of convents in their compassion dragging him out of the mud in which he had stuck, and by their charity bringing him to the bank, excited him. He chose to go to the Avenue de Saxe, to pray in the home of the sisters of those who suffered for him.

This time there were no lights, no crowds, as on the morning when he had been present at a Procession, no odour of wax or incense, no sweeping by of robes of scarlet and cope of gold, all was deserted and dark.

He was there alone, in the sombre and dank chapel, smelling like stagnant water, and without saying rosaries mechanically, or repeating prayers by rote, he fell into a reverie, endeavouring to look somewhat clearly into his life, and take stock of himself. And while he thus pulled himself together, far-off voices came behind the grating, drew nearer and nearer, passed by the black sieve of the veil, and dropped round the altar, whose form rose dimly in the shadow.

These voices of the Carmelites aided Durtal to probe his despair deeply.

Seated in a chair, he said to himself : " When any one is as incapable as I am when I speak to Him, it is almost shameful to dare to pray, for indeed, if I think of Him, it is that I may ask for a little happiness ; and that is foolish. In the immediate shipwreck of human reason, wishing to explain the terrible enigma of the meaning of life, one only idea comes to the surface, in the midst of the wreckage of thoughts which sink, the idea of an expiation felt rather than understood, the idea that the sole end assigned to life is sorrow.

" Every one has a sum of physical and moral suffering to pay, and whoever does not settle it here below, defrays it after death ; happiness is only lent, and must be repaid ; its very phantoms are like duties paid in advance on a future succession of sorrows.

Who knows in that case whether anæsthetics which suppress corporal pain do not bring into debt those who use them ? Who knows whether chloroform is not a means of revolt, and if the shrinking of the creature from suffering is not seditious, a rebellion against the will of Heaven ? If this be so, the arrears of torture, the balance of distress, the warrants of pain avoided must accumulate terrible interest above, and justify the war cry of Saint Teresa, ' Lord, let me always suffer, or die ; ' this explains why, in their trials, the saints rejoice, and pray the Lord not to spare them, for they know that the purifying amount of ills must be paid in order to be free from debt after death.

" To be just, human nature would be too ignoble without pain, for it alone can raise the soul while purifying it, but all that is nothing less than consoling," he added. " What an accompaniment to these sad thoughts are the wailing voices of these nuns ; it is truly frightful."

He ended by fleeing, and taking refuge, to shake off his depression, in the neighbouring convent at the bottom of the alley de Saxe, in a suburban lane, full of little cottages with gardens in front, where serpentine paths of pebbles wound round tufts of pot-herbs.

This was the convent of the Poor Clares of the Ave Maria,

an Order still more strict than that of the Carmelites, poorer,
less fashionable, more humble.

This cloister was entered by a little door, partly ajar ; you
ascended to the second storey without meeting anyone, and
found a little chapel, through whose windows trees were
visible, rocking to the chirping of riotous sparrows.

This too was a place of burial, but no longer, as though
opposite a tomb at the bottom of a dark cavern, but rather a
cemetery where birds sang in the sun among the branches,
you might have thought yourself in the country, twenty
miles from Paris.

The decoration of this bright chapel tried, however, to be
gloomy ; it was like those wine shops whose walls are made
to look like those of caves, with false stones painted in the
imitation plaster. Only the height of the nave manifested
the childishness of the imposture, and declared the vulgarity
of the deception.

At the end was an altar above a smooth waxed floor, and
on either side of it a grating with a black veil. According
to the rule of Saint Francis, all the ornaments, the crucifix,
the candlesticks, the tabernacle, were of wood, no object was
to be seen in metal, no flower, the only luxury in the chapel
consisted of two modern stained windows, one of which
represented Saint Francis, the other Saint Clare.

Durtal thought the sanctuary airy and delightful, but he
only stayed there a few minutes, for there was not here, as
at the Carmelites, an absolute solitude, a sombre peace ; here
there were always two or three Poor Clares trotting about
the chapel, who looked at him while they were arranging
the chairs, and seemed surprised at his presence.

They were annoying to him, and he feared he was the
same to them, so much so that he went away ; but this short
stay was enough to efface, or at least to lessen the funereal
impression of the neighbouring convent.

Durtal returned home, at once much appeased and much
disquieted—much appeased in regard to his temptations,
much disquieted about what he should do next.

He felt rising in him, and increasing ever more and more,
the desire to have done with these strifes and fears, but he
grew pale when he thought of reversing his life, once for
all.

But if he still had hesitation and fear, he had no longer

the firm intention of resisting ; he now accepted in principle the idea of a change of existence, only he tried to retard the day, and put off the hour ; he tried to gain time.

Then like people who grow angry at having to wait, on other days he wished to put off the inevitable moment no longer, and cried within himself that this must end; anything rather than remain as he was.

Then as this desire did not seem heard, he grew discouraged, would no longer think of anything, regretted the time past, and deplored that he felt himself carried along by such a current.

And when he was rather more cheerful, he tried again to examine himself. "In fact I do not at all know how I stand," he thought ; "this flux and reflux of different wishes alarms me, but how have I come to this point, and what is the matter with me ? " What he felt, since he became more lucid, was so intangible, so indefinite, and yet so continuous that he was obliged to give up understanding it. Indeed every time he tried to examine his soul, a curtain of mist arose, and hid from him the unseen and silent approach of he knew not what. The only impression which he carried with him as he rose, was that it was less that he advanced towards the unknown, but that this unknown invaded him, penetrated him, and little by little took possession of him.

When he spoke to the abbé of this state, at once cowardly and resigned, imploring and fearful, the priest only smiled.

" Busy yourself in prayer, and bow down your back," he said one day.

" But I am tired of bending my back, and of trampling always on the same spot," cried Durtal. "I have had enough of feeling myself taken by the shoulders and led I know not where, it is really time that in one way or another this situation came to an end."

" Plainly." And standing up, and looking him in the face, the abbé said, impressively,

" This advance towards God which you find so obscure and so slow is, on the contrary, so luminous and so rapid that it astonishes me, only as you yourself do not move, you do not take account of the swiftness with which you are borne along.

" Before long you will be ripe, and then without need to shake the tree you will fall off of yourself. The question we have now to answer is into what receptacle we must put you, when at last you fall away from your life."

CHAPTER VII.

" But . . . but . . ." thought Durtal, " we must at any rate come to an understanding ; the abbé wearies me with his quiet assumptions, his receptacle in which he must place me. He does not, I suppose, think of making me a seminarist or a monk ; the seminary, at my age, is devoid of interest, and as to the convent, it is attractive from the mystical point of view, and even enticing from the artistic standpoint, but I have not the physical aptitudes, still less the spiritual predispositions to shut myself up for ever in a cloister ; but putting that aside, what does he mean ?

" On the other hand he has insisted on lending me the works of Saint John of the Cross, and has made me read them ; he has then an aim, for he is not a man to feel his way as he walks, he knows what he wishes and where he is going ; does he imagine that I am intended for the perfect life, and does he intend to put me on my guard by this course of reading against the disillusions which, according to him, beginners experience ? His scent seems to fail him there. I have a very horror of bigotry, and pious polish, but though I admire, I do not feel at all drawn towards the phenomena of Mysticism. No, I am interested in seeing them in others, I like to see it all from my window, but will not go downstairs, I have no pretension to become a saint, all that I desire is to attain the intermediate state, between goody-goodiness and sanctity. This is a frightfully low ideal, perhaps, but in practice it is the only one I am capable of attaining, and yet !

" Then these questions have to be faced ! If I am mistaken and am obeying false impulses, I am, as I advance, on the verge of madness. How, except by a special grace, am I to know whether I am in the right way, or walking

in the dark towards the abyss ? Here, for instance, are
those conversations between God and the soul so common
in the mystical life ; how can one be sure that this interior
voice, these distinct words not heard with bodily ears, but
perceived by the soul in a clearer fashion than if they came
by the channels of sense, are true, how be sure that they
emanate from God, not from our imagination or from the
devil himself?

" I know, indeed, that Saint Teresa treats this matter at
length in her ' Castles of the Soul,' and that she points out
the signs by which we can recognize the origin of the words,
but her proofs do not seem to me always as easy to discern
as she thinks.

" ' If these expressions come from God,' she says, ' they
are always accompanied by an effect, and bring with them
an authority which nothing can resist ; thus a soul is in
affliction, and the Lord simply suggests the words " trouble
not thyself," and at once the whirlwind passes, and joy
revives. · In the second place, these words leave an indissoluble peace of mind, they engrave themselves on the
memory, and often cannot be effaced.

" ' In the other case,' she continues, ' if these words proceed from imagination or from the demon, none of these
effects are produced, a kind of uneasiness, anguish and
doubt torments you, moreover the expressions evaporate in
part, and fatigue the soul which endeavours in vain to recall
them in their entirety.'

" In spite of these tokens, we are, in fact, standing on
shifting ground in which we may sink at every step, but in
his turn Saint John of the Cross intervenes, and tells you
not to move. What then is to be done ?

" ' No one,' he says, ' ought to aspire to these supernatural
communications and rest there, for two motives ; first,
humility, the perfect abnegation of refusing to believe in
them ; the second, that in acting thus, we deliver ourselves
from the labour necessary to assure ourselves whether
these vocal visions are true or false, and so we are dispensed
from an examination which has no other profit for the
soul than loss of time and anxiety.'

" Good—but if these words are really pronounced by God,
we rebel against His will if we remain deaf to them. And
then, as Saint Teresa declares, it is not in our power not to

listen to them, and the soul can only think of what it hears when Jesus speaks to it. Moreover, all the discussions on this subject are uncertain, for one does not enter of one's own will into the strait way, as the Church calls it, we are led, and even thrown into it often against the will, and resistance is impossible, phenomena occur, and nothing in the world has power to check them ; witness Saint Teresa, who, resist as she would by humility, fell into ecstasy under the divine breath, and was raised from the ground.

"No, these superhuman conditions alarm me, and I do not hold to knowing them by experience. As to Saint John of the Cross, the abbé is not wrong in calling him unique, but though he sounds the lowest strata of the soul, and reaches where human auger has never penetrated, he wearies me all the same in my admiration, for his work is full of nightmares which repel me ; I am not certain that his hell is correct, and some of his assertions do not convince me. What he calls the ' night obscure ' is incomprehensible ; ' The sufferings of that darkness surpass what is possible,' he cries on each page. Here I lose foothold. I can imagine, though I have not experienced them, the moral and terrible pangs, of the deaths of friends and relations, love betrayed, hopes which failed, spiritual sorrows of all kinds, but such a martyrdom as he proclaims as superior to all others, is beyond me, for it is outside our human interests, beyond our affections ; he moves in an inaccessible sphere, in an unknown world very far off.

"I am certainly afraid that this terrible saint, a true man of the south, abuses metaphor, and is full of Spanish affectation.

"Moreover I am astonished at the abbé on another point. He, who is so gentle, shows a certain leaning to the dry bread of Mysticism ; the effusions of Ruysbröck, of Saint Angela, of Saint Catherine of Genoa, touch him less than the arguments of saints who are hard reasoners ; yet by the side of these he has advised me to read Marie d'Agreda, whom he ought not to fancy, for she has none of those qualities which are admired in the works of Saint Teresa and Saint John of the Cross.

"Ah ! he may flatter himself that he has inflicted on me a complete disillusion, by lending me her ' Cité Mystique.'

"From the renown of this Spanish woman, I expected the

breath of prophecy, wide outlooks, extraordinary visions. Not at all ; her book is simply strange and pompous, wearisome and cold. Then the phraseology of her book is intolerable. All the expressions which swarm in those ponderous volumes, ' my divine princess,' ' my great queen,' when she addresses Our Lady, who in her turn speaks to her as ' my dearest,' just as Christ calls her ' my spouse,' ' my well-beloved,' and speaks of her continually as ' the object of my pleasure and delight,' the way in which she speaks of the angels as ' the courtiers of the great King,' set my nerves on edge and weary me.

" They smell of perriwigs and ruffles, bows and dances like Versailles, a sort of court mysticism in which Christ pontificates, attired in the costume of Louis XIV.

" Moreover Marie d'Agreda enters into most extravagant details. She tells us of the milk of Our Lady which cannot grow sour, of female complaints from which she was exempt, she explains the mystery of the conception by three drops of blood which fell from the heart into the womb of Mary, and which the Holy Ghost used to form the child ; lastly, she declares that Saint Michael and Saint Gabriel played the part of midwives, and stood living, under human forms, at the lying-in of the Virgin.

" This is too strong. I know well that the abbé would say that we need not concern ourselves with these singularities and these errors, but that the ' Cité Mystique ' is to be read in relation to the inner life of the Blessed Virgin. Yes, but then the book of M. Ollier, which treats of the same subject, seems to me curious and trustworthy in quite a different way."

Was the priest forcing the note, playing a part ? Durtal asked himself this, when he saw how determined he was not to avoid the same questions during a certain time. He tried now and then, in order to see how the matter was, to turn the conversation, but the abbé smiled, and brought it back to the point he wished.

When he thought that he had saturated Durtal with mystical works, he spoke of them less, and seemed to attach himself mainly to the religious Orders, and especially to that of Saint Benedict. He very cleverly induced Durtal to become interested in this institution, and to ask him about it, and when once he had entered on this ground, he did not depart from it.

It began one day when Durtal was talking with him about plain chant.

"You have reason to like it," said the abbé, "for even independently of the liturgy and of art, this chant, if I may believe Saint Justin, appeases the desires and concupiscences of the flesh, ' affectiones et concupiscentias carnis sedat,' but let me assure you, you only know it by hearsay, there is no longer any true plain chant in the churches, these are like the products of therapeutics, only more or less audacious adulterations presented to you.

"None of the chants which are to some extent respected by choirs, the ' Tantum ergo,' for example, are now exact. It is given almost faithfully till the verse ' Præstet fides,' and then it runs off the rails, taking no account of the shades, which are, however, quite perceptible, that the Gregorian melody introduces when the text declares the impotence of reason and the powerful aid of Faith ; these adulterations are still more apparent, if you listen to the ' Salve Regina ' after Compline. This is abridged more than half, is enervated, blanched, half its pauses are taken away,. it is reduced to a mere stump of ignoble music, if you had even heard this magnificent chant among the Trappists, you would weep with disgust at hearing it bawled in the churches at Paris.

"But besides the textual alteration of the melody as we now have it, the way in which the plain chant is bellowed is everywhere absurd. One of the first conditions for rendering it well, is that the voices should go together, that they should all chant in the same time syllable for syllable and note for note, in one word it must be in unison.

"Now, you can verify it yourself, the Gregorian melody is not thus treated ; every voice takes its own part, and is isolated. Next, plain music allows no accompaniment, it must be chanted alone, without organ, it bears at most that the instrument should give the intonation and accompany it very softly, just enough if need be to sustain the pitch taken by the voices ; it is not so that you will hear it given in the churches."

"Yes, I know it well," said Durtal. "When I hear it at St. Sulpice, St. Severin, or Notre Dame des Victoires, I am aware that it is sophisticated, but you must admit

that it is even then superb. I do not defend the tricks,
the addition of fiorituri, the falseness of the musical pauses,
the felonious accompaniment, the concert-room tone
inflicted on you at Saint Sulpice, but what can I do ? in
default of the original I must be content with a more or
less worthless copy, and I repeat, even executed in that
fashion the music is so admirable that I am enchanted by
it."

"But," said the abbé quietly, "nothing obliges you to
listen to the false plain chant, when you can hear the true,
for saving your presence, there exists, even in Paris, a chapel
where it is intact, and given according to the rules of which
I have spoken."

"Indeed, and where is that ?"

"At the Benedictine nuns of the Blessed Sacrament in the
Rue Monsieur."

"And can anyone enter the convent and be present at
the offices ?"

"Anyone. Every day in the week, Vespers are sung
at three o'clock, and on Sundays High Mass is said at
nine."

"Ah, had I but known this chapel earlier," said Durtal,
the first time he came out.

In fact it combined all the conditions he could wish.
Situated in a solitary street, it had the completest privacy.
The architect who built it had introduced no innovations or
pretentiousness, had built a Gothic church, and introduced
no fancies of his own.

It was cruciform, but one of the arms was scarcely the
full length, for want of room, while the other was
prolonged into a hall, separated from the choir by an
iron grating above which the Blessed Sacrament was
adored by two kneeling angels, whose lilac wings were
folded over thin rose-coloured backs. Except these two
figures, of which the execution was truly sinful, the rest
was at least veiled by shadow, and was not too afflicting to
the eyes. The chapel was dim, and always at the time of
the offices, a young sacristan-sister, tall and pale, and
rather bent, entered like a shadow, and each time that
she passed before the altar she fell on one knee and bowed
her head profoundly.

She seemed strange and scarcely human, gliding noiselessly over the pavement, her head bowed, with a band as low as her eyebrows, and she seemed to fly like a large bat when standing before the tabernacle she turned her back, moving her large black sleeves as she lighted the tapers. Durtal one day saw her features, sickly but charming, her eyelids dark, her eyes of a tired blue, and he guessed that her body was wasted by prayers, under her black robe drawn together by a leathern girdle ornamented by a little medal of the Blessed Sacrament of gilt metal, under the trimming, near her heart.

The grating of the enclosure, on the left of the altar, was large, and well lighted from behind, so that even when the curtains were drawn it was possible to see the whole chapter drawn up in file in their oaken stalls surmounted at the end by a higher stall in which the abbess sat. A lighted taper stood in the middle of the hall, and before it a nun prayed day and night, a cord round her neck, to expiate the insults offered to Jesus under His Eucharistic form.

The first time Durtal had visited the chapel, he had gone there on Sunday a little before the time of Mass, and he had been thus able to be present at the entry of the Benedictine nuns, behind the iron screen. They advanced two and two, stopped in the middle of the grating, turned to the altar and genuflected, then each bowed to her neighbour, and so to the end of this procession of women in black, only brightened by the whiteness of the head-band and the collar, and the gilt spot of the little monstrance on the breast. The novices came last, to be recognized by the white veils which covered their heads.

And when an old priest, assisted by a sacristan, began the mass softly at the end of the chapter, a small organ gave the tone to the voices.

Then Durtal might well wonder, for he had never before heard a sole and only voice made up of perhaps some thirty, of a tone so strange, a superterrestrial voice, which burnt upon itself, in the air, and intertwined its soft cooings.

This bore no resemblance to the icy and obstinate lament of the Carmelites, nor was it like the unsexed tone, the child's voice, squeaking, rounded off at the end of the Franciscan nuns, but quite another thing.

At La Glacière in fact those raw voices, though softened
and watered by prayers, kept somewhat of the drawling,
almost vulgar, inflexion of the people from whom they
came ; they were greatly purified, but remained none the less
human. Here the tenderness of tones was rendered
angelic, that voice with no defined origin long bolted through
the divine sieve, patiently modelled for the liturgical chant,
caught fire as it unfolded, blazed in virginal clusters of white
sound, died down, flowered out again in pale pleadings,
distant, seraphic at the end of certain chants.

Thus interpreted the Mass gave a special accent to the
sense of the sequences.

Standing, behind the grating, the convent answered the
priest.

Durtal had then heard, after a mournful and solemn
" Kyrie Eleison," sharp and almost tragic, the decided cry,
so loving and so grave, of the " Gloria in Excelsis," to the
true plain chant ; he had listened to the Credo, slow and
bare, solemn and pensive, and he was able to affirm that
these chants were totally different from those which were
sung everywhere in the churches. St. Severin and St.
Sulpice now seemed to him profane ; in the place of their
gentle warmth, their curls and their fringes, the angles of
their polished melodies, their modern endings, their inco-
herent accompaniments arranged for the organ, he found
himself in the presence of a chant, thin, sharp and nervous,
like the work of an early master, and saw the ascetic severity
of its lines, its sonorous colouring, the brightness of its metal
hammered out with the rude yet charming art of Gothic
jewels, he heard under the woven robe of sound, the beating
of a simple heart, the ingenuous love of ages, and he noticed
that curious shade in Benedictine music ; it ended all cries
of adoration, all tender cooings in a timid murmur, cut short,
as though shrinking in humility, effacing itself modestly as
though asking pardon of God for daring to love Him.

" Ah, you were very right to send me there," said Durtal
to the abbé when next he saw him.

" I had no choice," answered the priest, smiling, " for the
plain chant is respected only in convents under the Benedictine rule. That grand Order has restored it. Dom
Pothier has done for it what Dom Guéranger has done for
the liturgy.

" Moreover, beyond the authenticity of the vocal text, and the manner of rendering it, there are still two essential conditions for restoring the special life of these melodies, and they are hardly found except in cloisters, first Faith, and next the understanding the meaning of the words sung."

"But," interrupted Durtal, " I do not suppose that the Benedictine nuns know Latin."

" I beg your pardon, among the nuns of Saint Benedict, and even among the cloistered sisters of other Orders there are a certain number who study the language enough to understand the Breviary and the Psalms. That is a serious advantage which they have over the choirs, composed for the most part of artisans without instruction and without piety, only simple workers with their voices.

" Now without wishing to abate your enthusiasm for the musical honesty of these nuns, I am bound to say, that in order to understand this magnificent chant in its height and breadth, you must hear it, not winnowed by the mouths of virgins, even if unsexed, but as it issues, unsmoothed, untrimmed from the lips of men. Unfortunately, though there are at Paris, in the Rue Monsieur and the Rue Tournefort, two communities of Benedictine nuns, there is not on the other hand a single monastery of Benedictine monks."

" At the Rue Monsieur do they absolutely follow the rule of Saint Benedict ? "

" Yes ; but over and above the usual vows of poverty, chastity, remaining in the cloister, obedience, they make a further vow of separation and adoration of the Blessed Sacrament, as formulated by Saint Mechtilde.

" And so they lead the most austere existence of any nuns. They scarcely taste flesh ; they rise at two in the morning to sing Matins and Lauds, night and day, summer and winter, they take turns before the taper of reparation, and before the altar. It need not be said," continued the abbé after a pause, " that woman is stronger and braver than man ; no male ascetic could live and lead such a life, especially in the enervating atmosphere of Paris."

" What perhaps astounds me still more," said Durtal, " is the kind of obedience exacted of them. How can a creature endowed with free will annihilate herself to such an extent ? "

" Oh," said the abbé, " the obedience is the same in all

the great Orders, absolute, without reserve ; its formula is well summed up by Saint Augustine. Listen to this sentence which I remember to have read in a commentary on his rule :

" ' We must enter into the feelings of a beast of burthen, and allow ourselves to be led like a horse or a mule, which have no understanding ; or rather, that obedience may be still more perfect, since these animals kick against the spur, we must be in the hands of a superior like a block, or the stock of a tree, which has neither life, nor movement, nor action, nor will, nor judgment.' Is that clear ? "

" It is most frightful ! I quite admit," said Durtal, " that in exchange for such abnegation, the nuns must be power-fully aided from on high, but are there not some moments of falling away, some cases of despair, some instants in which they pine for a natural life in the open air, in which they lament that death in life which they have made for themselves ; are there not days in which their senses wake and cry aloud ? "

" No doubt ; in the cloistered life the age of twenty-nine is terrible to pass, then a passionate crisis arises ; if a woman doubles that cape, and she almost always does so, she is safe.

" But carnal emotions are not, to speak correctly, the most troublesome assault they have to undergo. The real punishment they endure in those hours of sorrow is the ardent, wild regret for that maternity of which they are ignorant ; the desolate womb of woman revolts, and full of God though she be, her heart is breaking. The child Jesus whom they have loved so well then appears so far off and so inaccessible, and His very sight would hardly satisfy them, for they have dreamed of holding Him in their arms, of swathing and rocking Him, of giving Him suck, in one word, of being mothers.

" Other nuns undergo no precise attack, no assault to which a name can be given, but without any definite reason they languish and die suddenly, like a taper, blown out. The torpor of the cloister kills them."

" But indeed, Monsieur l'abbé, these details are far from encouraging."

The priest shrugged his shoulders. " It is the poor reverse of a splendid stuff," he said, " wonderful recom-

penses are granted, even in this world, to souls in convents."

"Nor do I suppose that if a nun fall, stricken in the
flesh, she is abandoned. What does the Mother abbess in
such a case?"

"She acts according to the bodily temperament and state
of the soul of the sick person. Note that she has been able
to follow her during the years of her probation, that she
has necessarily gained an influence over her ; at such times
therefore she will watch her daughter very closely, endeavour to turn the course of her ideas, breaking her by hard
work, and by occupying her mind ; she must not leave her
alone, must diminish her prayers, if need be, restrict her
hours of office, lessen her fasts, give her, if the case demands
it, better food. In other cases, on the contrary, she will
have recourse to more frequent communions, lessen her
food or cause her to be blooded, mix cooling meats with
her diet, and above all things she and all the community
must pray for her.

"An old Benedictine abbess, whom I knew at Saint-
Omer, an incomparable guide of souls, limited before all things
the length of confessions. The moment she saw the least
symptoms arise she gave two minutes, watch in hand, to the
penitent, and when the time was up she sent her back
from the confessional, to mix with her companions."

"Why so?"

"Because in convents, even for souls which are well,
confession is a most dangerous relaxation, it is as it were
too long and too warm a bath. In it nuns go to excess,
open their hearts uselessly, dwell upon their troubles,
accentuate them, and revel in them ; they come out more
weakened and more ill than before. Two minutes ought
indeed to be enough for a nun in which to tell her little
sins.

"Yet . . . yet . . . I must admit it, the confessor is a danger
for a convent, not that I suspect his honour, that is not at
all what I mean, but as he is generally chosen from among
the bishop's favourites, there are many chances that he may
be a man who knows nothing, and quite ignorant of how
to deal with such souls, ends by unsettling them while he
consoles them. Again, if demoniac attacks, so common in
nunneries, occur, the poor man can only gape, gives all sorts

of confused counsel, and hinders the energy of the abbess, who in such matters knows far better than he."

" And," said Durtal, who chose his words carefully, " tell me, I suppose that tales like those which Diderot gives in his foolish volume ' La Religieuse ' are incorrect ? "

" Unless a community is rotted by a superior given over to Satanism, which, thank God, is rare, the filthy stories told by that writer are false, and there is moreover a good reason why it should be so, for there is a sin which is the very antidote of the other, the sin of zeal."

" What ? "

" Yes : the sin of zeal which causes the denunciation of our neighbour, gives scope to jealousy, creates spying to satisfy hate, that is the real sin of the cloister. Well, I assure you that if two sisters became quite shameless they would be denounced at once."

" But I thought, Monsieur l'Abbé, that tale-bearing was allowed by the rules of most orders ? "

" It is, but perhaps there is a temptation to carry it somewhat to excess, especially in convents of women ; for you can imagine that if nunneries contain pure mystics, real saints, they have in them also some nuns less advanced in the way of perfection, and who even still retain some faults . . . "

" Come, since we are in the chapter of minute details, dare I ask if cleanliness is not just a little neglected by these good women ? "

" I cannot say ; all that I know is, that in the Benedictine abbeys I have known, each nun was free to act as seemed good to her ; in certain Augustinian constitutions, the case was provided for in contrary fashion, it was forbidden to wash the body, except once a month. On the other hand, amongst the Carmelites cleanliness is exacted. Saint Teresa hated dirt, and loved white linen, her daughters have even, I think, a right to have a flask of Eau de Cologne in their cells. You see this depends on the order, and probably also, when the rule does not expressly mention it, on the ideas which the superior may have on the subject. I will add that this question must not be looked at only from the worldly point of view, for corporal dirt is for certain souls an additional suffering and mortification which they impose on themselves, as Benedict Labre."

" He who picked up vermin which left him, and put them piously in his sleeve. I prefer mortifications of another kind."

" There are harder ones, believe me, and I think they would suit you better. Would you like to imitate Suso, who, to subdue his passions, bore on his naked shoulders, for eighteen years, an enormous cross set with nails, whose points pierced his flesh ? More than that, he imprisoned his hands in leather gloves which also bristled with nails, lest he should be tempted to dress his wounds. Saint Rose of Lima treated herself no better, she bound a chain so tightly round her body that it penetrated the skin, and hid itself under the bleeding pad of flesh, she wore also a horse-hair girdle set with pins, and lay on shards of glass ; but all these trials are nothing in comparison of those inflicted on herself by a Capuchin nun, the venerable Mother Pasidée of Siena.

" She scourged herself with branches of juniper and holly, then poured vinegar into her wounds, and sprinkled them with salt, she slept in winter on the snow, in summer on bunches of nettles, or pebbles, or brushes, put drops of hot lead in her shoes, knelt upon thistles, thorns and sticks. In January she broke the ice in a cask and plunged into it, and she even half-stifled herself by hanging head downwards in a chimney in which damp straw was lighted, but that is enough ; indeed," said the abbé laughing, " if you had to choose, you would like best the mortifications which Benedict Labre imposed on himself."

" I would rather have none at all," answered Durtal.

There was a moment's pause.

Durtal's thoughts went back to the Benedictine nuns : " But," said he, " why do they put in the ' Semaine reli-gieuse,' after their title Benedictine Nuns of the Blessed Sacrament, this further name, ' Convent of Saint Louis du Temple ? ' "

" Because," said the abbé, " their first convent was founded on the actual ruins of the Temple prison, given them by royal warrant, when Louis XVIII. returned to France.

" Their foundress and superior was Louise Adélaïde de Bourbon Condé, an unfortunate princess of many wanderings, almost the whole of whose life was spent in exile. Expelled from France by the Revolution and the Empire, hunted in

almost every country in Europe, she wandered by chance
among convents seeking shelter, now among the nuns of
the Annunciation at Turin and the Capuchins in Piedmont,
now among the Trappistines in Switzerland and the Sisters
of the Visitation at Vienna, now among the Benedictines of
Lithuania and Poland.   At last she found shelter among the
Benedictines in Norfolk, till she could again enter France.

" She was a woman singularly trained in monastic science
and experienced in the direction of souls.

" She desired that in her abbey every sister should offer
herself to heaven in reparation for crimes committed ;
and that she should accept the most painful privations to
make up for those which might be committed ; she
instituted there the perpetual adoration, and introduced
the plain chant, in all its purity, to the exclusion of all
others.

" It is, as you have been able to hear, there preserved
intact ; it is true that since her time, her nuns have had
lessons from Dom Schmitt, one of the most learned monks
in that matter.

" Then, after the death of the princess, which took place, I
think, in 1824, it was perceived that her body exhaled the
odour of sanctity, and though she has not been canonized
her intercession is invoked by her daughters in certain
cases.   Thus, for example, the Benedictine nuns of the Rue
Monsieur ask her assistance when they lose anything, and
their experience shows that their prayer is never in vain,
since the object lost is found almost at once.

" But," continued the abbé, " since you like the convent
so well, go there, especially when it is lighted up."

The priest rose and took up a " Semaine religieuse,"
which lay upon the table.

He turned over the leaves.   " See," he said, and read,
" ' Sunday 3 o'clock, Vespers chanted ; ceremony of clothing,
presided over by the Very Reverend Father Dom Etienne,
abbot of the Grande Trappe, and Benediction.' "

" That is a ceremony which interests me much."

" I too shall probably be there."

" Then we can meet in the chapel ? "

" Just so."

" These ceremonies of clothing have not now the gaiety
they had in the eighteenth century in certain Benedictine

institutions, amongst others the Abbey de Bourbourg in Flanders," said the abbé smiling, after a silence.

And since Durtal looked at him questioningly—

"Yes, there was no sadness about it, or at least it had a special sadness of its own ; you shall judge. On the eve of the day that the postulant was to take the habit, she was presented to the abbess of Bourbourg by the governor of the town. Bread and wine were offered to her, and she tasted them in the church itself. On the morrow she appeared, magnificently dressed, at a ball which was attended by the whole community of nuns, where she danced, then she asked her parents' blessing, and was conducted, with violins playing, to the chapel, where the abbess took possession of her. She had for the last time seen, at the ball, the joys of the world, for she was immediately shut up, for the rest of her days in the cloister."

"The joy of the Dance of Death," said Durtal, "monastic customs and congregations were strange in old days."

",No doubt, but they are lost in the night of time. I remember, however, that in the fifteenth century there existed under the rule of Saint Augustine an order strange indeed, called the Order of the Daughters of Saint Magloire, whose convent was in the Rue Saint Denys at Paris. The conditions of admission were the reverse of those of all other charters. The postulant had to swear on the holy Gospels that she had been unchaste, and no one believed her oath ; she was examined, and if her oath were false, she was declared unworthy to be received. Nor might she have brought about this condition expressly in order to enter the convent, she must have well and truly given herself over to sin, before she came to ask the shelter of the cloister.

"They were in fact a troop of penitent girls, and the rule of their subjection was savage. They were whipped, locked up, subjected to the most rigid fasts, made their confessions thrice in the week, rose at midnight, were under the most unremitting surveillance, were even attended in their most secret retirement ; their mortifications were incessant and their closure absolute. I need hardly add that this nunnery is dead."

"Nor likely to revive," cried Durtal. "Well then, Monsieur l'Abbé, we meet on Sunday in the Rue Monsieur ? "

And on the assent of the abbé, Durtal went his way,
with the strangest ideas in his head about the monastic
orders.   The thing would be, he thought, to found an abbey
where one could work at ease in a good library, there
should be several monks, with decent meals, plenty of
tobacco, and permission to take a turn on the quays now
and then.   And he laughed ; but then that would not be a
monastery! or only a Dominican monastery, with monks who
dine out, and have, at least, the amusement of preaching.

CHAPTER VIII.

ON Sunday morning, on his way to the Rue Monsieur, Durtal chewed the cud of his reflections on the Monasteries. "It is certain," he thought, "that in the accumulated filth of ages, they alone have remained clean, are truly in relation with heaven, and serve as interpreters between it and earth. But we must thoroughly understand and specify that we are speaking only of the cloistered orders, which have remained, as far as possible, poor . . . "

And thinking of the communities of women, he murmured as he hastened his steps : " Here is a surprising fact, which proves once more the incomparable genius with which the Church is endowed ; she has been able to bring into common life women who do not assassinate each other, and obey without recalcitrancy the orders of another woman—wonderful !

"Well, here I am "—and Durtal, who knew he was late, hastened into the court of the Benedictine nunnery, took the steps of the little church four at a time, and pushed the door open. He paused in hesitation on the threshold, dazzled by the blaze of the lighted chapel. Lamps were lit everywhere, and overhead the altar flamed with a forest of tapers against which stood out as on a gold ground, the ruddy face of a bishop all in white.

Durtal glided among the crowd, elbowing his way till he saw the Abbé Gévresin beckoning to him. He joined him, and sat down on the chair the priest had kept for him, and examined the abbot of Grande Trappe, surrounded by priests in chasubles, and choir boys some in red and others in blue, followed by a Trappist with shaven crown, surrounded by a fringe of hair, holding a wooden cross, on the reverse of which was carved the small figure of a monk.

Clad in a white cowl, with long sleeves and a gold button

on his hood, his abbot's cross on his breast, his head covered
with an old French mitre of low form, Dom Etienne, with
his broad shoulders, his greyish beard, his ruddy colour,
had a look of an old Burgundian, tanned by the sun while
working at his vines ; he seemed, moreover, a good sort of
man, uneasy under his mitre, oppressed by his honours.

A sharp perfume which burnt the nose as a spice burns
the tongue, the perfume of myrrh, floated in the air, the
crowds surged ; behind the grating from which the curtain
was withdrawn, the nuns standing sang the hymn of Saint
Ambrose, " Jesu corona virginum," while the bells of the
abbey rang a peal ; in the short aisle leading from the porch
to the choir, a bending line of women on either side, a cross-
bearer and torch-bearers entered, and behind them appeared
the novice dressed as a bride.

She was dark, slight, and very short, and came forward
shyly with downcast eyes, between her mother and sister.
At first sight Durtal thought her insignificant, scarcely pretty,
a mere nobody ; and he looked instinctively for the other
party, put out in his sense of fitness, by the absence of a
man in the marriage procession.

Striving against her agitation the postulant walked up
the nave into the choir, and knelt on the left before a large
taper, her mother and sister on either side as bridesmaids.

Dom Etienne genuflected to the altar, mounted the
steps, and sat down in a red velvet arm-chair, placed on
the highest step.

Then one of the priests conducted the girl, who knelt
alone, before the monk.

Dom Etienne was motionless as a figure of Buddha ; with
the same gesture, he lifted one finger, and said gently to
the novice,—

" What is it you ask ? "

She spoke so low as scarcely to be heard.

" Father, feeling in myself an ardent desire to sacrifice
myself to God, as a victim in union with our Lord Jesus
Christ, immolated on our altars, and to spend my life in
perpetual adoration of His divine Sacrament, under the
observance of the rule of our glorious Father Saint
Benedict, I humbly ask of you the grace of the holy
habit."

" I will give it you willingly if you believe you can

conform your life to that of a victim devoted to the Holy Sacrament."

And she answered in a firmer tone,

" I trust so, leaning on the infinite goodness of my Saviour Jesus Christ."

" God give you perseverance, my daughter," said the prelate ; he rose, turned to the altar, genuflected, and with uncovered head began the chant " Veni Creator," taken up by the voices of the nuns behind the light screen of iron.

Then he replaced his mitre, and prayed, while the chanted psalms rose under the arches. The novice, who in the meantime had been reconducted to her place at the prie-Dieu, rose, genuflected to the altar, and then knelt between her two bridesmaids before the abbot of La Trappe, who had reseated himself.

Her two companions lifted the veil of the bride, took off her wreath of orange flowers, unrolled the coils of her hair, while a priest spread a napkin on the knees of the prelate, and the deacon presented a pair of long scissors on a salver.

Then before the gesture of this monk, making himself ready, like an executioner, to shear the condemned person, whose hour of expiation was at hand, the terrible beauty of innocence becoming like crime, in substitution for sins of which she was ignorant, which she could not even understand, was evident to the public who had come to the chapel out of curiosity, and in consternation at the superhuman denial of justice, it trembled when the bishop seized the entire handful of her hair, and drew it towards him over her brow.

Then there was as it were a flash of steel in a dark shower.

In the death-like silence of the church the grinding of the scissors was heard in the mass of hair which fell under the blades, and then all was silent. Dom Etienne opened his hand, and the rain fell on his knees in long black threads.

There was a sigh of relief when the priests and bridesmaids led away the bride, looking strange in her train, with her head discrowned and her neck bare.

The procession returned almost immediately. There

was no longer a bride in a white skirt, but a nun in a black robe.

She bowed before the Trappist, and again knelt between her mother and sister.

Then, while the abbot prayed the Lord to bless his handmaid, the master of the ceremonies and the deacon took, from a credence near the altar, a basket, wherein under loose rose leaves were folded a girdle of untanned leather, emblem of the end of that luxury which the Fathers of the Church placed in the region of the reins, a scapular, symbol of a life crucified to the world, a veil, which signifies the solitude of the life hidden in God, and the prelate explained the sense of these emblems to the novice, then taking the lighted taper from the candlestick before her, he gave it to her, declaring in one phrase the meaning of his action : " Accipe, charissimà soror, lumen Christi."

Then Dom Etienne took the sprinkler which a priest handed him with an inclination, and as in the general absolution of the dead, he sprinkled the girl with holy water in the form of a cross, then he sat down and spoke gently and quietly without using a single gesture.

He spoke to the postulant alone, praising the august and humble life of the cloister. " Look not back," he said, " have no regrets, for by my voice Jesus repeats to you the promise once made to the Magdalen, ' yours is the better part, which shall not be taken away from you.' Say also to yourself, my daughter, that, henceforward, taken away from the eternal trifling of labours in vain, you will accomplish a useful work upon earth, you will practise charity in its highest form, you will make expiation for others, you will pray for those who never pray, you will aid, so far as your strength permits, to make amends for the hate the world bears to the Saviour.

" Suffer and you will be happy ; love your spouse, and you will see how tender He is to His elect. Believe me, His love is such that He will not even wait till you are purified by death to recompense you for your miserable mortifications, your poor sufferings. Even before your hour is come, He will heap His graces upon you, and you will beg Him to let you die, so greatly will the excess of these joys exceed your strength."

Little by little the old monk grew warm, and returned to the words of Christ to the Magdalen, showing how in reference to her Jesus set forward the excellence of the contemplative over the other Orders, and gave brief advice, dwelling on the necessity of humility and poverty, which are, as Saint Clare says, the two great walls of cloistered life. Then he blessed the novice, who kissed his hand, and when she had returned to her place, he prayed to the Lord, lifting his eyes to heaven, that He would accept this nun, who offered herself as a victim for the sins of the world. Then, standing, he intoned the " Te Deum."

Every one rose, and preceded by the cross and torch bearers, the procession passed out of the church, and was massed in the court.

Then Durtal might have believed himself carried back far from Paris, into the heart of the Middle Ages.

The court, surrounded by buildings, was closed opposite the entrance-gate by a high wall, in the midst of which was a folding-door ; on each side six thin pines rocked to and fro, and chanting was heard behind the wall.

The postulant, in front, alone, near the closed door, held her torch, with her head bent. The abbot of La Trappe, leaning on his crosier, waited, unmoving, a few paces from her.

Durtal examined their faces, the girl, so commonplace in her bridal costume, had become charming, her body was now full of a timid grace, the lines, somewhat too marked under her worldly dress, were softened, under her religious shroud her outline was only a simple sketch, it was as though the years had rolled back, and as though there was a return to the forms only prophesied in childhood.

Durtal drew near to examine her better, he tried to look at her face, but under the chill bandage of her head-dress, she remained mute, and as if absent from life, with her eyes closed, and as though she lived only in the smile of her happy lips.

Seen nearer, the monk who had seemed so stout and ruddy in the chapel, seemed also changed, his frame remained robust, and his complexion bright, but his eyes of a light blue, like chalk water, water without reflections or waves, eyes wonderfully pure, changed the common expression of his features, and took away from him that look of a vine-dresser which he had at a distance.

"It is clear," thought Durtal, "that the soul is everything in these people, and their faces are modelled by it.
There is a holy clearness in their eyes, and their lips, in
those only apertures through which the soul comes to look
out of the body, and almost shows itself."

The chants behind the wall suddenly ceased, the girl
made a step forward, and knocked with her closed fingers
at the door, and then with a failing voice she sang,—

"Aperite mihi portas justitiae : Ingressa in eas,
confitebor Domino."

The door opened. Another large court, paved with
pebbles was seen, bounded at the end by a building, and all
the community, in a sort of semicircle, with black books in
their hands, cried,—

"Haec porta Domini : Justi intrabunt in eam."

The novice made another step to the sill and answered in
her far-away voice,—

"Ingrediar in locum tabernaculi admirabilis : usque ad
domum Dei."

And the choir of nuns, unmoving, answered,—

"Haec est domus Domini firmiter aedificata : Bene
fundata est supra firmam petram."

Durtal hastily looked at those faces which could only be
seen for a few minutes and on the occasion of such a ceremony. It was a row of dead bodies standing in black
shrouds. All were bloodless, with white cheeks, lilac
eyelids and grey lips, the voices of all were exhausted and
fined down by prayer, and most of them, even the young,
were bent. "Their poor bodies are worn with austere
fatigue," thought Durtal.

But his reflections were cut short, the bride, now kneeling
on the threshold, turned to Dom Etienne and chanted in a
low voice,—

"Haec requies mea in saeculum saeculi : Hic habitabo
quoniam elegi eam."

The monk laid aside his mitre and crosier and said,—

"Confirma hoc Deus, quod operatus es in nobis."

And the postulant murmured,—

"A templo sacro tuo quod est in Jerusalem."

Then before re-covering his head and resuming his
crosier, the prelate prayed God Almighty to pour the dew
of His blessing on His handmaid ; then directing the girl

towards a nun who left the group of sisters and advanced to the threshold, he said to her,—

"Into your hands, Madame, we commit this new bride of the Lord, sustain her in the holy resolution she has so solemnly taken upon her, in asking to sacrifice herself to God as a victim, and to dedicate her life in honour of our Lord Jesus Christ, sacrificed on our altars. Lead her in the way of the divine Commandments, in the practice of the counsels of the Holy Gospel, and in the observance of the monastic rule. Prepare her for the eternal union to which the heavenly Spouse invites her, and from this blessed increase of the flock committed to your charge draw a new motive for maternal care. The peace of the Lord rest upon you."

This was all : the nuns one by one turned and disappeared behind the wall, while the girl followed them like a poor dog, who with drooping head accompanies at a distance a new master.

The folding doors closed.

Durtal remained stupefied, looking at the outline of the white bishop, the backs of the priests who were mounting the steps to give Benediction in the church, while behind them came in tears, their faces in their handkerchiefs, the mother and sister of the novice.

"Well?" said the abbé, passing his arm through Durtal's.

"Well, this scene is to my mind the most touching alibi of death that· it is possible to see, this living woman, who buries herself in the most frightful of tombs—for in it the flesh continues to suffer—is wonderful.

"I remember that you have yourself told me of the pressure of this observance, and I shivered in thinking of perpetual Adoration, in those winter nights, when a child like this is awakened out of her first sleep, and cast into the darkness of a chapel where unless she faints from weakness or terror, she must pray alone, through the freezing hours on her knees on the pavement.

"What passes in that conversation with the unknown, that interview with the Shadow ? Does she succeed in escaping from self, and in leaving the earth, in gaining, on the threshold of Eternity, the inconceivable Spouse, or does the soul, powerless to spring on high, remain riveted to the soil ?

"We figure her to ourselves, her face bent forward, her hands joined, making appeal to herself, concentrating herself, in order to pour herself forth the better, and we imagine her thus sickly, with no strength left, trying to set her soul on fire in a shivering frame. But who can tell if on certain nights she attains to it?

"Ah! those poor lamps of exhausted oil, of flames almost dead, which tremble in the obscurity of the sanctuary, what will God make of them?

"Then there was the family present at the taking the habit, and if the daughter filled me with enthusiasm I could not restrain myself from pitying the mother. Think if the daughter died, the mother would embrace her, would perhaps speak to her, or if she did not recognize her, it would at least not be with her own good will; but in this case it is not the body, but the very soul of her child that dies before her eyes. Of her own accord her child knows her no longer, it is the contemptuous end of an affection. You will admit that for a mother this is very hard."

"Yes, but this so-called ingratitude, gained at the price of God knows what struggles, is it not, even apart from the divine vocation, the most equitable repartition of human love? Think that this elect creature becomes the scapegoat of sins committed, and like a lamentable daughter of Danaus she will unceasingly pour the offering of her mortifications and prayers, of her vigils and fastings, into the bottomless vessel of offences and crimes. Ah! if you knew what it was to repair the sins of the world. In regard to this I remember that one day the abbess of the Benedictines in the Rue Tournefort said to me: 'Since our tears are not holy enough, nor our souls pure enough, God makes trial of us in our bodies.' Here are long illnesses which cannot be cured, illnesses which doctors fail to understand, and we make thus much expiation for others.

"But if you will think over the ceremony which is just ended, you need not be affected beyond measure or compare it to the well-known ceremonies of a funeral; the postulant whom you saw has not yet pronounced her final vows, she can if she choose leave the convent, and return to her own home. At present she is in regard to her mother, a child in a foreign country, a child at school, but she is not a dead child.

"You may say what you please, but there is a tragedy in that door which closed upon her."

"Therefore in the Benedictine convent in the Rue Tournefort, the scene takes place in the interior of the convent, and the family is not present, the mother is spared, but mitigated thus, the ceremony is but a mere form, almost a foolish rule in the seclusion wherein the Faith is hidden."

"Those nuns are also Benedictines of the perpetual Adoration, are they not?"

"Yes, do you know their convent?"

And as Durtal shook his head, the abbé continued,—

"It is older, but less interesting than that in the Rue Monsieur, the chapel is mean, full of plaster statuettes, cotton flowers, bunches of grapes and ears of corn in gold paper, but the old building of the nunnery is curious. It contains, what shall I call it? a school dining-room, and a retreatant's drawing-room, and so gives at once the impression of old age and childhood."

"I know that class of convents," said Durtal. "I used often to see one, when I used to visit an old aunt at Versailles. It always used to impress me as a Maison Vauquer, brought to devotional uses, it had the air at once of a *table d'hôte* in the Rue de la Clef and the sacristy of a country church."

"Just so," and the abbé went on with a smile,—

"I had many interviews with the abbess in the Rue Tournefort; you guess at rather than see her, for you are separated from her by a screen of black wood, behind which is stretched a black curtain which she draws aside."

"I can see it," thought Durtal, who, remembering the Benedictine custom, saw in a second a little face confused in neutral tinted light, and lower, at the top of her habit, the gleam of a medal of the Blessed Sacrament in red enamelled in white.

He laughed and said to the abbe,—

"I laugh, because having had some business to transact with my nun aunt of whom I was speaking, only visible like your abbess through a trellis, I found out how to read her thoughts a little."

"Ah! how was that?"

"In this way. Since I could not see her face, which

was hidden behind the lattice of her cage, and disappeared behind her veil, and if she should answer me, having nothing to guide me but the inflexions of her voice, always circumspect and always calm, I ended by trusting only to her great glasses, round, with buff frames, which almost all nuns wear. Well, all the repressed vivacity of this woman burst out there ; suddenly in a corner of her glasses, there was a glimmer, and I then understood that her eye had lighted up, and gave the lie to the indifference of her voice, the determined quietness of her tone."

The abbé in his turn began to laugh.

" Do you know the Superior of the Benedictines, in the Rue Monsieur ? " said Durtal.

" I have spoken with her once or twice ; there the parlour is monastic, there is not the provincial and middle-class side of the Rue Tournefort, it is composed of a sombre room, of which all the breadth at the end is taken up by an iron grating, and behind the grating are again wooden bars, and a shutter painted black. You are quite in the dark, and the abbess, scarcely in the light, appears to you like a phantom."

" The abbess is, I suppose, the nun, elderly, fragile and very short, to whom Dom Etienne committed the novice ? "

" Yes. She is a remarkable shepherdess of souls, and what is more, a very well educated woman of most distinguished manners."

" Oh," thought Durtal : " I can imagine that these abbesses are charming, but also terrible women. Saint Teresa was goodness itself, but when she speaks in her ' Way of Perfection ' of nuns who band themselves together to discuss the will of their mother, she shows herself inexorable, for she declares that perpetual imprisonment should be inflicted on them as soon as possible and without flinching, and in fact she is right, for every disorderly sister infects the flock, and gives the rot to souls."

Thus talking they had reached the end of the Rue de Sèvres, and the abbé stopped to rest.

" Ah," he said, as if speaking to himself, " had I not had all my life heavy expenses, first a brother, then nephews to maintain, I should many years ago have become a member of Saint Benedict's family. I have always had an attraction towards that grand Order, which is, in fact, the intellectual Order of the Church. Therefore, when I was stronger and younger, I always went for my retreats to one of their monasteries, sometimes to the black monks of Solesmes, or of Ligugé, who have preserved the wise traditions of Saint Maurus, sometimes to the Cistercians, or the white monks of La Trappe."

"True," said Durtal, "La Trappe is one of the great branches of the tree of Saint Benedict, but how is it that its ordinances do not differ from those which the Patriarch left?"

"That is to say that the Trappists interpret the rule of Saint Benedict, which is very broad and supple, less in its spirit than in its letter, while the Benedictines do the contrary.

"In fact, La Trappe is an off-shoot of Citeaux, and is much more the daughter of Saint Bernard, who was during forty years the very sap of that branch, than the descendant of Saint Benedict."

"But, so far as I remember, the Trappists are themselves divided, and do not live under a uniform discipline."

"They do so now, since a pontifical brief dated March 17th, 1893, sanctioned the decisions of the general Chapter of the Trappists assembled in Rome, and ordered the fusion into one sole order, and under the direction of a sole superior, of the three observances of the Trappists, who were in fact ruled by discordant constitutions."

And seeing that Durtal was listening attentively, the abbé continued,—

"Among these three observances, one only, that of the Cistercian Trappists, to which belonged the abbey of which I was a guest, followed in their integrity the rules of the twelfth century, and led the monastic life of Saint Bernard's day. This alone recognized the rule of Saint Benedict, taken in its strictest application, and completed by the Charte de Charité, and the use and customs of Citeaux ; the two others had adopted the same rule, but revised and modified in the seventeenth century by the Abbé de Rancé, and again one of them, the Belgian congregation, had changed the statutes imposed by that abbot.

" At the present day, as I have just said, all the Trappists form only one and the same institute under the name, Order of Reformed Cistercians of the Blessed Virgin Mary of La Trappe, and all resume the rules of Citeaux, and live again the life of the cenobites of the Middle Ages."

" But if you have visited these ascetics," said Durtal, " you must know Dom Etienne ? "

" No, I have never stayed at La Grande Trappe, I prefer the poor and small monasteries where one is mixed up with the monks, to those imposing convents where they isolate you in a guest-house, and in a word keep you separate.

" There is one in which I make my retreats, Notre Dame de l'Atre, a small Trappist monastery a few leagues from Paris, which is quite the most seductive of shelters. Besides that the Lord really abides there, for it has true saints among its children, it is delightful also with its ponds, its immemorial trees, its distant solitude, far in the woods."

" Yes, but," observed Durtal, " the life there must be un-bending, for La Trappe is the most rigid order which has been imposed on men."

For his only answer the abbé let go Durtal's arm, and took both his hands.

" Do you know," he said, looking him in the face, " it is there you must go for your conversion ? "

" Are you serious, Monsieur l'Abbé ? "

And as the priest pressed his hands more strongly Durtal cried,—

" Ah, no indeed, first I have not the stoutness of soul, and if that be possible I have still less the bodily health needed for such a course, I should fall ill on my arrival, and then . . . and then . . . "

" And then, what ? I am not proposing to you to shut you up for ever in a cloister."

" So I suppose," said Durtal, in a somewhat piqued tone.

" But just to remain a week, just the necessary time for a cure. Now a week is soon over, then do you think that if you make such a resolution God will not sustain you ? "

" That is all very fine, but . . . "

" Let us speak on the health question, then ; " and the abbé smiled a smile of pity that was a little contemptuous.

"I can promise you at once that as a retreatant, you will not be bound to lead the life of a Trappist in its austerest sense. You need not get up at two in the morning for Matins, but at three, or even at four o'clock, according to the day."

And smiling at the face Durtal made, the abbé went on,—

"As to your food it will be better than that of the monks ; naturally you will have no fish nor meat, but you may certainly have an egg for dinner, if vegetables are not enough for you."

"And the vegetables, I suppose, are cooked with salt and water, and no seasoning ? "

"No, they are dressed with salt and water only on fasting days ; at other times you will have them cooked in milk and water, or in oil."

"Many thanks," said Durtal.

"But all that is excellent for your health," continued the priest, "you complain of pains in the stomach, sick headaches, diarrhœa, well, this diet, in the country, in the air, will cure you better than all the drugs you take.

"Now let us leave, if you like, your body out of the question, for in such a case, it is God's part to act against your weakness. I tell you, you will not be ill at La Trappe, that were absurd ; it would be to send the penitent sinner away, and Jesus would not then be the Christ ; but let us talk of your soul. Have the courage to take its measure, to look it well in the face. Do you see that ? " said the abbé after a silence.

Durtal did not answer.

"Admit," said the priest, "that you are horrified at it."

They took a few steps in the street, and the abbé continued,—

"You declare that you are sustained by the crowds of Notre Dame des Victoires and the emanations of St. Severin. What will it be then, in the humble chapel, when you will be on the ground huddled together with the saints ? I guarantee you in the name of the Lord an assistance such as you have never had ; " and he went on with a laugh, "I may add that the Church will take pleasure in receiving you, she will bring out her ornaments which she has now left off : the authentic liturgies of the Middle Ages, true plain chant, without solos or organs."

"Listen, your propositions astound me," said Durtal with
an effort. "No : I assure you I am not at all disposed to
imprison myself in such a place. I know well that at Paris
I shall never come to any good. I swear to you that I am
not proud of my life, nor satisfied with my soul, but from
thence . . . to . . . where I cannot tell ; I want at least a
mitigated asylum, a quiet convent. There must be, on
those conditions, somewhere, hospitals for souls."

"I could only send you to the Jesuits, who make a
specialty of retreats for men : but knowing you as I think I
know you, I feel sure you would not stay there two days.
You would find yourself among amiable and very clever
priests, but they would overwhelm you with sermons,
would wish to interfere with your life, mix themselves up
with your art, they would examine your thoughts with a
magnifying glass, and then you would be under treatment
with good young people, whose unintelligent piety would
horrify you, and you would flee in exasperation.

"At La Trappe it is the contrary. You would certainly
be the sole retreatant there, and no one will have the least
idea of troubling himself about you ; you will be free, you
can if you choose leave the monastery just as you entered
it, without having confessed or approached the Sacraments,
your will will be respected there, and no monk will attempt
to sound it without your authority. To you only it will
appertain to decide whether you will be converted or no.

"And you will like me to be frank to the last, will you
not ? You are, as indeed I have already said to you, a
sensitive and distrustful man ; well, the priest as you see
him in Paris, even the religious not cloistered, seem to you,
how shall I express it ? second rate souls, not to go
further . . . "

Durtal protested vaguely, with a gesture.

"Let me go on. An afterthought will come to you in
regard to the ecclesiastic to whom will fall the task of
cleansing you, you will be quite certain that he is not a
saint ; this is not very theological, for were he even the
worst of priests his absolution would have just the same
value, if you merit it, but indeed here is a question of
sentiment which I respect, you will think of him in a word :
he lives as I do, he is not more self-denying than I am,
nothing shows that his conscience is very superior to mine,

and thence to losing all confidence, and throwing up the
whole thing there is but a step.   At La Trappe, I will defy
you to reason in this way, and not to become humble.
When you see men, who after having abandoned everything to serve God, lead a life of privations and penance
such as no government would dare to inflict on its convicts,
you will indeed be obliged to admit that you are no great
thing by their side."

Durtal was silent.   After the astonishment he had felt at
the suggestion of such an issue, he became dully irritated
against this friend, who hitherto so discreet, had suddenly
rushed upon his soul and opened it by force.   There came
out the disgusting vision of an existence stripped, used up,
reduced to a state of dust, a condition of rags.   And Durtal
shrank from himself, convinced that the abbé was right,
that he must at any rate stanch the discharge of his senses,
and expiate their inappeasable desires, their abominable
covetousness, their rotten tastes, and he was seized with a
terror irrational and intense.   He had the giddy fear of the
cloister, a terror which attracted him to the abyss over
which Gévresin made him lean.

Enervated by the ceremony of taking the habit, stunned
by the blow with which the priest had assailed him as they
left the church, he now felt an anguish almost physical, in
which everything ended in confusion.   He did not know
to what reflections he should give himself, and only saw,
swimming on this whirlpool of troubled ideas, one clear
thought, that the moment had come so dreaded by him in
which he must make a resolution.

The abbé looked at him, saw that he was really suffering,
and was full of pity for a soul so unable to support a
struggle.

He took Durtal's arm, and said gently,—

" My son, believe me that the day you go yourself to the
house of God, the day you knock at its door, it will open
wide, and the angels will draw aside to let you pass.
The Gospel cannot lie, and it declares that there is
more joy over one sinner that repents than over ninety
and nine just persons who need no repentance.   You will
be much better welcomed than you expect, and be
sufficiently my friend to think that the old priest you
leave here will not remain inactive, and that he and the

convents he can influence will pray their best for you."

"I will see," said Durtal, really moved by the affectionate tone of the priest, "I will see. I cannot decide thus, unexpectedly ; I will think. Ah ! it is not simple."

"Above all things pray," said the priest, who had reached his door. "I have on my side sought the Lord much that He would enlighten me, and I declare to you that the solution of La Trappe is the only one He has given me. Ask Him humbly, in your turn, and you will be guided. I shall soon see you again, shall I not ? "

He pressed Durtal's hand, who, left alone, recovered himself at last. Then he recalled the strategic smiles, the ambiguous phrases, the dreamy silences of the Abbé Gévresin, he understood the kindness of his counsels, the patience of his plans ; and a little put out at having been, without knowing it, led so wisely, he exclaimed in spite of himself, " This, then, was the design the priest was ripening, with his air of not concerning himself with it at all."

CHAPTER IX.

HE experienced that painful awakening of a sick man whom a doctor deceives for months, who learns some fine morning that he is to be taken at once to an hospital to undergo an urgent surgical operation. " But that is not the way things should be done," cried Durtal, " people should be prepared, little by little, accustomed by words of warning, to the idea that they are to be cut up on a table, they are not struck down thus unexpectedly !

" Yes, but what does that matter ? since I know very well, in the depths of my soul, that this priest is right ; I must leave Paris if I wish to amend ; but all the same, the treatment he inflicts is hard indeed to follow ; I know not what to do."

And from this moment his days were haunted by Trappists. He turned over the thought of his departure, and examined it on all sides, chewed the cud of for and against, and ended by saying to himself, " That he would take stock of his reflections and open an account, and this with a debit and credit side, that he might know himself the better.

" The debit is terrible. To gather up his life, and cast it into the stove of a cloister ; and again, he ought to know if his body were in a state to bear such a remedy ; mine is frail and soft, accustomed to rise late ; it becomes weak if not nourished by flesh meat, and is subject to neuralgia at any change of the hour of meals. I should never be able to hold out down there with vegetables cooked in warm oil or in milk ; first I detest oily cookery, and I hate milk still more, which I cannot digest.

" Then I think I see myself on my knees, on the floor for hours, I who suffered so much at La Glacière in remaining in that posture, on a step, for scarce a quarter of an hour.

" Again, I am so accustomed to cigarettes that it is

absolutely impossible to give them up, and it is pretty certain they will not let me smoke in a monastery.

"No, indeed, from the bodily point of view, this plan is madness ; in my state of health there is no doctor who would not dissuade me from undertaking such a risk.

"If I place myself in a spiritual point of view I must then again recognize that it is terrible to enter La Trappe.

"I am afraid indeed that my dryness of soul, my want of love will remain, and then what would become of me in such surroundings ? then it is equally probable, that in that solitude and absolute silence, I should be wearied to death, and if it be so, what a miserable existence is it to stalk about a cell and count the hours. No, for that one needs to be firmly fixed on God, to be dwelt in wholly by Him.

"Moreover, there are two formidable questions which I have never properly weighed, because it has been painful to think of them, but now that they come before me, and stop the road, I must face them, the questions of Confession and Holy Communion.

"Confession ? Yes, I will consent to it, I am so tired of myself, so disgusted with my wretched existence that this expiation appears to me as deserved, even necessary. I desire to humble myself, I would ask pardon with all my heart, but again this penance must be assigned me under possible conditions. At La Trappe, if I believe the abbé, no one will trouble himself about me, in other words no one will encourage me, and aid me to submit to this sorrowful extraction of my shames. I shall be somewhat like a sick man operated on in hospital, far from his friends and relatives.

"Confession," he went on, "is an admirable discovery, for it is the most sensitive touchstone of souls, the most intolerable act which the Church has ever imposed on the vanity of men.

"Is this strange ? We speak easily of our lapses, of our grosser actions, even, indeed, to a priest in conversation, that does not seem to lead to any consequences, and perhaps a little bragging enters into our admission of easy sins, but to tell the same thing on one's knees, accusing oneself, after prayer, is different, that which was only rather amusing becomes a very painful humiliation, for the soul is not the dupe of this false seeming, it knows so well in its inner tribunal that all is changed, it feels so well the terrible power of the Sacrament, that he who but now smiled, now trembles at the very thought.

"Now, were I to find myself face to face with an old monk who emerges from an eternity of silence to listen to me, a monk who will not aid me, perhaps cannot even understand me, this will be terrible. I shall never get to the end of my troubles if he does not hold out a staff to me, if he lets me stifle and gives no air to my soul, nor brings me help.

"The Eucharist also seems terrible. To dare to come forward, to offer Him as a tabernacle the sewer of self scarce purified by repentance, a sewer drained by absolution, but still hardly dry, is monstrous. I am quite without such courage as to offer Christ this last insult, and so there is no good in fleeing to a monastery.

"No ; the more I think of it, the more I am obliged to conclude that I should be mad if I ventured into a Trappist house.

"Now for the Credit side. The only proper work of my life would be to make a parcel of my life, and take it to a cloister to disinfect it, and if that cost me nothing, where is the merit ?

"Nothing shows me, on the other hand, that my body, however weakened, cannot support the regimen of La Trappe. Without believing or pretending to believe with the Abbé Gévresin that that kind of food will be even helpful to me, I ought to count on Divine consolations, to admit the principle that, if I am sent there, it is not that I may take at once to my bed, or be obliged to leave again as soon as I arrive—at least, unless that is the chastisement prepared me, the expiation demanded, and again no, for that would be to ascribe to God pitiless tricks, and would be absurd !

"As to the cookery, it matters little that it is uncivilized, if my stomach can digest it ; to have bad food, and get up in the middle of the night is nothing, provided the body can stand it, and no doubt I shall find some means of smoking cigarettes by stealth in the woods.

"After all, a week is soon over, and I am not even obliged, if I feel poorly, to remain a week.

"From the spiritual point of view, I must again count on the mercy of God, believe that it will not abandon me, will dress my wounds, and change the very foundation of my soul. I know well that these arguments do not rest on any earthly certainty, but yet if I have proofs that Providence has already taken part in my affairs, I have no reason to suppose that these arguments are weaker than the purely physical motives which served to support my other thesis. Now I must recall that conversion, so outside my will ; I must take account of a fact which should encourage me, the weakness of the temptations which I now experience.

"It is difficult to have been more rapidly and more completely heard. Whether I owe this grace to my own prayers or to those of the convents which have shielded me without knowing me, it is the case that for some time past my brain has been silent and my flesh calm. That monster Florence appears to me still at certain times, but she does not approach me, she remains in the shade, and the end of the Lord's Prayer, the 'ne nos inducas in tentationem,' puts her to flight.

"That is an unaccustomed fact, and yet a precise one. Why should I doubt, then, that I shall be better upheld at La Trappe than I am in Paris itself ?

"There remain confession and communion."

"Confession ? It will be what the Lord chooses it should be. He will choose the monk for me ; I shall only be able to make use of him ; and then the more disagreeable it is, the better worth it will be ; and if I suffer much, I shall think myself less unworthy to communicate.

"That is," he went on, "the most painful point ! Communicate ! But let us consider, it is certain that I shall be base in proposing to Christ that He should descend like a scavenger into my ditch ; but if I wait till it is empty, I shall never be in a state to receive Him, for my bulkheads are not closed, and sins would filter through the fissures.

"All this well considered, the abbé spoke truth when he answered me one day : 'But I too am not worthy to approach Him ; thank God, I have not those sewers of which you speak, but in the morning, when I go to say my mass, and think of all the dust of the evening, do you not think that I am ashamed ? 'it is always necessary, you see, to go back to the Gospels, and say to yourself that He came for the weak and the sick, the publicans and lepers ; and, in fact, you must convince yourself that the Eucharist is a lookout post, a help, that it is given, as it is written in the ordinary of the Mass "ad tutamentum mentis et corporis et ad medelam percipiendam." It is, if I may say so, a spiritual medicine; you go to the Saviour just as you go to a doctor, you take your soul to Him to care for it, and He does so ! '

"I stand before the unknown," pursued Durtal, "I complain that I am arid, and have wandered from the right way, but who will declare to me that, if I determine to communicate, I shall remain in the same mind; for indeed, if I have Faith, I ought to believe in the occult work of Christ in the Sacrament. Lastly, I am afraid of being wearied by solitude; I am not much amused here as it is, but at La Trappe I shall no longer have those vacillations at every minute, those constant fears; I shall at least have the advantage of having my time to myself; and then . . . and then . . . how well I know solitude. Have I not lived apart since the deaths of des Hermies and Carhaix? Indeed, whom do I see? A few publishers, a few literary men, and my relations with these people are not interesting. As to silence, it is a blessing. I shall not hear any foolish sayings at La Trappe; I shall not listen to pitiable homilies and poor sermons; but I ought to rejoice on being at last isolated, far from Paris, far from men."

He was silent, and made, as it were, a return in upon himself; and said to himself, in a melancholy manner: "These strifes are useless, these reflections vain. I need not try to take account of my soul, to make out the debit and credit; I know, without knowing how, that I must go; I am thrust out of myself by an impulse which rises from the very depths of my being, to which I am quite certain I have to yield."

At that moment Durtal had decided, but ten minutes afterwards the attempt at resolution vanished. He felt his cowardice gain on him once more, he chewed once more the cud of arguments against his moving; came to the conclusion that his reasons for remaining in Paris were palpable, human, certain, while the others were intangible, extra-natural, and consequently subject to illusions, perhaps false.

And he invented for himself the fear of not obtaining the thing he feared, said to himself that La Trappe would not receive him, or certainly that it would refuse him communion; and then he suggested to himself a middle term : to confess at Paris and communicate at La Trappe.

But then there passed in him an incomprehensible fact :
his whole soul revolted at this idea, and the formal order
not to deceive himself was truly breathed into him, and he
said to himself : " No, the bitter draught must be drained
to the last drop, it is all or nothing ; if I confess to the abbé
it will be in disobedience to absolute and secret directions ;
I should be capable of not going afterwards to Notre Dame
de l'Atre.

" What shall I do ? "   And he accused himself of distrust,
called to his aid once more the memory of benefits received,
how scales had fallen from his eyes, his insensible progress
towards Faith, his encounter with that singular priest,
perhaps the only one who could understand him, and treat
him in a way so benign and so elastic ; but he tried in vain
to reassure himself, then he called up the dream of the
monastic life, the sovereign beauty of the cloister ; he
imagined the joy of renunciation, the peace of exalted prayers,
the interior intoxication of the spirit, the delight of not
being at home any longer in his own body.   Some words
of the abbé about La Trappe served as a spring-board for
his dreams, and he perceived an old abbey, grey and warm,
immense avenues of trees, clouds flying confusedly amid
the song of waters, silent strolls in the woods at nightfall ;
he called up the solemn liturgies of Saint Benedict's time ;
he saw the white pith of monastic chants rise under the
scarcely pruned bark of sound.   He succeeded in his
decision, and cried : " You have dreamed for years of the
cloisters, now rejoice that you will know them at last," and
he wished to go at once and live there ; then suddenly he
fell down into reality, and said to himself : " It is easy to
wish to live in a monastery, to tell God that you would desire
to take shelter therein, when life in Paris weighs you down,
but when it comes to the real point of emigration, it is quite
another matter."

He turned over these thoughts everywhere, in the street, at
home, in the chapels.   He hurried like a shuttle from one
church to another, hoping to solace his fears by changing his
place, but they persisted, and rendered every place intolerable.

Then in the sacred places came always that dryness of
soul, the broken spring of impulse, a sudden silence
within, when he desired consolation in speaking to Him.
His best moments, his pauses in the hurly-burly, were a

few minutes of absolute torpor, which rested like snow on
the soul and he heard nothing.

But this drowsiness of thought lasted but a while, the
whirlwind blew once more, and the prayers which were
wont to appease it refused to leave his lips, he tried
religious music, the despairing sequences of the psalms,
pictures of the Crucifixion by the Early Masters, to excite
him, but his prayers ran on and became confused on his
lips, were divested of all sense, mere words, empty shells.

At Notre Dame des Victoires, where he dragged himself that he might thaw a little under the warmth of his
neighbours' prayers, he did in fact feel less chilly, and
seemed to break up a little, fell drop by drop into sorrows
which he could not formulate, and were all summed up in
the cry of a sick child, in which he said to Our Lady, in low
tones : " My soul is sorrowful."

Thence he returned to St. Severin, sat down under
those arches browned by the rust of prayers, and, haunted
by his fixed idea, he pleaded for himself extenuating
circumstances, exaggerated the austerities of La Trappe,
tried almost to exasperate his fear to excuse his weakness
in a vague appeal to Our Lady.

" But I must go and see the Abbé Gévresin," he murmured,
but his courage still failed him to pronounce the " Yes "
which the priest would surely require from him. He ended
by discovering a reason for his visit, without thinking
himself obliged to promise just yet.

" After all," he thought, " I have no precise information
about this monastery ; I do not even know whether it may
not be necessary to take a long and expensive journey to
get there ; the abbé indeed declares that it is not far from
Paris, but it is impossible to decide on this simple declara-
tion ; it will be useful also to know the habits of these
cenobites before going to stay with them."

The abbé smiled when Durtal mentioned these objections.

" The journey is short," he said. " You start from the
Gare du Nord at eight o'clock in the morning for Saint
Landry, where you arrive at a quarter to twelve ; you lunch
at an inn close to the station, and while you are drinking
your coffee they get you a carriage, and after a drive of
four hours you arrive at Notre Dame de l'Atre for dinner.
There is no difficulty there.

"Then the cost is moderate. As far as I remember the railway fare is about fifteen francs, add two or three francs for lunch, and six or seven for the carriage . . . "

And as Durtal was silent, the abbé went on : " Well ? "

" Ah yes, yes . . . if you knew . . . I am in a pitiable state, I will and will not, I know well that I ought to take refuge there, but in spite of myself, I wish to gain time and put off the hour of departure."

And he continued : " My soul is out of gear, when I would pray, my senses go all astray, I cannot recollect myself, and if I succeed in pulling myself together, five minutes do not pass but I am all astray again ; no, I have neither fervour nor true contrition, I do not love God enough, if it must be said.

" And, indeed, during the last two days, a frightful certainty has grown up in me ; I am sure that, in spite of my good intentions, if I found myself in the presence of a certain person, whose sight troubles me, I should send religion to the devil, I should return eagerly to my vomit ; I only hold on because I am not tempted, I am no better than when I was sinning. You will admit that I am in a wretched state to enter a Trappist monastery."

" Your reasons are at least weak," answered the abbé. "You say first that your prayers are distracted, that you are unable to concentrate your attention ; but in fact you are just like everybody else. Even Saint Teresa declares that often she was unable to recite the Credo without distraction, it is a weakness in which we must just take our portion humbly : above all things it is necessary not to lay too much stress on these evils, for the fear of seeing them return ensures their assiduity ; you are distracted in prayer by the very fear of distraction, and by regret for it ; go forth more boldly, look at things more widely, pray as best you can, and do not trouble yourself.

" Again, you declare that if you meet a certain person whose attraction is a trouble to you, you will succumb. How do you know that ? why should you take care about seductions which God does not yet inflict upon you, and which He will perhaps spare you ? Why doubt His mercy ? Why not believe, on the contrary, that if He judge the temptation useful, He will aid you enough to prevent your sinking under it ?

"In any case you ought not, by anticipation, to fear disgust at your weakness ; the Imitation declares ' There is nothing more foolish and vain, than to afflict ourselves about future things which may perhaps never happen.' No, it is enough to occupy ourselves with the present, for ' Sufficient for the day is the evil thereof,'—' sufficit diei malitia sua.

"Finally you say you do not love God; again I answer, what do you know about it ? You have this love by the very token that you desire to have it, and that you regret you have it not ; you love our Lord by the very fact that you desire to love Him."

"That is special pleading," murmured Durtal. "But indeed," he went on, "suppose at La Trappe, the monk revolted at the long outrage of my sins, refused me absolution, and forbade me to communicate."

The abbé burst out laughing.

"You are mad ! What is your notion of Christ ? "

"Not of Christ, but of His intermediary the human being who replaces Him."

"You can only chance upon a man pointed out beforehand from above to judge you ; moreover, at Notre Dame de l'Atre you have every chance of kneeling at the feet of a saint, therefore God will inspire him, will be present, you have nothing to fear.

"As to the Communion, the prospect of being rejected terrifies you, but is not that one proof the more that, contrary to your opinion, God does not leave you insensible ? "

"Yes, but the idea of communicating alarms me none the less."

"I say to you again : if Jesus were indifferent to you, it would be just the same to you, to consume or not to consume the sacred species."

"All that does not convince me," sighed Durtal. "I do not know where I am ; I am afraid of a confessor, of others, of myself ; it is foolish, but it is stronger than I. I cannot gain the upper hand."

"You are afraid of the water ; imitate Gribouille, throw yourself in boldly ; look, suppose I write to La Trappe this very day to say you are coming ; when ? "

"Oh ! " cried Durtal, "wait a while."

"To get an answer, we need two days each way; will you go there five days hence?"

And, as Durtal was astounded and silent,

"Is that settled?"

Then, at that moment, Durtal had a strange experience, as often at St. Severin, a sort of caressing touch and gentle push; he felt a will insinuate itself into his own, and he drew back disquieted at seeing he had a double self, to find he was no longer alone in the depth of his being; then he was inexplicably reassured, and gave himself up, and as soon as he had said "Yes" he felt immensely relieved; then passing from one extreme to the other, he was troubled at the idea that his departure could not take place at once, and was sorry that he had still to pass five days in Paris.

The abbé laughed. "But the Trappists must have notice, it is a simple formality, for with a word from me, you will be received at once, but wait at least until I have sent this word; I will post it this evening, so have no anxiety, and sleep in peace."

Durtal in his turn laughed at his own impatience. "You must think me very ridiculous," he said.

The priest shrugged his shoulders. "Come, you asked me about my little monastery; I must try to satisfy you. It is very small, if compared with the grande Trappe at Soligny, or the establishments at Sept Fonds, Meilleray or Aiguebelle, for there are only about ten choir fathers, and about thirty lay brothers or 'conversi.' There are also a certain number of peasants who work with them, and help them to till their land, and make their chocolate."

"They make chocolate!"

"That surprises you. How do you think they live? Ah! I warn you, you are not going into a sumptuous monastery."

"I like it so. But in regard to the stories of La Trappe, I suppose the monks do not greet each other with 'Brother, we must die,' and that they do not dig their graves every morning?"

"All that is false. They take no trouble about their graves, and they salute each other silently, since they are forbidden to speak."

"Then what am I to do if I need anything?"

" The abbot, the confessor, and the guestmaster have the right of conversing with the guests, you will have to do with them alone ; the others will bow when you meet them, but if you speak to them they will not answer."

" It is well to know that. What is their dress ? "

" Before the foundation of Citeaux, the Benedictines wore, or so it is supposed, the black habit of Saint Benedict ; the Benedictines properly so-called wear it still, but at Citeaux the colour was changed, and the Trappists, who are a twig of this branch, have adopted the white robe of Saint Bernard."

" Pray pardon all these questions, which must seem childish, but since I am about to visit these monks, I ought to be in some measure acquainted with the customs of their order."

" I am wholly at your disposition," replied the abbé.

Durtal asked him about the situation of the abbey itself, and he replied,

" The present monastery dates from the eighteenth century, but you will see in the gardens the ruins of the old cloister, which was built in the time of Saint Bernard. In the Middle Ages there was a succession of Blessed in this convent ; it is a truly sanctified land, fit for meditation and regret.

" The abbey is situated at the bottom of a valley, according to the orders of Saint Bernard ; for you know that if Saint Benedict loved the hills, Saint Bernard sought the low and moist plains wherein to found his convents. An old Latin line has preserved the different tastes of these two saints :

" ' Bernardus valles, colles Benedictus amabat.' "

" Was it on account of his own personal liking, or for a pious end, that Saint Bernard built his hermitages in unwholesome and flat places ? "

" In order that his monks, whose health was enfeebled by the fogs, might have constantly before their eyes the salutary image of death."

" The deuce he did ! "

" I may add at once that the valley in which Notre Dame de l'Atre rises is now drained, and the air is very pure. You will stroll by delightful ponds, and I may recommend you, on the borders of the enclosure, an avenue of secular chestnuts, where you may take some refreshing walks at daybreak."

And after a silence the Abbé Gévresin continued,—

"Walk there a good deal, traverse the woods in all directions; the forests will tell you more about your soul than books: 'Aliquid amplius invenies in sylvis quam in libris,' wrote Saint Bernard—'pray and your days will seem short.'"

Durtal went away from the priest's house comforted, almost joyful; he felt at least the solace of a fixed decision, a resolution taken at last. He said to himself that the only thing now to be done was to prepare himself as best he could for the retreat, and he prayed and went to bed for the first time for months with his mind at rest.

But next day, when he woke, his mood changed, all his preconceived ideas, all his fears returned; he asked himself if his conversion were ripe enough to allow him to cut it separate, and carry it to La Trappe; the fear of a confessor, the dread of the unknown, assailed him afresh. "I was wrong to have answered so soon," and he asked himself, "Why did I say 'yes'?" The recollection of this word pronounced by his lips, conceived by a will which was still his own and yet other than his, came back to his mind. "It is not the first time that such a thing happened to me," he thought, "I have already experienced when alone in the churches unexpected counsels, silent orders, and it must be admitted that it is terrifying to feel this infusion into self of an invisible being, and to know that he can, if he choose, almost turn you out of the domain of your personality.

"But no, it is not that, there is no substitution of an exterior will to one's own, for one's free will is absolutely intact; neither is it one of those irresistible impulses endured by certain sick persons, for nothing is more easy than to resist it; it is still less a suggestion, since, in this case, there are no magnetic passes, no somnambulism induced, no hypnotism; no, it is the irresistible entrance into oneself of a strange will, the sudden intrusion of a precise and discreet desire, a pressure on the soul at once firm and gentle. Ah! again I am incorrect, and play the fool, but nothing can describe that close pressure, which vanishes at the least movement of impatience—it is felt but cannot be expressed.

" Its introduction is always attended by surprise, almost with anguish, since it does not make use of even an interior voice to make. itself heard, and is formulated without the aid of words, all is blotted out, the breath which has thrilled you disappears. You would wish that this incitement should be confirmed, that the phenomenon should be repeated in order to be more closely observed, to try to analyze it and understand it, when lo ! it is gone ; you remain alone with yourself, are free not to obey, your will is unfettered and you know it, but you know also that if you reject these invitations you take on yourself unspeakable risks for the future.

" In fact," pursued Durtal, " it is an angelic influx, a divine touch, something analogous to the interior voice so well known by the mystics, but it is less complete, less precise, and yet it is quite as certain."

He ended his dreams concluding, " I am consumed and collared by myself, before being able to answer this priest, whose arguments would scarce persuade me, unless I had had this help, this unexpected succour.

" But then, since I am thus led by the hand, what have I to fear ? "

He feared all the same, and could not be at peace with himself ; then if he profited by the comfort of a decision, he was consumed for the moment by the expectation of his departure.

He tried to kill time in reading, but he had to admit once more that he could not expect consolation from any book. None came even distantly into relation with his state of mind. High Mysticism was so little human, soared at such heights far from our mire, that no sovereign aid could be expected from it. He ended by falling back on the " Imitation," in which Mysticism, placed within the reach of the crowd, was like a trembling and plaintive friend who stanched your wounds within the cells of its chapters, prayed and wept with you, and in any case compassionated the desolate widowhood of souls.

Unfortunately, Durtal had read so much, and was so saturated with the Gospels, that he had temporarily exhausted their sedative and soothing virtues. Tired of reading, he again began his courses in the churches. " And suppose the Trappists will not have me," he thought, " what will become of me ? "

" But I tell you that they will receive you," said the abbé, whom he went to see. He was not easy till the day the priest handed him the answer from La Trappe.

He read :—

" We will receive with pleasure, for a week, in our guest-house the retreatant whom you wish to commend to us, and I do not see at the moment any reason why the retreat should not begin next Tuesday.

" In the hope, Monsieur l'Abbé, that we shall also have the pleasure of seeing you again in our solitude, I beg to assure you that I am yours most respectfully,

"F. M. ETIENNE,
" *Guestmaster.*"

He read and re-read it, at once delighted and terrified. " There is no further doubt ; it is irrevocable," he said, and he went at once in haste to St. Severin, having less need of prayer than of going near to Our Lady ; of showing himself to her, paying her, as it were, a visit of thankfulness, and expressing his gratitude by his very presence.

He was taken by the charms of that church, its silence, the shadow which fell on the apse, from the height of its palm trees of stone, and he ended by caring for nothing and sinking on a chair, filled with one sole desire, not to enter again on the life of the streets, never to leave his refuge, never to move.

The next day, which was a Sunday, he went to the Benedictine nuns to hear High Mass. A black monk celebrated; he recognized a Benedictine when the priest chanted "Dominous vobiscoum," for the Abbé Gévresin had told him that the Benedictines pronounced Latin like Italian.

Though he was not inclined to like that pronunciation which took away from Latin the sonorous tones of its words, and turned after a fashion the phrases of that tongue into a ring of bells with their clappers muffled or their vases stuffed with tow, he let himself go, taken hold of by the unction, by the humble piety of the monk, who almost trembled with reverence and joy when he kissed the altar,

and he had a deep voice, to which, behind the grating,
answered the clear high voices of the nuns.

Durtal panted, listening to the fluid pictures of the Early
Masters sketch and form and paint themselves on the air ;
he was affected to his very marrow, as he had formerly
been during High Mass at St. Severin. He had lost that
emotion now in that church, where the flower of melody
had faded for him since he knew the Benedictine plain song,
and he now found it again, or rather he took it with him
from St. Severin to this chapel.

And for the first time he had a wild desire, a desire so
violent that it seemed to melt his heart.

It was at the moment of the Communion. The monk,
elevating the Host, uttered the "Domine non sum
dignus." Pale, with drawn features, sorrowful eyes, and
serious mouth, he seemed to have escaped from a monastery
of the Middle Ages, cut out of one of those Flemish pictures
where the monks are standing in the background, while,
before them, nuns are praying on their knees with joined
hands, near the donors, to the child Jesus on whom the
Virgin smiles, while lowering her long lashes under her
arching brow.

And while he descended the steps and communicated
two women, Durtal trembled, and his desires went forth
towards the ciborium.

It seemed to him that if he were nourished on that Bread,
there would be an end of all his dryness and all his fears ;
it would seem to him that the wall of his sins, higher and
higher from year to year, and now barring his view, would
roll away, and at last he would see. And he was in haste to
set off for La Trappe, that he too might receive the Sacred
Body from the hands of a monk.

That mass gave him new strength like a tonic, he came
out of the chapel joyful and firmer, and when the impression
grew somewhat feebler in the course of hours, he remained
perhaps less affected, but still resolute, joking in the evening with a gentle melancholy about his condition : "There
are many people who go to Barèges or Vichy to cure
their bodies, and why should not I go and cure my soul in
a Trappist monastery?"

CHAPTER X.

"I SHALL make myself a prisoner in two days," sighed Durtal ; "it is time to think about packing. What books shall I take to help me to live down there ? "

He searched his library, and turned over the mystical books, which had, by degrees, replaced profane works on the shelves.

"I will not talk of Saint Teresa," he thought ; "neither she, nor Saint John of the Cross, would be indulgent enough to me in solitude ; I have need of more pardon and consolation."

"Saint Denys the Areopagite, or the apocryphal book known under that name ? He is the first of the Mystics, and perhaps has gone the furthest in his theological definitions. He lives in the rarefied air of the mountain tops, above the gulfs, on the threshold of the other world which he sees in part by flashes of grace, and he remains lucid, undazzled in the blaze of light around him.

"It seems that in his 'Celestial Hierarchies,' in which he brings out in procession the armies of heaven, and shows the meaning of angelic attributes and symbols, he has already passed the limits assigned to man, and yet in his 'Divine Names' he ventures even a step further, and then he raises himself into the super-essence of metaphysics at once calm and stern.

"He over-heats the human word to give it greater force, but when after all his efforts he endeavours to define the Indescribable, to distinguish those never to be confounded Persons of the Trinity who in their plurality never lose their unity, words fail on his lips, and his tongue is paralyzed under his pen ; then tranquilly and without any astonishment he makes himself again a child, comes down from those heights among us, and in order to try and explain to us what he understands, he has recourse to comparisons with domestic life ; and that he may explain the Trinity in Unity he notices how, if many torches be lighted in one hall, lights, though distinct, mingle in one, and are in fact no more than one.

"Saint Denys," thought Durtal, "is one of the boldest explorers of the eternal regions, but he would be dry reading at La Trappe."

"Ruysbröck ? " he thought—"perhaps, and yet I hardly am sure—I might put him in my bag as well as for a cordial the little collection distilled by Hello ; as for the Spiritual Marriages, so well translated by Maeterlinck, they are disconnected and obscure, they stifle me, this Ruysbröck oppresses me less. This hermit is singular, all the same, for he does not enter into us, but rather goes round about us ; he endeavours, like Saint Denys, to arrive at God, rather in heaven than in the soul, but in wishing to take such a flight, he strains his wings, and stammers incomprehensibly when he comes down.

"We will leave him behind, then. Now let us see. Saint Catherine of Genoa ? Her discussions between the soul, the body, and self-love are unmeaning and confused, and when in her ' Dialogues,' she treats of the operations of the interior life, she is greatly below Saint Teresa and Saint Angela. On the other hand her Treatise on Purgatory is clear. It declares that she alone has penetrated into the spaces of unknown sorrows, and that she has disentangled and taken hold of the joys ; she has in fact succeeded in reconciling two contraries which seemed eternally repugnant ; the suffering of the soul in its purification from sin, and the joy of the same soul, which at the very moment it is enduring frightful torment experiences immense happiness, for little by little it draws near to God, and feels His rays attract it more and more, and His love inundate it with such excess, that it would seem the Saviour desires nought but only it.

"Saint Catherine sets forth also that Jesus forbids heaven to none, that it is the soul herself who, deeming herself unworthy to attain it, flings herself by her own motion into Purgatory there to cleanse herself, for she has only one end, to re-establish herself in her primitive purity, only one desire, to attain her last end, by destroying herself, annihilating herself, losing herself in God.

"This is a conclusive study," murmured Durtal, "but not that which would lead to La Trappe. We must try again."

He touched other volumes in the book-cases.

"Here, for instance, is one which obviously I should use," he went on, as he took down the "Seraphic Theology" of Saint Bonaventure, "for he condenses the means of self-examination, of meditation for communion, of thoughts on death, then in these 'Selections' is a treatise on the Contempt of the World, whose terse phrases are admirable; it is the true essence of the Holy Spirit, a jelly of unction firm set—we will put that on one side.

"I shall hardly find a better help to remedy the probable weariness of solitude," murmured Durtal, turning over new ranks of volumes. He looked at the titles. "The Life of the Blessed Virgin," by M. Olier.

He hesitated, saying to himself, "Under a style which is like water with scarcely the chill off, there are some interesting observations, some tasteful comments. M. Olier has in a way traversed the mysterious territory of hidden designs, and has there discovered the unimaginable truths which the Lord is sometimes pleased to reveal to His saints. He has made himself the liege-man of Our Lady, and living near her has made himself also the herald of her attributes, the legate of her graces. His Life of Mary is certainly the only one which seems really inspired and is possible to read. Where the abbess of Agreda wanders, he alone remains vigorous and clear. He shows us the Virgin existing from all eternity in God, conceiving without ceasing to be immaculate, like the crystal which receives and reflects the rays of the sun, yet loses nothing of its lustre, and indeed shines with greater brightness, bringing forth without pain, but suffering at the death of her Son the pangs she would have borne at His birth. Then he gives us learned dissertations on Her whom he calls the Treasure-house of all good, the Mediatrix of love and impetration. Yes, but to converse with Her nothing is so good as the 'Officium parvum beatæ Virginis,' and that," concluded Durtal, "I will put in my bag with my Prayer-book; we will not disturb M. Olier's volume."

"My stock begins to give out," he continued. "Angela of Foligno? Certainly she is a brasier at which one may warm one's soul. I will take her with me. What more— Tauler's Sermons? I am tempted to do so, for never has any treated better than this monk the most abstruse subjects with a more perfectly lucid mind. By aid of familiar images, humble analogies, he has rendered accessible the highest speculations of Mysticism. He is homely and deep, then he borrows a little from quietism, and, perhaps, it will be no bad thing to absorb, down there, a few drops of that mixture. Yet on the whole, no; I have rather need of nerve tonics. As to Suso, he is a remedy far inferior to Saint Bonaventure, or Saint Angela. I put aside also Saint Bridget of Sweden, for in her conversations with heaven she seems aided by a God morose and tired, who reveals to her nothing unexpected, nothing new.

"There is also Saint Magdalen of Pazzi, that voluble Carmelite whose work is a series of apostrophes. An exclamatory person, clever at analogies, expert in coincidences, a saint infatuated with metaphors and hyperboles. She talks directly with God the Father, and stammers out in ecstasy explanations of the mysteries revealed to her by the Ancient of days. Her books contain one sovereign page on the Circumcision, another magnificent one, entirely made up of antitheses, on the Holy Spirit, others, very strange, on the deification of the human soul, on its union with heaven, and on the part assigned in this operation to the wounds of the Word.

"These are inhabited nests; the eagle which is the symbol of Faith resides in the eyrie of the left foot; in the hole of the right foot resides the melancholy sweetness of the turtle-doves; in the wound of the left hand the dove ensconces herself, the symbol of surrender, and in the cavity of the right hand reposes the pelican, the emblem of love.

"These birds leave their nests and come to seek the soul that they may lead it to the nuptial chamber of the wound which bleeds in the side of Christ.

"Was it not also that Carmelite nun who, ravished by the power of grace, despised so greatly the certitude acquired by the way of the senses, as to say to the Lord :

' If I saw Thee with mine eyes, I should have Faith no more, because Faith ceases where evidence comes in ' ?

"All things considered," he said ; "Magdalen of Pazzi, with her dialogues and contemplations, opens eloquent horizons, but the soul, snared in the bird-lime of its sins, cannot follow her. No ; this saint cannot reassure me in the cloister.

"Ah ! " he went on, shaking the dust from a volume in a grey cover ; "ah ! it is true I have The Precious Blood, of Father Faber." And he began to dream as he turned over its pages where he stood.

He remembered the impression, till now forgotten, produced on him when he read it. The work of this Oratorian was at least strange. The pages boiled over, ran forth tumultuously, carrying with them grandiose visions, such as Hugo conceived, developing historical perspectives such as Michelet loved to paint. In this volume was seen advancing the solemn procession of the Precious Blood, starting from the confines of humanity, from the origin of the ages, and it broke the bounds of the worlds, overwhelmed the nations, submerged history.

Father Faber was less a mystic, properly so-called, than a visionary and a poet ; in spite of the abuse of rhetoric transferred from the pulpit to a book, he tore up souls by roots, carried them away on the rush of the stream, but when one regained footing, and sought to remember what had been heard and seen, one could recall nothing ; on reflection one recognized that the theme of the work was very thin, too slender to have been executed by so noisy an orchestra, and there remained of that reading something distracting and feverish which made you uneasy, and made you think that this kind of book had only very distant relation to the heavenly fulness of the great mystics.

"No, not that," thought Durtal. "Now what have we selected ? I keep the little collection of Ruysbröck, the Life of Angela of Foligno, and Saint Bonaventure, and the best of all for my state of soul," he said, striking his fore-head. He went back to his book-case, and seized a little book, which lay alone in a corner.

He sat down, and turned it over, saying, "Here is the tonic, the stimulant in weakness, the strychnine for failure of Faith, the goad which drives you in tears to the feet of Christ, the ' Dolorous Passion ' of Sister Emmerich."

She was no chemist of the spiritual being, like Saint Teresa ; she had nothing to do with our interior life; in her book she forgot herself, and left us on one side, for she saw only Jesus crucified, and wished only to show the stages of His agony, and to leave marked on her pages, as on the veil of Veronica, the imprint of the Holy Face.

Though she was of our time, for Catherine Emmerich died in 1824, this great work dates from the Middle Ages. It is a picture which seems to belong to the early schools of Franconia and Swabia. This woman was the sister of the Zeitbloms and the Grünewalds, she had their clear visions, their vivid colouring, their wild scent ; but she seemed to bring back also, by her care for exact detail, by her precise indication of places, the old Flemish Masters, Roger Van der Weyden and Bouts ; she united in herself two currents, springing one from Germany, the other from Flanders, and this painting brushed in with blood, and varnished with tears, was transposed by her into a prose style which has no relation to any known literature, of which we can only find by analogy the ancestry in the panels of the fifteenth century.

Moreover, she was quite illiterate, had never read a book, nor seen a painting ; she told quite plainly what she saw in her ecstasies.

The pictures of the Passion unfolded themselves before her while she was bed-ridden, crushed by suffering, bleeding from the wounds of her stigmata ; she mourned and wept, brought to nothingness by love and pity, before the torments of Christ.

According to her words, which a scribe took down, Calvary rose, and the whole rascaldom of the soldiers rushed at the Saviour and spat on Him ; frightful episodes took place where Jesus, chained to a pillar, twisting like a worm, under the lashes of the scourgers, then falling, looking with His failing eyes, at the fallen women who held Him by the hand, and turned away in disgust from His lacerated body, from His face covered with threads of blood as with a red net.

Then slowly, patiently, only stopping to sob, and cry for mercy, she described the soldiers tearing away the stuff

which had stuck to the wounds, the Virgin weeping ; her
face livid and her lips blue, she related the agony of
His bearing His Cross, how He fell on His knees, grew
weaker and more worn when death came.

It was a frightful spectacle, told in its every particular,
forming a sublime and frightful whole. The Redeemer was
extended on a cross laid on the ground, one of the executioners placed a knee against His side, while another
spread His fingers abroad, and a third hammered in a flat-
headed nail as broad as a crown, and so long that the point
came out behind the wood. And when the right hand was
riveted the torturers saw that the left would not reach to
the place they intended to pierce, therefore they attached
a rope to the arm, pulled it with all their force, dislocated
the shoulder, and the cries of the Saviour were heard above
the blows of the hammer, His breast was seen heaving,
while His body was anguished and furrowed by terrible
shuddering.

The same scene was repeated to fix His feet. They also
did not reach the place which the executioners had marked.
The body had to be tied and the arms bound so as not to
tear the hands from the wood, and then it was necessary
to hang on the legs so as to lengthen them as far as the
bracket on which they were to rest ; all at once the entire
body yielded, the ribs moved under the skin ; the shock was
so fearful, that the executioners believed that the bones
would start, and burst the flesh, wherefore they made haste
to rest the left foot on the right, but their difficulties began
again, the feet turned over, and it was necessary to bore
them with an auger to fasten them.

This continued till Jesus died, when Sister Emmerich
fainted from terror, her stigmata bled afresh, and her
wounded head rained blood.

In this book the whole pack of Jewish hounds was seen
in full cry, the imprecations and shouts of the crowd were
heard, the Virgin was shown trembling with fever, the
Magdalen, beyond herself, was terrible by her cries, and
towering above this lamentable group, Christ appeared, pale
and swollen, His legs entangled in His robe, when He
mounted to Golgotha clenching His broken nails on the
cross as it slipped from His grasp.

This extraordinary visionary, Catherine Emmerich,

also described the surroundings of these scenes, the land-scapes of Judæa, which she had never visited, but have since been recognized as exact ; without knowing it, without willing it, this illiterate woman became an unique and powerful artist.

"Wonderful visionary, wonderful painter," cried Durtal, "and also wonderful saint," he added, running over the life of this nun, placed as a preface to the book.

She was born in 1774, in the diocese of Münster, the child of poor peasants. From her infancy she had conversations with the Virgin, and possessed the gift which also was given to Saint Sibylline of Pavia, Ida of Louvain, and more recently to Louise Lateau, of discerning, when she looked at, or touched them, objects which had been blessed from those which had not. She entered, as a novice, the Augustinian convent at Dulmen, made her profession when she was twenty-nine ; her health failed and incessant pain tortured her, which she increased, for, like Blessed Lidwine, she obtained from Heaven permission to suffer for others, and succour the sick by taking their maladies. In 1811, under the government of Jerome Bonaparte, King of West-phalia, the convent was suppressed and the nuns dispersed. Infirm and penniless, she was carried to a room in an inn where she had to bear every sort of curiosity and insult. Christ added to her martyrdom in giving her the stigmata for which she asked ; she could neither rise, nor walk, nor sit, could take no food but the juice of a cherry, but she was transported by long ecstasies. In these she visited Palestine, following the Saviour step by step, dictated with groans this fond book, then said with her death-rattle, "Let me die in shame with Jesus on the Cross," and died overwhelmed with joy, thanking Heaven for the life of suffering she had endured.

"Ah, yes ; I will take the 'Dolorous Passion !' cried Durtal to himself.

"Take the Gospels also," said the abbé, who came in meanwhile ; "they are the heavenly phials from which you will draw the oil you need to dress your wounds."

"It will be equally useful, and truly in accordance with the atmosphere of La Trappe, to be able to read in the abbey itself the works of Saint Bernard, but they consist of unmanageable folios, and the abridgments and extracts in

volumes of a more convenient form are so ill-chosen, that I
have never had the courage to buy them."

"They have Saint Bernard at La Trappe, and will lend
you the volumes if you ask them ; but where are you from
the spiritual point of view ?   How are you getting on ?"

"I am melancholy, badly prepared and resigned.   I cannot tell if weariness has come from my turning always on
the same round, like a circus horse, but at this moment I
am not suffering.   I am .persuaded that this change of place
is necessary, and that it would be useless to hesitate.   All
the same," he said, after a silence, "it is very odd that I am
going to imprison myself in a monastery, and in truth, in
spite of myself, that astonishes me."

"I will admit," said the abbé, laughing, "that when I
first met you at Tocane's, I never thought I was pointed
out to direct you to a monastery ; ah, you see I must
evidently belong to that category of people whom I may
call mere bridges, involuntary brokers of souls who are imposed on you for a certain end which you do not suspect,
and of which even themselves are ignorant."

"Rather, if any one were a mere bridge in this matter,"
answered Durtal, "it was Tocane, for it was he who brought
us together, and we kick him away as soon as he has
finished his unconscious task ; it was evidently designed that
we should know each other."

"That is true," said the abbé, with a smile ; "now I do
not suppose I shall see you again before you start, for I go
to-morrow to Mâcon, where I shall stay five days, time to
see my nephews and to sign some law papers : at any rate
keep up your courage, and do not forget to send me news
of yourself.   Write to me without much delay, that I may
find your letter when I return to Paris."

And as Durtal thanked him for his constant kindness, he
took his hand and held it in his own.

"Say nothing about that," he said ; "you have only to
thank Him, whose fatherly impatience has broken the
obstinate slumber of your Faith ; you owe thanks to God
only.

"Thank Him in getting rid of your nature as soon as
possible, and leaving the house of your conscience empty
for Him.   The more you die to yourself the better will He
live in you.   Prayer is the most powerful ascetic means

by which you can renounce yourself, empty yourself and render yourself humble in this matter ; pray therefore without ceasing at La Trappe. Implore our Lady especially, for like myrrh which consumes the proud flesh of wounds, she heals the ulcers of the soul ; I on my side will pray for you as best I can ; you can thus in your weakness lean, so as not to fall, on that firm and protecting pillar of prayer of which Saint Teresa speaks. Once again, a safe journey to you ; we shall meet soon again, my son, good-bye."

Durtal remained much disturbed. " It is most tiresome," he thought, " that this priest is leaving Paris before me, for indeed if I have need of spiritual help or counsel, to whom shall I go ? It is clearly written that I must end as I have begun, alone, but ... but ... solitude under these conditions is alarming. I am no spoilt child, whatever the abbé may say."

Next morning Durtal awoke ill ; furious neuralgia bored his temples like a gimlet ; he tried to stop it with antipyrine, but this medicine in a large dose put his stomach out of order without abating the strokes of the machine which penetrated his skull. He wandered about his rooms, changing from one seat to another, coiling himself up in an arm-chair, getting up to lie down again, jumping from his bed in fits of sickness, upsetting his furniture from time to time.

He could assign no precise cause for this attack ; he had slept his fill, and had not exceeded in any way the night before.

He thought, with his head in his hands, " There are still two days counting to-day before I leave Paris, and very fit I am for it ! I shall not be in a state to travel by train, and if I travel, the food at La Trappe will finish me."

He had a minute's comfort from the idea that through no fault of his own he might perhaps avoid his painful duty, and remain at home ; but the reaction was immediate ; he understood that if he did not go, he was lost ; the vacillation of his soul had become chronic, the crisis of disgust of self, the acute regret of an effort consented to with pain, and suddenly missed, the certainty that it would only be postponed for a time, that he would have to pass again through alternations of revolt and terror, and begin again to fight with himself for conviction.

" Admitting that I am not in a state to travel, I have

always the resource of making my confession to the abbé when he returns, and of communicating in Paris," he thought, but he shook his head, saying to himself once more that he felt and knew that was not his duty. "But then," he said to God : " since Thou dost implant this idea in me so violently that I cannot even discuss it, in spite of its entire common sense—for after all it is not necessary to immure myself in a Trappist monastery in order to reconcile myself to Thee—then let me go ! "

And he spoke to God quietly.

" My soul is an evil place, sordid and infamous ; till now it has loved only perverse ways ; it has exacted from my wretched body the tithe of illicit pleasures and unholy joys, it is worth little, it is worth nothing, and yet down there near Thee, if Thou wilt succour me, I think that I shall subdue it, but if my body be sick, I cannot force it to obey me ; this is worse than all, I am disarmed if Thou do not come to my aid.

" Take count of this, O Lord ; I know by experience that when I am ill-fed, I have neuralgia ; humanly, logically speaking, I am certain to be horribly ill at Notre Dame de l'Âtre ; nevertheless, if I can get about at all, the day after to-morrow, I will go all the same.

" In default of love, this is the sole proof I can give that I truly desire Thee, that truly I hope and believe in Thee, but then, O Lord, aid me."

He added sadly, " Ah ! indeed I am no Lidwine or Catherine Emmerich, who when Thou didst strike them cried out, More, more !—Thou dost scarce touch me, and I protest ; but what wouldest Thou ? Thou dost know better than I ; physical suffering breaks me down, drives me to despair."

He went to sleep at last to kill the day in bed ; slumbering to wake again suddenly from frightful nightmares.

The next day his head seemed empty and his heart feeble, but his neuralgia was less violent. He rose, saying to himself that he must eat, though he was not hungry, for fear his pain should return. He went out and wandered in the Luxembourg, saying to himself that he must arrange his time, that after breakfast he would visit St. Severin, then he would go home and pack, and afterwards finish the day at Notre Dame des Victoires.

The walk did him good, his head was lighter, and his heart free. He went into a restaurant, where because of the early hour nothing was ready ; he spent the time before a newspaper, on a bench. How often he had held papers thus without reading them, how many evenings he had waited in cafés with his nose in an article, thinking of other matters, at those times especially when he was striving with his vices ; when Florence appeared to him, still keeping the clear smile of a little girl on her way to school, her eyes cast down, her hands in the pockets of her apron.

Suddenly the child changed into a ghoul who whirled round him wildly, and made him silently understand the horror of his desires. . . .

All that was now far distant ; almost in one day the charm was broken, without any real strife or true effort, without inward struggles ; he had abstained from seeing her, and now when she roused his memory again she was no more in fact than a recollection odious and sweet.

"After all," thought Durtal, as he cut up his beefsteak, "I wonder what she thinks of me ; she must certainly suppose me dead or lost ; happily I have never met her, and she does not know my address.

"Well," he went on, "there is no use in stirring the mud, it will be time to cleanse it when I am at La Trappe," and he shuddered, for the idea of the confessor again took root in him, and he was obliged to tell himself for the twentieth time that the expected never happens, and to declare that he should find some good fellow of a monk who would listen to him ; then he was afraid again, putting things at their worst, and fancying himself turned out, like a mangy dog.

He finished his breakfast, and went to St. Severin ; there the crisis declared itself, the overcharged soul gave way, struck down by a congestion of sadness.

He lay on a chair in such a state of depression that he could think no more, he remained inert without the power of suffering, till little by little the soul, recovered from its torpor, came to itself in a flood of tears.

These tears gave him solace ; he wept over his lot, thought himself so unhappy, so worthy of pity, that he hoped still more for help, yet he dare not address himself to Christ, whom he thought less accessible, but he spoke

in low tones to the Virgin, murmuring that prayer in which
Saint Bernard reminds the Mother of Christ that never in
human memory was it heard that she abandoned any of
those who sought her aid.

He left St. Severin, consoled and more resolved, and,
when once at home, was taken up with preparations
for departure. Afraid that he would find nothing he
wanted down there, he determined to stuff his portmanteau
full; he crammed into the corners sugar, packets of
chocolate, that he might try to deceive if needful the
anguish of a fasting stomach, took towels thinking there
would be few at La Trappe, prepared a stock of tobacco and
matches; then besides books, paper, pencils, ink, packets of
antipyrine, a phial of laudanum, which he wrapped in
handkerchiefs and wedged into his slippers.

When he had strapped his portmanteau, he said to
himself, looking at the clock : "To-morrow at this time I
shall be jolting in a cab, and my seclusion will be near at
hand ; never mind, I shall do well, in anticipation of bodily
ailment, to ask for the confessor as soon as I get there, and
suppose that turns out badly, I shall have time to make
arrangements and take the train back at once.

" All the same this will not prevent my having a wretched
moment this evening when I enter Notre Dame des
Victoires," but his anxieties and emotions vanished when
the hour of Benediction came. He was seized by the giddy
infection of the church, and he wrapped, steeped, and lost
himself in the prayer which arose from all those souls, in
the chant which went up from every mouth, and when
the monstrance was brought forward to make its sign in the
air, he felt a vast peace descend upon him.

At evening as he undressed he sighed : " To-morrow I shall
lie down in a cell, amazing when I think of it ! I should
have considered anyone mad, who, a few years ago, had
prophesied that I should take refuge in a Trappist monastery;
yet now I am going there of my own accord, and yet no,
I am going driven by an unknown power, I am going as a
whipped cur.

" After all, what a symptom of the time it is ! Society
must indeed be unclean, if God has no longer the right to
be hard, and is reduced to pick up what He finds, and to
content Himself with gathering to Himself people like me !

SECOND PART.

CHAPTER I.

DURTAL awoke, gay and brisk, astonished at not hearing himself groan, when the moment had come in which he should set off for La Trappe ; he was wonderfully reassured. He tried to recollect himself, and to pray, but he felt his thoughts more scattered and wandering than usual ; he remained indifferent and unmoved. Surprised at this result, he tried to examine himself, and touched the void ; he was slack that morning, in one of those sudden dispositions in which a man becomes a child again, incapable of attention, in which the wrong side of things disappears, and everything distracts.

He dressed hastily, got into a cab, was too early at the station ; and there experienced a perfectly childish attack of vanity. Looking at the people who hurried through the waiting rooms, thronged the ticket offices, or resignedly followed their luggage, he was not far from admiring himself. "If these travellers who think only of their pleasures or their business, knew where I am going," he thought.

Then he reproached himself for the stupidity of these reflections, and as soon as he was settled in his compartment, in which he chanced to be alone, he lighted a cigarette, saying to himself, "Let us profit at least by the time there is still for smoking," and he began to wander, to dream about the position of the monastery, and rove about the neighbourhood of La Trappe.

He remembered that a review had recently estimated the number of nuns and monks in France at two hundred thousand.

" Two hundred thousand persons, who, in such an epoch, have understood the wickedness of the struggle for life, the filth of sexual relations, the horror of lyings-in, those are they who save the honour of the country," he thought.

Then, passing at a bound from cloistered souls to the treatises he had put in his portmanteau, he went on : " It is, all the same, curious how completely the temperament of French art rebels against Mysticism !

" All exalted writers are foreigners. Saint Denys the Areopagite was a Greek ; Eckhart, Tauler, Suso, Sister Emmerich, were Germans ; Ruysbröck came from Flanders ; Saint Teresa, Saint John of the Cross, Saint Marie d'Agreda, were Spaniards ; Father Faber was English ; Saint Bonaventure, Angela of Foligno, Magdalen of Pazzi, Catherine of Genoa, Jacopo de Voragine, were Italians. . . .

" Ah ! " he said, struck by the last name he had cited, " I ought to have brought his Golden Legend in my bag ; how was it I did not remember it, for that book is, in fact, the very crowning work of the Middle Ages, the stimulant for hours rendered languid by the prolonged uneasiness of fasting, the simple aid of pious vigils ? For the most incredulous souls of our time, the Golden Legend at least still seems like one of those pure parchments, on which simple illuminators painted the faces of saints with gum water, or white of egg on golden backgrounds. Jacopo de Voragine is the Jehan Fouquet, the André Beaunevue, of literary miniature, of mystic prose !

" It is quite absurd to have forgotten that book, for it would have made me pass precious days, like those of old, in La Trappe.

" Yes, it is strange," he thought, returning on his thoughts, and coming back to his first idea ; " France can count religious authors, more or less celebrated, but very few mystical writers, properly so-called, and it is just the same also in painting. The true Early Masters are Flemish, German or Italian, none are French, for our Burgundian School descended from the Flemish.

" No, it cannot be denied, the genius of our race cannot easily follow and explain how God acts when He works in the central depths of the soul, which is the ovary of thought, the very source of conception; it is refractory at explaining, by the expressive power of words, the crash or the silence of grace; bursting forth in the domain which is wasted by sin, it is inapt at extracting from that secret world, works of psychology like those of Saint Teresa and Saint John of the Cross, works of art, like those of Voragine or Sister Emmerich.

"Besides that our field is scarcely arable, and our soil harsh, where shall we now find the labourer who sows and harrows it, who prepares not even a mystical harvest, but even any spiritual fruit, capable of assuaging the hunger of the few who stray and are lost, and fall from inanition in the icy desert of our time?

"He who should be the cultivator of that land, the farmer of souls, the priest, has not strength to clear the ground.

"The seminary has made him arbitrary and puerile, life outside has made him lukewarm. Therefore it seems that God has withdrawn Himself from him, and the proof of this is that He has taken away all ability from the priesthood. There are no priests now who have talent, either in the pulpit or in books; the laity have inherited that grace which was so common in the Church of the Middle Ages. Another example proves it still more, priests make so few conversions. In these days the being who pleases Heaven does without them, the Saviour Himself strikes him down, handles him, works directly on him.

"The ignorance of the clergy, their want of education, their unintelligence of their surroundings, their dislike for Mysticism, their incomprehension of art, have taken away all their influence on the aristocracy of souls. Their only action is now on the childish brains of bigots and pretenders; and this is no doubt providential; it is better so, for if the priest became the master, if he succeeded in raising and vivifying the wearisome tribe he manages, it would be like a waterspout of clerical stupidity beating down on a country, would be the end of all literature and all art in France.

"To save the Church there remains the monk, whom the priest detests, for the life of the cloister is a constant reproach to his own existence," continued Durtal; "always supposing that my illusions are not again destroyed when I see a monastery . . . . but no, I am lucky; I have discovered in

Paris one of those few abbés who is neither indifferent nor
a pedant ; why should I not, in an abbey, come into contact
with authentic monks ? "

He lighted a cigarette, and looked at the landscape from
the carriage window ; the train was passing through fields
in front of which the telegraph wires danced in puffs of
steam ; the landscape was flat and uninteresting. Durtal
fell back sulkily in his corner.

"The arrival at the convent disturbs me," he murmured ;
" since there are no useless words to proffer, I shall confine
myself to giving his letter to the Father Guestmaster ; ah !
and then all will arrange itself."

He felt, in fact, a pèrfect calm, and was astonished at not
finding in himself any disgust or fear, at being almost in high
spirits : " Well, my good priest was right in declaring that I
was creating monsters in advance ; " and he thought of
the Abbé Gévresin, was surprised that long as he had visited
him, he knew nothing whatever of his antecedents, that he
was no more intimate with him than on the very first day ;
" In fact, it only rested with me to question him discreetly,
but the idea never entered my head : it is true that our
intercourse has been strictly limited to matters of religion
and art ; this perpetual reserve does not create very thrilling
friendships, but it institutes a sort of Jansenism of the
affections which is not without charm.

" In any case that ecclesiastic is a holy man ; he has not
even that manner at once caressing and reserved of other
priests.   Apart from certain gestures, his habit of rolling his
arms in his cincture, of wrapping his hands in his sleeves, of
liking to walk backwards when in conversation ; apart from
his innocent mania of interlarding his phrases with Latin,
he does not recall either the attitude or the unfashionable
speech of his brethren.   He loves mysticism and plain song ;
he is exceptional, and therefore he must have been also carefully chosen for me in heaven.

" Ah well ! we must be getting near," he sighed, looking
at his watch, " I am beginning to feel hungry ; come, that is
all right, we shall be at Saint Landry in a quarter of an
hour."

He strummed on the windows of the carriage, saw the
fields and woods fly past, smoked a cigarette or two, took his
bag from the rack, at last arrived at the station and got out.

Close to the tiny station he recognized the inn of which the abbé had told him. He found a good woman in the kitchen who said, " All right, sir, sit down, they will put the horse to while you breakfast."

He fed himself on uneatable things, they brought him a calf's head forgotten in a tub, some cutlets that were high, vegetables blackened with gravy from the stove.

In his present mood he was amused at this infamous meal, fell back upon a thin wine which rasped his throat, and resignedly drank coffee which left a sediment of peat at the bottom of the cup.

Then he climbed into a jolting car driven by a young man, and the horse went off at a smart pace through the village and into the country.

On the way he asked the driver for some information about La Trappe, but the peasant knew nothing. " I often go there," he said, " but never enter, the carriage stays at the gate, so you see I can tell you nothing."

They went for an hour rapidly through the lanes, and the peasant saluted a roadmaker with his whip, and said to Durtal,

" They say that the eminets eat their bellies."

And as Durtal asked what he meant,

" They are idle dogs, they lie all the summer on their bellies in the shade."

And he said no more.

Durtal thought of nothing ; he digested and smoked, dizzy with the rumbling of the carriage.

At the end of another hour they came into the heart of the forest.

" Are we near ? "

" Oh, not yet ! "

" Can we see La Trappe from a distance ? "

" Oh no, you must have your nose just over it to see it, it is quite in a bottom, at the end of a lane, like that," said the peasant, pointing to a grassy lane into which they turned.

" There is a fellow coming from the place," he said, pointing out a vagabond, who was crossing the copse at a great pace.

And he explained to Durtal that every beggar had a right to food and even to lodging at La Trappe ; they gave

them the ordinary fare of the community in a room close
to the brother porter's lodge, but did not let them into
the convent.

When Durtal asked him the opinion which the villagers
round about had of the monks, the peasant was evidently
afraid of compromising himself, for he answered,

" Some say nothing about them."

Durtal began to be rather weary, when suddenly as they
turned out of a lane, he saw an immense building below
him.

" There is La Trappe ! " said the peasant, gathering his
reins for the descent.

From the height where he was, Durtal looked over the
roofs, and saw a large garden, with thickets, and in front of
them a formidable crucifix.

Then the vision disappeared, the carriage again went
through the wood, descending by zig-zag roads where the
foliage intercepted the view.

They came at last, by long circuits, to an open place, at
the end of which rose a wall with a large gate in the
middle.   The carriage stopped.

" You have only to ring," said the peasant, showing
Durtal an iron chain along the wall ; and he added,

" Shall I come for you again to-morrow ? "

" No."

" Then you remain here ? " and the peasant looked at
him with astonishment, turned about, and drove up the
hill.

Durtal remained as one crushed, his portmanteau at his
feet, before the door ; his heart beat violently ; all his
assurance, all his enthusiasm, had vanished, and he
stammered : " What will happen to me within ? "

And with a swift feeling of dread, there passed before
him the terrible life of the Trappists ; the body ill-nourished,
exhausted from want of sleep, prostrate for hours on the
pavement ; the soul trembling, squeezed like a sponge in
the hand, drilled, examined, ransacked even to its smallest
folds ; and at the end of its failure of an existence, thrown
like a wreck against this rude rock, into the silence of a
prison, and the dreadful stillness of the tomb !

" My God, my God, have pity upon me ! " said he, as he
wiped his brow.

Mechanically he looked around, as if he expected some help ; the roads were deserted and the woods were empty ; no sound was heard in the country, or in the monastery.

"At any rate I must make up my mind to ring ; " and, his limbs sinking under him, he pulled the chain.

The sound of the bell, hard, rusty, grumbling, sounded on the other side of the wall.

"Get up and don't be a fool," he said to himself, as he heard the clatter of a pair of sabots behind the door.

This opened, and a very old monk, clad in the brown cloth of the Capuchins, looked at him inquiringly.

"I come to make a retreat, and I wish to see Father Etienne."

The monk bowed, took up the portmanteau, and made a sign to Durtal to follow him. He went with bent head and short steps across an orchard. They reached a grating, passed on the right of the vast building a sort of dilapidated chateau, flanked by two wings advancing on a court.

The brother entered the wing close to the grating. Durtal followed him along a corridor into which several grey doors opened ; on one of these he read the word "Auditorium." The Trappist stopped before it, lifted the wooden latch, ushered Durtal into the room, and after some minutes he heard repeated calls on the bell.

Durtal sat down and looked at this gloomy chamber, for the window was half closed by shutters. There was little furniture ; the most important a dining-table with an old cover ; in the corner, a "prie-Dieu" above which was nailed a figure of Saint Antony of Padua rocking the infant Jesus in his arms ; a large crucifix on the other wall, and here and there were placed two high-backed chairs and four ordinary chairs.

Durtal took from his pocket-book the letter of introduction to the father. "What sort of reception will he give me ?" he asked himself ; "he at any rate can speak ; well, we shall soon see," he said, as he heard steps.

A monk in white with a black scapular whose two ends fell, one on his shoulders, the other on his breast, appeared ; he was young and smiling.

He read the letter, then he took Durtal's hand, and led

him in silent astonishment across the court to the other
wing of the building, opened a door, dipped his finger in
a holy-water stoup, and offered it to him.

They were in a chapel. The monk invited Durtal by a
sign to kneel on a step before the altar, and he prayed
in a low voice ; he then rose, returned slowly to the
threshold, offered Durtal holy water again, still without
opening his lips, and leading him by the hand they went
the way they came to the Auditorium.

There, he inquired after the health of the Abbé Gévresin,
seized the portmanteau, and mounted an immense staircase falling into ruin. At the top of this staircase, which
had only one story, there extended a vast landing bounded
at each of its extremities by a door.

Father Etienne entered that on the right, crossed a
broad vestibule, and led Durtal into a room, which a ticket
printed in large letters placed under the invocation of St.
Benedict, and said, " I am sorry, sir, to be only able to
put at your disposal this room, which is not very comfortable."

" But it will do very well," said Durtal, " and the view is
charming," he continued, approaching the window.

" At least you will be in good air," said the monk, opening the casement.

Below stretched the orchard through which Durtal had
passed under the conduct of the brother porter. An
enclosure full of apple trees stunted and clipped, silvered by
lichens, and gilt by moss ; then beyond the monastery,
and above the walls, rose fields of clover intersected by a
great white road, extending to the horizon, which was
notched by the foliage of trees.

" You will see, sir," Father Etienne went on, " if you need
anything in this cell, and tell me quite simply, will you not ?
for otherwise we should heap up regret for both of us, for
you who have only to ask for what might be useful to you,
for me who should only discover it later and be sorry for
my forgetfulness."

Durtal looked at him reassured by this frank greeting ;
he was a young priest, about thirty years old. His face
bright, and finely cut, was streaked with red fibres on the
cheeks ; this monk wore a beard, and round his shaven
head was a crown of brown hair. He spoke somewhat

rapidly, and smiled, with his hands pushed into the large leathern belt round his waist. " I will come back directly, for I have some important work to finish," he said ; " try to make yourself at home as much as possible, and if you have time glance over the rule which you have to follow in this monastery—it is written on one of these cards on the table ; we will talk about it after you have mastered it, if you like."

And he left Durtal alone.

He soon made an inventory of the room ; it was very high and extremely narrow like a gun-barrel, the door was at one end, the window at the other.

At the bottom, in a corner, near the casement, was a little iron bed, and a small round table in chestnut wood. At the foot of the bed which stood along the wall was a prie-Dieu in faded rep, upon which was a crucifix, and a branch of dried fir below it ; on the same side was a table of white wood covered with a towel, on which were placed an ewer, a basin, and a glass. On the opposite wall was a wardrobe, and by the fireplace, on the mantelpiece of which a crucifix was placed, was a table opposite the bed near the window ; three straw chairs completed the furniture of this room. " I shall never have water enough to wash in," thought Durtal, gauging the miniature jug, which held about a pint ; " since Father Etienne shows himself so obliging, I must ask him for a larger ration." He unpacked his portmanteau, undressed, put on flannel instead of his starched shirt, arranged his toilet things on the washing-stand, folded his linen in the wardrobe ; then sat down, looked around the cell, and thought it sufficiently comfortable, and above all very clean. He then went towards the table on which were laid a ream of ruled paper, an ink-stand, and some pens ; he was grateful for this attention of the monk, who knew no doubt by the Abbé Gévresin's letter that his business was writing, opened two volumes bound in leather and shut them again. The one was " The Intro-duction to the Devout Life," by Saint Francis de Sales, the other was " Manresa," or " The Spiritual Exercises " of Saint Ignatius of Loyola, and he arranged his own books on the table.

Then he took up, just as it came, one of the cards spread on the table and read :—

"Exercises of the Community for ordinary days—from Easter to the Invention of the Cross in September.

> Rise. 2.
> Prime and Mass. 5.15.
> Work after the Chapter.
> End of work and leisure time. 9.
> Sext. 11.
> Angelus and Dinner. 11.30.
> Siesta after Dinner.
> End of Siesta. 1.30.
> None and work, five minutes after waking.
> End of work and leisure. 4.30.
> Vespers followed by prayer. 5.15.
> Supper and leisure. 6.
> Compline. 7.25.
> Retire to rest. 8."

He turned the card, and on the other side was a new horary, entitled :—

"Winter Exercises, from the Invention of the Cross in September to Easter."

The hour of rising was the same, but bed-time was an hour earlier ; dinner was changed from 11.30 to 2 ; siesta and supper at 6 o'clock were suppressed ; the canonical hours were the same, except vespers and compline, which were changed from 5.15 and 7.25 to 4.30 and 6.15.

"It is not pleasant to drag oneself from bed in the middle of the night," sighed Durtal, " but I am inclined to think that the Retreatants are not subject to this rule of wakefulness," and he took up another card. " This must be the one intended for me," he said, reading the head of the card :—

Rules of Retreat from Easter to the Invention of the Cross in September.

Let us look at these rules rather more closely.

He examined the two tables, brought together, one for the morning, and one for the evening.

MORNING.

> 4.   Rise at the Angelus bell.
> 4.30. Prayer and Meditation.

5.15.   Prime and Mass.
6–7.   Examination of Conscience.
7.   Breakfast.
7.30.   Way of the Cross.
8.   Sext and None.
8.30.   Second Meditation.
9.   Spiritual Reading.
11.   Adoration and Examination.   Tierce.
11.30.   Angelus.   Dinner.   Recreation.
12.15.   Siesta.   Absolute Silence.

Evening

1.30.   End of Siesta.   Rosary.
2.   Vespers and Compline.
3.   Third Meditation.
3.15.   Spiritual Reading.
4.15.   Matins and Lauds.
5.15.   Reflections.   Choir Vespers.
5.30.   Examination and Prayer.
6.   Supper and Recreation.
7.   Litanies.   Absolute Silence.
7.15.   Assist at Compline.
7.30.   Salve Regina.   Angelus.
7.45.   Private Examination.   Retire to rest.

" This at any rate is more practical—four o'clock in the morning is an almost possible hour, but I do not understand it, the canonical hours on this tablet do not agree with those of the monks, and then why these double Vespers and Compline ?   Lastly, these little points in which you are invited to meditate so many minutes, to read so many more, scarcely suit me.   My mind is scarcely malleable enough to run in those channels—it is true that after all I am free to do as I please, for no one can verify what tricks I may play, can know, for instance, if I meditate. . . .

" Ah, here is again a regulation at the back," he went on, as he turned the card, " the regulation for September, I need not trouble myself about it, it differs, moreover, little from the other ; but here is a postcript which concerns both horaries."

Note.

1. Those who are not bound to say the Breviary will say the Little Office of the Blessed Virgin.

2. The Retreatants are requested to make their Confessions at an early date, in order to have their mind more free for meditation.

3. After each meditation an analogous chapter of the Imitation must be read.

4. The best time for confessions and the Way of the Cross is from 6—9 in the morning, 2—5 in the afternoon, and in summer from 9 in the morning till 5 in the afternoon.

5. To read the table of notices.

6. It is well to be punctual at meals to keep no one waiting.

7. The Father Guestmaster alone is charged with providing for the wants of guests.

8. Guests may ask for books for the retreat, if they have none themselves.

Confession ! He saw this word only in the whole series of rules. He must at once have recourse to it. He felt a cold shiver down his back ; and knew that he must speak to Father Etienne about it as soon as he returned.

He had not long to wrestle with himself, for the monk entered almost at once and said,

" Have you noticed anything you need, and the presence of which may be useful to you ? "

" No, Father ; yet if you could let me have a little more water."

" Nothing is easier ; I will send you up a large pitcher every morning."

" Thank you . . . see, I have been studying the rules."

" I will at once put you at ease," said the monk. " You are compelled to nothing but the strictest punctuality. You must follow the canonical offices to the letter. As to the exercises marked on the card, they are not of obligation ; they may be useful, as they are laid down, for people who are very young and devoid of all initiative, but, as I think at least, they somewhat hamper others, and as a general rule we do not trouble the retreatants here, we let solitude act on them ; it belongs to yourself to discriminate and distinguish the best mode of occupying your time holily. Therefore I will not impose on you any of the reading laid down on this

card, and only take leave to get you to say the Little
Office of the Blessed Virgin. Have you it ? "

" Here it is," said Durtal, holding out a bound book.

" Your volume is charming," said Father Etienne, as he
turned over the pages exquisitely printed in red and black.
He paused at one of them, and read aloud the third lesson
of Matins.

" Is it not fine ? " he cried. A sudden joy sprang up
in his face ; his eyes grew bright, his hands trembled on the
cover. " Yes," he said, closing it, " read this office, here
especially, for you know our true patroness, the true
Abbot of the Trappists, is the Blessed Virgin ! "

After a silence he continued : " I have fixed a week as
the duration of your retreat, in the letter I sent to the
Abbé Gévresin, but I need not say that if you are not
too weary here, you can stay as long as seems good to
you."

" I hope to be able to prolong my stay among you, but
this must depend upon the way in which my body stands
the struggle ; my stomach is somewhat weak, and I am
not without some fear ; I shall, therefore, be much
obliged to you if you will let me see the confessor as soon
as possible."

" Good ; you shall see him to-morrow. I will tell you
the time this evening, after compline. As for the food, if
you think it insufficient, I will see that you have an extra
egg, but there ceases the discretion I can exercise, for the
rule is precise, no fish, no flesh—vegetables, and I am bound
to admit they are not first rate.

" But you shall judge, and, indeed, as it is just upon supper-
time, I will show you the room where you will dine in
company with M. Bruno."

And as they descended the staircase, the monk went on :
" M. Bruno is a person who has renounced the world, and,
without having taken the vows, lives enclosed. He is what
our rule calls an oblate, he is a holy and learned man,
whom you will certainly like ; you can talk with him
during the meal."

" Ah ! " said Durtal, " and before and after I must keep
silence ? "

" Yes, unless you have anything to ask, in which case
I shall be always at your service, ready to answer you.

As for that question of silence, as for those of the hours of rising and going to bed, and the offices, the rule allows no modification, it must be observed to the letter."

" Good," said Durtal, a little taken aback by the decided tone of the Father, " but I saw on my card a note directing me to consult a table of regulations, and I have not that table."

" It hangs on the wall of the staircase, near your room ; you can read it when your head is rested to-morrow. Will you go in ? " he said, opening a door in the lower corridor, just opposite that of the auditorium.

Durtal bowed to an old gentleman who came to meet him ; the monk introduced them and vanished.

The dishes were on the table, two poached eggs, a bowl of rice, another of French beans, and a pot of honey.

M. Bruno said grace, and proceeded to help Durtal.

He gave him an egg.

" This is a poor supper for a Parisian," he said, with a smile.

" Ah, as long as there is an egg and wine it is bearable. I was afraid, I confess, that my only drink would be cold water."

They talked as friends.

The man was pleasant, and distinguished, with ascetic features, but with a bright smile, lighting up a grave face, yellow and wrinkled.

He lent himself with perfect good grace to Durtal's inquiries, and told him, that after a tempestuous life, he felt that Grace had touched him, and he had retired from the world to expiate by years of austerities and silence his own sins and those of others.

" And you have never grown tired of being here ? "

" Never, during the five years that I have spent in this cloister, time, cut up as it is at La Trappe, seems short."

" You are present at all the exercises of the Community ? "

" Yes ; I only replace manual labour by meditation in my cell ; my position as oblate, however, dispenses me, if I so wish, from getting up at two o'clock to follow the night office, but it is a great joy to me to recite the magnificent Benedictine Psalter before daybreak—but you are listening to me, and eat nothing. Let me give you a little more rice."

"No, thank you, but I will take, if you will allow me, a spoonful of honey.

"The food is not bad," he said, "but I do not quite understand the same strange and identical taste in all the dishes ; it smells, how shall I express it ? like burnt fat or suet."

"That is the warm oil with which the vegetables are dressed, you will soon grow accustomed to it, in a couple of days you will cease to notice it."

"But in what consists, precisely, the part of an oblate ? "

"His life is less austere, and more contemplative than that of a monk ; he may travel if he will, and though he is not bound by vows, he shares in all the spiritual advantages of the order.

"In old times the rule admitted those whom it styled ' familiars.'

"Those were oblates who received the tonsure, wore a distinct costume, and pronounced the three greater vows ; they led in fact a mitigated life, half layman, half monk. This rule, which still exists among the true Benedictines, has disappeared among the Trappists since the year 1293, the date at which it was suppressed by the Chapter General.

"At the present time, in the Cistercian abbeys are only the fathers, the lay brothers, the oblates, when there are any, and the peasants employed in field labour."

"The lay brothers, I suppose, are those whose heads are completely shaven, and who are clothed in a brown habit, like the monk who opened the door to me ? "

"Yes ; they do not sing office, and have only manual tasks."

"By the way, the rule for retreat which I read in my room does not seem clear. As far as I recall it, it doubles certain offices, places Matins at four in the afternoon, and Vespers at two ; in any case the horary is not the same as that of the Trappists ; how am I to understand and reconcile them ? "

"You have only to take into consideration the exercises set out on your card ; Father Etienne must, I think, have said so ; that mould was only made for people who cannot occupy and guide themselves. That explains to you how, to prevent them from becoming idle, the priests' breviary has been in some degree taken to pieces, and their time has

been distributed in small slices, so that, for instance, they
may be obliged to recite the psalms for Matins at hours
when there is no psalm."

Dinner was over ; M. Bruno said grace, and said to
Durtal,

" You have twenty minutes free from now to Compline ;
you can make acquaintance with the garden and woods."
He bowed politely and went out.

" I can smoke a cigarette," thought Durtal, when he was
alone. He took his hat and left the room. Night was
coming on. He passed through the great court, skirted
a small building surmounted by a long chimney-stack,
discovered by the smell that it was a chocolate factory, and
entered an avenue of trees.

The sky was so obscure that he could scarcely see the
group of trees he entered, and not seeing anyone he rolled
his cigarettes, and smoked them slowly, with enjoyment,
consulting his watch from time to time by his cigar lights.

He was astonished at the silence of the monastery ; not a
sound, however hushed, however distant, save now and then
a gentle rustle of boughs ; he went to the side whence the
noise came, and saw a piece of water, on which a swan was
sailing, which came towards him.

He saw its white plumage oscillate against the darkness
which it displaced with a splash, when a bell sounded with
slow strokes ; " Ah," said he, looking again at his watch,
" that is the hour of Compline."

He went to the chapel, which was still empty ; and he
took occasion of the solitude to examine it at his ease.

It was in the form of a truncated cross, a cross without a
foot, rounded at the summit, holding out two square arms,
with a door at either end.

The upper part of the cross, below a cupola painted blue,
formed a little circular apse, round which was a circle of
stalls placed back against the wall ; in the middle rose a great
altar of white marble, surmounted by wooden chandeliers,
flanked on the left and right by candelabra also of wood,
placed on marble shafts.

The lower part of the altar was hollow, and closed in front
by a glass, behind which appeared a shrine in Gothic style,
which reflected in its copper gilt mirror the light of the
lamps.

The apse opened into a large porch, with three steps in front, on the arms of the cross, which were prolonged into a kind of vestibule serving at once as nave and side aisles to this stumpy church.

The hollowed arms, at their extremities near the doors, held two very small chapels set back in niches painted blue, like the cupola, containing above two stone altars without ornament, two mediocre statues, one of Saint Joseph, the other of Christ.

Lastly, a fourth altar, dedicated to the Virgin, was situated in this vestibule opposite the steps leading to the apse, opposite therefore to the high altar. It was relieved against a window whose lights represented Saint Bernard in white on one hand, and Saint Benedict in black on the other, and it appeared to recede into the church, because of the two ranges of seats which stood on the left and right before the two other little chapels, leaving only room necessary to pass along the vestibule, or to go in a straight line from this altar of the Virgin in the apse, to the high altar.

"This sanctuary is alarmingly ugly," said Durtal, who had sat down on a bench in front of the statue of Saint Joseph. "To judge by the few subjects carved along the walls, this edifice dates from the time of Louis XVI., an abominable date for a church."

He was disturbed in these thoughts by the sound of bells, and at the same time all the doors were opened ; one situated in the apse itself, on the left of the altar, gave passage to about half a score monks, wrapped in great white cowls, who spread out into the choir, and occupied the stalls on either side.

Then, by the two doors of the vestibule, came a crowd of brown monks, who knelt at the benches on the two sides of Our Lady's altar.

Durtal had some of them near him ; but they bowed their heads, and joined their hands, he dared not observe them ; moreover, the vestibule had become almost dark, the light was concentrated in the choir, where the lamps were kindled.

He could make out the faces of the white monks in their stalls in the part of the apse he could see, and among them he recognized Father Etienne on his knees near a short monk ; but another at the end of the stalls near the

porch, almost opposite the altar, and in full light, attracted
him.

He was tall and strong, and looked like an Arab in his
white burnous. Durtal could only see him in profile, and he
distinguished a long grey beard, a shaven skull, surrounded
by the monastic crown, a high forehead, and a nose like an
eagle's beak. He had a grand appearance, with his imperious
features, and his fine figure as it swayed under the cowl.

"That is probably the abbot of La Trappe," thought
Durtal, and he felt certain when this monk struck a little
bell hidden under the desk before him, and directed the
office.

All the monks bowed to the altar ; the abbot recited the
opening prayers, then there was a pause, and, from the other
side of the apse, which Durtal could not see, rose the frail
voice of an old man, a voice which had returned to the clear
tones of childhood, but was just a little cracked, growing
higher as it declaimed the antiphon,

" Deus in adjutorium meum intende."

And the other side of the choir, that on which were
Father Etienne and the abbot, answered, scanning the
syllables very slowly, with voices of bass pitch,—

" Domine ad adjuvandum me festina."

And all bowed their heads over the folios placed before
them, and took up the words,—

" Gloria Patri et Filio et Spiritui Sancto."

And they lifted their heads while the other part of the
Fathers pronounced the response, " Sicut erat in principio,
etc."

The office began.

It was not chanted but declaimed, now rapid and now
slow. The side of the choir which Durtal saw made all the
vowels sharp and short letters ; the other, on the contrary,
altered them all into long letters and seemed to cap all the
Os with a circumflex accent. It might be said that one
side had the pronunciation of the South, the other that of
the North ; thus chanted, the office became strange, and
ended by rocking like an incantation, and soothing the soul
which fell asleep in the rolling of the verses, interrupted by
the recurrent doxology like a refrain after the last verse of
each of the psalms.

"Ah well, I cannot understand it," thought Durtal,

who had his Compline at his fingers' ends, "they are not singing the Roman office at all."

The fact is that one of the psalms was wanting. He caught indeed, at one moment, the hymn of Saint Ambrose, the "Te lucis ante terminum," sung to a simple and rugged tune of the old plain chant, and yet the last stanza was not the same ; but he lost himself afresh, and waited for the "Short Lessons" and the "Nunc Dimittis" which never came.

"Yet Compline does not vary like Vespers," he thought, "I must ask Father Etienne the meaning of this to-morrow."

Then his reflections were disturbed by a young white monk, who passed him, genuflected to the altar, and lighted two tapers.

Suddenly all rose, and with a great shout, the "Salve Regina" shook the arches.

Durtal was affected as he listened to this admirable chant, which had nothing in common with that which is bellowed at Paris in the churches. This was at once flexible and ardent, sustained by such suppliant adoration, that it seemed to concentrate in itself alone, the immemorial hope of humanity, and its eternal lamentation.

Chanted without accompaniment, unsustained by the organ, by voices indifferent to themselves and blending in one only, masculine and deep, it rose with quiet boldness, sprang up with irresistible flight towards Our Lady, then made, as it were, a return upon itself, and its confidence was lessened ; it advanced more tremblingly, but so different, so humble, that it felt itself forgiven, and dared then in passionate appeals to demand the undeserved pleasures of heaven.

It was the absolute triumph of the neumes, those repetitions of notes on the same syllable, the same word, which the Church invented to paint the excess of that interior joy or sorrow which words cannot render ; it was a rush, a going forth of the soul, escaping in the passionate voices, breathed forth by the bodies of the monks as they stood and trembled.

Durtal followed in his prayer-book this work with so short a text, so long a chant ; and as he listened to, and read it with recollection, this magnificent prayer seemed to decompose as a whole, and to represent three different states of the soul, to exhibit the triple phase of humanity, during its youth, its maturity, and its decline ; it was, in a word, an essential summary of prayer for all ages.

First, there was the canticle of exultation, the joyous welcome of a being yet little, stammering forth respectful caresses, petting with gentle words, and fondness of a child who seeks to coax his mother—this is the " Salve Regina, Mater misericordiæ, vita, dulcedo et spes nostra, salve." Then the soul so candid, so simply happy, has grown, and knowing the wilful failings of thought, the repeated loss through sin, joins her hands, and asks, sobbing, for help. She adores no longer with a smile, but with tears ; it is " Ad te clamamus, exsules filii Hevae ; ad te suspiramus, gementes et flentes in hac lachrymarum valle." At last old age comes ; the soul lies, tormented by the memory of counsels neglected, by regret for lost graces ; and having become weaker, and more full of fears, is alarmed before her deliverance, before the destruction of that prison of the flesh which she feels at hand, and then she thinks of the eternal death of those whom the Judge condemns. On her knees she implores the Advocatress of earth, the Consultrix of heaven ; it is the " Eia ergo Advocata nostra ; illos tuos misericordes oculos ad nos converte ; et Jesum, benedictum fructum ventris tui, nobis post hoc exilium ostende."

And to that essence of prayer composed by Peter of Compostella or Hermann Contract, Saint Bernard, in an excess of hyperdulia, added the three invocations at the end, " O clemens, O pia, O dulcis Virgo Maria," sealing the inimitable prose with a triple seal, by those three cries of love which recall the hymn to the affectionate adoration of its beginning.

" This is unprecedented," thought Durtal, as the Trappists chanted these sweet and eager appeals ; the neumes were prolonged on the Os, which passed through all the colours of the soul, through the whole register of sound ; and these interjections summed up again, in the series of notes which clothed them, the inventory of the human soul, which now recapitulated the whole body of the hymn.

And suddenly at the word " Maria," at the glorious cry of that name, the chant fell, the tapers were extinguished, the monks fell on their knees, a silence like death came upon the chapel. The bells rang slowly, and the Angelus unfolded under the arches the separated petals of its clear sounds.

All, now prostrate, their faces buried in their hands, were praying, and this lasted long ; then the sound of the little hand-bell was heard, everyone rose, genuflected to the altar, and in silent file the monks disappeared through the door in the apse.

" Ah ! the true creator of plain music, the unknown author who cast into the brain of man the seed of plain chant, was the Holy Ghost," said Durtal, sick and dazzled, with tears in his eyes.

M. Bruno, whom he had not noticed in the chapel, came and joined him. They crossed the court without speaking, and when they had entered the guest-house, M. Bruno lighted two candles, gave one to Durtal, and said gravely, " I wish you a good night, sir."

Durtal went up the staircase behind him. They bowed again on the landing, and Durtal entered his cell.

The wind blew under the door, and the room, scarcely lighted by the low flame of the candle, seemed to him gloomy, the high ceiling vanished in shadow, and rained down darkness.

Durtal sat down by his bed, discouraged.

And yet he was thrust forward by one of those impulses it is impossible to translate into words, in which it seems that the heart swells almost to bursting, and before his inability to get away and fly from self, Durtal ended by becoming a child again, by weeping without definite cause, simply from the need of relieving himself by tears.

He sank down at the prie-Dieu, expecting he knew not what, which never came ; then before the crucifix which stretched its arms above him, he began to speak to Him, and to say to Him in low tones :

" Father, I have driven the swine from my being, but they have trampled on me, and covered me with mire, and the very stye is in ruins. Have pity on me, for I return from a distant land. Have mercy, O Lord, on the swine-herd without a house. I have entered into Thy house ; do not send me away, be to me a kindly host, wash me."

"Ah," he said suddenly, " that reminds me that I have not seen Father Etienne, who was to tell me the hour at which the confessor would receive me to-morrow ; he has no doubt forgotten to ask him ; so much the better. At any rate it will put it off for a day ; my soul is so cramped that I have indeed need of rest."

He undressed, sighing : " I must be up at half-past three to be in the chapel at four : I have no time to lose if I wish to sleep. If only I have no neuralgia to-morrow, and can wake before dawn ! "

CHAPTER II.

He passed a most terrible night ; it was so special, so dreadful, that he did not remember, in the whole of his existence, to have endured such anguish, undergone the like fears.

It was an uninterrupted succession of sudden wakings and of nightmares.

And these nightmares overpassed the limits of abomination that the most dangerous madness dreams. They developed themselves in the realm of lust ; and they were so special, so new to him, that when he woke Durtal remained trembling, almost crying out.

It was not at all that involuntary and well known act, that vision which ceases just at the moment when the sleeper clasps an amorous form ; it was as and more complete than in nature, long and accomplished, accompanied by all the preludes, all the details, all the sensations, and the orgasm took place with a singularly painful acuteness, an incredible spasm.

A strange fact, which seemed to point the difference between this state, and the unconscious uncleanness of night, was, beyond certain episodes and caresses which could only follow each other in reality, but were united at the same moment in the dream, the sensation clear and precise of a being, of a fluid form disappearing, with the sharp sound of a percussion cap, or the crack of a whip close by, on waking. This being was felt near him so distinctly, that the sheet, disarranged by the wind of the flight, was still in motion, and he looked at the empty place in terror.

"Ah," thought Durtal, when he had lighted his candle, "this carries me back to the time when I used to visit

Madame Chantelouve, and reminds me of the stories of the Succubus."

He remained sitting up in bed, astonished, and looked with real uneasiness round the cell steeped in shadow. He looked at his watch, it was only eleven o'clock at night. " God," he said, " if the nights are always like this in monasteries ! "

He had recourse to bathing with cold water in order to recover himself, opened his window to change the air, and lay down again, thoroughly chilled.

He hesitated to blow out his candle, uneasy at the darkness which seemed to him inhabited, full of ambushes and threats. He decided at last to extinguish it, and repeated the stanza he had already heard sung that evening in chapel :

> Procul recedant somnia
> Et noctium phantasmata,
> Hostemque nostrum comprime,
> Ne polluantur corpora.

He ended by falling asleep and dreamt again of impurity, but he came to himself in time to break the charm, experiencing again the impression of a shadow evaporating before he could seize it in the sheets. He looked at his watch ; it was two o'clock.

" If this goes on, I shall be broken down to-morrow," he thought, but he succeeded somehow or other in dozing, and waking every ten minutes to wait for three o'clock.

" If I fall asleep again, I shall not be able to wake at the moment I wish," he thought, " suppose I get up."

He sprang out of bed, dressed, prayed, reduced his thoughts to order.

Real excesses would have exhausted him less than these sham freaks, but what seemed to him especially odious was the want of satisfaction left by the completed rape of these ghosts. Compared with their greedy tricks, the caresses of a woman only diffused a temperate pleasure, and ended in a feeble shock, but with this Succuba one remained in a fury at having clasped only the void, at having been the dupe of a lie, the plaything of an appearance, of which one could not remember the form or the features. It necessarily brought with it the desire of the flesh, the wish to clasp a real body, and Durtal began to think of Florence ; she at least quenched his desires, and did not leave him thus, panting and feverish, in quest of he knew not what, in an atmosphere where he was surrounded, spied upon by an unknown whom he could not discern, by a phantom he could not escape.

Then Durtal shook himself, and would repulse the assault of these memories. "At any rate I will go and breathe the fresh air, and smoke a cigarette ; we will see afterwards."

He descended the staircase, whose walls seemed not to keep their place, and danced in the light of his candle, threaded the corridors, blew out his light, placed the candlestick near the auditorium, and rushed out.

It was pitch dark ; at the height of the first story a round window in the wall of the chapel cut a hole through the darkness like a red moon.

Durtal took a few whiffs of a cigarette, and then made his way to the chapel. He turned the latch of the door gently ; the vestibule into which he entered was dark, but the apse, though it was empty, was lighted by numerous lamps.

He made a step, crossed himself, and fell back, for he had stumbled over a body ; and he looked down at his feet.

He had come upon a battle-field.

On the ground human forms were lying, in the attitudes of combatants mowed down by grape shot, some flat on their faces, others on their knees, some leaning their hands on the ground as if stricken from behind, others extended with their fingers clenched on their breast, others again holding their heads or stretching out their arms.

And from this group in their agony rose no groan, no complaint.

Durtal was stupefied as he looked at this massacre of monks, and suddenly stopped with open mouth. A shaft of light fell from a lamp which the Father Sacristan had just placed in the apse, and crossing the porch, it showed a monk on his knees before the altar dedicated to the Virgin.

He was an old man of more than four-score years ; motionless as a statue, his eyes fixed, leaning forward in such an access of adoration, that the faces in ecstasy in the Early Masters seemed, compared with his, forced and cold.

Yet his features were vulgar, his shaven skull, without a crown, tanned by many suns and rains, was brick-coloured, his eye was dim, covered with a film by age, his face was wrinkled, shrivelled, stained like an old log, hidden in a thicket of white hair, while his somewhat snub nose made the general effect of the face singularly common.

But there went out, not from his eyes, nor his mouth, but from everywhere and nowhere, a kind of angelic look which was diffused over his head, and enveloped all his poor body, bowed in its heap of rags.

In this old man the soul did not even give herself the trouble to reform and ennoble his features, she contented herself in annihilating them with her rays ; it was, as it were, the nimbus of the old saints not now remaining round the head, but extending over all the features, pale and almost invisible, bathing his whole being.

He saw nothing and heard nothing ; monks dragged themselves on their knees, came to warm themselves, and to take shelter near him, and he never moved, dumb and deaf, so rigid that you might have believed him dead, had not his lower lip stirred now and then, lifting in this movement his long beard.

The dawn whitened the windows, and as the darkness was gradually dissipated, the other brethren were visible in turn to Durtal ; all these men, wounded by divine love, prayed ardently, flashed out beyond themselves noiselessly before the altar. Some were quite young, on their knees, with their bodies upright ; others, their eyeballs in ecstasy, were leaning back, and seated on their heels ; others again were making the way of the cross, and were often placed each opposite another face to face, and they looked without seeing, as with the eyes of the blind.

And among these lay brethren, some fathers buried in their great white cowls lay prostrate and kissed the ground.

" Oh to pray, pray like these monks ! " cried Durtal within himself.

He felt his unhappy soul grow slack within him ; in this atmosphere of sanctity he unbent himself, and sank down on the pavement, humbly asking pardon from Christ, for having soiled by his presence the purity of this place.

He prayed long, unsealing himself for the first time, recognizing his unworthiness and vileness so that he could not imagine how, in spite of His mercy, the Lord could tolerate him in the little circle of His elect ; he examined himself, saw clearly, and avowed that he was inferior to the least of these lay brothers who perhaps could not even spell out a book, understood that the culture of the mind was naught and the culture of the soul was all, and little by little, without perceiving it, thinking only of stammering forth acts of gratitude, he disappeared from the chapel, his soul borne up by the souls of others, away, away from the world, far from his charnel-house, far from his body.

In this chapel, the impulse had come at last, the going forth from self, till now refused, was at last permitted ; he no longer strove with self as in the time when he escaped with so great difficulty from his prison-house, as at St. Severin or Notre Dame des Victoires.

Then he again realized this chapel, where his animal part had alone remained, and he looked round him with astonishment ; the greater part of the brethren had gone, one father remained prostrate before our Lady's altar ; he quitted it in his turn, and went back to the apse, as the other fathers entered it.

Durtal looked at them ; they were of all sizes and all kinds ; one fat and bald, with a long black beard and spectacles, some little fair and puffy men, some very old, bristling with skin like a wild boar, others very young, with a vague air of German dreaminess, with their eyes under their glasses ; and almost all except the very young had this feature in common : a large belly, and cheeks with little red streaks.

Suddenly through the open door in the apse itself appeared the tall monk who had conducted the office the evening before. He threw back on his chasuble the woollen hood which covered his head, and assisted by two white monks went up to the high altar to say mass.

And it was not one of those masses served as so many are cooked in Paris, but a mass slow, meditated, and profound, a mass where the priest takes long to consecrate, overwhelmed before the altar, and when he elevated the Host no little bell tinkled, but the bells of the monastery spread abroad their slow peal, brief dull strokes, almost plaintive, while the Trappists disappeared, crouched on all-fours, their heads hidden below their desks.

When the mass ended it was nearly six o'clock. Durtal took the same way as the evening before, passed before the little chocolate factory, and saw through the windows the fathers wrapping up the tablets in lead paper, and in another room a tiny steam engine which a lay brother was directing.

He reached the walk where he had smoked the cigarettes in the shade. So gloomy at night, it was now charming with its two rows of aged limes which rustled gently while the wind wafted to him their enervating scent.

Seated on a bench, he could see at a glance the whole front of the abbey.

Before it was a long kitchen garden, with here and there some rose trees spread over the blueish basins and large balls of cabbages, and the old house, built in the monumental style of the seventeenth century, extended, solemn and immense, with eighteen windows in a row, and a pediment, in the span of which was placed a mighty clock.

It was roofed with slate, and surmounted by a ring of small bells, and was reached by a flight of several steps. It reached a height of at least five stories, though it had in reality only a ground and a first floor, but to judge by the unexpected height of the windows, the rooms had to accommodate their ceilings to the vast altitude of the church; on the whole the building was striking and cold, more apt, since it had been converted into a convent, to shelter the disciples of Jansen, than the sons of Saint Bernard.

The weather was warm that morning; the sun was filtered through the moving sieve of foliage, and the daylight, thus screened, was changed to rose colour as it touched the white. Durtal, who was about to read his prayer-book, saw the pages growing red, and by the law of complementary colours all the letters printed in black ink grew green.

He was amused by these details, and with his back to the warmth, he brightened up in this aromatic breeze, rested in this bath of sunshine from his fatigues of the night, when at the end of the walk he saw some of the brothers. They walked in silence, some carrying under their arms great round loaves, others holding milk cans, or baskets full of hay and eggs; they passed before him, and bowed respectfully.

All had a joyous and serious aspect. "Ah, good fellows," he thought, "for they helped me this morning, it is to them I owe it that I could keep silence no longer, and was able to pray, to have at last known the joy of supplication which at Paris was only a snare for me ! to them, and above all to Our Lady de l'Atre, who had pity on my poor soul."

He sprang from his bench in an access of joy, went into the lateral walks, reached the piece of water he had partially seen the evening before ; in front of it rose the huge cross he had seen at a distance from the carriage, in the wood, before he reached La Trappe.

It was placed opposite the monastery itself, and turned its back upon the pond ; it bore an eighteenth-century Christ, of natural size, in white marble ; the pond also took the form of a cross such as is shown on the greater part of the plans of churches.

This brown and liquid cross was spotted by duckweed, which the swan displaced as he swam.

He came towards Durtal, with extended beak, expecting, no doubt, a piece of bread.

Not a sound arose in this deserted spot, save the rustle of dry leaves which Durtal brushed as he walked. The clock struck seven.

He remembered that breakfast would be ready, and he walked quickly to the abbey. Father Etienne was waiting for him, shook hands, asked if he had slept well, then said :

"What would you like ? I can only offer you milk and honey ; I will send to-day to the nearest village and try to get you a little cheese, but you will have only a poor meal this morning."

Durtal proposed to exchange the milk for wine, declaring that he should then do very well, and said, "In any case I should do ill to complain, for you are fasting."

The monk smiled. "Just now," he said, "we are doing penance, on account of certain feasts of our order." And he explained that he only took food once a day, at two o'clock in the afternoon, after Nones.

"And you have not even wine and eggs to keep up your strength ! "

Father Etienne smiled again. "One gets accustomed to it," he said. "What is this rule in comparison with that adopted by Saint Bernard and his companions, when they went to till the valley of Clairvaux ? Their meal consisted of oak leaves, salted, cooked in muddy water."

And after a silence the Father continued : " No doubt
the Trappist rule is hard, but it is mild if we carry our
thoughts back to the rule of Saint Pacomius in the
East. Only think ; whoever wished to join that order
had to remain ten days and nights at the door of the
convent, and had to endure spitting and insults ; if he still
desired to enter, he fulfilled a three years' novitiate, inhabited
a hut where he could not stand up, nor lie at full length,
ate only olives and cabbage, prayed twelve times in the
morning, twelve times in the afternoon, twelve times in the
night ; the silence was perpetual, and his mortifications
never ceased. To prepare himself for this novitiate, and to
learn to subdue his appetite, Saint Macarius thought of the
plan of soaking his bread in a vessel with a very narrow
neck, and only fed on the crumbs which he could take out
with his fingers. When he was admitted into the monastery,
he contented himself with gnawing leaves of raw cabbage on
Sunday. Ah ! they could stand more than we. We, alas !
have no longer souls nor bodies stout enough to bear such
fasts ; but do not let that stop your meal ; make as good an
one as you can. Ah, by the way," said the monk, " be in
the auditorium at ten precisely, where the Father Prior
will hear your confession."

And he left the room.

If Durtal had received a blow on his head with a mallet,
he could not been more overwhelmed. All the scaffold-
ing of his joys, so rapidly run up, fell. This strange
fact had occurred, in the impulse of joy he had felt
since daybreak he had wholly forgotten that he had
to confess. He had a moment of aberration. " But I
am forgiven," he thought ; " the proof is that state of
happiness, such as I have never known, that truly wonderful
expansion of soul which I experienced in the chapel and in
the wood."

The idea that nothing had begun, that all was still to do,
terrified him ; he had not the courage to swallow his bread,
he drank a little wine, and rushed out of doors in a wind of
panic.

He went, wildly, with great strides. Confession ! The
prior ? Who was the prior ? He sought in vain among the
fathers whose faces he remembered the one who would
hear him.

"My God!" he said, all at once, "but I do not even know
how a confession is made."

He sought a deserted corner, where he could recollect
himself a little. He was striding along without even knowing how he came there, along a walnut-tree walk with a
wall on one side. There were some enormous trees, he hid
himself behind the trunk of one of them, and sitting on
the moss, turned over the leaves of his prayer-book, and
read : " On arriving at the confessional, place yourself on
your knees, make the sign of the cross, and ask the priest for
his blessing, saying, ' Bless me, Father, for I have sinned ; '
then recite the Confiteor as far as *mea culpa* . . . and . . ."

He stopped, and without any need of probing it his life
sprang out in jets of filth.

He shrank from it, there was so much, of every kind, that
he was overwhelmed with despair.

Then by an effort of his will he pulled himself together,
endeavoured to control and bank up these torrents, to
separate them so as to understand them, but one affluent
rolled back all the others, ended by overwhelming them,
and became the river itself.

And this sin appeared at first ape-like and sly, at school
where everyone tempted and corrupted others ; then there
was all his greedy youth, dragged through tap-rooms, rolled
in swine troughs, wallowing in the sinks of prostitution,
and then an ignoble manhood. To his regular tasks had
succeeded toll paid to his senses, and shameful memories
assailed him in a crowd ; he recalled to mind how he had
sought after monstrous iniquities, his pursuit of artifices
aggravating the malice of the act, and the accomplices and
agents of his sins passed in file before him.

Among all, at one time, there was a certain Mme.
Chantelouve, a demoniacal adulteress who had drawn him
headlong into frightful excesses, who had linked him to
nameless crimes, sins against holy things, to sacrileges.

"How can I tell all this to the monk ?" thought Durtal,
terrified by the remembrance ; "how can I even express
myself, so as to make him understand without defilement ?"

Tears rushed from his eyes. "My God, my God !" he
sighed, " this is indeed too much."

And in her turn Florence appeared with her little
street-arab smile, and her childish haunches. "I can never

tell the confessor all that was brewed in the perfumed shade of her vices," cried Durtal. "I can by no means make him face these torrents of pus.

"Yet they say this has to be done ;" and he bowed under the weight of the foulness of this girl.

"How shameful to have been riveted to her, how disgusting to have satisfied the abominable demands of her desires !"

Behind this sewer extended others. He had traversed all the districts of sin which the prayer-book patiently enumerated. He had never confessed since his first communion, and with the piling up of years had come successive deposits of sins. He grew pale at the thought that he was about to detail to another man all his dirt, to acknowledge his most secret thoughts, to say to him what one dares not repeat to one's own self, lest one should despise oneself too much.

He sweated with anguish, then nausea at his being, remorse for his life solaced him, and he gave himself up ; regret for having lived so long in this cesspool was a very crucifixion to him ; he wept long, doubting pardon, not even daring to ask it, so vile did he feel himself.

At last he sprang up ; the hour of expiation must be at hand, in fact his watch pointed to a quarter to ten. His agony as he thus wrought with himself had lasted more than two hours.

He hurriedly reached the main path which led to the monastery. He walked with his head down, forcing back his tears.

He slackened his pace somewhat as he drew near the little pond ; he lifted his eyes in supplication to the cross, and as he lowered them he met a look so moved, so compassionate, so gentle, that he stopped, and the look disappeared with the bow of a lay brother, who passed on his way.

"He read my thoughts," said Durtal to himself. "Oh, this charitable monk has good reason to pity me, for indeed I suffer. Ah, Lord, that I might be like that humble brother !" he cried, remembering that he had seen that very morning the young tall lad, praying in the chapel with such fervour that he seemed to rise from the ground, before Our Lady.

He arrived at the auditorium in a frightful state, and

sank on a chair ; then, like a hunted animal that thinks itself discovered, he sprang up, and, disturbed by his fears, moved by a wind of disorder, he thought of flight, that he would pack his bag, and make for the train.

He mastered himself, undecided and trembling, his ear on the watch, his heart beating with great strokes, and he heard the sound of distant steps. " My God," he said, waiting for the steps that drew near, " what manner of monk is coming ? "

The steps were silent, and the door opened. Durtal in his alarm dared not look at the confessor, in whom he recognized the tall Trappist, with the imperious profile, whom he believed to be the abbot of the monastery.

His breath was taken away, and he drew back without saying a word.

Surprised at this silence, the prior said,—

" You have asked to make your confession, sir ? "

And at a sign from Durtal, he pointed out the prie-Dieu placed against the wall, and himself knelt down, turning his back.

Durtal braced himself, fell down at the prie-Dieu, and then completely lost his head. He had vaguely prepared how to enter on the matter, noted the points of his statement, classified his sins in some degree, and now remembered nothing.

The monk rose, sat down on a straw chair, leant towards the penitent, his hand behind his ear to hear the better.

He waited.

Durtal wished rather to die than speak ; he succeeded, however, in mastering himself, and bridling his shame ; he opened his lips, but no word came ; he remained overwhelmed, his head in his hands, repressing the tears he felt ready to fall.

The monk did not move.

At last he made a desperate effort, stammered the beginning of the Confiteor, and said,

" I have not confessed, since my childhood ; since then I have led a shameful life, I have . . ."

The words would not come.

The Trappist remained silent, and did not assist him at all.

"I have committed every kind of debauch, I have done
everything . . . everything . . ."

He choked, and the tears he had repressed flowed, he
wept, his body was shaken, his face hidden in his hands.

And as the prior, still bending over him, did not move,

"But I cannot," he cried; "I cannot."

All that life he could not bring out, stifled him; he
sobbed in despair at the view of his sins, and crushed also
at finding himself thus abandoned, without a word of
kindness, without help. It seemed to him that all was
giving way, that he was lost, repulsed even by Him who yet
had directed him to this abbey.

Then a hand was laid on his shoulder, while a gentle, low
voice said,

"Your soul is too tired for me to fatigue you with
questions, come back at nine o'clock to-morrow, we shall
have time before us, we shall not then be hurried by any
office; from now till then, think of the story of
Calvary; the cross, which was made for the sins of the
whole world, lay so heavily on the shoulders of the Saviour,
that His knees bent and He fell. A man of Cyrene passed
by who helped the Lord to bear it. You, in detesting, in
weeping for your sins, have alleviated and rendered lighter,
if one may say so, the cross of the burthen of your sins, and
having made it less heavy, have thus allowed Our Lord to
lift it.

"He has recompensed you by the most astonishing of
miracles, the miracle of having brought you here from so
far off. Thank Him, then, with all your heart, and be not
discomforted. You will say to-day for your penancè, the
Penitential Psalms, and the Litany of the Saints. I will
give you my blessing."

And the prior blessed him and went out. Durtal raised
himself up after his tears; what he feared so much had
happened; the monk who would take him in hand was
impassive, almost dumb. "Alas!" he thought, "my
abscesses are ripe, but it needs the cut of a lancet to open
them."

"After all," he went on, as he went upstairs to bathe
his eyes in his cell, "this Trappist was compassionate at
last, not so much in what he said, as the tone in which he

said it ; then, to be just, he was perhaps confused by my tears ; the Abbé Gévresin certainly did not tell Father Etienne that I was taking refuge in La Trappe in order to be converted, let us put ourselves in the place of a man living in God, far from the world, over whose head a shower bath is suddenly discharged.

"Well, we shall see to-morrow ;" and Durtal made haste to sponge his face, for it was nearly eleven o'clock and the office of Sext was about to begin.

He went to the chapel, which was almost empty, for the brothers were working at that time in the chocolate factory, and in the fields.

The fathers were in their places in the apse. The prior struck his bell, all signed themselves with a large cross, and on the left, where he could not see, for Durtal had taken the same place as in the morning, near Saint Joseph's altar, a voice arose :

"Ave Maria, gratia plena, Dominus tecum."

And the other part of the choir answered :

"Et benedictus fructus ventris tui, Jesus."

There was a moment's pause, and the pure thin voice of the old Trappist sang as before the office of Compline the evening before :

"Deus in adjutorium meum intende."

And the liturgy continued its course, with its "Gloria Patri," etc., during which the monks bowed their foreheads on their books, and with its series of psalms, accented in short tones on the one side, and long on the other.

Durtal, as he knelt, allowed himself to be rocked by the psalmody, too tired to be able to pray himself.

Then, when Sext was ended, all the fathers meditated, and Durtal caught a look of pity from the prior, who turned a little towards his bench. He understood that the monk implored the Saviour for him, and perhaps asked God to show him the way in which he might conduct himself on the morrow.

Durtal rejoined M. Bruno in the court ; they shook hands, and the oblate announced the presence of a new guest.

"A retreatant ?"

"No ; a curate from the neighbourhood of Lyons, he has come to see the abbot, who is ill."

"But I thought the abbot of Notre Dame de l'Atre was the
tall monk who led the office ? "

" Oh no ; that was the prior Father Maximin, you have
not seen the abbot, and I doubt if you will see him, for I
do not think he will leave his bed before you go."

They reached the guest-house, and found Father Etienne
making excuses to a short fat priest for the poor fare he
could offer.

He was a jovial priest, with strong features moulded in
yellow fat.

He joked M. Bruno, whom he seemed to have known
some time, on the sin of gluttony which must so often be
committed at La Trappe, then tasted, pretending a chuckle
of delight, the scentless bouquet of the poor wine he poured
out, and lastly, when he divided with a spoon the omelette
which was the main dish of their dinner, he pretended to
cut up a fowl, and to be delighted with the fine appearance
of the flesh ; saying to Durtal, "This is a barley-fed fowl,
may I offer you a wing ? "

This kind of pleasantry exasperated Durtal, who had no
wish to laugh that day ; he therefore was satisfied to make a
vague bow, wishing to himself that the end of dinner was at
hand.

The conversation continued between the priest and M.
Bruno.

After it had spread over various commonplaces, it took
a more definite form, in regard to an invisible otter which
plundered the abbey ponds.

"But, no doubt," said the curate, "you have found its lair ?"

" Never ; it is easy to see in the lain grass the paths it
traverses to get to the water, but we always lose its traces
at the same spot. We have watched for days with Father
Etienne, but it has never shown itself."

The abbé explained various traps which might be set
with advantage. Durtal thought of the otter-hunt which
Balzac tells so pleasantly at the beginning of his " Paysans,"
when the dinner came to an end.

The curate said grace, and said to M. Bruno, " Suppose we
take a turn ; the fresh air will do instead of the coffee,
which they forget to give us."

Durtal returned to his cell.

He felt himself emptied, injured, cheated, reduced to a

state of fibre, a state of pulp. His body, crushed by the nightmares of the night, enervated by the scene of the morning, needed entire rest, and if his soul had not still that infatuation which had broken it in tears at the monk's feet, it was sad and restless, and it also asked for silence, repose, and sleep.

"Let us see," said Durtal, "I must not give way, let me bestir myself."

He read the Penitential Psalms and the Litanies of the Saints; then he hesitated between two volumes of Saint Bonaventure and Saint Angela.

He decided on the Blessed Angela. She had sinned and had been converted, and she seemed less far from him, more intelligible, more helpful than the Seraphic Doctor, than a Saint who had always remained pure, sheltered from falls. For she too had been a carnal sinner; she too had reached the Saviour from afar.

A married woman, she lived in adultery and shame; lovers succeeded one another, and when she had exhausted them she threw them aside like husks. Suddenly grace rose in her and made her soul break forth; she went to confession, not daring to avow the more awful of her sins, and she communicated, thus grafting sacrilege upon her other faults.

She lived, day and night tortured by remorse, and finally prayed to Saint Francis of Assisi to help her; and the next night the saint appeared to her. "My sister," he said, "if you had called on me sooner, I should have granted your prayer before this." The next day she went to church, heard a priest preaching, understood she must address herself to him, and laid all before him in a full confession.

Then began the trials of an appalling life of purification. In blow after blow she lost her mother, her husband, her children; she went through such violent temptations to impurity that she was obliged to seize on lighted coals and cauterize the plague of her senses with fire.

During two years the demon sifted her. She parted her goods among the poor, assumed the habit of the Third Order of Saint Francis, gathered in the sick and infirm, and begged for them in the streets.

One day a feeling of sickness came over her before a leper whose sores were stinking. To punish herself she drank the water in which she had washed the sores; she was overcome with nausea ; and punished herself yet more by forcing herself to swallow a scab which had not gone down with the water and remained dry in her throat.

For years she dressed ulcers and meditated on the Passion of Christ. Then her novitiate of sorrows drew to a close and a radiant day of visions dawned on her. Jesus treated her as a spoilt child, called her, " My sweetest, my well-beloved daughter ; " He dispensed her from the necessity of eating, and nourished her only with the Sacred Species ; He called her, drew her, absorbed her in uncreated light, and by anticipating her inheritance, enabled her to understand, in life, the joys of heaven.

And she was so simple and timid that she feared in spite of all, for the memory of her sins alarmed her. She could not believe herself forgiven, and said to Christ ; " Ah, if I could but put myself in an iron collar and drag myself to the market-place to proclaim my shame."

And He consoled her : " Be easy, My daughter, My sufferings have atoned for your sins ; " and as she reproached herself for having lived in opulence and having delighted in clothes and jewels, He addressed her, smiling : " To buy you riches, I have wanted for everything ; you required a great number of clothes, and I had but one garment of which the soldiers stripped Me, for which they drew lots ; My nakedness was the expiation of your vanity in ornaments."

And all her conversations with Christ were in this tone. He passed His time in comforting this humble creature whom His benefits overwhelmed; and this has made her the most loving of the saints ! her work is a succession of spiritual outpourings and caresses ; her book is such a living hearth that beside it the volumes of other mystics seem but dull coal.

" Ah," said Durtal to himself, in turning over these pages, " it was indeed the Christ of Saint Francis, the God of mercy who spoke to this Franciscan ! " and he went on : " that ought to give me courage, for Angela of Foligno was as great a sinner as I am, but all her sins were remitted ! Yes, but then what a soul she had, while mine is good for nothing ; instead of loving, I reason ; nevertheless it is right to remember that the conditions of the Blessed Angela were more favourable than mine. Living in the thirteenth century

she had a shorter journey to make to approach God, for since
the Middle Ages, each century takes us further from Him!
she lived in a time full of miracles, which overflowed with
Saints. For me, I live in Paris in an age when miracles
are rare and Saints scarcely abound. And once away from
here, what a vista is before me of falling away, of soaking
myself in a stew of infamy, in a bath of the sins of great
cities."

"By the way " . . . he looked at his watch and started ; it
was two o'clock—"I have missed the office of Nones," he
said ; "I must simplify my complicated horary, or I shall
never know where I am ;" and at once he traced in a few
lines :

"Morning. Rise at 3 o'clock, or rather at 3.30. Breakfast at 7—Sext at 11, dinner at 11.30——Nones at 1.30—
Vespers at 5.15—Supper at 6, and Compline at 7.25."

"There, at least that is clear and easy to remember—If
only Father Etienne have not noticed my absence from
chapel ! "

He left his room. "Ah, here is the famous rule," he said
to himself, on seeing a framed table hung on the landing.

He approached and read :—

"Rule for Visitors."

It was composed of numerous paragraphs, and opened as
follows :—

"Those whom Divine Providence has guided to this
monastery are requested to note the following :—

"They will at all times avoid meeting the religious and
lay brothers, and will not go near their places of work.

"They are forbidden to leave the cloister for the farm or
the neighbourhood of the monastery."

Then came a series of instructions which he had already
seen on the printed horary.

Durtal skipped several paragraphs, and read again :—

"Visitors are requested not to write anything on the
doors, not to strike matches on the wall, and not to spill
water on the floor.

"They are not allowed to visit each other's rooms or to
speak to one another.

"Smoking is not allowed in the house."

"Nor indeed outside," thought Durtal. "But I want a cigarette badly ; " and he went down.

In the corridor he ran against Father Etienne, who immediately observed that he had not seen him in his place during the office. Durtal excused himself as well as he could. The monk said no more, but Durtal understood that he was observed, and that under his childlike aspect the guest-master would, where discipline was concerned, hold him in an iron grip. He was confirmed in this impression when at Vespers he noticed that the monk's first glance on entering the chapel was at him, but that day he felt so sore and broken that he cared but little. This sudden change of existence, and of the manner in which he had been accustomed to spend his time, astounded him, and since the crisis of the morning he had been in a kind of torpor which took from him all power of recovery. He drifted to the end of the day, no longer thinking of anything, sleeping as he stood, and when the evening came he fell on his bed a mere inert mass.

CHAPTER III.

He woke with a bound at eleven o'clock, with an impression of someone looking at him in his sleep. Lighting a match, he ascertained the time, and seeing no one, fell back in bed again, and slept at a stretch till four o'clock. Then he dressed himself in haste and ran to the church.

The vestibule, which had been dark on the previous evening, was lit up that morning, for an old monk was celebrating mass at the altar of St. Joseph. He was bald and infirm, with a white beard waving from side to side in long threads with every gust of wind.

A lay brother was assisting him, a small man with black hair and a shaven head, like a ball painted blue ; he looked like a bandit, with his beard in disorder and his worn-out robe of felt.

And the eyes of this bandit were gentle and startled like those of a little boy. He served the priest with an almost timid respect and a suppressed joy which was touching to see.

Others, kneeling on the flagstones, prayed with concentrated attention or read their mass. Durtal noticed the old man of eighty, immovable with outstretched face and closed eyes ; and the youth whose look of pity had helped him near the pond, was following the office in his prayer-book with attentive meditation. He looked about twenty years old, tall and strong ; his face, with an air of fatigue, was at once masculine and tender, with emaciated features, and a light beard which fell over his habit in a point.

Durtal gave way to his emotions in this chapel, where everyone did a little to help him, and thinking of the confession he was about to make, he implored the Saviour to help him, and prayed that the monk would completely explore his soul.

And he felt himself less dismayed, more master of himself, and firmer. He collected and pulled himself together, feeling a melancholy confusion, but he had no longer the sense of desolation which had overcome him the evening before. He set his mind on the idea that he would not abandon himself, that he would help himself with all his might, and that in any case he could not collect himself better.

These reflections were interrupted by the departure of the old Trappist, who had finished offering the sacrifice, and by the entry of the prior, who went up in the rotunda between two white fathers to say mass at the high altar.

Durtal was absorbed in his prayer-book, but he ceased reading when the priest had consumed the Species, for all rose, and he was amazed at a sight of which he had never dreamed, a communion of monks.

They advanced in single file, silent and with downcast eyes, and when the first arrived before the altar, he turned round to embrace the comrade who followed ; he in turn took in his arms the religious who followed him, and so on to the last. All, before receiving the Eucharist, exchanged the kiss of peace, then they knelt, communicated, and came back in single file, turning into the rotunda behind the altar.

And the return was unexpected ; with the white fathers at the head of the line, they made their way very slowly with closed eyes and joined hands. The faces seemed to be somewhat altered ; they were differently lit from within ; it seemed that the soul, driven by the power of the Sacrament against the sides of the body, filtered through the pores and lit up the skin with a special light of joy, with that kind of brightness which pours from white souls, and makes way like a rose-coloured vapour along the cheeks, and shines, as if concentrated, on the brow.

Watching the mechanical and hesitating gait of these monks, it seemed as if their bodies were no more than automata moving from habit, and that the souls, being elsewhere, gave no heed to them.

Durtal recognized the old lay brother, bent so much that his face disappeared in his beard which pressed against his chest, and his two great knotty hands trembled as he clasped them; he also noticed the tall young brother, his features seeming drawn on a dissolved surface, gliding with short steps, his eyes closed.

By a fatal chance he thought upon himself. He was the only one who did not communicate, for he saw M. Bruno coming last from behind the altar and returning to his place with folded arms. This exclusion brought home to him clearly how different he was, and how far apart, from those around him! All were admitted, and he alone remained outside. His unworthiness was more apparent, and he grew sad at being put aside, looked on, as he deserved to be, as a stranger, separated like the goat of the Scriptures, penned, far from the sheep, on the left of Christ.

These reflections were of use to him, for they relieved him of the terror of confession which was again coming over him. This act seemed to him so natural and just, in his necessary humiliation and unavoidable suffering, that a desire came over him to accomplish it at once, so that he might appear in this chapel purified and washed, and with at least some resemblance to the others.

When the mass was over, he made his way towards his cell to get a tablet of chocolate.

At the top of the stairs M. Bruno, with a large apron round him, was getting ready to clean the steps.

Durtal looked on him with surprise. The oblate smiled and shook hands with him.

" This is an excellent task for the soul," he said, showing his broom ; " it recalls modest sentiments which one is too inclined to forget after living in the world."

And he began sweeping vigorously, and collecting into a pan the dust which like pepper filled every crevice in the floor.

Durtal carried his tablet into the garden. " Let us consider," he said to himself as he nibbled it ; " supposing I took another walk and tried an unknown part of the wood ?" And he felt no wish to do so. " No, placed as I am, I would rather haunt the same spot and not leave the places to which I am accustomed ; I am already so little under control, and so easily disturbed, that I do not wish to risk anything by curiosity to see new places." And he went down to the cross pond. He went along the banks, and having reached the end, was astonished to find, a few steps farther, a stream spotted with green pellicules, hollowing its way between two hedges which fenced in the monastery. The fields stretched out beyond, and the roofs of a large farmhouse were visible in the trees, and all round the horizon on hills were forests which seemed to stop the way before the sky.

"I imagined the grounds were larger," he said to himself, retracing his steps ; and having reached the end of the cross pond, he gazed on the huge wooden crucifix reared in the air which was reflected in that black mirror. It sank down, seen from behind, trembling in the small waves stirred up by the breeze, and seemed to fall whirling round in that stretch of ink. And as the body of the marble Christ was hidden by the wood, only the two white arms which hung below the tree could be seen, twisted in the blackness of the water.

Seated on the grass, Durtal gazed on the hazy image of the recumbent cross, and thinking of his soul, which, like the pond, was tanned and stained by a bed of dead leaves and a dunghill of sins, he pitied the Saviour whom he was about to invite to bathe Himself there, for it would no longer be the Martyr of Golgotha to whom at all events death came on a hill, His head high, by daylight, in the open air ! but it would be by an increase of outrages, the abominable plunging of the crucified body, the head low, by night, into a depth of mud.

"Ah ! it would be time to spare Him, in filtering and clarifying me," he cried to himself. And the swan, till then motionless in an arm of the pond, swept over the lamentable image in advancing, and whitened the moving mourning of the waters with its peaceful reflection.

And Durtal thought of the absolution which he would perhaps obtain, and he reopened his prayer-book and numbered his faults ; and, slowly, as on the day before, he tapped, in his innermost being, a fountain of tears.

"I must control myself," he said, trembling at the idea that he would suffocate again and be unable to speak ; and he resolved to begin his confession at the other end, first going over the minor sins, keeping the great ones for the end so as to finish with the avowal of his carnal misdeeds : "if I succumb then I can explain myself in two words. My God ! may the prior only not remain silent as he did yesterday, may he only absolve me ! "

He shook off his sadness, left the pond, and returning to the lime avenue, he interested himself in a closer inspection of the trees. They raised huge trunks, covered with reddish-brown stonecrop, silvered grey by mosses ; and several that morning were wrapped as in a mantle trimmed with pearls, gossamer threads studded with drops of dew.

He sat down on a bench, but fearing a shower, for it looked threatening, he retired to his cell.

He felt no desire to read ; he was eager for, while yet he dreaded, the arrival of nine o'clock, to have done with, to get rid of the weight upon his soul, and he prayed mechanically, without knowing what he mumbled, always thinking on this confession, full of alarm and harassed with fears.

He went down a little before the time, and when he entered the auditorium his heart failed him.

In spite of himself, his eyes were fixed upon the prie-Dieu, where he had suffered so cruelly.

To think that he had to put himself on that hurdle again, to stretch himself on that rack of torture ! He tried to collect himself, to compose himself—and he drew himself up quickly ; he heard the footsteps of the monk. The door opened, and, for the first time, Durtal dared to look the prior in the face ; it seemed to be hardly the same man, nor the face, he had noticed from a distance ; the profile was so haughty, and the full face so sweet ; the eye dulled the proud energy of the features, an eye familiar and deep, when at the same time there was a quiet joy and a sad pity.

" Come," he said, " do not be disturbed, you are about to speak to our Saviour alone, who knows all your faults." And he knelt down and prayed for some time and came, as on the day before, to sit by the prie-Dieu ; he bent towards Durtal and listened.

Somewhat reassured, the penitent began without too great anguish. He accused himself of faults common to all men, want of charity towards his neighbour, evil speaking, hate, rash judgment, abuse, lies, vanity, anger, etc.

The monk interrupted him for a moment.

" You said, just now, I think, that in your youth you contracted debts ; have you paid them ? "

And on an affirmative sign from Durtal, he said, "Good," and went on,

"Have you belonged to any secret society? have you fought a duel?—I am obliged to ask these questions for they are reserved cases."

"No?—Good"—and he was silent.

"Before God, I accuse myself of everything," resumed Durtal; "as I confessed to you, yesterday, since my first communion I have given up everything; prayers, mass, everything; I have denied God, I have blasphemed, I had entirely lost faith."

And Durtal stopped.

He was reaching the sins of the flesh. His voice fell.

"Here I do not know how to explain myself," he said, keeping back his tears.

"Let us see," the monk said gently; "you told me yesterday that you had committed all those acts which are comprised in the sin of lust."

"Yes, father;" and trembling, he added, "Must I go into the details?"

"No, it is useless. I will confine myself to asking you, for it alters the nature of the sin, whether in your case there have been any private sins, or any sins committed between persons of the same sex?"

"Not since I left school."

"Have you committed adultery?"

"Yes."

"Am I to understand that in your relations with women, you have committed every possible excess?"

Durtal made an affirmative sign.

"That is sufficient."

And the monk was silent.

Durtal choked with disgust; the avowal of these horrors was a terrible effort to him; yet crushed as he was by shame, he was beginning to breathe, when suddenly he plunged his head again in his hands.

The remembrance of the sacrilege in which Madame Chantelouve had made him share, came back to him.

Hesitatingly he confessed that he had from curiosity assisted at a black mass, and that afterwards, without wishing it, he had defiled a Host which that woman, saturated with Satanism, concealed about her.

The prior listened without moving.

" Did you continue your visits to that woman ? "

" No ; that had given me a horror of her."

The Trappist reflected and said,

" That is all ? "

" I think I have confessed everything," replied Durtal.

The confessor was silent for some minutes, and then in a pensive voice, he murmured,

" I am struck, even more than yesterday, by the astonishing miracle which Heaven has worked in you.

" You were sick, so sick that what Martha said of the body of Lazarus might truly have been said of your soul, ' Iam foetet ! ' And Christ has, in some manner, raised you. Only do not deceive yourself, the conversion of a sinner is not his cure, but only his convalescence ; and this convalescence sometimes lasts for several years and is often long.

" It is expedient that you should determine from this moment to fortify yourself against any falling back, and to do all in your power for recovery. The preventive treatment consists of prayer, the sacrament of penance, and holy communion.

" Prayer ?—you know it, for without much prayer you could not have decided to come here after the troubled life you had led."

" Ah ! but I prayed so badly ! "

"It does not matter, as your wish was to pray well ! Confession ?—It was painful to you ; it will be less so now that you no longer have to avow the accumulated sins of years. The communion troubles me more ; for it is to be feared that when you have triumphed over the flesh the Demon should await you there, and endeavour to draw you away, for he knows well that, without this divine government, no healing is possible. You will therefore have to give this matter all your attention."

The monk reflected a minute, and then went on,

" The holy Eucharist . . . you will have more need of it than others, for you will be more unhappy than less cultured and simpler beings. You will be tortured by the imagination. It has made you sin much ; and, by a just recompense, it will make you suffer much ; it will be the badly closed door of your soul by which the Demon will enter and spread himself in you. Watch over this, and pray fervently that the Saviour may help you. Tell me, have you a rosary?"

"No, father."

"I feel," said the monk, "that the tone in which you said 'No' shows a certain hostility to the rosary."

"I admit that this mechanical manner of saying prayers wearies me a little; I do not know why, but it seems to me that at the end of some seconds I can no longer think of what I am saying; I should mock, and should certainly end by stammering out something stupid."

"You have known," quietly answered the prior, "some fathers of families. Their children stammer forth caresses, and tell them no matter what, and yet they are delighted to listen! Why should not our Lord, who is a good Father, love to hear His children when they drawl, or even when they talk nonsense?"

And after a pause he went on,

"I scent the devil's artifice in what you say, for the highest graces are attached to this crown of prayers. The most Blessed Virgin herself revealed to the saints this means of prayer; she declared she delighted in it; that should be enough to make us love it.

"Do it, then, for her who has powerfully assisted in your conversion, who has interceded with her Son to save you. Remember, also, that God wished that all graces should come to us through her. St. Bernard expressly declares 'Totum nos habere voluit per Mariam.'"

The monk paused anew, and added,

"However, the rosary enrages fools, and that is a sure sign. You will for a penance recite ten every day for a month."

He ceased, and then went on again, slowly,

"All of us, alas! retain that scar of original sin which is the inclination towards evil; each man encourages it more or less; as for you, since you grew up, the scar has been always open, but as you hate the wound God will close it.

"So I will say nothing of your past, as your repentance and your firm resolve to sin no more efface it. To-morrow, you will receive the pledge of reconciliation, you will communicate; after so many years the Lord will set out on the way to your soul and will rest there; approach

Him with great humility, and prepare yourself from this moment, by prayer, for this mysterious meeting of hearts which His goodness desires. Now say your act of contrition and I will give you holy absolution."

The monk raised his arms, and the sleeves of his white cowl rose above him like two wings. With uplifted eyes he uttered the imperious formula which breaks the bonds, and the three words, "Ego te absolvo," spoken more distinctly and slowly, fell upon Durtal, who trembled from head to foot. He almost sank to the ground, incapable of collecting himself or understanding himself, only feeling, in the clearest manner, that Christ Himself was present, near him in that place, and finding no word of thanks, he wept, ravished and bowed down under the great sign of the cross with which the monk enveloped him.

He seemed to be waking from a dream as the prior said to him,

" Rejoice, your life is dead ; it is buried in a cloister, and in a cloister it will be born again ; it is a good omen ; have confidence in our Lord and go in peace."

And the father added, pressing his hand, " Do not be afraid of disturbing me, I am entirely at your service, not only for confession, but for interviews and for any advice which may be of use to you ; you quite understand me ? "

They left the auditorium together ; the monk bowed to him in the corridor and disappeared. Durtal hesitated whether to meditate in his cell or in the church, when M. Bruno met him. Approaching Durtal he said,

" Well ? that is a fine weight the less on your stomach ! "

And as Durtal looked at him in astonishment he laughed.

" Do you think that an old sinner like me could not tell from a thousand nothings, if only from the way your poor eyes are now shining, that you had not been reconciled when you landed here ? Now I have just met the reverend father returning to the cloister, and I find you coming out of the auditorium ; there is no need to be particularly sly to guess that the great wash has just taken place."

" But," said Durtal, " you could not have seen the prior with me, for he had left before you came in, and he might have been performing some other duty."

" No, for he was not in his scapular ; he had his cowl

on. And as he never puts on that robe except to go to church or at confessions, I was quite certain that he came from the auditorium, as there is no office at this hour. I may also point out that as the Trappists do not come to confession in this room, two persons only could have been with him, you or I."

" You may say as much," replied Durtal, laughing.

Father Etienne met them in the midst of all this, and Durtal asked him for a rosary.

" But I have not one," exclaimed the monk.

" I have several," said M. Bruno, " and shall be most happy to offer you one. You will allow me, father ? . . ."

The monk acquiesced by a sign.

" Then if you will come with me," replied the oblate, addressing Durtal, " I will hand it you without delay."

They went upstairs together, and Durtal then learnt that M. Bruno lived in a room at the bottom of a small corridor, not far from his own.

His cell was very simply furnished with old middle-class furniture, a bed, a mahogany bureau, a large bookcase full of ascetic books, an earthenware stove and some arm-chairs. These articles were evidently the property of the oblate, for they were nothing like the furniture of La Trappe.

" Pray be seated," said M. Bruno, indicating an arm-chair ; and they conversed.

Having first discussed the Sacrament of Penance, the talk came round to the subject of Father Maximin, and Durtal admitted the high bearing of the prior had terrified him at first.

M. Bruno laughed. " Yes," he said, " he produces that effect on those who never come near him, but when one associates with him, one finds that he is only strict for himself, for no one is more indulgent to others. In every acceptation of the term he is a true and holy monk ; besides, he has great judgment. . . ."

And as Durtal spoke to him of the other cenobites, and wondered that there were some quite young men among them, M. Bruno replied,

" It is a mistake to suppose that most Trappists have lived in the world. The idea, so widespread, that people take refuge in La Trappe after long sorrows or disorderly lives, is bsolutely false ; besides, to be able to stand the weakening rule of the cloister it is necessary to begin young, and not to come in worn out with every kind of abuse.

"It is also necessary to avoid confounding misanthropy with the monastic vocation ; it is not hypochondria, but the divine call, which leads to La Trappe. There is a special grace, which makes all young men who have never lived in the world long to bury themselves in silence and therein suffer the hardest privations ; and they are happy as I hope you will be ; and yet their life is still more rigorous than you would think ; take the lay brothers, for example.

"Think of their giving themselves up to the most painful labour, and that they have not, like the fathers, the consolation of singing and assisting at all the offices ; remember that even their reward, the communion, is not very often conceded to them.

"Now think of the winter here. The cold is frightful ; in these decayed buildings nothing shuts properly, and the wind sweeps the house from top to bottom ; they freeze without fires, they sleep upon pallets, and they cannot help or encourage each other, for they hardly know each other, as all conversation is forbidden.

"Think, also, that these poor people never hear a kindly word, a word which would soothe and comfort them. They work from dawn till night, and the master never thanks them for their zeal, never tells the good workman that he is pleased.

"Consider, also, that in summer when men are hired from the neighbouring villages to reap the harvest, these rest when the sun scorches the fields ; they sit in their shirt sleeves under the shade of the ricks, and drink, if they are thirsty, and eat ; and the lay brother in his heavy clothes looks at them and goes on with his work, and neither eats nor drinks. Ah ! men must have well-tempered souls to stand such a life."

"But surely there must be some off days," said Durtal, "when the rule is relaxed ? "

"Never ; there is not even, as in some very strict orders—the Carmelites, to take one instance—an hour of recreation, when the religious may talk and laugh. Here, the silence is eternal."

"Even when they are together in the refectory ? "

" Then they read the Conferences of Cassien, the ' Holy Ladder ' of Climacus, the Lives of the Fathers of the Desert, or some other pious book."

" And on Sunday ? "

" On Sunday they rise an hour earlier ; but on the whole it is their best day, for they can follow all the offices and pass their whole time in church."

" Humility and self-denial carried to such an extent are superhuman ! " cried Durtal. " But they are surely given a sufficient quantity of strong nourishment to enable them to give themselves up from morning till evening to exhausting work in the fields ? "

M. Bruno smiled.

" They simply get vegetables which are not even as good as those which are served to us, and, by way of wine, they quench their thirst with a sour and insipid liquid, which leaves half a glass full of sediment. They get a pint each, and if they are thirsty they can add water."

" And how often do they eat ? "

" That depends. From the 14th September to Lent they only eat once a day, at half-past two—and during Lent this meal is put off till four o'clock. From Easter to the 14th September, when the Cistercian fast is less strict, dinner is at about half-past eleven, and to this may be added a light meal in the evening."

" It is frightful ! to work for months on one meal a day, two hours after noon, after being up since two o'clock in the morning ; having had no dinner the evening before."

" It is sometimes necessary to relax the rule a little, and when a monk fails from weakness he is not refused a morsel of bread.

" It would be well," continued M. Bruno, pensively, " to relax still further the grasp of these observances, for this question of food is becoming a veritable stumbling-block in recruiting for La Trappe ; souls which delight in these cloisters are forced to fly them, because their bodies cannot stand the rule." [1]

" And the fathers lead the same life as the lay brothers ? "

The opinion of M. Bruno has been lately adopted by all the abbeys of the order. In a General Chapter of La Trappe, held from the 12th to the 18th September, 1894, in Holland, at Tilburg, it was decided that except

" Absolutely—they set the example ; they all swallow the same pittance, and sleep in the same dormitory on similar beds ; there is complete equality. Only, the fathers have the advantage of singing the office and obtaining more frequent communions."

" Among the lay brothers there are two who have interested me particularly, one quite young, a tall fair man with a pointed beard, the other a very old man, quite bent ? "

" The young one is Brother Anacletus ; this young man is a veritable column of prayer, and one of the most precious recruits whom Heaven has bestowed upon our abbey. As for old Simeon, he is a child of La Trappe, for he was brought up in an orphanage of the order. There you have an extraordinary soul, a true saint, who already lives absorbed in God. We will talk of him at greater length another day, for it is time we went down ; the hour of Sext is near.

" Wait, here is the rosary which I am pleased to offer you. Allow me to add to it a medal of Saint Benedict." And he made over to Durtal a small wooden rosary, and the strange circle engraved with cabalistic letters, the amulet of Saint Benedict.

" Do you know the meaning of these signs ? "

" Yes ; I read it once in a pamphlet of Dom Guéranger."

" Good. And, by-the-bye, when do you communicate ? "

" To-morrow."

" To-morrow ; it is impossible ! "

" Why impossible ? "

" Because there will be only a single mass to-morrow, that of five o'clock, and at that the rule prevents your communicating alone. Father Benedict, who usually says an earlier mass, went away this morning and will not return for two days. There is some mistake."

in seasons of fasting, the monks might eat a little in the morning, dine at eleven, and sup in the evening.

Article CXVI. of the new constitutions, voted by this assembly of the Chapter and approved by the Holy See, is in effect thus conceived :—

'· Diebus quibus non jejunatur a Sancto Pascha usque ad Idus Septembris, Dominicis per totum annum et omnibus festis Sermonis aut feriatis extra Quadrigesimam, omnes monachi mane accipiant mixtum, hora undecima prandeant et ad seram cœnent.''

"But the prior positively declared to me that I should communicate to-morrow!" exclaimed Durtal. "Not all the fathers here, then, are priests?"

"No, in fact, as to priests, there is the abbot who is ill, the prior who will offer the sacrifice to-morrow at five o'clock, Father Benedict of whom I spoke to you, and another whom you have not seen and who is travelling. And then, if it had been possible, I also should have approached the Holy Table."

"Then, if the fathers are not all ordained, what difference is there between those who have obtained the priesthood and the simple lay brothers?"

"Education—to be a father a man must have studied, must know Latin, and in a word must not be what the lay brothers are, peasants or workmen. In any case I shall see the prior, and as to the communion to-morrow, I will let you know, after the office. But it is tiresome; it is a pity you could not have come up this morning, with us."

Durtal made a gesture of regret. He went into the chapel, dwelling on this misfortune and praying God not to delay his re-entry into grace any longer.

After Sext, the oblate came to rejoin him. "It is just as I thought," he said, "but nevertheless you will be admitted to take the Sacrament. The father prior has arranged with the curate who dines with us. He will say a mass to-morrow morning before leaving, and you will then communicate."

"Oh!" groaned Durtal.

This news broke his heart. That he should have come to La Trappe to receive the Eucharist from the hands of a priest of passage, from a jovial priest such as this man! "Ah, no, I have confessed to a monk, and I wished to receive the communion from a monk!" he exclaimed. "It would have been better to wait till Father Benedict returned—but what can I do? I can hardly explain to the prior how repugnant this unknown priest is to me, and how terribly painful it would be to me, after having gone through so much, to end by being thus reconciled in a cloister."

And he complained to God, telling Him that all the joy he might have felt in being purified and clean at last, was now spoilt by this disappointment,

He arrived at the refectory hanging his head.

The curate was there already. Seeing Durtal's sad demeanour, he charitably tried to cheer him, but the jokes he attempted produced the opposite effect. Durtal smiled in order to be polite, but his air was so wearied that M. Bruno, who saw it, turned the conversation and monopolized the priest.

Durtal was in a hurry for his dinner to be over. He had eaten his egg and was painfully swallowing a warm potato soup made with hot oil, which from its appearance might have been mistaken for vaseline ; but he now cared little about his food.

He said to himself, " It is dreadful to carry away an irritating and painful recollection of a first communion— and I know it will haunt me for ever. I know well enough that from a theological point of view it does not matter whether I am dealing with a priest or a Trappist ; both are but interpreters between God and me, but yet, I feel very well that it is not at all the same thing. For once at least I need a guarantee of certain holiness, and how can I have it with an ecclesiastic who hawks about jokes like a bagman ? " He stopped, remembering that the Abbé Gévresin, fearing this mistrust, had specially sent him to a Trappist monastery. " What a run of ill-luck ! " he said to himself.

He did not even hear the conversation which was going on beside him between the curate and the oblate.

He struggled with himself all alone, as he chewed, with his nose in his plate.

" I do not wish to communicate to-morrow," he went on, and he was shocked. He was cowardly, and becoming foolish at the last. Would not the Saviour give Himself to him all the same ?

He rose from the table, stirred by a dull anguish, and he wandered in the park and went down the paths as chance led him.

Another idea was now growing in him, an idea that Heaven was inflicting a trial upon him. " I want humility," he repeated. " Well, it is to punish me that I am refused the joy of being sanctified by a monk. Christ has forgiven me, that is much. Why should He do more by taking note of my preferences and granting my wishes ? "

This thought appeased him for a few minutes, and

reproaching himself for rebelling, he accused himself of
being unjust towards a priest who, after all, might be a
saint.

" Ah, enough of that," he said ; " I must accept the fact,
and try for once to be a little humble ! but I have to recite
my rosary." He seated himself on the grass and began.

He had not reached the second bead, when misunder-
standing again pursued him. He began again on the Pater
and Ave, and went on thinking no more of the sense of his
prayers, reflecting : " What ill-luck that the one monk who
says mass every day should be away, so that I have to go
through such a disappointment to-morrow ! "

He was silent and had a moment of calm, when suddenly
a new element of trouble burst upon him.

He looked at the rosary, of which he had told ten beads.

" Let me see, the prior told me to recite ten every day—
ten beads or ten rosaries ? "

" Beads," he said, and almost at the same moment
answered, " Rosaries."

He remained perplexed.

" But that is idiotic, he could not have told me to go
through the rosary ten times a day ; that would amount
to something like five hundred prayers on end ; no one
could do such a task without losing his wits. There is no
doubt, it is clear he meant ten beads !

" But no ! for if a confessor gives a penance, it must be
admitted that he would proportion it to the greatness of
the sins. And as I have such repugnance for these drops
of devotion taken in globules, it is natural that he should
gorge me with a large dose of the rosary !

" Still . . . still . . . it cannot be ! I should not have even
time for it all in Paris ; it is absurd ! "

And the idea that he was deceiving himself came inter-
mittently charging back.

"Still, there must be no haggling ; in ecclesiastical language
' ten ' means ten beads ; no doubt . . . but I remember very
well that after he pronounced the word rosary, the father
expressed himself thus : ' you will say ten,' that means ten
rosaries, for otherwise he would have specified ten . . . of a
rosary."

And so he thrust and parried with himself—" The father
had no need to put the dots on all the i's, if he were using

an ordinary phrase, known to everyone. This cavilling about the value of a word is ridiculous."

He tried to get rid of this torment by appealing to his reason ; and suddenly there came out some argument which unsettled him.

He found out that it was through cowardice, idleness, desire for contradiction and the necessity of rebelling, that he did not wish to wind his ten reels. "Of the two interpretations I have chosen the one which would relieve me of all effort and trouble, it is really too easy !—that alone proves that I deceive myself when I try to persuade myself that the prior only ordered me to pick out ten beads ! "

"Then a Pater, ten Aves, and a Gloria are nothing ; it is not heavy as a penance ! "

And then he answered himself, "But it is much for you, for you cannot even attempt so much without wandering."

He was turning on himself without advancing a step.

"I have never felt such hesitation," he said, trying to pull himself together ; "I am not stupid and yet I am fighting against my good sense, for it is not a matter of doubt, I know it, I ought to say ten Aves and not one more ! "

He remained nonplussed, almost frightened at his condition which was new to him.

And, to get out of the difficulty, to silence himself, he thought of a new idea to conciliate both parties, which seemed most concise and which presented at least a provisional solution.

"In any case," he reflected, " I cannot communicate to-morrow if I do not complete my penance to-day ; in the doubt, the wisest course is to yoke myself to the ten rosaries ; later I shall see ; if necessary I shall be able to consult the prior. It is true that he will think me an idiot if I speak to him of these rosaries ! so I shall not be able to ask him that ! "

"But then, you see, you admit yourself, it can only be ten beads ! "

He was furious with himself, and for silence' sake rushed upon the rosary.

He might well shut his eyes, and try to collect himself, it was impossible for him at the end of the second ten to follow his prayers ; he hesitated, forgetting the large beads of the Paters, losing his way in the small beads of the Aves, stamping on the ground.

To check himself, he thought of transporting himself in imagination at each dose, into one of the chapels of the Virgin which he loved to attend in Paris, at Notre Dame des Victoires, at St. Sulpice, at St. Severin ; but these Virgins were not numerous enough for him to dedicate each set of ten to them, so he evoked the Madonnas of the early masters, and, absorbed before their images, he turned the windlass of his prayers, not understanding what he mumbled, but praying the Mother of the Saviour to accept his pater-nosters, as she would receive the lost smoke of a censer forgotten before the altar.

" I cannot force myself any more," he said. He left this toil worried and crushed and wanting to take breath ; there were still three rosaries to exhaust.

And as soon as he had stopped, the question of the Eucharist, which had been dropped, came up again.

" Better not to communicate than to communicate badly ; " and it was impossible that after such debates and with such prejudices he could properly approach the Holy Table.

" Yes, but then what shall I do ?—in reality, was it not monstrous of me to dispute the monk's orders, to wish to carry them out in my own way, to take them up at my convenience ! If this goes on, I shall sin so much to-day that I shall have to confess again," he said.

To break through this feeling, he threw himself again upon his wheel, but then stupefied himself completely ; the device he had tried to keep himself before the Virgin at least was used up. When he wished to abstract himself and to bring up a recollection of Memling, he could not succeed, and his lip-prayers, wearying him, distressed him.

" My soul is worn out," he thought, " I should do well to let it rest, while I stay quiet."

He wandered round the pond, not knowing what to do next.

" Suppose I go to my cell ! " He went there, tried to become absorbed in the Little Office of the Virgin, and did not grasp a single word of the phrases he was reading. He went down and began to prowl about the park again.

" This is enough to drive me mad," he cried—and mournfully he exclaimed, " I ought to be happy, to pray in

peace and prepare myself for to-morrow's act, yet never
have I been so restless, so upset, so far from God !

" But I must finish this penance ! " Despair seized him,
and he was on the point of letting all go ; he mortified
himself again, and compelled himself to tell the beads.

He finished by despatching them ; he was at the end of
his powers. And he immediately found a new means of
torture.

He reproached himself with having moaned the prayers
negligently, without having even seriously tried to follow
their meaning. And he was on the point of beginning the
rosary over again, but in the face of the evident folly of
this suggestion he pulled himself up, refused to listen,
and then he worried himself again.

" It is none the less true that you have not literally
fulfilled the task assigned you by the confessor, for your
conscience reproaches you for your want of reflection and
your wandering."

" But I am half dead ! " he exclaimed. " I cannot go
through the exercises again in this condition ! "—and once
again he ended, by giving a casting vote, and finding a new
weakness.

By saying over another ten, thoughtfully pronouncing the
prayers with care, he might make up for all the beads of the
rosary which he had mumbled without understanding them.

And he tried to turn the crank, but as soon as he had got
out the Pater, he wandered ; he was obstinate in wishing to
grind out the Aves, but then his mind gave way and
became thoroughly distracted.

He stopped, thinking, " What is the use of it ? besides,
would one set of ten, however well said, be equal to five
hundred prayers that have missed fire ? and then why one
set of ten and not two, why not three ? it is absurd ! "

He grew angry ; " After all," he concluded, " these
repetitions are absurd ; Christ positively declared that we
should not use vain repetitions in our prayers. Then what
is the object of this wheel of Aves ? "

" If I dwell upon such ideas, if I cavil at the injunctions of
the monk, I am lost," said he suddenly ; and by an effort
of will, he stifled the revolt which was rumbling in him.

He took refuge in his cell ; the hours lengthened inter-
minably ; he killed the time by recapitulating all the same

objections with all the same answers. It was a repetition
of which he was himself ashamed.

" So much is certain, that I am the victim of an aberration," he said. " I do not speak of the Eucharist ; there
my thoughts may not be exact, but at least they are not
maddening, while as for this question of paternosters ! "

He confused himself so much that he felt hammered like
an anvil between these two opposing ideas, and finally sank
drowsily on a chair.

Thus he passed the time till the hour of vespers and
supper. After this meal he returned to the park.

And then the slumbering dispute revived and all came
back. A furious battle was raging within him. He remained
there, immovable, astounded, listening to himself, when
a rapid footstep approached and M. Bruno said to him,

" Take care, you are possessed by the devil ! "

And as Durtal, stupefied, did not answer,

" Yes," he said, " God sometimes allows me intuitions, and
I am certain at this moment that the devil is working in
you. Let us see, what is wrong with you ? "

" I . . . I do not know myself ; " and Durtal told him of
the extraordinary conflict about the rosary which had
been raging in him since the morning.

" But this is madness," exclaimed the oblate ; " it is ten
beads the prior ordered you to tell ; ten rosaries would be
impossible."

" I know it . . . and yet I doubt still."

" Always the same tactics," said M. Bruno ; " contriving
to render disgusting the thing you ought to do. Yes, the
devil wished to make the rosary odious to you by crushing
you with it. And what is there besides ? You do not wish
to communicate to-morrow ? "

" True," replied Durtal.

" I thought as much, when I was watching you at
supper. Ah ! well, after conversions the Evil One is at
work ; and it is nothing, believe me ; he was harder on me
than that."

He slipped his arm under Durtal's, and leading him to
the auditorium, begged him to wait, and disappeared.

Some minutes afterwards, the prior entered.

" Well," said he, " M. Bruno tells me that you are suffering. What is it, exactly ? "

" It is so stupid that I am ashamed to explain myself."

"You will never astonish a monk," said the prior, smiling.

" Well, I know precisely, I am certain that you gave me ten beads of the rosary to recite every day for a month, and, since this morning, I have been arguing with myself against all common sense, to convince myself that my daily penance is to be the rosary ten times."

" Hand me your rosary," said the monk, " and look at these ten beads ; well, that is all I prescribed for you, and all you have to recite. So you have told all the beads ten times to-day ? "

Durtal signified assent.

" And naturally you were perplexed, you lost all patience, and ended up by rambling."

And seeing Durtal's pitiful smile,

"Well, listen to me," declared the father, in an energetic tone, " I absolutely forbid you for the future to begin a prayer again ; it has been badly said ; so much the worse, go on, do not repeat it.

" I need not ask you if the idea of abstaining from communion occurred to you, for that comes of itself ; it is there that the enemy directs all his efforts. Do not listen to the devil's voice which would keep you away ; whatever happens you will communicate to-morrow. You should have no scruple, for I command you to receive the Sacrament ; I take it all upon myself.

" And now another question ; what sort of nights have you ? "

Durtal told him of the awful night of his arrival at La Trappe, and of the feeling of being spied upon which had awakened him the day before.

" We have long known these manifestations, they are without imminent danger ; do not therefore let them trouble you. At the same time, if they continue you will let me know, and we will not neglect attending to them."

And the Trappist left quietly, while Durtal remained thinking.

"I never doubted that those phenomena were satanic," he thought, " but I did not understand these attacks upon the soul, this charge at full speed against my reason which remains untouched, and yet is overcome ; that is remarkable ; if only this lesson may be useful to me so that I may not be unhorsed on the first alarm ! "

He went up to his cell again and a great peace fell upon him. All had died down at the voice of the monk ; he now only felt surprise at having been off the rails for hours ; he understood now that he had been assailed unawares and that the struggle had not been with himself.

He said his prayers and lay down. And, suddenly, the assault began again by new tactics he had not guessed at.

"No doubt I shall communicate to-morrow," he said to himself ; " but . . . but . . . am I prepared for such an act ? I ought to have collected my thoughts in the day-time, I ought to have thanked the Lord for having absolved me, and I have lost my time in nonsense."

" Why did I not say that just now to Father Maximin ? how is it I did not think of it ? Then I ought to have confessed again. And this priest who will give me the communion, this priest ! "

The horror which he felt for this man increased suddenly and became so vehement that he was astonished. " Ah, but there I am again knocked about by the enemy," he said, and he went on :

" All that shall not prevent me from receiving the Heavenly Bread to-morrow, for I have quite decided ; only how frightful it is that the Spirit of Malice should be allowed to oppress and harass me without respite while I have no sign from Heaven which does not interfere, and I know nothing.

" Ah ! Lord, if I were only certain this communion would please Thee ! Give me a sign, show me that I may ally my-self with Thee without remorse ; let the impossible take place so that, to-morrow, it may be a monk and not this priest . . ."

And he stopped himself, astonished at his boldness, asking himself how he dared ask for, and indicate a sign.

"It is idiotic ! " he exclaimed ; "in the first place, no one has a right to claim such favours from God ; and then, as He will not grant my prayer, what shall I have gained ? I shall infer from the refusal that my communion will be worth nothing ! "

And he prayed the Lord to forget his wish, excused himself for having formed it, and wished to convince himself that He should not take it into account, and, helped by the agitations of the day, he ended by falling asleep as he prayed.

CHAPTER IV.

WHEN he left his cell he said to himself, " This morning I shall communicate," and these words, which should have thrilled him through and through, woke no zeal in him. He remained dull, tired and caring for nothing, feeling cold in the depth of his being.

Nevertheless a fear stimulated him when he was outside. " I do not know," he said to himself, " when I must leave my seat and go to kneel before the priest ; I know that the congregation should communicate after the celebrant ; but at what moment exactly ought I to move ? It is indeed another misfortune that I should have to go up, alone, towards this Table which so disturbs me ; otherwise I shall only have to follow the others and at least be sure of not doing anything improperly."

He scrutinized the chapel as he went in, looking round for M. Bruno who, had he been by his side, might have kept off his scruples, but the oblate could not be found. Durtal sat down, disabled, dreaming of the sign he had asked for the evening before, endeavouring to throw off the recollection, thinking of it all the same.

He wished to examine himself and collect himself, and he was praying Heaven to forgive him his mental vacillations when M. Bruno came in, and went to kneel before the statue of the Virgin.

Almost at the same minute a brother, who had a beard like seaweed growing from a face like a pear, took up to the altar of St. Joseph a small rustic table on which he placed a basin, a towel, two vases and a napkin.

Before these preparations, which recalled the imminence of the Sacrifice, Durtal stiffened himself and succeeded by an effort in keeping back his anxieties and overthrowing his troubles, and escaping from himself he ardently implored

Our Lady to intervene so that he might, for this hour at
least, without wandering, pray in peace.

And when he had finished his prayer he lifted his eyes
and looked with a start at the priest who was advancing,
preceded by a lay brother, to celebrate mass.

This was not the curate whom he knew, but another,
younger, very tall, with a majestic air, with cheeks pale
and shaven, and a bald head.

Durtal was watching him solemnly marching towards the
altar with his eyes cast down when he suddenly noticed a
violet flame light up his fingers.

"He wears an episcopal ring, he is a bishop," thought
Durtal, who leant forward to see the colour of the vestment underneath the chasuble and alb.   It was white.

"Then it is a monk," he said, astounded ; and, mechanically, he turned towards the statue of the Virgin, summoning
the oblate by a hasty glance, who came to sit beside him.

"Who is he ? "

"Dom Anselm, the abbot of the monastery."

"He who was ill ? "

"Yes, he will give us communion."

Durtal fell upon his knees, suffocated, almost trembling :
he was not dreaming !   Heaven was answering him by the
sign on which he had fixed.

He ought to abase himself before God, to be overwhelmed
at His feet, to spread himself in a passion of gratitude ; he
knew and wished it !   And without knowing how, he was
exercising himself in seeking natural causes which might
account for the substitution of a monk for the priest.

No doubt it was very simple ; for on the whole, before
admitting a kind of miracle. . . . "anyhow, I will keep an
open mind, for after the ceremony I wish to clear the matter
up."

And he repelled the insinuations which crept into him.
Well ! what interest could there be in the motive of this
change ? there clearly must be a motive, but it was only a
consequence, an accessory ; the important point was the
supernatural will which had produced it.   "In any case
you have obtained more than you asked ; you have even a
better than the simple monk you wished for, you have the
abbot of La Trappe himself ! "   And he cried :   "Oh, to
believe, to believe like these poor lay brothers, not to be

endowed with a soul which is blown about by every wind ;
to have the faith of a child, an immovable faith, a faith
which cannot be rooted up ! Ah, Father, Father, bury it,
rivet it in me ! "

And such was his enthusiasm that he came out of
himself ; all around him seemed to disappear and he cried,
stammering, to Christ : " Lord, go not far from me. Let
Thy pity curb Thy justice ; be unjust, forgive me ; receive
Thy poor bedesman for communion, the poor in spirit ! "

M. Bruno touched his arm, and with a glance invited him
to accompany him. They went up to the altar and knelt
upon the flagstones, then, when the priest had blessed
them, they knelt closer on the single step, and the lay
brother handed them a napkin, for there was no bar or
cloth.

And the abbot of La Trappe gave them the communion.

They returned to their places. Durtal was in a state of
absolute torpor ; the Sacrament had, in a manner, anæsthe-
tized his mind ; he fell on his knees at his bench, incapable
even of unravelling what might be moving within him,
unable to rally and pull himself together.

And all of a sudden the impression came over him that he
was suffocating and wanted air ; the mass was finished ; he
rushed out and ran to his walk ; there he wished to take an
account of himself and he found nothing.

And in front of the cross pond, in whose waters the Christ
was drowning, there came over him an infinite melancholy,
a vast sadness.

It was a true syncope of the soul ; it lost consciousness ;
and when it came to itself, he was astonished that he had
not felt an unknown transport of joy ; then he dwelt on a
troublesome recollection, on the all too human side of the
deglutition of a God ; the Host had stuck against his palate,
and he had had to seek it with his tongue and roll it about
like a pancake in order to swallow it.

Ah ! it was still too material ! he only wanted a fluid, a
perfume a fire, a breath !

And he tried to explain to himself the treatment that the
Saviour made him follow.

All his anticipations had returned ; it was the absolution
and not the communion which had worked. When with
the confessor he had very clearly perceived the presence

of the Redeemer ; all his being had, in a manner, been injected with divine effluvia, and the Eucharist had only brought him suffocation and trouble.

It seemed that the effects of the two Sacraments had changed places the one with the other ; they had worked the wrong way with him ; Christ had been perceptible to his soul before and not afterwards.

"But it is easy enough to see," he reflected, "that the great question for me is to have an absolute certainty of my forgiveness ! By a special favour, Jesus has ratified my faith in the healing power of Penance. Why should He have done more ? "

"And then, what bounties would He reserve for His saints ? After all I am astonishing. It is too much that I should wish to be treated as He certainly treats Brother Anacletus and Brother Simeon."

"I have obtained more than I deserve. And what an answer I had, this very morning ? Yes, indeed, but why should such advances end suddenly in this recoil ? "

And making his way towards the abbey to eat his bread and cheese, he said to himself : " My error towards God is to be always arguing, when I ought to adore stupidly as these monks here do. Ah ! to be able to keep silence, silence to one's self, that is indeed a grace ! "

He reached the refectory, which, as a rule, he had to himself, M. Bruno never coming to the meal at seven o'clock in the morning. He was beginning to cut himself a piece of bread, when the father guest-master appeared.

He had a whetstone and some knives in his hand, and smiling at Durtal, he said : " I am going to polish the knives of the monastery, for they want it badly." And he placed them on a table in a small room attached to the refectory.

" Well, are you satisfied ? " he said, on coming back.

" Certainly—but, what happened this morning, how is it I was communicated by the abbot of La Trappe, when I should have been by the curate who dines with me ? "

" Ah ! " exclaimed the monk, " I was as much surprised as you. On waking, the Father Abbot suddenly declared that he must say mass this morning. He got up in spite of the observations of the prior, who as a doctor, forbade him to leave his bed. Neither I, nor any one else, knows what took him. Then they told him that a retreatant would communicate and he answered ' Just so, I shall communicate him.' And then M. Bruno took the opportunity of also approaching the Sacrament, for he loves to receive our Saviour from the hands of Dom Anselm."

"And this arrangement also satisfied the curate," the monk went on, smiling ; " for he left La Trappe at an earlier hour this morning and has been able to say his mass in a parish where he was expected. . . . By the way, he told me to make his excuses to you for not having been able to bid you good-bye."

Durtal bowed. "There is no doubt about it," he thought, "God wished to give me an unmistakable answer."

" And your health ? "

" It is good, father ; I am astounded ; my digestion has never been so good as it is here ; to say nothing of the fact that the neuralgia, which I feared so much, has spared me."

" That shows that Heaven protects you."

" Yes, indeed. But now that I remember it, I have long wished to ask you this—how are your offices arranged ? They do not correspond with those printed in my prayer-book."

" No, they differ from yours, which belong to the Roman ritual. At the same time, the Vespers are almost similar, except sometimes the lessons, and then what may put you out is that ours are often preceded by the Vespers of the Blessed Virgin. As a general rule we have a psalm less in the office, and the lessons are nearly always short.

" Except," Father Etienne went on, smiling, " in Compline, the very one you recite. Thus you may have noticed we know nothing of ' In manus tuas, Domine,' which is one of the few short lessons sung in parish churches.

" We have also a special Proper of Saints ; we celebrate the commemoration of the Blessed of our order which you will not find in your books. In fact we follow the letter of the monastic breviary of Saint Benedict."

Durtal had finished his breakfast. He rose, fearing to trouble the father by his questions.

One word of the monk, however, was troubling his brain, that relating to the prior as a doctor; and before going out he spoke of this again to Father Etienne.

"No—the Reverend Father Maximin is not a doctor, but he understands simples very well, and he has a small pharmacy which is enough as long as no one is seriously ill."

"And in that case?"

"In that case the practitioner can be called in from one of the nearest towns, but no one is ever so ill as that; or else the end is approaching and the doctor's visit would be useless . . ."

"So on the whole the prior looks after soul and body at La Trappe."

The monk signified assent.

Durtal went out. He hoped to get rid of his suffocation by a long walk.

He took a road which he had not been along before, and came out on a glade where stood the ruins of an ancient convent, some bits of wall, truncated columns and capitals in the Roman style; unhappily these remains were in a deplorable condition, rough, covered with moss and riddled with holes like pumice stones.

He went on and came to the end of a long walk, at the top of which was a pond five or six times as large as the small one in the form of a cross, which he frequented.

The walk was planted with old oaks on each side, and in the middle, near a wooden bench, stood a cast-iron statue of the Virgin.

He groaned as he looked at it. The crime of the church followed him once more; even in this little chapel so full of divine compassion, all the statues came from the religious bazaars of Paris or Lyons.

He took his position below, near the pond whose banks were bordered by reeds surrounded by tufts of osiers; and he amused himself by examining the colours of these shrubs, with their smooth green leaves and stalks of citron yellow, or blood red, noticing the curling water which began to foam with a gust of wind. And the martins skimmed it, touching it with the tips of their wings from which drops of water fell like pearls of quicksilver. And the birds rose whirling above and giving out their cries of weet, weet, weet, while the dragon-flies shone brightly in the air which they slashed with blue flames.

"Peaceful refuge ! " thought Durtal ; " I ought to have come to rest here before." He sat down on a bed of moss and interested himself in the noiseless and active life of the waters. Now the splash and flash of the turn of a leaping carp ; now great spiders skating on the surface, making little circles and driving one against another, stopping, going back and making new rounds ; then, near him on the ground, Durtal noticed jumping, green grasshoppers with vermilion bellies, or, scaling the oaks, colonies of queer insects on whose backs a devil's head was painted in red lead on a black ground.

And above all that, if he raised his eyes, there was the silent upturned sea of heaven, a blue sea crested with surging white clouds like waves ; and at the same time this firmament moved in the water where it billowed under a blueish gray glass.

Durtal felt himself expand as he smoked cigarettes ; the melancholy which had oppressed him since the dawn began to melt away, and joy crept into him as he felt his soul was washed in the pool of the Sacraments and dried in the air of a cloister. And he was at once happy and uneasy ; happy, for the meeting he had had with the father guestmaster, had removed all the doubts he had entertained as to the supernatural side to the sudden change of a priest for a monk to communicate him ; happy, also, to know that not only had Christ not repulsed him in spite of all the disorders of his life, but that He was encouraging him and giving him pledges, ratifying the signs of His favours by perceptible acts. And nevertheless he was uneasy, for he knew himself to be barren, and felt that it was necessary for him to be grateful for this goodness by a struggle with himself and an entirely new existence differing completely from that he had hitherto led.

" Well, we shall see ! " and he went off to the office of Sext almost calmed, and thence to dinner, where he found M. Bruno.

" We will go for a walk to-day," said the oblate, rubbing his hands.

Durtal looked at him with astonishment.

"Yes, indeed, I thought that after a communion a little air outside the walls would do you good, and I proposed to the Reverend Father Abbot to free you from the rule for to-day, if the offer is not disagreeable to you."

"I gladly accept, and thank you sincerely for your kind attention," said Durtal.

They dined off a soup made with oil in which a stick of cabbage and some peas were swimming ; it was not bad, but the bread made at La Trappe reminded him, when stale, of the bread in the siege of Paris, and made the soup turn sour.

Then they tasted an egg with sorrel and some rice steeped in milk.

"If it suits you," said the oblate, "we will begin by paying a visit to Dom Anselm, who has expressed a wish to know you."

And M. Bruno led Durtal through a labyrinth of passages and staircases to a small cell where the abbot was. He was dressed like the fathers in a white robe and a black scapular ; only at the end of a violet cord he bore on his breast an abbot's cross of ivory, in the centre of which, under a round glass, some relics were inserted.

He gave his hand to Durtal and begged him to sit down.

Then he asked if the food seemed to be enough for him. And on receiving a reply in the affirmative from Durtal he inquired if the long silence did not weigh upon him too much.

"Not at all, this solitude suits me perfectly."

"Well," said the abbot, laughing, "you are one of the few laymen who have borne our rule so easily. Generally those who have tried to make a retreat here have been devoured by home sickness and spleen, and have had but one idea, to get away."

"Let us see," he said after a pause ; "it is not possible, all the same, that such a sudden change of habits should not bring with it some painful privations ; there must be at least one which you feel above all the others ? "

"True, I feel the want of being able to light a cigarette whenever I like."

The abbot answered smiling, "But I suppose you have not been entirely without smoking, since you came here ? "

"I should tell a lie if I said I had not smoked in secret."

" Why, bless me, tobacco was not foreseen by St. Benedict ; there is no mention of it in his rule, and I am therefore free to allow its use ; so smoke as many cigarettes as you like without being uneasy."

And Dom Anselm added :

" I hope shortly to have a little more time to myself, unless, indeed, I am obliged to keep my room, in that case I shall be happy to have a longer talk with you."

And the monk, who seemed exhausted, shook them by the hand.

Going down into the court with the oblate Durtal exclaimed,

" The Father Abbot is charming, and quite young."

" He is hardly forty."

" He appears to be really ill."

" Yes, he is not well, and he required no common energy to say his mass this morning ; but let us see, we will first of all visit the grounds of La Trappe which you can hardly have been over completely, then we will leave the enclosure and push on to the farm."

They started, skirting the remains of the ancient abbey, and as they walked, turning by the piece of water near which Durtal had been seated in the morning, M. Bruno entered into explanations about the ruins.

" This monastery was founded in 1127 by St. Bernard, who installed the Blessed Humbert as abbot, an epileptic Cistercian, whom he had cured by a miracle. At that time there were apparitions in the convent ; a legend relates that two angels came and cut one of the lilies planted in the cemetery every time one of the monks died.

" The second abbot was the Blessed Guerric, who was famous for his knowledge, his humility and his patience in enduring evils. We possess his relics and they are enclosed in the shrine under the high altar.

" But the most remarkable of the superiors, who succeeded each other here in the middle ages, was Peter Monoculus, whose story was written by his friend, the member of the synod, Thomas de Reuil.

" Pierre, called Monoculus, or the one-eyed, was a saint thirsting for austerities and sufferings. He was assailed by horrible temptations at which he laughed. Exasperated, the Devil attacked his body and, by fits of neuralgia, broke his

skull, but Heaven came to his aid and cured it. By
shedding tears from a spirit of penitence, Peter lost an eye,
and he thanked our Lord for this blessing, ' I had ' he said,
' two enemies ; I have escaped the first, but the one I
retain troubles me more than the one I have lost.'

"He worked miracles of healing. The king of France,
Louis VII., venerated him so much that, on seeing the
empty eyelid, he wished to kiss it. Monoculus died in
1186 ; they soaked linen cloths in his blood, and washed
his entrails in wine which was distributed, for the mixture
was a powerful remedy.

" The property of the abbey was then immense ; it
comprised all the country which surrounds us, kept up
several lazar houses in the neighbourhood, and was the
home of more than three hundred monks. Unfortunately
what happened to others happened to Notre-Dame de l'Atre.
Under the rule of abbots in commendam it declined, and
it was dying with only six religious to look after it when
the Revolution suppressed it. The church was then
pulled down and afterwards replaced by the rotunda
chapel.

"Only in 1875 the present house, which I think dates
from 1733, was reconciled and became a monastery again.
Trappists were brought here from Sainte Marie de la Mer,
in the diocese of Toulouse, and this small colony has
made Notre-Dame de l'Atre the Cistercian nursery you
see.

" Such, in few words, is the history of the convent," said
the oblate. " As for the ruins they are buried underground,
and no doubt precious fragments might be discovered, but
for want of money and men no excavations have been
made.

" In addition to the broken columns and the capitals we
passed, there remains from the old church a large statue of
the Virgin which has been erected in one of the corridors
of the abbey ; besides this there are two angels fairly well
preserved and which you may see down there at the end of
the cloister in a small chapel, hidden behind a curtain of
trees."

" A virgin, before which St. Bernard may possibly have
knelt, ought surely to have been put in the church on the
altar dedicated to Mary, for the coloured statue, which

surmounts it, is of crying ugliness—like that one also," said Durtal, pointing out in the distance the cast-iron Madonna which towered above the pond."

The oblate bowed his head and did not reply.

"Do you know," exclaimed Durtal, who in the face of this silence did not persist and changed the conversation, "do you know that I envy you living here?"

"It is certain that I do not deserve this favour, for, on the whole, the cloister is less an expiation than a reward; it is the only place where, far from the world and near heaven, the only place where a man may give himself up to this mystic life which only develops in solitude and silence."

"Yes, and if possible, I envy you yet more that you should have had the courage to venture into regions which, I confess, frightened me. And I know so well that, in spite of the spring-board of prayers and fasts, in spite of the green house, or orchid house atmosphere, wherein mysticism is grown, I should wither away in these regions without ever expanding again."

The oblate smiled. "What do you know about it?" he replied, "the thing is not done in an hour; the orchid you speak of does not flower in a day; the advance is so slow, that mortifications space themselves out, fatigues are distributed over years, and, on the whole, are easily borne.

"As a general rule it is necessary, to cross the distance which separates us from the Creator, to go through three grades to attain that science of Christian perfection which is called mysticism; we must live in turn the life of Purification, of Illumination and of Unity—to join the uncreated Good and be poured out in Him.

"It matters little that these three grand phases of ascetic existence subdivide themselves into an infinity of stages; which are degrees according to Saint Bonaventure, dwelling places according to Saint Teresa, steps according to Saint Angela; they may vary in length and number, according to the will of the Lord and the temperament of those who go through them. It is not disputed that the journey of the soul towards God includes, first, perpendicular and breakneck roads—these are the roads of the life of Purification—next, narrower paths still, but well marked out and accessible—these are the paths of the life of Illumination—

at length, a wide road almost smooth, the road of the life of unity, at the end of which the soul throws itself into the furnace of Love, and falls into the abyss of the most adorable Infinity !

" On the whole, these three ways are successively reserved to those who start in Christian asceticism, to those who practise it, and finally to those who attain to the supreme end, the death of self and the life in God.

"Long," pursued the oblate, " I have placed my desires beyond the horizon, yet I progress little ; I am scarcely disengaged from the life of Purification, scarcely . . ."

"And you do not fear—how shall I say—material infirmities, for if at last you succeed in attaining the limits of contemplation, you risk the ruin of your body for ever. Experience seems to show, in effect, that the deified soul acts on the constitution and brings incurable troubles."

The oblate smiled. " In the first place I should, no doubt, fail to attain to the last degree of initiation, the extreme point of mysticism ; then, supposing I attain it, what would corporal accidents be in the face of such results ?

" Let me also assure you that these accidents are neither so frequent nor so certain as you seem to think.

"A man may be a great mystic, or an admirable saint, and not be the subject of visible phenomena for those who surround him. Would you not think, for example, that levitation, or the flight of bodies in the air, which seems to constitute the highest state of rapture, is one of the rarest ? Whom can you quote to me ? Saint Teresa, Saint Christina the Admirable, Saint Peter of Alcantara, Dominic of Mary Jesus, Agnes of Bohemia, Margaret of the Blessed Sacrament, the Blessed Gorardesca of Pisa, and above all Saint Joseph of Cupertino, who raised himself at will from the ground. But they are ten or twenty out of thousands of the elect !

"And note well that these gifts do not prove their superiority over other Saints. Saint Teresa declares expressly : it must not be imagined that anyone, blessed as he may be in this respect, is better than those who are not so blessed, for our Lord directs each one according to his particular need.

"And then the doctrine of the Church is seen in the untiring prudence shown in the canonization of the dead.

Qualities and not extraordinary acts decide this; for the Church, miracles themselves are only secondary proofs, for she knows that the Spirit of Evil imitates them.

"In the lives of the Blessed you will find, too, the most unusual deeds, and more amazing phenomena than in the biographies of the Saints. These phenomena have rather hindered than helped them. After having beatified them for their virtues, the Church has put off—and no doubt for a long time—their promotion to the sovereign dignity of Saints.

"It is difficult, on the whole, to formulate an exact theory on this subject, for if the cause, if the mental action is the same in all mystics, it differs a little, as I have said, according to God's will and the character of the subjects; the difference of sex often changes the form of the mystic flow, though in essence it never varies; the rush of the Spirit from on High may produce different effects, but is none the less identical.

"The only observation we dare make in these matters is that women, as a rule, are more passive and less reserved, while men resist more violently the wishes of Heaven."

"That makes me think," said Durtal, "that even in religion there are souls which seem to have mistaken their sex. Saint Francis of Assisi, who was all love, had rather the feminine soul of a nun, and Saint Teresa, who was the most attentive of psychologists, had the virile soul of a monk. We might correctly speak of Saint Francis as a woman and Saint Teresa as a man."

The oblate smiled. "To return to your question," he resumed, "I do not at all believe that illness can be the necessary consequence of phenomena aroused by the impetuous force of mysticism."

"But look at Saint Colette, Lidwine, Saint Aldegonde, Jane-Mary of the Cross, Sister Emmerich and how many more who passed their existence, half paralyzed, upon a bed! They are a small minority. Besides, the Saints or Blessed ones whose names you quote were victims of substitution, expiating the sins of others, a part God had reserved to them; it is not, therefore, surprising that they were bed-ridden and cripples, and were constantly half dead.

"No, the truth is that mysticism can modify the needs of the body, without, for all that, having much effect on, or

destroying the health.   I know well, you would answer me
with that terrible phrase of Saint Hildegarde, a phrase at
once just and sinister : 'the Lord dwells not in the bodies
of the healthy and vigorous,' and you might add, with Saint
Teresa, that evils are more frequent in the last of the
castles of the soul.   Yes, but these saints hoist themselves
on the summit of life and retain God in a permanent
manner in their carnal shell.   Having reached this point,
nature, too feeble to support a perfect state, gives way, but,
I assert again, these cases are an exception and not a rule.
And, alas, such maladies are not contagious.

"I am quite aware," resumed the oblate, after a pause,
"that the very existence of mysticism is resolutely denied
by some who in consequence can never admit the possibility
of any influence over the bodily organs, but the experience
of this supernatural reality is from all time, and proofs
abound.

"Let us take the stomach for example.   Well, under the
heavenly influence, it becomes transformed, omits all
earthly nourishment and consumes the Holy Species only.

"Saint Catherine of Sienna and Angela of Foligno lived
for years exclusively on the Sacrament ; and this gift
devolved equally upon Saint Colette, Saint Lidwine,
Dominic of Paradise, Saint Columba of Rieti, Mary
Bagnesi, Rose of Lima, Saint Peter of Alcantara, Mother
Agnes of Langeac and on many others.

"Under the divine impress the senses of smell and taste
presented no less strange metamorphoses.   Saint Philip
Nevi, Saint Angela, Saint Margaret of Cortona recognized
a special taste in unleavened bread, when after the consecration there was no longer any wheat, but the very flesh of
Christ.   Saint Pacomius knew heretics by their foul smell ;
Saint Catherine of Siena, Saint Joseph of Cupertino and
Mother Agnes of Jesus discovered sins by their evil odours ;
Saint Hilarion, Saint Lutgarde, Gentilla of Ravenna, could
tell merely by the scent of those whom they met what faults
they had committed.

"And the Saints themselves, whether living or dead,
exhaled powerful perfumes.

"When Saint Francis de Paul and Venturini of Bergamo
offered the Sacrifice they smelt sweet.   Saint Joseph of
Cupertino secreted such fragrant odours that his track

could be followed ; and sometimes it was during illness that these aromas were diffused.

"The pus of Saint John of the Cross and of the Blessed Didée gave forth strong and distinct scent of lilies ; Barthole, the tertiary, gnawed to the bones by leprosy, gave out pleasant emanations, and the same was the case with Lidwine, Ida of Louvain, Saint Colette, Saint Humiliana, Maria-Victoria of Genoa, Dominic of Paradise, whose wounds were boxes of perfume, whence fresh scents escaped.

"And thus we can enumerate organs and senses one after another, and declare marvellous effects. Without speaking of those faithful stigmata which open or shut according to the Proper of the liturgical year, what is more astounding than the gift of bilocation, the power of doubling oneself, of being in two places at the same time, at the same moment ? And yet what numerous examples exist of this incredible fact : many are celebrated, amongst others those of Saint Antony of Padua, Saint Francis Xavier, Marie of Agreda, who was at the same time in her monastery in Spain and in Mexico when she was preaching to infidels, Mother Agnes of Jesus, who came to visit M. Olier at Paris without leaving her convent at Langeac. And, again, the action from on High seems singularly energetic when it takes hold of the central organ of circulation, the motor which drives the blood into all parts of the body.

"Numbers of the elect had such a burning heart that the linen they wore was singed ; the fire which consumed Ursula Benincasa, the foundress of the Theatines, was so strong that this saint breathed columns of smoke as soon as she opened her mouth ; Saint Catherine of Genoa dipped her feet or her hands in iced water and the water boiled ; snow melted round Saint Peter of Alcantara, and, one day when the blessed Gerlach was crossing a forest in the depth of winter he advised his companion, who walked behind him, and who could not go on, as his legs were numb, to put his feet into his footsteps, and immediately he ceased to feel cold.

"I will add that certain of these phenomena, which make freethinkers smile, have been renewed and have been verified quite recently.

"Linen scorched by the fire of the heart has been observed by Dr. Imbert-Gourbeyre on the stigmatized Palma d'Oria,

and phenomena of high mysticism, which no science can
explain, were watched in the case of Louise Lateau, minute
by minute, and noted and controlled by Professor Rohling,
Dr. Lafebvre, Dr. Imbert Gourbeyre, Dr. de Noüe, by
medical delegates from all countries. . . .

"But here we are," said the oblate; "excuse me, I will
go first to show you the way."

They had left the enclosure as he spoke, and cutting
across the fields, reached an immense farm. Trappists bowed
respectfully as they entered the court yard. M. Bruno,
addressing himself to one of them, asked him to be good
enough to take them over the property.

The lay brother took them to the cattle sheds, then to
the stables, then to the poultry yard ; Durtal, who was not
interested in such sights, confined himself to admiring the
grace of these good people. No one spoke, but they replied
to questions by signs and winks.

"But how do they communicate with each other ? " asked
Durtal, when they were outside the farm.

"You have just seen ; they correspond by signs ; they
have a simpler alphabet than that of the deaf and dumb, for
each idea that they may require to express for their common
work is foreseen.

"Thus the word 'wash' is translated by one hand
tapping on the other ; the word 'vegetable' by scratch-
ing the left forefinger ; sleep is feigned by leaning the
head upon the fist ; drink by raising a closed hand to the
lips. And for more spiritual expressions they employ a
like method. Confession is translated by a finger kissed
and laid upon the heart ; holy water by five fingers of the
left hand clasped on which a cross is made with the thumb
of the right hand ; fasting by fingers which close the mouth ;
the word 'yesterday' by turning the arm back towards the
shoulder ; shame by covering the eyes with the hand."

"But supposing they wished to indicate me, who am
not one of themselves, how would they set about it ? "

"They would use the sign of 'guest,' which they make
by stretching out the hand and bringing it near the body."

"That means that I come to them from far, an open and
even transparent fact if you like."

They went silently along a walk which led down into the
labour fields.

" I have not noticed Brother Anacletus or old Simeon among these monks," exclaimed Durtal, suddenly.

" They are not occupied on the farm ; Brother Anacletus is employed in the chocolate factory, and Brother Simeon looks after the pigs ; both are working in the immediate neighbourhood of the monastery. If you like, we will go and wish Simeon good-morning."

And the oblate added, " You can tell them, when you go back to Paris, that you have seen a real saint, such as existed in the eleventh century ; he carries us back to the time of St. Francis of Assisi ; he is in some sense the reincarnation of that astonishing Juniper whose innocent exploits the Fioretti celebrate for us. You know that work ? "

" Yes ; after the Golden Legend it is the book on which the soul of the Middle Ages is most clearly impressed."

" But to return to Simeon ; this old man is a saint of uncommon simplicity. Here is one proof out of a thousand. Several months ago I was in the prior's cell when Brother Simeon appeared. He made use of the ordinary formula in asking permission to speak, ' Benedicite.' Father Maximin replied ' Dominus,' and on this word, which permitted him to speak, the brother showed his glasses and said he could no longer see clearly.

" ' That is not very surprising,' said the prior, ' you have been using the same glasses for nearly ten years, and since then your eyes may well have become weaker ; never mind, we will find the number which suits your sight now.'

" As he spoke, Father Maximin mechanically moved the glass of the spectacles between his hands, and suddenly he laughed, showing me his fingers, which were black. He turned round, took a cloth, cleaned the spectacles, and replacing them on the brother's nose, said to him, ' Do you see, Brother Simeon ? '

" And the old man, astonished, cried ' Yes . . . I see ! '

" But this is only one side of this good man. Another is the love of his beasts. When a sow is going to bring forth, he asks permission to pass the night by her, and delivers her, looking after her like his child, weeps when they sell his little pigs or when the big ones are sent to the slaughter-house ! And how all the animals adore him ! "

" Truly," the oblate went on, after a silence, " God loves simple souls above all, for he loads Brother Simeon with graces. Alone, here, he can reabsorb and even prevent the demoniacal accidents which arise in cloisters. Then we assist at strange performances : one fine morning all the pigs fall on their sides ; they are ill and at the point of death.

" Simeon, who knows the origin of these evils, cries to the Devil : ' Wait, wait, and you will see ! ' He runs for holy water, and sprinkles them with it, praying the while, and all the beasts who were dying jump up, frisking about and wagging their tails.

" As for diabolic incursions into the convent itself, they are but too real, and sometimes are only driven back after persistent prayers and energetic fastings ; at certain times in most convents the Demon sows a harvest of hobgoblins of whom no one knows how to get rid. Here, the father abbot, the prior, and all those who are priests have failed ; it was necessary, to give efficacy to the exorcisms, that the humble lay brother should intervene ; so, to forestall new attacks, he has obtained the right to wash the monastery with holy water and to use prayers whenever he thinks well to do so.

" He has the power of feeling where the Evil One is hidden, and he follows him, tracks him, and finally casts him out."

" Here is the piggery," continued M. Bruno, showing a tumble-down old place in front of the left wing of the cloister, surrounded by palisades ; and he added,

" I warn you, the old man grunts like a pig, but he will not answer your questions except by signs."

" But he can speak to his animals ? "

" Yes, to them only."

The oblate opened a small door, and the lay brother, all bent, lifted his head with difficulty.

" Good-day, brother," said M. Bruno ; " here is a gentleman who would like to see your pupils."

There was a grunt of joy on the lips of the old man. He smiled and invited them by a sign to follow him.

He introduced them into a shed, and Durtal recoiled, deafened by horrible cries, suffocated by the pestilential heat of the liquid manure. All the pigs jumped up behind their barrier, and howled with joy at the sight of the brother.

"Peace, peace," said the old man, in a gentle voice ; and lifting an arm over the paling, he caressed the snouts which, on smelling him, were almost suffocated by grunting.

He drew Durtal aside by the arm, and making him lean over the trellis work, showed him an enormous sow with a snub nose, of English breed, a monstrous animal surrounded by a company of sucking pigs which rushed, as if mad, at her teats.

"Yes, my beauty ; go, my beauty," murmured the old man, stroking her bristles with his hand.

And the sow looked at him with little languishing eyes, and licked his fingers ; she ended by screaming abominably when he went away.

And Brother Simeon showed off other pupils, pigs with ears like the mouth of a trumpet and corkscrew tails, sows whose stomachs trailed and whose feet seemed hardly outside their bodies, new-born pigs which sucked ravenously at the teats, larger ones, who delighted in chasing each other about and rolled in the mud, snorting.

Durtal complimented him on the beasts, and the old man was jubilant, wiping his face with his great hand ; then, on the oblate inquiring about the litter of some sow, he felt his fingers in a row ; replying to the observation that the animals were very greedy, by stretching his arms to heaven, showing the empty troughs, lifting ends of wood, tearing up tufts of grass which he carried to his lips, grunting as if he had his muzzle full.

Then he took them into the courtyard, placed them against the wall, opened a door beyond, and hid himself. A formidable boar passed like a waterspout, upset a wheelbarrow, scattering everything round him with a noise like a shell bursting ; then he broke into a gallop all round the courtyard, and ended by taking a header into a sea of liquid manure. He wallowed, turned head over heels, kicked about with his four feet in the air, and got up black and disgusting as the inside of a chimney.

After this he halted, grunted a cheerful note, and wished to fawn on the monk, who checked him with a gesture.

"Your boar is splendid !" said Durtal.

And the lay brother looked on Durtal with moist eyes
as he rubbed his neck with his hand, sighing.

" That means they are going to kill him soon," said the
oblate.

And the old man acquiesced with a melancholy shake of
his head.

They left him, thanking him for his kindness.

" When I think of how this being, who is devoted to the
lowest duties, prays in church, I long to kneel before him
and, like his pigs, kiss his hands ! " exclaimed Durtal after
a silence.

" Brother Simeon is an angelic being," replied the oblate.
" He lives the Unitive life, his soul plunged, drowned in the
divine essence.   Under a rough exterior an absolutely
white soul, a soul without sin, lives in this poor body ; it is
right that God should spoil him !   As I have told you, He
has given him all power over the Demon ; and in certain
cases He allows him also the power of healing by the imposi-
tion of hands.   He has renewed here the wonderful cures of
the ancient saints."

They ceased speaking, and, warned by the bells which
were ringing for Vespers, they moved towards the church.

And, coming to himself again, trying to recover, Durtal
remained astounded.   Monastic life retarded time.   How
many weeks had he been at La Trappe, and how many days
since had he approached the Sacraments ? that was lost in
the distance.   Ah, life was double in these cloisters !
And yet he was not tired of it ; he had bent himself easily
to the hard rule, and, in spite of the scanty meals, he felt no
sick headaches or failing ; he had never felt so well !—but
what remained was a feeling of stifling, of restrained sighs,
this burning melancholy for hours, and, more than all, this
vague anxiety at listening again within himself, and hearing
united in his person the voices of this Trinity, God, the
Devil, and Man.

" This is not the peace of the soul I dreamed of—and it is
even worse than at Paris," he said to himself, recalling the
maddening trial of the rosary—" and yet—how can I explain
it ? I am happy here all the same."

CHAPTER V.

RISING, somewhat earlier than his wont, Durtal went down to the chapel. The office of Matins was over, but some lay brothers, amongst whom was Brother Simeon, were praying on their knees on the ground.

The sight of this holy swine-herd threw Durtal into a long train of thought. He tried in vain to penetrate into the sanctuary of that soul, hidden like an invisible chapel behind the dung-hill rampart of a body ; he did not even succeed in representing to himself the docile and clinging soul of this man, who had attained the highest state to which the human creature can reach here below.

" What a power of prayer he has," thought he, as he looked at the old man.

He remembered the details of his interview the evening before. " It is true," he thought, " that in this monk I find something of the charm of that brother Juniper, whose surprising simplicity has come down through the ages."

And he brought to mind the adventures of that Franciscan whom his companions left one day by himself in the convent, telling him to prepare dinner against their return.

Juniper reflected, " What an amount of time is spent in preparing food ! The brothers who take turns in that work have not even time to pray "—and desiring to lighten the work of those who should succeed him in the kitchen, he determined to cook such plentiful dishes that the community might dine on them for a fortnight.

He lighted all the stoves, procured, we are not told how, enormous boilers, filled them with water, threw into them, pell-mell, eggs with their shells, chickens with their feathers,

vegetables he had neglected to trim, and before a fire which
would roast an ox, he exerted himself to pile up and stir the
ridiculous jumble of his stock-pots.

When the brothers came home, and sat down in the
refectory, he ran, his face browned and his hands burnt,
and joyously served up his stew. The superior asked him
if he were not mad, while he remained stupefied that no
one gobbled up this astonishing mess. He declared in all
humility that he thought he was doing a service to his
brethren, and only when he observed that so much food
would be wasted, did he weep hot tears, and declare himself
a wretch ; he cried that he was good for nothing but to
spoil the property of Almighty God, while the monks
smiled, admiring this debauch of charity, and the excess of
Juniper's simplicity.

" Brother Simeon would be humble enough and simple
enough to renew again such splendid jokes," thought
Durtal, " but better still than the good Franciscan, he
recalls the memory of that astonishing Saint Joseph of
Cupertino, of whom the oblate spoke yesterday."

He, who called himself brother Ass, was a charming and
poor creature, so modest, and so ignorant, that he was
turned away wherever he went. He passed through life,
with open mouth, thrusting himself eagerly against all the
cloisters that repulsed him. He wandered about unable to
perform even the lowest tasks. He was, to use a popular expression, a regular butter-fingers, and broke whatever he
touched. They ordered him to go and fetch water, and he
wandered without understanding, absorbed in God, and at
the end, when no one thought about it any more, brought
some after a month.

A monastery of Capucins which had received him, got
rid of him. He went his way, vaguely, out of his orbit
among the towns, stumbled into another convent where he
employed himself in taking care of the animals, whom
he adored, and he rose into a perpetual ecstasy, revealing
himself as the most singular of wonder workers, putting the
demons to flight, and healing the sick. He was at once
idiotic and sublime ; in the hagiography he stands alone,
and seems to figure there to furnish a proof that the soul
is identified with Eternal Wisdom, rather by ignorance
than by science.

" He also loves animals," said Durtal to himself, as he looked at old Simeon ; " and he too puts to flight the Evil One, and works cures by his sanctity.

" In a time when all men are exclusively haunted by the thoughts of luxury and lucre, the soul appears extraordinary when divested of its bark, as the candid and naked soul of this good monk. He is eighty years old and more, and he has led from his youth up the restricted life of the Trappists ; he probably does not know in what time he lives, nor what latitudes he inhabits, whether he is in America or in France, for he has never read a newspaper, and outside rumours do not reach him.

" He does not even know the taste of flesh meat or wine ; he has no notion of money, of which he does not suspect the value nor the appearance ; he does not imagine how a woman is made ; and save for the breeding of his pigs, he perhaps cannot even guess the meaning and the consequences of the sin of the flesh.

" He lives alone ringed round by silence, and buried in the shade ; he meditates on the mortifications of the Fathers in the Desert, which are read to him as he eats, and the frenzy of their fasts makes him ashamed of his miserable repast, and he accuses himself that he is so well to do.

" Ah ! this Father Simeon is innocent ; he knows nothing that we know, and knows that of which all others are ignorant ; his education has been taken in hand by the Lord Himself, who teaches him truths which we cannot comprehend, models his soul after heaven, infuses Himself into him, possesses him, and deifies him in the union of Blessedness.

" This puts us somewhat at a distance from hypocrites and devout persons ; as far indeed as modern Catholicism is from Mysticism, for certainly that religion is as grovelling on the ground as Mysticism is high !

" And that is true. Instead of directing all our forces to that unknown end, of taking our soul to fashion it in that form of a dove which the Middle Ages gave to the pyxes ; instead of making it the shrine where the Host reposes in the very image of the Holy Spirit, the Catholic confines himself to trying to conceal his conscience, to deceive his Judge by the fear of a salutary hell ; he acts not by choice, but by fear : he with the aid of his clergy, and the help of his imbecile literature, and his feeble press, has made of religion a mere fetishism, a ridiculous worship composed of statuettes and alms boxes ; candles and chromo-lithographs ; he has materialized the ideal of Love, in inventing an entirely physical devotion to the Sacred Heart.

"What baseness of conception!" continued Durtal, who had come out of the chapel, and was strolling along the bank of the great pond. He looked at the reeds, which bent like an harvest still green, under a puff of wind ; then he half saw as he leant forward, an old boat, which bore almost effaced on its blueish hull the name "Alleluia." This bark disappeared under the tufts of leaves round which were twined the bells of the convolvulus, a symbolic flower, since it widens out like a chalice, and has the dead white of a wafer.

The scent of the water, at once enticing and bitter, intoxicated him. "Ah!" he thought, "happiness certainly consists in being restricted to a place closely locked, a prison very confined, or a chapel always open," and he caught himself up : "Ah! there is Brother Anacletus ;" the lay brother was coming towards him, bending under a hamper.

He passed before Durtal, smiling at him with his eyes : and while he went his way, Durtal thought, "This man is a true friend of mine ; when I was suffering so much before my confession, he expressed all to me in a look. To-day when he believes me serener, and more joyous, he is content, and shows it to me by a smile ; and I shall never speak to him, I shall never thank him, I shall never even know who he is, I shall perhaps never even see him again.

"In leaving this place, I shall keep a friend, for whom I too feel affection ; yet neither of us has even exchanged a gesture with the other.

"After all," he thought, "does not this absolute reserve make our friendship more perfect ? it is stamped in the eternal distance, it remains mysterious and incomplete, and more certain."

While thinking over these reflections, Durtal went towards the chapel, where the Office called him, and thence to the refectory.

He was surprised to find the table laid only for one. "What has happened to M. Bruno ? Yet I may as well wait a while," and to kill time, he occupied himself by reading a printed card, hung upon the wall.

It was a sort of advertisement which began thus :

" ETERNITY.

" Fellow sinners, you will die.   Be ye always ready.

" Watch then, pray without ceasing, never forget the Four Last Things which you see here traced

> " Death, the gate of Eternity,
> Judgment, which decides Eternity,
> Hell, the abode of unhappy Eternity,
> Paradise, the abode of blessed Eternity."

Father Etienne interrupted Durtal, telling him that M. Bruno had gone to Saint Landry to make some purchases, and would only return at bed-time at eight o'clock.   " Dine then without waiting, and make haste, or all your dishes will be cold."

" And how is the father abbot ? "

" Better, he keeps his room still, but he hopes to be able to come down a while, the day after to-morrow, and assist at least at some of the offices."

And the monk bowed and disappeared.

Durtal seated himself at table, ate some bean broth, swallowed a soft-boiled egg and a spoonful of warm beans, then once outside, he passed along the chapel, entered it, and knelt before the altar of the Virgin ; but at once the spirit of blasphemy filled him ; he wished, whatever it cost him, to insult the Virgin ; it seemed to him that he would experience a sharp joy, an acute pleasure in soiling her ; but he restrained himself, he wrinkled his face not to allow the coal-heaver's abuse, which was on his lips, to escape.

And he detested these abominations ; he revolted against them, strove against them with horror ; and the impulse became so irresistible, that in order to keep silence he was obliged to bite his lips till they bled.

" This is somewhat strong," he said, " to hear grumbling in oneself, the contrary of what one is thinking ; " but he had need to call to his help all his will, he felt that he should yield, and spit out all these impurities ; wherefore he fled, thinking, that should he find no means of resistance, it were better to vomit this filth in the court rather than in the church,

And so soon as he quitted the chapel this madness of
blasphemy ceased ; he walked along the pond astonished
by the strange violence of the attack.

Little by little there came to him the unexplained intuition of a danger that menaced him. As a beast that scents
a hidden enemy, he looked with precaution within himself,
and ended by seeing a black point on the horizon of his
soul, and suddenly, before he had time to reconnoitre, and
take account of the danger he saw arising, this point
extended, and covered him with its shadow ; there was no
more light in him.

He had that minute of unrest which precedes the storm,
and in the anxious silence of his being, arguments fell like
drops of rain.

The painful effects of the Sacrament justified themselves,
had he not proceeded in such a way that his communion
could not but be unfaithful ? Evidently ; instead of collecting
and straining himself, he had passed an afternoon of revolt
and anger ; the very evening before he had unworthily
judged an ecclesiastic whose only wrong was that he took
pleasure in the vanity of easy jokes. Had he confessed this
injustice, and these revolts ? Not the least in the world ;
and after the communion still less ; had he, as he should
have done, shut himself up alone with his Guest ? He had
abandoned Him, without thinking more of Him ; had quitted
his innermost cell, had taken a walk in the wood, had
not even been present at the Offices.

" But come, come, this blame is foolish. I communicated,
just as I was, on the formal order of the confessor ; as for
the walk, I did not ask for it nor wish for it. M.
Bruno, in agreement with the abbot of La Trappe,
decided it would do me good ; I have then nothing to
reproach myself with ; I am blameless.

" This does not prove that you would not have done better
to spend the day in prayer, in the church.

" But," he cried, " with such a system one could not move,
one could not eat, nor sleep, for one should never leave the
church. There must be time for everything, or the devil
take it all !

" No doubt, but a more diligent soul would have refused
that excursion, just because it was pleasant ; would have
avoided it, out of mortification, in a spirit of penance."

"Evidently, but " . . . these scruples tortured him ; " the fact is," he said, "I might have employed my afternoon more wholesomely than that ; " to believe that he had spent it ill was but a step, and he made it. He pelted himself for an hour, sweating with agony, heaping on himself imaginary sins, and entering so far on that road that he ended by suddenly realizing his position and understanding he was out of the right track.

The story of the rosary returned to his memory, and then he blamed himself for allowing himself to be again driven into a corner by the demon. He began to breathe again, to regain his footing, when other attacks equally formidable presented themselves.

It was no longer an insinuation of arguments which ran drop by drop, but a furious rain, which threw itself like an avalanche on his soul. The storm, of which the wave of scruples was only the prelude, burst in its fulness ; and in the panic of the first moment, in the violence of the tempest, the enemy unmasked his batteries, and struck him to the heart.

He had got no good from that communion, but he was also too young at it. Ah ! indeed, was he to believe that because a priest uttered five Latin words over a bit of unleavened bread, that bread was transubstantiated into the flesh of Christ ? That a child should accept such nonsense, might be possible, but that a man past forty should listen to such formidable shams, was excessive ; almost disquieting.

And these insinuations lashed him like hail showers : how could bread made of wheat before, have only the appearance of wheat afterwards ; what is flesh that is neither seen nor felt ; what is a body, which has such ubiquity as to be at the same time on the altars of divers countries ; what is that power which is annihilated when the Host is not made of pure wheat ?

And this became a regular deluge which overwhelmed him, and yet like an impenetrable pile, that Faith he had acquired without ever having known how, remained immovable, disappeared under torrents of interrogation, but never stirred.

He revolted, and said to himself : " This only proves that the sacramental darkness of the Eucharist cannot be sounded. Moreover, if it were intelligible, it would not be divine. If the God whom we serve could be comprehended by reason,

He could not be worth the trouble of serving, said Tauler ; and the 'Imitation' declares plainly also at the end of the IVth book that if the works of God were such as man's intelligence could easily grasp, they would cease to be marvellous, and could not be qualified as ineffable."

And a mocking voice replied,

"That is what you call answering, avowing that there is nothing to answer."

"In fact," said Durtal, who reflected, "I have been present at spiritualistic experiences, where no trickery was possible. It was quite evident that there was no fluid from the spectators, no suggestion of persons surrounding the table who dictated the responses ; then in giving its raps, the table expressed itself suddenly in English, though no one spoke that language, then a few minutes later, addressing itself to me, who was at a distance from it, and consequently was not touching it, it told me this time in French, facts which I had forgotten, and I alone could know. I am then certainly obliged to suppose an element of the supernatural, using a table in guise of an interpreter, to accept if not the evocation of the dead, but at least the proved existence of ghosts.

"Then it is not more impossible, more surprising that Christ should substitute Himself for a piece of bread, than that a ghost should hide and brag in the foot of a table. These phenomena equally put our senses to rout ; but if one of them be undeniable, and spiritualistic manifestation certainly is so, what motives can we invoke to deny the other, which is moreover attested by thousands of saints ?

"After all," he went on with a smile, "we have already demonstration by the absurd, but this may be called demonstration by the abject, for if the Eucharistic mystery is sublime, it is not the same with spiritualism, which is after all only the latrine of the supernatural !"

"If this were the only enigma," began the voice again, "but all the Catholic doctrines are on the same model ; examine religion from its birth, and see if it do not always issue by an absurd dogma.

"Here is a God, infinitely perfect, infinitely good, a God who is not ignorant of past, present, or future. He knew then that Eve would sin ; therefore of two things, one ; either He is not good, in that He submitted her to that proof knowing that she had not power to stand it ; or again, He was not certain of her defeat ; in that case He is not omniscient, He is not perfect."

Durtal gave no answer to this dilemma ; which is in fact difficult to resolve.

" Yet," he thought, " we may at once exclude one of these two propositions, the latter ; for it is childish to concern ourselves about the future, when we have to do with God ; we judge Him by our miserable understanding, and there is for Him neither present nor past, nor future ; He sees them all at the same moment in light uncreate. For Him distance has no figure, and space is nought. It is consequently impossible to doubt that the Serpent will conquer. This amputated dilemma is then out of order."

" Be it so, but the other alternative remains ; what do you make of His goodness ? "

" His goodness ? " And Durtal had need to repeat again the arguments drawn from free will, and the promised coming of the Saviour ; and he was obliged to admit that these answers were weak.

And the voice became more pressing,

" Then you admit original sin ? "

" I am obliged to admit it, because it exists. What are heredity and atavism, save, under another name, the terrible sin of the beginning ? "

" And does it appear to you just that innocent generations should make amends now and always for the sin of the first man ? "

And as Durtal did not reply, the voice insinuated gently,

" This law is so iniquitous that it seems as if the Creator were ashamed of it, and that in order to punish Himself for His ferocity, and not to make Himself for ever execrated by His creature, He wished to suffer on the Cross, and expiate His crime in the person of His own Son."

" But," cried Durtal, exasperated, " God could not commit a crime and punish Himself : were that so, Jesus would be the Redeemer of His Father, and not ours ; it is madness ! "

Little by little he recovered his balance ; he recited slowly the Apostles' Creed, while the objections which demolished it, pressed one after the other within him.

" There is one fact certain," he said to himself, for in all

this tumult, he was perfectly lucid, " that for the moment
we are two persons in one. I can follow my reasonings,
and I hear on the other side, the sophisms my double
breathes in me. This duality has never appeared so clear
to me."

And the attack grew feebler, on this reflection ; it might
have been believed that the enemy now discovered was
beating a retreat.

But nothing of the kind ; after a short truce, the
assault began again on another point,

" Are you very sure that you have not suggested and
shown the blow to yourself? By having wished, you
have ended by begetting belief, and by implanting in yourself a fixed idea, disguised under the name of grace, round
which everything now clings. You complain that you did
not experience sensible joys after your communion ; this
simply proves that you were not careful enough, or that,
tired by the excess of the evening before, your imagination
showed itself unready to play the infatuating fairy story
you expected from yourself after the mass.

" Moreover, you ought to know that in these questions all
depends on the more or less feverish activity of the brain and
the senses ; see what takes place in the case of women, who
deceive themselves more easily than men ; for that again
declares the difference of conformations, the variety between
the sexes ; Christ gives Himself carnally under the appearances of bread ; that is mystical marriage, the divine union
consummated by the way of the lips ; He is indeed the
spouse of women, while we men, without willing it, by the
very lodestone of our nature, are more attracted by the
Virgin. But she does not give herself, like her Son, to us ;
she does not reside in the Sacrament ; possession is in her
case impossible ; she is our Mother, but she is not our
Spouse, as he is the Spouse of virgins.

" We conceive, therefore, that women are more violently
duped, that they adore better, and imagine more easily the
more they are petted. Moreover, M. Bruno said to you
yesterday, ' Woman is more passive, less rebellious to the
action of Heaven . . .'

" Well, what has that to do with me ; what does that
prove ? that the more we love the better we are loved : but
if that axiom is false, from the earthly point of view, it is

certainly exact from the divine point of view ; which would be monstrous, and would come to this, that the Lord would not treat the soul of a Poor Clare better than mine."

There was again a time of rest, and the attack turned and rushed on a new place.

" Then you believe in an eternal hell ? You suppose a God · more cruel than yourself, a God who has created people, without their having been consulted, without their having asked to be born ; and after having suffered during their existence, they will be again punished without mercy after their death ; but consider, if you were to see your worst enemy in torture, you would be taken by pity, and would ask pardon for him. You would pardon, and the Almighty be implacable ; you will admit this is to have a singular idea of Him."

Durtal was silent ; hell going on infinitely became in fact wearisome. The reply that it is legitimate, that punishment should be infinite, because rewards are so, was not decisive, since indeed it were the property of perfect goodness, to abridge the chastisements and prolong the joys.

" But, in fact," he said to himself, " Saint Catherine of Genoa has elucidated the question. She explains very well that God sends a ray of mercy, a current of pity into hell, that no damned soul suffers as much as it deserves to suffer ; that if expiation ought not to cease, it may be modified, and weakened, and become at length less rigorous, less intense.

" She remarks also, that at the moment of its separation from the body, the soul becomes obstinate or yields ; if it remain hardened and shows no contrition for its faults, its guilt cannot be remitted, since, after death, free will subsists no more ; the will which we possess at the moment of quitting the world remains invariable.

" If, on the contrary, it does not persist in those impenitent sentiments, a part of the repression will no doubt be removed ; and consequently is not devoted to a continual gehenna, as that which deliberately, while there is yet time, will not return to amendment, refuses in fact to lay aside its sins.

" Let us add that according to the saint, God does not even make the soul empty to be never polluted by sin, for it goes there of itself ; it is led there by the very nature of

its sins, it flings itself in as into its own good ; is, if one may
say so, naturally engulfed there.

"In fact we may imagine to ourselves a very small hell,
and a very large purgatory ; may imagine that hell is scantily
peopled, is only reserved for cases of rare wickedness,
that in reality the crowd of disincarnate souls presses into
Purgatory and there endures punishments proportioned to
the misdeeds it has willed here below. These ideas have
nothing which cannot be sustained, and they have the
advantage of being in accord with the ideas of mercy and
justice."

"Exactly," replied the voice in railing tones. "Man then
will do well to constrain himself ; he may steal, rob, kill
his father, and violate his daughter ; the price is the same ;
provided he repent at the last minute, he is saved ! "

"But no, contrition takes away the eternity of punishment
only, and not punishment itself ; everyone must be
punished or rewarded according to his works. He who
will be soiled by a parricide or an incest will bear a
chastisement different in pain and length to him who has
not committed them ; equality in expiatory suffering, in
reparative pain, does not exist.

"Moreover this idea of a purgative life after death is so
natural, so certain, that all religions assume it. All consider
the soul is a sort of air balloon, which cannot mount and
attain its last end in space except by throwing away its
ballast. In the religions of the East, the soul is re-incarn-
istic ; in order to purify itself it rubs itself against a new
body, like a blade in sandstone troughs, to brighten it. For
us Catholics it undergoes no terrestrial avatar, but it lightens
and scours itself, clears itself in the Purgatory, where God
transforms it, draws it out, extracts it little by little from
the dross of its sins, till it can raise itself and lose itself in
Him.

"To have done with this irritating question of a perpetual
hell, why not conceive that divine justice hesitates in
the majority of cases to pronounce inexorable decrees?
Humanity is for the most part composed of unconscious
rascals and fools, who do not take any count of the reach of
their faults. These are saved by their complete want of
comprehension. As for others who rot, knowing what they
do, they are evidently more blameworthy, but society

which hates superior beings takes on itself their punishment, humiliates and persecutes them ; and it is therefore
allowed us to hope that our Lord will pity these poor souls
so miserably pelted during their stay upon earth by a horde
of fools."

"Then there is every advantage in being imbecile, since
one is spared both on earth and in heaven ? "

"Ah ! certainly, and yet . . . and yet. . . What is the
good of discussion, since we cannot frame for ourselves the
least idea of the infinite justice of a God ? "

"Moreover, this is enough, these debates overwhelm me."
He tried to distract his thoughts from these subjects, and
would feign to break the obsession, betake himself to Paris ;
but five minutes had not passed before his double returned
to the charge.

He entered once more on that halting dilemma which
had so recently assailed the goodness of the Creator in
regard to the sins of man. "Purgatory is then exorbitant,
for after all," said he, "God knew that man would yield to
temptations ; then why allow them, and above all why
condemn them ? Is that goodness, is that justice ? "

"But it is a sophism," cried Durtal, growing angry.
"God has left to every man his liberty ; no one is tempted
beyond his power. If in certain cases, he allows the seduc-
tion to overpass our means of resistance, it is to recall us to
humility, to bring us back to Him by remorse, for other
causes which we know not, which it is not His business to
show us. Then probably those transgressions are appreci-
ated in a different way to those which we have practised
with our full accord."

"The liberty of man ! it is a pretty thing. Yes, let us
speak of it, and atavism, and our surroundings and diseases
of the brain, and of the marrow. Is a man driven by the
impulses of sickness, overwhelmed by troubles of the
generative organs, responsible for his acts ? "

"But what can be said if under these conditions these acts
are imputed to him on high. It is after all idiotic always
to compare divine justice to man's tribunals ; for it is
exactly the contrary ; human judgments are often so
infamous that they attest the existence of another equity.
Rather than the proofs of a theodicy, the magistrature proves
God ; for without Him, how can be satisfied that instinct of

justice so innate in each of us, that even the humblest beast
possesses it ? "

" Yet," replied the voice, " all this does not hinder the
change of character according as the stomach does its work ill
or well ; slander, anger, envy are accumulated bile, or faulty
digestion ; good temper, joy, come from a free circulation of
blood, the expansion of the body at will ; mystics are anemo-
nervous people ; your ecstatics are hysterical patients badly-
fed, madhouses are full of them ; they depend on science
when visions begin."

All at once Durtal recovered himself, the material arguments were but little disquieting, for none could remain
standing : all confounded the function and the organ, the
lodger and the lodging, the clock and the hour. Their
assertions rested on no base. To liken the happy lucidity
and unequalled genius of a Saint Teresa to the extravagances
of nymphomaniacs and other mad women were so obtuse,
so clumsy, that it could only raise a smile !

The mystery would remain complete ; no doctor has been
able to discover or could discover the psyche in those
round or fusiform cells, in the white matter or grey substance of the brain. They would recognize more or less
justly the organs which the soul uses to pull the strings of
the puppet, which it is condemned to move, but itself remains invisible ; it has gone, when after death they force
open the rooms of its habitation.

" No ; these newsmongers have no effect on me," Durtal
assured himself.

" But does this one do any better ?   Do you believe in the
utility of life, in the necessity of this endless chain, this tow-
age of sufferings, to be prolonged for the most part after
death ?   True goodness would have consisted in inventing
nothing, creating nothing, in leaving all as it was, in
nothingness, in peace."

The attack turned round on itself, and after apparent
variations, returned always to the same starting point.

Durtal lowered his head, for this argument dismasted him ;
all the replies which could be imagined were remarkably
weak, and the least feeble, that which consists in denying
to ourselves the right to judge because we only see the
details of the divine plan, because we can possess no general
view of it cannot avail against that terrible phrase of

Schopenhauer : "If God made the world I would not be that God, for the misery of the world would break my heart ! "

"There is no haggling in the matter," he said to himself. "I can quite understand that sorrow is the true disinfectant of souls, yet I am obliged to ask myself why the Creator has not invented a less atrocious way of purifying us ?

"Ah ! when I think of the sufferings shut up in madhouses, and hospital wards, I am revolted, and inclined to doubt everything.

"If, again, grief were an antiseptic for future misdeeds or a detersive for past faults, one might again understand, but now it falls indifferently on the bad and on the good ; it is blind. The best proof is the Virgin who was without spot, and who had not like her Son to expiate for us. She consequently ought not to be punished ; yet she too underwent at the foot of Calvary the punishment exacted by this horrible law.

"Good ; but then," replied Durtal, after a silence of reflection, "if the innocent Virgin has given us an example, by what right do we who are culpable dare to complain ?

"No ; we must therefore resolve to dwell in darkness, to live surrounded by enigmas. Money, love, nothing is clear ; chance if it exist is as mysterious as Providence, and indeed still more so; it is inexplicable. God is at least an origin of the unknown, a key.

"An origin which is itself another secret, a key which opens nothing !

"Ah ! it is irritating," he said to himself, "to be thus harassed in every sense. Enough of it ; besides these are questions which a theologian is alone able to discuss ; I am unarmed, the game is not equal ; I will not answer any more."

And he could not but hear a vague laughter which arose in him.

He quitted the garden, and directed his steps towards the chapel, but the fear of being seized again by the madness of blasphemy turned him away from it. Knowing not whither to go, he regained his cell, saying to himself, that he ought not to wrangle thus ; yes, but how could he help hearing the cavils which rose he knew not whence ? He almost shouted aloud : " Be silent, let the other speak ! "

When he was in his chamber he desired to pray, and fell on his knees at his bedside.

This was abominable ; for memories of Florence recurred to him. He rose, but the old aberrations returned.

He thought of that creature, her strange tastes, her mania for biting his ears, for drinking toilet scents in little glasses, for nibbling bread and butter with caviare, and dates. She was so wild, and so strange ; a fool no doubt, but obscure.

"And if she were in this room, before you, what would you do ? "

He stammered to himself : " I would try not to yield."

" You lie ; admit then that you would send your conversion, the monastery, all, to the devil."

He grew pale at the thought ; the possibility of his cowardice was a punishment. To have communicated, when one was no more certain of the future, no more certain of oneself, was almost a sacrilege, he thought.

And he became angry. Up till now he had kept right, but the vision of Florence subdued him. He threw himself, in desperation, on a chair, no longer knowing what would become of him, gathering what of courage remained to him to descend to the church, where the Office was beginning.

He dragged himself there, and held himself down, assailed by filthy temptations, disgusted with himself, feeling his will yielding, wounded in every part.

And when he was in the court he remained overwhelmed, asking himself where he could take shelter. Every place had become hostile to him ; in his cell were carnal memories, outside were temptations against Faith, " or rather," he cried, " I carry these with me always. My God, my God ! I was yesterday so tranquil."

He strolled by chance into an alley, when a new phenomenon arose.

He had had, up to this hour, in the sky within him, a rain of scruples, a tempest of doubts, a thunderstroke of lust ; now was silence and death.

Complete darkness was within him.

He sought his soul by groping for it, and found it inert, without consciousness, almost icy. He had a body living and healthy ; all his intelligence, all his reason, and his other powers, his other faculties, were benumbed little by

little, and stopped. In his being there was manifested an
effect at once analogous and contrary to that which curara
produces on the organism, when it circulates in the network
of the blood ; the members are paralyzed, no pain is
experienced, but cold rises, the soul ends by being sequestered
alive in a corpse ; in this case it was the living body that
detained a dead soul.

Harassed by fear, he disengaged himself with a supreme
effort, he would make a visit to himself, see where he was,
and like a sailor who descends into the hold in a ship
that has sprung a leak, he had to step backwards, for the
gangway was cut, the steps opened upon an abyss.

In spite of the terror which rushed upon him, he hung
fascinated over the hole, and by fixing the black point he
distinguished appearances ; in a light as of eclipse in
rarefied air, he perceived at the basis of himself the
panorama of his soul, a desert twilight on the horizons
that approached the night, and under this doubtful light
there seemed something like bare fields, a marsh heaped
with rubbish and cinders ; the place of the sins torn up by
the confessor remained visible, but besides the dry darnel
of dead vices which grew still, nothing budded.

He saw himself exhausted ; he knew that he had no further
force to extirpate the last roots, and he fancied that he
had again to sow the seed of virtues, to till this arid soil,
manure this dead ground. He felt himself incapable of all
work, and had at the same time the conviction that God
rejected him, that God would aid him no more. This
certainty tore him to pieces. It could not be expressed, for
nothing could translate the anxiety, the anguish of a
state through which he must have passed who could
understand it. The terror of a child who has never left its
mother's petticoats, and who is deserted, without warning,
in the open country in a fog, could only give a vestige of
an idea of it, and again by reason of his age the child after
having felt desolate would end by growing calmer, by
distracting himself from his grief, no longer seeing the
danger which surrounds him, while in this state is danger,
clinging and absolute, the immovable thought of abandonment, obstinate fear, which nothing diminishes, nothing
appeases.

One dare not advance nor retreat ; rather cast oneself on

the ground, with bowed head, and wait the end of what we know not, and be assured that the menaces we ignore, and those at which we guess, are removed. Durtal was at this point ; he could not return on his steps, for the way he had quitted horrified him. He would rather have died than return to Paris, there to begin again his carnal experiences, to live again his hours of libertinage and lassitude ; but if he could not again retrace his road, neither could he advance, for the road ended in a blind alley. If earth repulsed him, heaven at the same time was closed for him.

He was lying, half on his side, in the darkness, in the shade, he knew not where.

And this state was aggravated by an absolute failure to understand the causes which brought him there, was exaggerated by the memory of graces before received.

Durtal remembered the sweetness of the beginning, the caress of the divine touches, the steady progress without obstacles, the encounter with a solitary priest, his being sent to La Trappe, the very ease with which he bent to the monastic life, the absolution which had such truly sensible effects, the rapid and clear answer that he might communicate without fear.

And suddenly, without his will, he had in fact failed. He who had till then held him by the hand, refused to guide him, cast him off into the darkness without a word.

"All is over," he thought ; " I am condemned to float here below, like a waif which no one wants ; no shore is henceforward accessible, for if the world refuses me, I disgust God. Ah ! Lord, remember the garden of Gethsemani, the tragic defection of the Father whom Thou didst implore in unspeakable pangs." In the silence which received his cry he gave way, and yet he desired to react against this desolation, endeavoured to escape from his despair ; he prayed, and had again that very precise sensation that his petitions did not carry, were not even heard. He called her who superintends allegiance, the Mediatrix of pardon, to his aid, and he was persuaded that the Virgin heard him no longer.

He was silent and discouraged, while the shade grew still more dense, and complete darkness covered him. He did not then suffer any longer in the true sense of the word, but it was worse, for this was annihilation in the void, the giddiness of a man who is bent over a gulf ; and the scraps of reasoning which he could gather and knit together in this breaking up, ended by branching out into scruples.

He sought for any sins which since his communion might justify such a trial, and he could not find them. He even tried to magnify his small faults, enlarge his want of patience ; he wished to convince himself that he had taken a certain pleasure in finding the image of Florence in his cell, and he tortured himself so violently that he reanimated the soul, which had half fainted, by these moxas, and placed it again, without wishing it, in that acute state of scruples, in which it was when the crisis declared itself.

And in these brawling reflections he did not lose the sad faculty of analysis. He said to himself while gauging himself at a glance : " I am like the litter in a circus, trodden down by all the sorrows which go and come to play their parts. Doubts about Faith, which seemed to stretch into every sense, turned in fact in the same circle. And now scruples, from which I thought myself freed, reappear and course through me."

How should he explain this ? Was he who inflicted this torture on him the Spirit of Malice, or God ?

That he had been bruised by the Evil One was certain, the very nature of his attacks showed his handiwork, but how could this abandonment of God be explained, for in fact, the Demon could not prevent the Saviour from assisting him, and he was quite obliged to conclude that if he were martyrized by the one, the Other took no interest in him, let him be, and retired from him completely ?

This certainty deduced from precise observations, this reasoned assurance, finished him. He cried out from the anguish of it, looking at the pond by which he was walking, wishing he might fall in, thinking that death by drowning were preferable to such a life.

Then he trembled before the water which attracted him, and carried away his sorrows to the charm of the woods. He tried to wear himself out by long walking, but he wearied himself without effect, and he ended by sinking down worn and broken at the refectory table.

He looked at his plate, with no courage to eat, no desire to drink ; he breathed hard, and, exhausted as he was, could not keep in one place. He rose and wandered in the

court till Compline, and there in the chapel, where at least
he hoped to find some solace, was the crowning point of all ;
the mine went off ; the soul, sapped since the morning,
exploded.

On his knees, desolate, he tried again to invoke help,
and nothing came ; he choked, immured in so deep a
trench, under a vault so thick, that every appeal was stifled,
and no sound vibrated. Without courage, he wept with
his head in his hands, and while he complained to God that
He had brought him thither to punish him in a Trappist
monastery, ignoble visions assailed him.

Fluids passed before his face, and peopled the space with
priapisms. He did not see them with the eyes of his body,
which were in no degree hallucinated, but perceived them
outside him, and felt them within him ; in a word, the touch
was external, and the vision internal.

He tried to gaze on the statue of Saint Joseph, before
which he kept himself, and to see nothing but it, but
his eyes seemed to revolve, to see only within, and
were filled with indecencies. It was a medley of apparitions with undecided outlines, and confused colours, which
gained precision only in those parts coveted by the secular
infamy of man. And this changed again. The human
forms vanished. There remained only, in invisible land-
scapes of flesh, marshes reddened by the fires of what
sunset it was impossible to say, marshes shuddering under
the divided shelter of the grasses. Then the sensual spot
grew smaller still, but remained, and this time did not
move ; it was the growth of an unclean flood, the spreading
of the daisy of darkness, the unfolding of the lotos of the
caverns, hidden at the bottom of the valley.

And there, burning gasps excited Durtal, enwrapped
him, stifled him with furious gasps which drank his mouth.

He looked in spite of himself, unable to withdraw himself
from the outrages imposed by these violations, but the body
was still and remained calm, while the soul revolted with a
groan ; the temptation was then of no effect ; but if the
tricks only succeeded in suggesting to him disgust and
horror, they made him suffer beyond measure, while they
delayed ; all the days of his shameful existence came to the
surface, all these enticements to greedy desires crucified him.
Joined to the sum of sorrows accumulated since the dawn,

the overcharge of these sorrows overwhelmed him, and a cold sweat bathed him from head to foot.

He was in agony, and suddenly, as though he had come to overlook his ministers, and to see if his orders were carried out, the executioner himself entered on the scene. Durtal did not see him, but felt him, and it was indescribable. Since he had the impression of a real demoniac presence, his whole soul trembled and desired to fly, like a terrified bird that clings to the window-panes.

And it fell back exhausted ; then unlikely as it may appear, the parts of his life were inverted, the body was upright, and held its own, commanding the terrified soul, repressed this panic in a furious tension.

Durtal perceived very plainly and clearly for the first time the distinction, the separation of the soul from the body, and for the first time also, he was conscious of the phenomenon of a body, which had so tortured its companion by its needs and wants, to forget all its hatred in the common danger, and hinder her who resisted it, the habit of sinking.

He saw that in a flash, and suddenly all vanished. It seemed that the Demon had taken himself off, the wall of darkness which encompassed Durtal opened, and light issued from all parts ; with an immense impulse the " Salve Regina," springing up from the choir, swept aside the phantoms, and put the goblins to flight.

The elevated cordial of this chant restored him. He took courage, and began again to hope that this frightful desertion might cease ; he prayed, and his petitions found vent ; he understood that they were at last heard.

The Office was at an end ; he gained the guest-house, and when he appeared so worn out and pale before Father Etienne and the oblate, they cried : " What is the matter with you ? "

He sank on a chair, and endeavoured to describe to them the terrible Calvary he had climbed. " This has lasted," he said, " for more than nine hours ; I wonder that I have not gone mad ; " and he added, " Yet I never could have believed that the soul could suffer so much."

The face of the father was illuminated. He pressed Durtal's hands and said,

" Rejoice, my brother, you have been treated here like a monk."

"How is that?" said Durtal, surprised.

"Yes, this agony, for there is no other word to define the horror of the state, is one of the most serious trials which God inflicts on us; it is one of the operations of the purgative life. Be happy, for it is a great grace which Jesus does to you."

"And this proves that your conversion is good," affirmed the oblate.

"God! But it was not He at any rate who insinuated doubts about the Faith, who caused to be born in me that madness of scruples, who raised in me that spirit of blasphemy, who caressed my face with disgusting apparitions."

"No, but He allows it. It is frightful, I know it," said the guest-master. "God conceals Himself, and however you may call on Him, He does not answer you. You think yourself deserted, yet He is very near you; and while He effaces Himself, Satan advances. He twists you about, places a microscope over your faults, his malice gnaws your brain like a dull file, and when to all this are joined, to try you to the utmost, impure visions. . . ."

The Trappist stopped; then, speaking to himself, he said, slowly,

"It would be nothing to be in presence of a real temptation, of a true woman in flesh and bone, but these appearances on which imagination works, are horrible!"

"And I used to think there was peace in the cloister!"

"No, we are here on this earth to strive, and it is just in the cloister that the Lowest works; there, souls escape him, and he will at all price conquer them. No place on earth is more haunted by him than a cell, no one is more harassed than a monk."

"A story which is told in the Lives of the Fathers in the Desert, is typical from this point of view. One demon only was charged to watch a town; and he went to sleep while two or three hundred demons who had orders to guard a monastery had no rest, but behaved themselves, here is the place for the phrase, like very devils.

"And indeed, the mission to increase the sin of the towns is a sinecure, for Satan holds them, though they are not aware of it; all then he has to do is to torment them so as to take from them trust in God, since all obey him without his taking the least trouble about it.

"And so he keeps his legions to besiege convents where resistance is determined. And indeed, you see the way in which he conducts the attack."

" Ah ! " exclaimed Durtal, " it is not he who makes you suffer the most ; for what is worse than scruples, worse than temptations against purity, or against the Faith, is the supposed abandonment of Heaven ; no, nothing can describe that."

"That is what mystical theology calls 'the Night Obscure,'" answered M. Bruno.

And Durtal exclaimed,

" Ah ! now I am with you ; I remember . . . That is why Saint John of the Cross declares that it is impossible to describe the sorrows of that night, and why he exaggerates nothing when he says, that one is then plunged alive into hell.

" And I doubted the veracity of his books, I accused him of excess ; rather he minimized. Only one must have felt this oneself to believe it."

" And you have seen nothing," the oblate replied quietly; " you have passed through the first portion of that night, through the night of the senses ; it is terrible enough, as I know by experience, but it is nothing in comparison with the Night of the Spirit which sometimes succeeds it. That is the exact image of the sufferings which our Lord endured in the Garden of Olives, when, sweating blood, He cried at the end of His force, ' Lord, let this chalice pass from me.'

" This is so terrible . . ." and M. Bruno was silent and grew pale. " Whoever has undergone that martyrdom," he said, after a pause, " knows beforehand what awaits the damned in another life."

" But," said the monk, " the hour of bedtime has struck. There exists but one remedy for all these evils, the Holy Eucharist ; to-morrow, Sunday, the community approaches the Sacrament ; you must join us."

" But I cannot communicate in the state in which I am . . . ."

" Well, then, be up to-night, at three o'clock. I will come for you to your cell, and will take you to Father Maximin, who confesses us at that time."

And without waiting for his answer, the guest-master pressed his hand and went.

"He is right," said the oblate ; " it is the true remedy."

And when he had regained his room, Durtal thought,

"I now understand why the Abbé Gévresin made such a point of lending me Saint John of the Cross ; he knew that I should enter into the ' Night Obscure ' ; he did not dare warn me clearly, for fear of alarming me, and yet he would put me on my guard against despair, and aid me by the remembrance here of that reading. Only how could he think that in such a shipwreck I should remember anything !

" All this makes me think that I have omitted to write to him, and that to-morrow I must keep my promise by sending him a letter."

And he thought again of Saint John of the Cross, that extraordinary Carmelite who described so placidly that terrible phase of the mystic genesis.

He took count of the lucidity, the power of spirit of this saint, explaining the most obscure vicissitude of the soul and the least known, catching and following the operations of God, who dealt with that soul, pressed it in His hands, squeezed it like a sponge, then let it suck up again, fill itself out with sorrows, then wrung it again ; making it drip tears of blood to cleanse it.

CHAPTER VI.

"No," said Durtal, in a whisper, "I will not take the place of these good people."

"But I assure you it is quite the same to them."

And while Durtal was still refusing to go before the lay brothers who were waiting their turn for confession, Father Etienne insisted : "I will stay with you, and as soon as the cell is free, you will enter."

Durtal was then on the landing of a staircase on every step of which was posted a brother kneeling or standing, his head wrapped in his hood, his face turned to the wall. All were sifting and closely examining their souls.

"Of what sins can they really accuse themselves ? " thought Durtal. "Who knows ? " he continued, perceiving Brother Anacletus, his head sunk on his breast, and his hands joined, "who knows if he does not reproach himself for the discreet affection he has for me ; for in monasteries all friendship is forbidden ! "

And he called to memory in the " Way of Perfection " of Saint Teresa, a page at once glowing and icy in which she cries out on the nothingness of human ties, declares that friendship is a weakness, and asserts clearly that every nun who desires to see her relations is imperfect.

"Come," said Father Etienne, who interrupted these reflections, and pushed him towards the door of the cell out of which a monk came. Father Maximin was there, seated close to a prie-Dieu.

Durtal knelt, and told him briefly his scruples and strifes of the evening before.

"What has happened to you is not surprising after a conversion ; indeed, it is a good sign, for those persons alone

for whom God has views are submitted to these proofs,"
said the monk slowly, when Durtal had ended his story.

And he continued,

"Now that you have no more grave sins, the Demon
endeavours to drown you by spitting at you. In fact, in
these episodes of malice at bay, there is for you temptation
and no sin.

"You have, if I may sum up what you have said, undergone temptation of the flesh, and of Faith, and you have
been tortured by scruples.

"Let us leave on one side the sensual visions ; such as they
have been were produced independently of your will, painful
no doubt, but ineffectual.

"Doubts about Faith are more dangerous.

"Steep yourself in this truth that besides prayer there
exists but one efficacious remedy against this evil, to despise
it.

"Satan is pride ; despise him, and at once his audacity
gives way ; he speaks ; shrug your shoulders and he is
silent. You must not discuss with him ; however good a
reasoner you may be, you will be worsted, for he is a most
tricky dialectician."

"Yes, but what can I do ? I do not wish to listen to
him, but I hear him all the same. I was obliged to answer
him if only to refute him."

"And it was just on that he counted to subdue you ;
keep this carefully in your mind ; in order to let you give
him an easy throw, he will present you at need grotesque
arguments, and so soon as he sees you confident, simply
satisfied with the excellence of your replies, he will involve
you in sophisms so specious that you will fight in vain to
solve them.

"No ; I repeat to you, had you the best reasons to oppose
to him, do not riposte, refuse the strife."

The prior was silent ; then he began again, quietly,

"There are two ways of getting rid of a thing which
troubles you—to throw it far away, or let it fall. To throw
it to a distance demands an effort of which one may not be
capable ; to let it fall imposes no fatigue, is simple, without
danger, within the reach of all.

"To throw to a distance implies again a certain interest,
a certain animation, perhaps even a certain fear ; to let it

fall is indifference, complete contempt ; believe me, use this means and Satan will fly.

"This weapon of contempt will be also all-powerful to conquer the assault of scruples, if in combats of this nature the person assailed sees clear. Unfortunately, the peculiarity of scruples is to alarm people, to make them lose at once the clearing breeze, and then it is indispensable to have recourse to a priest to defend oneself.

"Indeed," pursued the monk, who had interrupted himself a moment to think—"the closer one looks the less one sees ; one becomes short-sighted the moment one observes ; it is necessary to place oneself at a certain point of view to distinguish objects, for when they are very close they become as confused as if they were far. Therefore in such a case we must have recourse to the confessor, who is neither too distant, nor too near, who holds himself precisely at the spot where objects detach themselves in their relief. Only it is with scruples as with certain maladies which, when they are not taken in time, become almost incurable.

"Do not allow them, then, to become implanted in you ; scruple cannot resist being told as soon as it begins. The moment you formulate it before the priest it dissolves ; it is a kind of mirage which a word effaces.

"You will object to me," continued the monk, after a silence, "that it is very mortifying to avow delusions which generally are absurd ; but it is for this very reason that the demon suggests to you less clever arguments than foolish. He takes hold of you thus by vanity, by false shame."

The monk was silent again ; then he continued,

"Scruples not treated, scruples not cured, lead to discouragement which is the worst of temptations ; for in other cases Satan attacks one virtue only in particular, and he shows himself ; while in this case he attacks all at once, and he hides himself.

"And this is so true that if you are seduced by lust, by the love of money, or by pride, you can, in examining yourself, give yourself account of the nature of the temptation which exhausts you ; in discouragement, on the contrary, your understanding is obscured to such a degree that you do not even suspect that the state in which you succmub is only a diabolic manœuvre which you must combat ; and you let go all, you give up the only arm which can save you, prayer, from which the demon turns you aside as a vain thing.

"Never hesitate, then, to cut the evil at its root, to take care of a scruple as soon as it is born.

"Now tell me ; you have nothing else to confess ? "

"No, except the indesire for the Eucharist, the languor in which I now faint."

" There is some fatigue in your case, for no one can endure such a shock with impunity ; do not be uneasy about that, have confidence, do not attempt to present yourself before God all neat and trim ; go to Him simply, naturally, in undress even, just as you are ; do not forget that if you are a servant you are also a son ; have good courage, our Lord will dispel all these nightmares."

And when he had received absolution, Durtal went down to the church to await the hour of mass.

And when the moment for communion came, he followed M. Bruno behind the lay brothers. All were kneeling on the pavement, and one after the other rose to exchange the kiss of peace, and reach the altar.

Though he repeated to himself the counsels of Father Maximin, though he exhorted himself to dismiss all his unrest, Durtal could not help thinking as he saw these monks approach the Table, " The Lord will find a change when I advance in my turn ; after having descended into the sanctuaries, He will be reduced to visit hovel." And sincerely, humbly, he was sorry for Him.

And as the first time that he approached this peace-giving mystery, he experienced a sensation of stifling, as if his heart were too large when he returned to his place. As soon as the mass was over, he quitted the chapel and escaped into the park.

Then gently, without sensible effects, the Sacrament worked ; Christ opened, little by little, his closed house and gave it air, light entered into Durtal in a flood. From the windows of his senses which had looked till then into he knew not what cesspool, into what enclosure, dank, and steeped in shadow ; he now looked suddenly, through a burst of light, on a vista which lost itself in heaven.

His vision of nature was modified ; the surroundings were transformed ; the fog of sadness which visited them vanished ; the sudden clearness of his soul was repeated in its surroundings.

He had the sensation of expansion, the almost childlike joy of a sick man who takes his first outing, of the convalescent, who having long crawled in a chamber, sets foot without; all grew young again. These alleys, this wood, through which he had wandered so much, which he began to know in all their windings, and in every corner, began to appear to him in a new aspect. A restrained joy, a repressed gladness emanated from this site, which appeared to him, instead of extending as formerly, to draw near and gather round the crucifix, to turn, as it were, with attention towards the liquid cross.

The trees rustled trembling, in a whisper of prayers, inclining towards the Christ, who no longer twisted His painful arms in the mirror of the pool, but He constrained these waters, and displayed them before Him, blessing them.

They were themselves different; the dark fluid was covered with monastic visions, in white robes, which the reflections of clouds left there in passing, and the swan scattered them, in a splash of sunlight, making as he swam great oily circles round him.

One might have said that these waves were gilt by the oil of the catechumens, and the sacred Chrism, which the Church exorcises on the Saturday of Holy Week, and above them heaven half-opened its tabernacle of clouds, out of which came a clear sun like a monstrance of molten gold in a Blessed Sacrament of flames.

It was a Benediction of nature, a genuflection of trees and flowers, singing in the wind, incensing with their perfume the sacred Bread which shone on high, in the flaming custody of the planet.

Durtal looked on in transport. He desired to cry aloud his enthusiasm and his Faith to the landscape; he felt a joy in living. The horror of existence counted for nothing when there were such moments, as no earthly happiness can give. God alone had the power of thus filling a soul, of making it overflow, and rush in floods of joy; and He alone could also fill the basin of sorrows, as no event in this world could do. Durtal had just tried it; his spiritual sufferings and joys attained under the divine imprint an acuteness, which people most humanly happy or unhappy cannot even suspect.

This idea brought him back to the terrible distresses of the evening before. He endeavoured to sum up what he had been able to observe of himself in this Trappist monastery.

First, the clear distinction between body and soul ; then the action of the demon, insinuating and obstinate, almost visible, while the heavenly action remained, on the contrary, dull and veiled, appeared only at certain moments, and seemed at others to vanish for ever.

And all this, when felt and understood, had an appearance simple in itself, but scarcely explaining itself. The body appearing to throw itself forward to the rescue of the soul, and no doubt borrowing from it its will, to help it when it fainted, was unintelligible. How a body could itself react obscurely, and yet show, all at once, so strong a decision that it pressed its companion into a vice, and prevented its flight—

" It is as mysterious as the rest," thought Durtal, and as in a dream he continued,

" The secret action of Jesus in His Sacrament is not less strange. If I may judge by what has happened to me ; a first communion exasperates the action of the devil, while a second represses it.

" Ah, and how I put myself in line with all my calculations ! In taking shelter here I thought myself pretty sure of my soul, and that my body would trouble me ; whereas just the contrary has been the case.

" My stomach has grown vigorous and shown itself fit to support an effort of which I should never have thought it capable, and my soul has been below everything, vacillating and dry, so fragile, so feeble !

" But we will let all that alone."

He walked about, lifted from earth by a confused joy. He grew vaporized in a sort of intoxication, in a vague etherization, in which arose, without his even thinking of formulating words, acts of thanksgiving ; it was an effort of thanks of his soul, of his body, of his whole being, to that God whom he felt living in him, and diffused in that kneeling landscape which also seemed to expand in mute hymns of gratitude.

The hour which struck by the clock in the portico reminded him it was breakfast time. He went to the guest-house, cut himself a slice of bread and butter with some cheese, drank half a glass of wine, and was about to go out again when he reflected that the horary of the offices was changed.

"They must be different from those of the week," he thought; and he went up into his cell to consult his placards.

He found only one, that of the rule of the monks themselves, which contained the regulations for the Sunday practices for the cloister ; and he read :

EXERCISES OF THE COMMUNITY FOR ALL ORDINARY SUNDAYS.

MORNING.

1.	Rise. Little Office. Prayer till 1.30.
2.	Grand Canonical Office chanted.
5.30.	Prime, Morning Mass, 6 o'clock.
6.45.	Chapter Instructions. Great Silence.
9.15.	Asperges, Tierce, Procession.
10.	High Mass.
11.10.	Sext and special examination.
11.30.	Angelus, Dinner.
12.15.	Siesta, Great Silence.

EVENING.

2.	End of Repose. None.
4.	Vespers and Benediction.
5.45.	Quarter of an hour for Prayer.
6.	Supper.
7.	Reading before Compline.
7.15.	Compline.
7.30.	Salve, Angelus.
7.45.	Examination of conscience and Retreat.
8.	Bed time, Great Silence.

Note.—After the Cross of September, no siesta. None is at 2 o'clock ; Vespers at 3 ; Supper at 5 ; Compline at 6, and bed time at 7.

Durtal copied this rule for his use on a scrap of paper. "In fact," he said to himself, " I have to be in chapel at 9.15 for Asperges, High Mass and the Office of Sext, afterwards at 2 for None, then at 4 for Vespers and Benediction, and lastly at 7.30 for Compline.

" Here is a day which will be occupied, without counting that I got up at half-past two this morning," he concluded ; and when he reached the chapel, about nine o'clock, he found the greater part of·the lay brothers on their knees, the others saying their rosary ; and when the clock struck all returned to their place.

Assisted by two fathers in cowls, the prior, vested in a white alb, entered, and while the antiphon "Asperges me, Domine, hyssopo, et mundabor " was sung, all the monks in succession defiled before Father Maximin, standing on the steps, turning his back to the altar ; and he sprinkled them with holy water, while they regained their stalls, each making the sign of the cross.

Then the prior descended from the altar, and came to the entrance to the vestibule, where he dispersed the water crosswise, traced by the sprinkler over the oblate, and over Durtal.

At last he vested, and went to celebrate the sacrifice.

Then Durtal was able to think over his Sundays at the Benedictine nuns.

The " Kyrie Eleison " was the same but slower and more sonorous, more grave on the prolonged termination of the last word ; at Paris the voices of the nuns drew it out and put a gloss on it at the same time, turned into satin its final sound, rendered it less dull, less spaced, less ample. The "Gloria in Excelsis " differed ; that of La Trappe was more primitive, more mounting, more sombre, interesting by its very barbarism, but less touching, for in its forms of adoration, in the "Adoramus te," for example, the " te " did not detach itself, did not drop like a tear of amorous essence, like an avowal retained by humility on the tip of the lips ; but it was when the Credo arose, that Durtal could uplift himself at ease.

He had never yet heard it so authoritative, and so imposing ; it advanced, chanted in unison, developing its slow procession of dogmas, in sounds well furnished and rigid, of a violet almost obscure, a red almost black, growing lighter towards the end, till it expired in a long and plaintive Amen.

In following the Cistercian office Durtal could recognize the morsels of plain chant still preserved in parish masses. All the part of the Canon, the " Sursum Corda," the " Vere

Dignum," the Antiphons, the "Pater," remained intact. Only the " Sanctus " and the " Agnus Dei" were changed.

Massive, built up, as it were, in the Roman style, they draped themselves in the colour, glowing and dull, which clothes, in fact, the offices of La Trappe.

" Well," said the oblate, when, after the ceremony, they sat at the table of the refectory ; " well, what do you think of our High Mass ? "

" It is superb," answered Durtal. And he said dreamily, " Would that one could have the whole complete ! to bring here, instead of this uninteresting chapel, the apse of St. Severin ; hang on the walls the pictures of Fra Angelico, Memling, Grünewald, Gerard David, Roger van den Weyden, Bouts ; add to these, admirable sculptures such as those of the great door of Chartres, altar screens of sculptured wood, such as those of the Cathedral of Amiens, what a dream ! "

" Yet," he went on after a silence, " this dream has been a reality, it is evident. This ideal church existed for ages, everywhere in the Middle Ages! The chant, the goldsmith's work, the panels, the sculptures, the tissues were all attractive ; the liturgies possessed, to give them value, fabulous caskets, but all that is far off."

" But you certainly cannot say," replied M. Bruno, with a smile, " that the church ornaments are ugly here ! "

" No ; they are exquisite. First, the chasubles have not the shapes of a miner's apron, and they do not hoist themselves up on the shoulders of the priest, that excrescence, that puffing like the ear of a little donkey lying back, which the vestment makers use at Paris.

" Nor is it any more that cross in stripe or woven, filling all the stuff, falling like a sack-coat over the back of the celebrant ; the Trappist chasubles have kept the old form, as the old image makers and the old painters preserved them in their religious scenes ; and that cross with four leaves, like those which the Gothic style chiselled on the walls of its churches, is related to the very expanded lotus a flower so full-blown that its falling petals droop."

" Without counting," pursued Durtal, " that the stuff which seems cut in a sort of flannel or thick soft felt must have been plunged in threefold dyes, for it takes a depth, and a magnificent clearness of tone. The religious trimming-

makers could trim these watered and plain silks with
silver and gold, yet never attain to give a colour at once so
vehement and so familiar to the eye as that crimson with
sulphur-yellow flowers, which Father Maximin wore the
other day."

"Yes, and the mourning chasuble with its lobed crosses,
and its discreet white fullings, in which the Father abbot
vested himself, the day on which he communicated us, is
not it also a caress for the eyes ? "

Durtal sighed : "Ah ! if the statues in the chapel showed
a like taste ! "

"By the way," said the oblate, "come and salute that
Notre Dame de l'Atre, of which I have spoken to you,
found among the remains of the old cloister."

They rose from table, passed along a corridor, and struck
into a lateral gallery, at the end of which they stopped
before a statue of life size, in stone.

It was heavy and massive, representing in a robe of long
folds, a peasant woman, crowned, and round-cheeked,
holding on her arm a child who blessed a ball.

But in this portrait of a robust peasant woman, sprung
from Burgundy or Flanders, there was a candour, a goodness
almost tumultuous, which sprang from her smiling face, her
innocent eyes, her good and large lips, indulgent, ready for
all forgiveness.

She was a rustic Virgin made for the humble lay brothers ;
she was not a great lady who could hold them at a distance,
but she was indeed the nursing mother of their souls, their
true mother. "How was it they had not understood her
here ? how instead of presiding in the chapel, did she grow
chill at the end of a corridor ? " cried Durtal.

The oblate turned the conversation—"I warn you," he
said, "that Benediction will not take place after Vespers as
your placard indicates, but directly after Compline ; this
latter office will therefore be advanced a quarter of an hour
at least."

And the oblate went up to his cell, while Durtal went
towards the large pond. There he lay down on a bed of
dry reed, looking at the water which broke in wavelets at his
feet. The coming and going of these limited waters, folding
back on themselves, yet never overpassing the basin they
had hollowed for themselves, led him on into long reveries.

He said to himself that a river was the most exact symbol of the active life ; one follows it from its source through all its courses across the territories it fertilizes ; it has fulfilled its assigned task before it dies, immersing itself in the gaping sepulchre of the seas ; but the pond, that tamed water, imprisoned in a hedge of reeds which it has itself caused to grow in fertilizing the soil of its bank, has concentrated itself, lived on itself, not seemed to achieve any known work, save to keep silence and reflect on the infinite of heaven.

"Still water troubles me," continued Durtal. "It seems to me that unable to extend itself, it grows deeper, and that while running waters borrow only the shadows of things they reflect, it swallows them without giving them back. Most certainly in this pond is a continued and profound absorption of forgotten clouds, of lost trees, even of sensations seized on the faces of monks who hung over it. This water is full, and not empty, like those which are distracted in wandering about the country and in bathing the towns. It is a contemplative water, in perfect accord with the recollected life of the cloisters.

"The fact is," he concluded, "that a river would have here no meaning ; it would only be passing, would remain indifferent and in a hurry, would be in all cases unfit to pacify the soul which the monastic water of the ponds appeases. Ah ! in founding Notre Dame de l'Atre, Saint Bernard knew how to fit the Cistercian rule and the site.

"But we must leave these fancies," he said, rising ; and, remembering that it was Sunday, he transferred himself to Paris, and revisited in thought his halts on this day in the churches.

In the morning St. Severin enchanted him, but he ought not to thrust himself into that sanctuary for the other Offices. Vespers there were botched and mean ; and if it were a feast day the organ master showed himself possessed by the love of ignoble music.

Occasionally Durtal had taken refuge at St. Gervais, where at least they played at certain times motets of the old masters ; but that church was, as well as St. Eustache, a paying concert, where Faith had nothing to do. No recollection was possible in the midst of ladies who fainted behind, their faces in their hands, and grew agitated in creaking chairs. These were frivolous assemblies for pious music, a compromise between the theatre and God.

St. Sulpice was better, where at least the public was silent. There, moreover, Vespers were celebrated with more solemnity and less haste.

In general the seminary reinforced the choir, and rendered by this imposing choir they rolled on majestically sustained by the grand organ.

Chanted, only in half, and not in unison, reduced to a state of couplets, given, some by a baritone, others by the choir, they were twisted and frizzled by a curling iron, but as they were not less adulterated at the other churches, there was every advantage in listening to them at St. Sulpice, whose powerful choir, very well led, had not, as for example at Notre Dame, those dusty voices which break at the least whisper.

This only became really odious when, with a formidable explosion, the first strophe of the Magnificat struck the arches.

The organ then swallowed up one stanza out of two, and under the seditious pretext that the length of the Office of incensing was too long to be filled up entirely by singing, M. Widor, seated at his desk, rolled forth stale fragments of music splashed about above, imitating the human voice and the flute, the bagpipe and the bassoon, or indeed, tired of affectations, he blew furiously on the keys, ending by imitating the roll of locomotives over iron bridges, letting all the stops go.

And the choirmaster, not wishing to show himself inferior to the organist in his instinctive hatred of plain chant, was delighted, when the Benediction began, to put aside Gregorian melodies and make his choristers gurgle rigadoons.

It was no longer a sanctuary, but a howling place. The "Ave Maria," the "Ave Verum," all the mystical indecencies of the late Gounod, the rhapsodies of old Thomas, the capers of indigent musicasters, defiled in a chain wound by choir leaders from Lamoureux, chanted unfortunately by children, the chastity of whose voices no one feared to pollute in these middle-class passages of music, these by-ways of art.

" Ah," thought Durtal, " if only this choirmaster, who is
evidently an excellent musician ; for indeed, when he must,
he knows how to get executed better than anywhere else in
Paris, the ' De Profundis ' with organ accompaniment, and
the ' Dies Iræ ' ; if only this man would as at St. Gervais
give us some Palestrina and Vittoria, some Aichinger and
Allegri, some Orlando Lasso and De Près ; but no, he must
detest these masters also, consider them as archaic rubbish,
good to send into the dust-heaps."

And Durtal continued,

" What we hear now at Paris, in the churches, is wholly
incredible ! Under pretence of managing an income for
the singers, they suppress half the stanzas of canticles and
hymns, and substitute, to vary the pleasure, the tiresome
divagations of an organ.

" There they howl the ' Tantum Ergo ' to the Austrian
National air ; or what is still worse, muffle it up with operatic
choruses, or refrains from canteens. The very text is
divided into couplets which are ornamented like a drinking
song with a little burthen.

" The other Church sequences are treated in the same
manner.

" And yet the Papacy has formally forbidden, in many
bulls, that the sanctuary should be soiled by those liberties.
To cite one only, John xxii., in his Extravagant ' Doctor
Sanctorum,' expressly forbade profane voices and music in
churches. He prohibited choirs at the same time to change
plain chant into fiorituri. The decrees of the Council of
Trent are not less clear from this point of view, and more
recently still a regulation of the Sacred Congregation of
Rites has intervened to proscribe musical rioting in holy
places.

" Then what are the parish-priests doing who, in fact,
have musical police charge in their churches ? Nothing,
they laugh at it.

" Nor is this a mere phrase, but with those priests who,
hoping for receipts, permit on fête days the shameless voices of
actresses to dance gambols to the heavy sounds of the organ,
the poor Church has become far from clean.

" At St. Sulpice," Durtal went on, " the priest tolerates
the villainy of jolly songs which are served up to him ; but
at least he does not, like the one at St. Severin, allow

strolling women players to lighten up the Office by the
shouts of such voices as remain to them.   Nor has he accepted
the solo on the English horn which I heard at St. Thomas
one evening during the Perpetual Adoration.   In short, if
the grand Benedictions at St. Sulpice are a shame, the
Complines remain in spite of their theatrical attitude really
charming."

And Durtal thought of those Complines of which the
paternity is often attributed to Saint Benedict ; they were
in fact the integral prayer of the evenings, the preventive
adjuration, the safeguard against the attempts of the
Demon, they were in some measure the advanced sentinels
of the out-posts placed round the soul to protect it during
the night.

And the regulation of this entrenched camp of prayer
was perfect.   After the benediction the best trained
voice, the most threadlike of the choir, the voice of the
smallest of the children, sang forth the short lesson taken
from the first Epistle of Saint Peter, warning the faithful
that they must be sober and watch, not allow themselves
to be surprised unexpectedly.   A priest then recited the
usual evening prayers ; the choir organ gave the intonation,
and the psalms fell, chanted one by one, the twilight psalms,
in which before the approaches of night peopled with
goblins, and furrowed by ghosts, man calls God to aid, and
prays Him to guard his sleep from the violence of the ways
of hell, the rape of the lamias that pass.

And the hymn of Saint Ambrose, the " Te lucis ante
terminum," made still more precise the scattered meaning
of these psalms, gathering it up in its short stanzas.   Unfortunately, the most important, that which foresees and
declares the luxurious dangers of darkness, was swallowed
up by the full organ.   This hymn was not rendered in plain
chant at St. Sulpice as at La Trappe, but was sung to a
pompous and elaborate air, an air full of glory, with a
certain proud attractiveness, originating no doubt in the
eighteenth century.

Then there was a pause—and man, feeling himself more
sheltered, behind a rampart of prayers, recollected himself,
more assured, and borrowed innocent voices to address new
supplications to God.   After the chapter read by the
officiant, the children of the choir chanted the short response

" In manus tuus Domine, commendo spiritum meum," which rolled out, dividing in two parts, then doubled itself, and resolved at the last its two separate portions by a verse, and part of an antiphon.

And after that prayer there was still the canticle of Simeon, who, as soon as he had seen the Messiah, desired to die. This "Nunc dimittis," which the Church has incorporated in Compline to stimulate us at eventide to self-examination—for none can tell whether he shall wake on the morrow—was raised by the whole choir, which alternated with the responses of the organ.

In fact, to end this Office of a besieged town, to take its last dispositions and try to repose in shelter from a violent attack, the Church built up again a few prayers, and placed her parishes under the tutelage of the Virgin, to whom it chanted one of the four antiphons which follow, according to the Proper.

" At La Trappe Compline was evidently less solemn, less interesting than at St. Sulpice," concluded Durtal, " for the monastic breviary is, for a wonder, less complete for that Office than the Roman breviary. " As for Sunday Vespers, I am curious to hear them."

And he heard them ; but they hardly differed from the Vespers adopted by the Benedictine nuns of the Rue Monsieur ; they were more massive, more grave, more Roman, if it may be said, for necessarily the voice of women drew them out into sharp points, made them like acute arches, as it were, in Gothic style, but the Gregorian tunes were the same.

On the other hand they resembled in nothing those at St. Sulpice, where the modern sauces spoilt the very essences of the plain chants. Only the Magnificat of La Trappe, abrupt, and with dry tone, was not so good as the majestic, the admirable Royal Magnificat chanted at Paris.

" These monks are astonishing with their superb voices," said Durtal to himself, and he smiled as they finished the antiphon of Our Lady, for he remembered that in the primitive Church the chanter was called " Fabarius cantor," " eater of beans," because he was obliged to eat that vegetable to strengthen his voice. Now, at La Trappe, dishes of beans were common ; perhaps that was the secret of the ever young monastic voices.

He thought over the liturgy and plain chant while smoking cigarettes, in the walks, after Vespers.

He brought to mind the symbolism of those canonical hours which recalled every day to the Christian the shortness of life in summing up for him its image from infancy to death.

Recited soon after dawn, Prime was the figure of childhood ; Tierce of youth ; Sext the full vigour of age ; None the approaches of old age, while Vespers were an allegory of decrepitude. They belonged, moreover, to the Nocturns, and were sung about six o'clock in the evening, at that hour when, at the time of the Equinoxes, the sun sets in the red cinder of the clouds. As for Compline, it resounds when night, the symbol of death, has come.

This canonical Office was a marvellous rosary of psalms ; every bead of each of these hours bore reference to the different phases of human existence, followed, little by little, the periods of the day, the decline of destiny, to end in the most perfect of offices, in Compline, that provisional absolution of a death, itself represented by sleep.

And if, from these texts so wisely selected, these Sequences so solemnly sealed, Durtal passed to the sacerdotal robe of their sounds, to those neumatic chants, that divine psalmody all uniform, all simple, which is plain chant, he had to admit, that except in Benedictine cloisters, an organ accompaniment was everywhere added, that plain chant had been put forcibly in modern tonality, and it disappeared under vegetations which stifled it, became everywhere discoloured, amorphous and incomprehensible.

One only of its executioners, Niedermayer, showed himself at least pitiful. He tried a system more ingenious and more honest. He reversed the terms of torture. Instead of wishing to make plain chant supple and to thrust it into the mould of modern harmony, he constrained that harmony to bend itself to the austere tonality of plain chant. He thus preserved its character, but how far more natural would it have been to leave it solitary and not obliged it to tow an useless companion and awkward following ?

Here at least at La Trappe it lived and spread in all security, without treason on the part of the monks. There was always sameness of sound, it was always chanted without accompaniment in unison.

He was able to satisfy himself about this truth once more after supper, that evening, when at the end of Compline the father sacristan lighted all the candles on the altar.

At that moment, in the silence of the Trappists on their knees, their head in their hands, or their cheek resting on the sleeve of their great cowl, three lay brothers entered, two carrying torches, and another preceding them with a censer, and behind them a few paces, came the prior with his hands joined.

Durtal looked at the changed costume of the three brothers. They had no longer their robes of serge, made of bits and scraps, stained mud colour, but robes of violet-brown, like plums on which was spread the white twilling of a new surplice.

While Father Maximin, vested in a copy of milky white, woven with a cross in orange yellow, placed the Host in the monstrance, the thurifer put down the censer, on the coals of which melted tears of real incense. Contrary to what takes place in Paris, where the censer, swung before the altar, sounds against its chains, and is like the clear tinkling of a horse which, as he lifts his head, shakes his curb and bit, the censer at La Trappe remained immovable before the altar, and smoked by itself behind the officiants.

And everyone chanted the imploring and melancholy antiphon " Parce Domine," then the " Tantum Ergo," that magnificent song, which could be almost acted, so clear in their changes are the sentiments which succeed each other in their rhymed sequence.

In the first stanza it seems indeed to shake the head gently, to put forward the chin, so to speak, so as to affirm the insufficiency of the senses to explain the dogma of the real presence, the finished avatar of the Bread. It is then admiring and reflective ; then that melody so attentive, so respectful, does not wait to affirm the weakness of the reason, and the power of faith, but in the second stanza it goes forward, adores the glory of the three Persons, exults with joy, only recovers itself at the end, where the music adds a new sense to the text of Saint Thomas, in avowing in a long and mournful Amen the unworthiness of those present to receive the Benediction of the Flesh placed upon that cross which the monstrance is about to trace in the air.

And slowly, while unrolling its coil of smoke, the censer spread, as it were, a blue gauze before the altar, while the Blessed Sacrament was lifted like a golden moon, amid the stars of the tapers, sparkling in the growing darkness of that fog, the bells of the abbey sounded with musical and sweet strokes. And all the monks bowed low with their eyes closed, then recovered themselves and entoned the " Laudate " to the old melody which is also sung at Notre Dame des Victoires at the Benediction in the evening.

Then one by one, having genuflected before the altar, they went out, while Durtal and the oblate returned to the guest-house, where Father Etienne was waiting for them.

He said to Durtal : " I would not go to bed without knowing how you have borne the day ; " and as Durtal thanked him, assuring him that this Sunday had been very peaceful, Father Etienne smiled and revealed in a word, that under their reserved attitude all at La Trappe were more interested in their guest than he had himself believed.

" The reverend Father abbot and the Father prior will be glad when I give them this answer," said the monk, who wished Durtal good-night, pressing his hand.

CHAPTER VII.

At seven o'clock, just as he was preparing to eat his bread, Durtal encountered Father Etienne.

"Father," he said, "to-morrow is Tuesday ; the time of my retreat has expired, and I am going ; how should I order a carriage for Saint Landry ? "

The monk smiled. "When the postman brings the letters I can charge him with the commission, but let us see ; are you in a great hurry to leave us ? "

"No, but I would not trespass. . . ."

"Listen, since you are so well broken in to the life at La Trappe, stay here two days more. The Father procurator must go to settle a dispute at Saint Landry. He will take you to the station in our carriage. So you will avoid some expense, and the journey hence to the railroad will seem to you less long, since there will be two of you."

Durtal accepted, and as it rained, he went up to his room. "It is strange," he said, as he sat down, "how impossible one finds it in a cloister to read a book ; one wants nothing, one thinks of God by Himself, and not by the volumes which speak about Him."

Mechanically he had taken up from a heap of books one in octavo, which he had found on his table the day he took possession of his cell ; it bore the title "Manresa," or the "Spiritual Exercises" of Ignatius of Loyola.

He had already run through the work at Paris, and the pages which he turned over afresh did not change the harsh, almost hostile, opinion which he had retained of this book.

The fact is that these exercises leave no initiative to the soul ; they consider it as a soft paste good to run into a mould ; they show it no horizon, no sky. Instead of trying to stretch it, and make it greater, they make it smaller deliberately ; they put it back into the cases of their wafer box, nourish it only on faded trifles, on dry nothings.

This Japanese culture of deformed toes which remain dwarf ; this Chinese deformation of children planted in pots, horrified Durtal, who closed the volume.

He opened another, the "Introduction to the Devout Life," by Saint Francis de Sales.

Certainly he found no need to read it again, in spite of its affectations, and its good nature, at first charming, but which ends by making you sick, by making the soul sticky with sweets with liqueurs in them, and lollypops ; in a word, that work so much praised by Catholics was a julep scented with bergamot and ambergris.   It was like a fine handkerchief shaken in a church in which a musty smell of incense remained.

But the man himself, the Bishop Saint Francis de Sales, was suggestive ; with his name was called up the whole mystical history of the seventeenth century.

And Durtal recalled the memories he had kept of the religious life of that time.   There were then in the Church two currents :

That of the high Mysticism, as it was called, originating from Saint Teresa and Saint John of the Cross ; and this current was concentrated on Marie Guyon.

And another that of so-called temperate Mysticism, of which the adepts were Saint Francis de Sales and his friend the celebrated Baroness de Chantal.

It was naturally this second current which triumphed. Jesus, putting Himself within the reach of drawing-rooms, descending to the level of women of the world, a moderate and proper Jesus, only dealing with the soul of His creature just enough to give it one attraction the more, this elegant Jesus became all the fashion ; but Madame Guyon, whose source was above all Saint Teresa, who taught the mystical theory of love, and familiar intercourse with heaven, raised the opposition of the whole clergy who abominated Mysticism without understanding it ; she exasperated the terrible Bossuet, who accused her of the fashionable heresy, Molinism and Quietism.   She refuted, unhappy as she was, this trouble without much difficulty, but he persecuted her for it none the less ; he was furious against her, and had her imprisoned at Vincennes ; revealed himself obstinate, surly, and atrocious.

Fenelon, who tried to conciliate these two tendencies in preparing a small Mysticism neither too hot nor too cold, a little less lukewarm than that of Saint Francis de Sales, and above all things much less ardent than that of Saint Teresa, ended in his turn by displeasing the cormorant of Meaux, and though he abandoned and denied Madame de Guyon, whose friend he had been for long years, he was persecuted and tracked down by Bossuet, condemned at Rome, and sent in exile to Cambrai.

And here Durtal could not but smile, for he remembered the desolate complaints of his partisans weeping for this disgrace, representing thus as a martyr this archbishop whose punishment consisted in quitting his post as courtier at Versailles to go at last and administer his diocese, in which he appeared till then to have never resided.

This mitred Job, who remained in his misfortune Archbishop and Duke of Cambrai, Prince of the Holy Roman Empire, and rich, so unhappy because he was obliged to visit his flock, well shows the state of the episcopate under the redundant reign of the great king. It was a priesthood of financiers and valets.

Only there was at any rate a certain attraction, there was talent in every case ; while now bishops are not for the most part less intriguing nor less servile, but they have no longer either talent or manners. Caught in part, in the fishpond of bad priests, they show themselves ready for everything, and turn out to be souls of old usurers, low jobbers, beggars, when you press them.

"It is sad to say it, but so it is," concluded Durtal. "As for Madame Guyon," he went on, "she was neither an original writer nor a saint ; she was only an unwelcome substitute for the true mystics ; she was presuming and certainly lacked that humility which magnified Saint Teresa and Saint Clare ; but after all she burst into a flame, she was overcome by Jesus ; above all, she was not a pious courtier, a bigot softened by a court like the Maintenon.

"After all, what a time for religion it was? All its saints have something formal and restricted, wordy and cold, which turns me away from them. Saint Francis de Sales, Saint Vincent de Paul, Saint Chantal. . . No, I prefer Saint Francis of Assisi, Saint Bernard, Saint Angela. . .The Mysticism of the seventeenth century is all the fashion with its emphatic and mean churches, its pompous and icy painting, its solemn poetry, its gloomy prose.

" But look," he said, " my cell is still neither swept nor set in order, and I am afraid that in lingering here I may give some trouble to Father Etienne. It rains, however, too hard to allow of my walking in the wood ; the simplest thing is to go and read the Little Office of Our Lady in the chapel."

He went down there ; it was at this hour almost empty ; the monks were at work in the fields or in the factory ; two fathers only, on their knees before the altar of Our Lady, were praying so absorbedly that they did not even hear the opening of the door.

And Durtal, who had placed himself near them opposite the porch which gave upon the high altar, saw them reflected in the sheet of glass, placed before the shrine of the Blessed Guerrie. This sheet had indeed the effect of a mirror, and the white fathers were in the depths of it, lived in prayers under the table, in the very heart of the altar.

And he also appeared there in a corner, reflected, at the back of the shrine, near the sacred remains of the monk.

At one moment he lifted his head, and saw that the round window in the apse, behind the altar, reproduced on its glass ornamented with grey and blue, the marks engraved on the reverse of the medal of Saint Benedict, the first letters of its imperative formulas, the initials of its distiches.

It might have been called an immense clear medal, sifting a pale light, straining it through prayers, not allowing them to penetrate to the altar till sanctified and blessed by the Patriarch.

And while he was dreaming, the clock struck ; the two Trappists regained their stalls, while the others entered.

Waiting thus in the chapel, the hour of Sext had struck. The abbot advanced. Durtal saw him again for the first time since their conversation ; he seemed less ill, less pale ; he marched majestically in his great white cowl, at the hood of which hung a violet acorn, and the fathers bowed, kissing their sleeve before him ; he reached his place, which was designated by a wooden cross standing before a stall, and all enfolded themselves with a great sign of the cross, bowed to the altar, and the feeble imploring voice of the old Trappist rose : " Deus in adjutorium meum intende."

And the Office continued, in the monotonous and charming pitch of the doxology, interrupted by profound reverences, large movements of the arm lifting the sleeve of the cowl as it fell to the ground, to allow the hand freedom to turn the pages.

When Sext was over Durtal went to rejoin the oblate.

They found on the table of the refectory a little omelette, leeks cooked in a sauce of flour and oil, haricots and cheese.

"It is astonishing," said Durtal, "how in regard to mystics, the world errs on preconceived ideas, on the old string. Phrenologists declare that mystics have pointed skulls ; now here that their form is more visible than elsewhere, because they are all hairless and shaven, there are no more heads like eggs than anywhere else. I looked this morning at the shape of their heads, no two are alike. Some are oval and depressed, others like a pear and straight, some have lumps on them, and some have none ; and it is just the same with faces ; when they are not transfigured by prayer they are ordinary. If they did not wear the habit of their order, no one could recognize in these Trappists predestined beings living out of modern society, in the full Middle Ages, in absolute dependence on a God. If they have souls which are not like those of other people, they have, after all, faces and bodies like those of the first comer."

"All is within," said the oblate. "Why should elect souls be enclosed in fleshly prisons different to others ? "

This conversation, which continued on different points of Trappist life, ended by turning on death in a monastery, and M. Bruno revealed some details.

"When death is near," he said, "the Father abbot traces on the ground a cross in blessed ashes covered with straw, and the dying man is placed on it wrapped in serge cloth.

"The brothers recite near him the prayers of the dying, and at the moment of his death the response 'Subvenite Sancti Dei' is chanted in choir. The Father abbot incenses the body, which is washed while the monks sing the Office of the Dead in another room.

"Then his regular habit is put on the dead monk, and he is borne in procession to the church, where he lies on a stretcher with his face uncovered, until the hour destined for the funeral.

"Then on the way to the cemetery the community intones no longer the chant of the dead, the psalms of grief, and the sequences of regret, but rather ' In exitu Israel de Ægypto,' which is the psalm of deliverance, the free song of joy.

"And the Trappist is buried without a coffin, in his robe of stuff, his head covered with his hood.

"Lastly, during thirty days, his place remains empty in the refectory, his portion is served as usual, but the brother porter distributes it to the poor.

"Ah! the happiness to die thus," said the oblate, as he ended, "for if one dies after having honestly fulfilled one's task in the order, one is assured of eternal happiness, according to the promises made by our Lord to Saint Benedict and to Saint Bernard!"

"The rain is over," said Durtal; "I should like to visit to-day that little chapel at the end of the park of which you spoke to me the other day. Which is the shortest way to reach it?"

M. Bruno told him the way, and Durtal went off, rolling a cigarette, to gain the great pond, thence he struck a path to the left and mounted a lane of trees.

He slipped on the wet ground, and got on with difficulty. At last, however, he gained a clump of chestnuts, which he skirted. Behind these rose a dwarf tower topped by a very small dome, pierced by a door. To the left and right of this door, on sockets where ornaments of the Romanesque epoch still were seen under the velvety crust of moss, two stone angels were still standing.

They belonged, evidently, to the Burgundian school, with their big round heads, their hair puffed and divided into waves, their fat faces with turned-up noses, their solid draperies with hard folds. They also came from the ruins of the old cloister, but the interior of the chapel was unfortunately thoroughly modern; it was so small that the feet of him who knelt at the altar almost touched the wall at the entrance.

In a niche veiled by white gauze a Virgin smiled with extended hands. She had blue plaster eyes and apple-shaped cheeks. She was wearisome in her insignificance, but her sanctuary retained the warmth of places always shut up. The walls, hung with red calico, were dusted, the floor was swept, and the holy water basins full; superb tea roses flourished in pots between the candelabra. Durtal then understood why he had so often seen M. Bruno walking in this direction with flowers in his hand; he was going to pray in this place, which he loved no doubt because it was isolated in the profound solitude of this Trappist monastery.

"Excellent man!" cried Durtal, thinking over the affectionate services, the fraternal care the oblate had had for him; and he added, "He is a happy man too, for he is self-contained, and lives so placidly here.

"And, indeed," he went on, "where is the good of striving, if not against oneself? to agitate oneself for money, for glory, to conduct oneself so as to keep others down, and gain adulation from them, how vain a task!

"Only the Church, in decking the temporary altars of the liturgical year, in forcing the seasons to follow step by step the life of Christ, has known how to trace for us a plan of necessary occupations, of useful ends. She has given us the means of walking always side by side with Jesus, to live day by day with the Gospels; for Christians she has made time the messenger of sorrows and the herald of joys; she has entrusted to the year the part of servant of the New Testament, the zealous emissary of worship."

And Durtal reflected on the cycle of the liturgy which begins on the first day of the religious year, with Advent, then turns with an insensible movement on itself till it returns again to its starting-point, to the time when the Church prepares by penitence and prayer to celebrate Christmas.

And turning over his prayer-book, seeing the extraordinary circle of offices, he thought of that prodigious jewel, that crown of King Recceswinthe preserved in the Museum of Cluny.

The liturgical year was, like it, studded with crystals and jewels by its admirable canticles and its fervent hymns set in the very gold of Benedictions and Vespers.

It seemed that the Church had substituted for that crown of thorns with which the Jews had surrounded the temples of the Saviour, the truly royal crown of the Proper of the

Seasons, the only one which was chiselled in a metal precious
enough, with art pure enough to dare to place itself on the
brow of a God.

And the grand Lapidary had begun his work by incrust-
ing, in this diadem of offices, the hymn of Saint Ambrose,
and the invocation taken from the Old Testament, the
"Rorate Cœli," that melodious chant of expectation and
regret, that obscure gem violet-coloured ; the lustre declares
itself then, when after each of its stanzas rises the solemn
prayer of the patriarchs, calling for the longed-for presence
of Christ.

And the four Sundays of Advent disappeared with the
turned pages of the prayer-book ; the night of the Nativity
was come. After the "Jesu Redemptor" of Vespers, the
old Portuguese chant, the "Adeste Fideles," arose at Benediction from every lip. It was a sequence of a truly charming
simplicity, an old carving wherein defiled the shepherds
and the kings to a popular air appropriate to great marches,
apt to charm, to aid by the somewhat military rhythm of its
steps, the long lines of the faithful quitting their cottages to
go to the distant churches in the towns.

And imperceptibly, like the year in an invisible rotation,
the circle turned, and stopped at the Feast of the Holy
Innocents, where there flourished out, like a flower from a
slaughter-house, on a shoot culled from a soil irrigated by
the blood of lambs, this sequence, red, and smelling of roses,
the "Salvate Flores Martyrum" of Prudentius ; the crown
moved again, and the hymn of the Epiphany, the "Crudelis
Herodes" of Sedudius, appeared in its turn.

Now the Sundays grew heavy, the violet Sundays when
the "Gloria in Excelsis" is no more heard, when the "Audi
Benigne" of Saint Ambrose is chanted, and the "Miserere,"
that cinder-coloured psalm, which is perhaps the most perfect
masterpiece which the Church has ever drawn from her
store-houses of plain chants.

It was Lent, when the amethysts fade in the moist grey
of onyxes, in the embrowned white of quartz, and the
magnificent invocation, "Attende Domine," rose beneath
the arches. Sprung like the "Rorate Cœli" from the
sequences of the Old Testament, this humble and contrite
chant, enumerating the deserved punishments of sins,
became, if not more sorrowful, at all events more grave and

more pressing when it confirmed, when it resumed in the initial stanza of its burthen, the avowal of shame already confessed.

And suddenly on this crown there burst out after the expiring fires of Lent, the flaming ruby of the Passion. On the upturned yellow of the sky a red cross was raised, while majestic shouts and despairing cries proclaimed the blood-stained fruit of the tree ; and the " Vexilla Regis " was again repeated the following Sunday at the Feast of Palms, which joined to that Sequence of Fortunatus the green hymn which it accompanied with a silky noise of palms, the " Gloria laus et honor " of Theodulph.

Then the fires of precious stones grew grey and died. To the glowing coals of gems succeeded the dead cinders of obsidians, black stones scarcely swelling, without a gleam above the tarnished gold of their mountings ; one entered no Holy Week, everywhere the " Pange Lingua " and the " Stabat Mater " wailed under the arches, and then came the " Tenebræ," the lamentations, and the psalms, whose knell shook the flame of the brown waxen tapers, and after each halt, at the end of each of the psalms, one of the tapers expired, and its column of blue smoke evaporated still under the lighted circumference of the arches, while the choir recommenced the interrupted series of complaints.

And the crown turned once more ; the beads of this musical rosary still ran on, and all changed. Jesus had risen, and songs of joy issued from the organs. The " Victimæ Paschali Laudes " exulted before the gospel of the masses, and at the Benediction the " O Filii et Filiæ," created indeed to be intoned by the wild jubilations of crowds, ran and sported in the joyous hurricane of the organs, which uprooted the pillars and unroofed the naves.

And the feasts rung in with bells followed at longer intervals. At Ascension the heavy and clear crystals of Saint Ambrose filled with their luminous water the tiny basin of the catkins ; the fire of rubies and garnets lighted up again with the crimson hymn and scarlet sequence of Pentecost the " Veni Creator " and " Veni Spiritus." The Feast of the Trinity passed, signalized by the stanzas of Gregory the Great; and for the Feast of the Blessed Sacrament, the liturgy could exhibit the most marvellous jewel case of its dower, the Office of Saint Thomas, the "Pange Lingua," the "Adore Te," the "Sacris Solemniis," the "Verbum Supernum," and above all the "Lauda Sion," that pure masterpiece of Latin poetry and scholasticism, that hymn so precise, so lucid in its abstraction, so firm in its rhymed words, round which is rolled the melody perhaps the most enthusiastic, the most supple in plain chant.

The circle displaced itself again, showing on its different faces the twenty-three to twenty-eight Sundays which defile after Pentecost, the green weeks of the time of Pilgrimage, and stopped at the last feast, at the Sunday after the Octave of All Saints, at the Dedication of Churches which the "Cœlestis Urbs" incensed, old stanzas of which the ruins were badly consolidated by the architects of Urban VIII., old jewels, on which the troubled water slept and was reanimated only in rare lights.

The juncture of the religious crown, of the liturgical year, was then made at the masses, in which the gospel of the last Sunday after Pentecost, the Gospel according to Saint Matthew, repeats, as well as the Gospel according to Saint Luke, recited on the first Sunday in Advent, the terrible predictions of Christ on the desolation of the time, on the end of the world.

"This is not all," Durtal continued, who was interested in this run through his prayer-book. "In this crown of the Proper of the Seasons are inserted, like smaller stones, the sequences of the Proper of Saints which fill the empty places, and finish the round of the circle.

First the pearls and gems of the Blessed Virgin, the limpid jewels, the blue sapphires and rose rubies of her antiphons; then the aquamarine, so lucid and pure, of the "Ave Maris Stella," the topaz, pale as tears, of the "O Quot nudis Lacrymarum" on the Feast of the Seven Dolours, the hyacinth, colour of dried blood, of the "Stabat;" then were told the feasts of the Angels and the Saints, the hymns dedicated to the Apostles and the Evangelists, to the Martyrs, whether solitary or in couples, both out of and during the Paschal season, to the Confessors, Pontiffs, and non-Pontiffs, to Virgins, to Holy Women, all Feasts differentiated by special Sequences, by special Proses of which some are very simple, like those stanzas made in honour of the Nativity of Saint John the Baptist, by Paul the Deacon.

There still remains All Saints, with the " Placare Christe," and the three blows on the alarm bell, the knell in triplets of the " Dies Iræ," which resounds on the day set apart for the Commemoration of the Dead.

" What an immense fund of poetry, what an incomparable estate of art the Church possesses ! " he cried, closing his book ; and many memories rose for him at this excursion into his prayer-book.

On how many evenings had the sadness of life been dissipated in listening to these proses chanted in the churches !

He thought over again of the suppliant voice of Advent, and recalled one evening, when he had wandered under a fine rain along the quays. He had been driven from home by ignoble visions, and at the same time had been harassed by the increasing disgust of his vices. He had ended by being brought up against his will at St. Gervais.

In the chapel of the Virgin, some poor women were prostrate. He had knelt, tired and dazed, his soul so ill at ease, that he slumbered without power to wake himself. Some men and boys of the choir were installed in the chapel, with two or three priests ; they had lighted candles, and the voice, light and sustained, of a child, had in the dark of the church chanted the long antiphons of the " Rorate."

In the state of overwhelming sadness in which he was stagnant, Durtal felt himself open and bleeding to the bottom of his soul ; then a voice older and less trembling, which understood the words it said, narrated ingenuously, almost without confusion, to the Just One, " Peccavimus et facti sumus tanquam immundus nos."

And Durtal took up these words, and spelt them over in terror, thinking, " Ah ! yes, we have sinned and become like the leprous, O Lord ! " And the chant continued, and in His turn, the Most High borrowed that same innocent organ of childhood, to declare to man His pity, and to confirm to him the pardon assured by the coming of the Son.

And the evening had ended by the Benediction in plain chant, in the midst of the silence and prostration of unhappy women.

Durtal remembered how he left the church refreshed,

freed from his hauntings, and he had gone away in the drizzling rain, surprised that the way was so short, humming the " Rorate," of which the air had taken possession of him, ending by seeing in it the personal touch of a kindly unknown.

And there were other evenings . . . the Octave of the Feast of All Souls at St. Sulpice and at St. Thomas Aquinas, where, after the Vespers of the Dead, they brought out again the old Sequence which has disappeared from the Roman Breviary, the " Lanquentilus in Purgatorio."

This church was the only one in Paris which had retained these pages of the Gallican hymnal, and had them sung by two basses without a choir ; but these singers, so poor as a rule, no doubt were fond of this air, for if they did not sing it with art, at least they put a little soul into its delivery.

And this invocation to the Madonna, in which she was adjured to save the souls in Purgatory, was as sorrowful as the souls themselves, and so melancholy, so languid, that the surroundings were forgotten, the ugliness of that sanctuary of which the choir was a theatre scene, surrounded by closed dressing-rooms and garnished with lustres, one might think oneself for a few moments far from Paris, far from that population of devout women and servant girls, which attend that place in the evening.

" Ah ! the Church," he said to himself, as he descended the path which led to the great pond, " what a mother of art is she ! " and suddenly the noise of a body falling into the water interrupted his reflections.

He looked behind the hedge of reeds and saw nothing but great circles running on the water, and all at once in one of these rings a small dog-like head appeared holding a fish in its mouth ; the beast raised itself a little out of the water, showed a thin body covered with fur, and gazed on Durtal quietly with its little black eyes.

Then in a flash it passed the distance which separated it from the bank, and disappeared under the grasses.

"It is the otter," he said to himself, remembering the discussion at table between the stranger priest and the oblate.

And he went to gain the other pond, when he encountered Father Etienne.

He told him his adventure.

"Impossible ! " cried the monk, " no one has ever seen the otter ; you must have mistaken it for a water rat, or some other animal, for that beast, for which we have watched for years, is invisible."

Durtal gave him a description of it.

" It is certainly the otter," admitted the guest-master, surprised.

It was evident that this otter lived in the pond in a legendary state. In monotonous lives, in days like those in a cloister, it took the proportions of a fabulous subject, of an event whereof the mystery would occupy intervals seized between prayers and offices.

" We must point out to M. Bruno the exact spot where you remarked it, for he will begin to hunt it again," said Father Etienne after a silence.

" But how can it trouble you in eating your fish, since you do not angle for them ? "

" I beg your pardon ; we fish for them to send them to the Archbishop," answered the monk, who went on : " Still, it is very strange that you saw the beast ! "

" When I leave this," thought Durtal, " they will certainly speak of me as the gentleman who saw the otter."

While talking, they had arrived at the cross pond.

" Look," said the father, pointing out the swan, who rose in a fury, beat his wings, and hissed.

" What is the matter with him ? "

" The matter is that the white hue of my habit infuriates him."

" Ah ! and why ? "

" I do not know ; perhaps he wants to be the only one who is white here ; he spares the lay brothers, while as for a father . . . wait, you will see."

And the guest-master walked quietly towards the swan.

" Come," he said to the angry creature, who splashed him with water ; and he held out his hand which the swan snapped.

" See," said the monk, showing the mark of a red pinch printed on the flesh.

And he smiled, holding his hand, and quitted Durtal, who asked himself whether, in acting thus, the Trappist were not wishing to inflict on himself some corporal punishment to

atone for some distraction the evening before ; some pecca-
dillo.

" That stroke of the beak must have pinched him horribly,
for the tears came into his eyes. How could he expose
himself with joy to such a bite ? "

And he remembered that one day at the office of None,
one of the young monks made a mistake in the tone of an
antiphon ; at the moment that the office ended, he knelt
before the altar, then he lay his whole length on the tiles on
his face, his mouth pressed on the ground, till the stroke of
the prior's bell gave him the order to get up.

This was a voluntary punishment for a negligence committed, a forgetfulness. Who knows whether Father
Etienne did not in his turn punish himself for a thought he
deemed to border on sin, in getting himself thus pinched ?

He consulted the oblate on the point in the evening, but
M. Bruno contented himself with a smile, without answering.

And when Durtal spoke to him of his speedy departure
for Paris, the old man shook his head.

" Considering," he said, " the fear and the discomfort that
Communion caused you, you would act wisely if you approach the Holy Table immediately on your return."

And seeing that Durtal did not reply, but hung his
head,

" Believe a man who has known these trials ; if you do
not force yourself while you are still under the warm impression of La Trappe, you will float between desire and
regret without advancing ; you will be ingenious in discovering excuses for not making your confession ; you will try
to think it impossible to find in Paris an abbé who understands you. Now allow me to assure you nothing is more
false. If you desire an expert and easy confidant, go to the
Jesuits ; if you wish above all a zealous-souled priest, go to
St. Sulpice.

" You will find there honest and intelligent ecclesiastics,
excellent hearts. In Paris, where the clergy of the parishes
are so mixed, they are at the top of the basket of the priesthood, and, as may be imagined, they form a community, live
in cells, do not dine out ; and as the Sulpician rule forbids
them to aspire to honours, or places, they do not run the
chance of becoming bad priests by ambition. Do you know
them ? "

" No ; but to resolve that question, which in fact constantly troubles me, I count on a priest whom I often see, on the very man who, in fact, sent me into this Trappist monastery.

" And that," he went on, " makes me remember," and he rose to go to Compline, " that I have as yet forgotten to write to him. It is true that now it is too late, I should arrive at his house almost as soon as my letter. It is strange, but by force of walking in one's own, by force of living to oneself, the days run by, and there is no time to do anything here ! "

CHAPTER VIII.

HE had hoped for his last day at La Trappe a morning of quiet, when his mind might lounge, a mixture of spiritual siesta and of working, charmed by a round of offices, and not at all that the idea persistent and obstinate that he must quit the monastery next day, would spoil all the pleasures he had promised himself.

Now that he had no longer to cleanse himself, and pass under the winnowing of confession, to present himself for the Communion in the morning, he remained irresolute, not knowing any longer how to occupy his time, terrified by the recommencement of that life of the world which would upset all the barriers of forgetfulness, and would get at him at once above all the broken defences of the cloister.

Like a captured animal, he began to rub against the bars of his cage, made the tour of the enclosure, filling his sight with those places where he had tasted hours so kindly and so cruel.

He felt in himself a shaking of the ground, a disturbance of soul, an absolute discouragement before the prospect of re-entering into his habitual existence, of mixing himself anew with the coming and going of men, and he experienced at the same time a great fatigue of brain.

He dragged himself along the walks in a state of complete discomfort, in one of those attacks of religious spleen which determine, while they last during years, the "tædium vitæ" of the cloisters. He had a horror of any life but this, and the soul overwrought by prayers was failing in a body insufficiently rested and ill-nourished ; it had no further desire, asked only to be let alone, to sleep, to fall into one of those states of torpor in which everything becomes indifferent, in which one ends by losing consciousness gently, by being stifled without suffering.

He might well, to re-act on him as a consolation, promise himself to assist in Paris at the offices of the Benedictine nuns, that he would keep himself on the outskirts of society, to himself; and he was at once obliged to answer that these subterfuges are impossible, that the very movement of the town is against all decoys, that isolation in a chamber is in no degree like the solitude of a cell, that masses celebrated in a chapel open to the public cannot be likened to the private Offices of the Trappists.

Then what is the good of trying to misunderstand? It is with the soul as with the body, which is better on the sea shore, or in the mountains, than shut up in a town. There is a better spiritual air even at Paris, in certain religious quarters of the left bank, than in the districts situated on the other bank, more lively in certain churches, more pure, for example, at Notre Dame des Victoires than in churches such as La Trinité and the Madeleine.

But the monastery was, as it were, the true shore and high plateau of the soul. There the atmosphere was balsamic, strength returned, lost appetite for God was there recovered, there was health succeeding weakness, a regimen, fortified and sustained, instead of languor and the restricted exercises of the towns.

The conviction that no trickery was possible to him at Paris brought him to the ground. He wandered from cell to chapel, from chapel to woods, awaiting the dinner hour with impatience, in order to be able to speak to someone, for in his disorder a new need arose. For more than a week he had spent the whole afternoon without opening his lips; he did not suffer from it, was even satisfied with his silence, but since he was pressed by this idea of departure he could not keep silence any longer, thought aloud in the walks to assuage the sensations of his swelling heart, that stifled him.

M. Bruno was too sagacious not to guess the uneasiness of his companion, who became by turns taciturn and over talkative during the meal. He made, however, as though he saw nothing, but after he had said grace he disappeared, and Durtal, who was strolling near the great pond, was surprised to see him coming in his direction with Father Etienne.

They greeted him, and the Trappist with a smile pro-

posed to him, if he had made no other plan, to pass his
time in visiting the convent, and especially the library, which
the Father prior would be delighted to show him.

"If convenient to me! I shall be delighted!" cried
Durtal.

All three returned towards the abbey; the monk lifted
the latch of a little door fashioned in a wall near the church,
and Durtal entered a minute cemetery, planted with
wooden crosses on grass graves.

There was no inscription, no flower in this enclosure
which they traversed; the monk pushed another door,
which opened on a long corridor smelling of rats.   At the
end of this gallery, Durtal recognized the staircase he had
ascended one morning for his confession in the prior's room.
They left it on their right, turned into another gallery, and
the guest-master led them into an immense hall, pierced by
high windows, decorated with eighteenth century pier-glasses,
and *grisailles;* it was furnished only with benches and
stalls, above which was a single chair sculptured and
painted with abbatial arms, which marked the place of
Dom Anselm.

"Oh! this chapter-house has nothing monastic," said
Father Etienne, designating the profane pictures on the
walls; "we have kept just as it was the drawing-room of
this old chateau, but I beg you to believe that this decoration hardly pleases us."

"And what takes place in this hall?"

"Well, we meet here after mass; the chapter opens by
reading the martyrology, followed by the concluding prayers
of Prime.   Then we read a passage from the rule, and the
Father abbot comments on it.   Lastly, we practise the
exercise of humility, that is to say, that whoever among us
has committed any fault against the rule, prostrates himself,
and avows it before his brethren."

They went thence to the refectory.   This room had also
a high ceiling, but was smaller, and garnished with tables
in form of a horse-shoe.   A kind of large cruets, each
containing two half-bottles of wine and water, separated by
a water bottle, and before them, instead of glasses, cups of
brown earthenware, with two handles, were placed at equal
distances.   The monk explained that these sham cruets
with three branches indicated the place of two covers, each

monk having a right to his half bottle of drink, and partaking with his neighbour the water in the bottle.

"This pulpit," said Father Etienne, pointing out a large wooden box fixed against the wall, "is destined for the reader of the week, the father who reads during the meal."

"How long does the meal last ? "

"Just half an hour."

"Yes ; and the cookery which we eat is delicate in comparison with that which is served to the monks," said the oblate.

"I should lie if I were to affirm that we make good cheer," answered the guest-master. "Do you know that the hardest thing to bear, in the earlier time especially, is the want of seasoning in our dishes. Pepper and spices are forbidden by our rule, and as no salt-cellar has place on our table, we swallow our food just as it is, and it is for the most part scarcely salted.

"On certain days in summer, when one sweats in big drops, this becomes almost impossible, the gorge rises. Yet one must begin upon this warm paste, and at least swallow a sufficient quantity not to give out before the next day ; we look at each other discouraged, unable to get any further ; there is not another word to define our dinner in the month of August, it is a punishment."

"And all, the Father abbot, the prior, the fathers, the brethren, have the same food ? "

"All. Now come and see the dormitory."

They ascended to the first floor. An immense corridor, furnished like a stable with wooden boxes, extended before them, closed at each end by a door.

"This is our lodging," said the monk, as he stopped before one of these cases. Cards were placed on them, affixing the name of each monk, and the first bore a ticket with this inscription : "The Father Abbot."

Durtal felt the bed against one of the two walls.

It was as rough as a carding comb, and as biting as a file. It was composed of a simple quilted paillasse extended on a plank ; no sheets, but a prison coverlet of grey wool, a sack of straw instead of pillows.

"God ! it is very hard," said Durtal, and the monk laughed.

"Our habits soften the roughness of this straw mattress,"

he said ; "for our rule does not allow us to undress, we may
only take off our shoes, therefore we sleep entirely clad, our
head wrapped in our hood."

" And it must be cold in this corridor swept by all the
winds," added Durtal.

" No doubt the winter is rough here, but it is not that
season which alarms us ; we live pretty well, even without
fire in time of frost, but the summer—! If you knew what
it is to wake in habits still steeped in sweat, not dried since
the evening before, it is terrible !

" Then, though because of the great heat we have often
hardly slept, we must before dawn jump out of bed, and
begin at once the great night office, the Vigils, which
last at least two hours. Even after twenty years of
Trappist life, one cannot but suffer at that getting up ; in
chapel you fight against sleep which crushes you, you sleep
while you hear a verse chanted, you strive to keep awake,
in order to be able to chant another, and fall asleep again.

" One ought to be able to turn the key on thought, and
one is incapable of it.

"Truly, I assure you that even beyond the corporal
fatigue which explains that state in the morning, there is
then an aggression of the demon, an incessant temptation to
make us recite the office badly."

" And you all undergo this strife ? "

" All ; and this does not hinder," concluded the monk,
whose face was radiant, "this does not hinder us from being
very happy here.

" Because all these trials are nothing beside the deep and
intimate joys which our good God gives us. Ah ! He is a
generous Master ; he pays us a hundred-fold for our poor
sorrows."

As they spoke, they had passed through the corridor and
had arrived at its other end.

The monk opened the door, and Durtal was astounded
to find himself in a vestibule just opposite his own cell.

"I did not think," he said, "that I was living so near
you."

"This house is a regular labyrinth—but M. Bruno will
take you to the library where the Father prior is waiting for
you ; for I must go to my business. We shall meet
presently," he said, with a smile.

The library was situated on the other side of the staircase by which Durtal reached his chamber. It was large, furnished with shelves from top to bottom, occupied in the middle by a sort of counter table on which also were spread rows of books.

Father Maximin said to Durtal,

"We are not very rich, but at any rate we possess tools for work fairly complete on theology and the monography of the cloisters."

"You have superb volumes," cried Durtal, who looked at magnificent folios in splendid bindings with armorial bearings.

"Wait ; here are the works of Saint Bernard in a fine edition," and the monk presented to Durtal enormous volumes, printed in heavy letters on crackling paper.

"When I think that I promised myself to make acquaintance with Saint Bernard in this very abbey which he founded, and here I am on the eve of my departure, and have read nothing ! "

"You do not know his works ? "

"Yes ; scattered fragments of his sermons and of his letters. I have run through some *selectæ mediocres* of his works, but that is all."

"He is our chief master here ; but he is not the only one of our ancestors in Saint Benedict whom the convent possesses," said the monk with a certain pride. "See," and he pointed out on the shelves some heavy folios, "here : ' Saint Gregory the Great,' ' Venerable Bede,' ' Saint Peter Damian,' ' Saint Anselm.' . . . And your friends are there," he said, following Durtal with a glance as he read the titles of the volumes, "' Saint Teresa,' ' Saint John of the Cross,' ' Saint Magdalen of Pazzi,' 'Saint Angela,' ' Tauler,' . . . and she who like Sister Emmerich dictated her conversations with Jesus during her ecstasy." And the prior took from the range of books in octavo, "The Dialogues of Saint Catherine of Siena."

"That Dominican nun is terrible for the priests of her time," the monk went on. "She insists on their misdeeds, reproaches them roundly with selling the Holy Spirit, with practising sortilege, and with using the Sacrament to compose evil charms."

"And there are besides the disorderly vices of which she

accuses them in the series concerning the sin of the flesh,"
added the oblate.

"Certainly, she does not mince her words, but she had
the right to take up that tone, aad menace in the name of
the Lord, for she was truly inspired by Him. Her doctrine
was drawn from divine sources. 'Doctrina ejus infusa non
acquisita,' says the Church in the bull of her canonization.
Her Dialogues are admirable ; the pages in which God exposes
the holy frauds which He sometimes uses to recall men to
good, the passages in which she treats of the monastic life,
of that barque which possesses three ropes : chastity,
obedience, and poverty, and which faces the tempest
under the conduct of the Holy Spirit, are delightful. She
reveals herself in her work the pupil of the well-beloved
disciple and of Saint Thomas Aquinas. One might believe
that one heard the Angel of the School paraphrasing the
last of the Evangelists."

"Yes," said the oblate, striking in, " if Saint Catherine of
Siena does not give herself to the high speculations of
Mysticism ; if she does not analyze like Saint Teresa the
mysteries of divine love, nor trace the itinerary of souls
destined to the perfect life, she reflects directly at least
the conversations of Heaven. She calls, she loves ! You
have read, sir, her treatises on Discretion and Prayer ? "

"No. I have read Saint Catherine of Genoa, but the
books of Saint Catherine of Siena have never fallen into my
hands."

"And what do you think of this collection ? "

Durtal looked at the title, and made a face.

"I see that Suso hardly delights you."

"I should tell a lie if I assured you that the dissertations
of this Dominican pleased me. First, however illuminated
the man may be, he does not attract me. Without speaking
of the frenzy of his penances, what scrupulousness of devotion
and narrowness of piety was his ! Think that he could not
decide on drinking till he had first, as a preliminary, divided
his beverage into five parts. He thought thus to honour
the five wounds of the Saviour, and, moreover, he swallowed
his last mouthful in two gulps to call up before himself the
water and the blood which flowed from the side of the
Word.

"No ! these sort of things would never enter into my

head ; I would never admit that such practices would glorify Christ.

"And remark well that this love of pounding things small, this passion for small blessings, is found in all his work. His God is so difficult to content, so scrupulous, so meddling, that no one would ever get to heaven if they believed what he said. This God of his is the fault-finder of eternity, the miser of paradise.

"On the whole, Suso expands himself in impetuous discourses on trifles ; then what with his insipid allegories, his morose 'Colloquy on the Nine Rocks' knocks me down."

"You will, however, admit that his study on the Union of the Soul is substantial, and that the 'Office of the Eternal Wisdom' which he composed is worth reading ? "

"I cannot say, Father, I do not now remember that Office ; but I recollect tolerably well the treatise on 'Union with God,' it seems to me more interesting than the rest, but you will admit that it is very short . . . and then Saint Teresa has also elucidated that question of human renunciation and divine fruition ; and, hang it then . . . ! "

"Come," said the oblate, with a smile, "I give up the attempt to make you a fervent reader of the good Suso."

"For us," said Father Maximin, " if we had a little time to work, this ought to be the leaven of our meditations, the subject of our reading ; " and he took down a folio which contained the works of Saint Hildegarde, abbess of the Convent of Rupertsberg.

"She, you see, is the great prophetess of the New Testament. Never, since the visions of Saint John at Patmos, has the Holy Spirit communicated to an earthly being with such fulness and light. In her 'Heptachronon' she predicts Protestantism and the captivity of the Vatican ; in her 'Scivias, or Knowledge of the Ways of the Lord,' which was edited, according to her recital, by a monk of the Convent of Saint Désibode, she interprets the symbols of the Scriptures, and even the nature of the elements. She also wrote a diligent commentary on our rules and enthusiastic pages on sacred music, on literature, on art, which she defines admirably ; a reminiscence, half-effaced, of a primitive condition from which we have fallen since Eden. Unfortunately, to understand her, it is necessary to give oneself to minute researches and patient studies. Her apocalyptic style has something retractile, which retreats and shuts itself up all the more when one will open it."

"I am well aware that I am losing my little Latin," said M. Bruno. "What a pity there is not a translation of her works, with glosses to help."

"They are untranslatable," said the father, who went on,

"Saint Hildegarde is, with Saint Bernard, one of the purest glories of the family of Saint Benedict. How predestinate was that virgin, who was inundated with interior light at the age of three, and died at eighty-two, having lived all her life in the cloister ! "

"And add that she was as a permanent state, prophetical!" cried the oblate. "She is like no other woman saint ; all in her is astonishing, even the way in which God addresses her, for He forgets that she is a woman, and calls her ' man.'

"And she," added the prior, "employs, when she wishes to designate herself, the singular expression, ' the paltry form.' But here is another writer who is dear to us," and he showed Durtal the two volumes of Saint Gertrude. "She is again one of our great nuns, an abbess truly Benedictine, in the exact sense of the word, for she caused the Holy Scriptures to be explained to her nuns, wished that the piety of her daughters should be based on science, that this faith should be sustained by liturgical food, if I may say so."

"I know nothing of her but her ' Exercises,'" observed Durtal, "and they have left with me the memory of echoed words, of things said again from the sacred books. So far as one may judge from simple extracts, she does not appear to have original expression, and to be far below Saint Teresa or Saint Angela."

"No doubt," answered the monk. "But she comes near Saint Angela by the gift of familiarity when she converses with Christ, and also by the loving vehemence of what she says ; only all this is transformed on leaving its proper source ; she thinks liturgically ; and this is so true, that the least of her reflections at once presents itself to her clothed in the language of the Gospels and the Psalms.

"Her ' Revelations,' her ' Insinuations,' her ' Herald of Divine Love,' are marvellous from this point of view ; and then her prayer to the Blessed Virgin is exquisite which opens with this phrase : 'Hail, O white lily of the Trinity, resplendent, and always at rest. . . .'

" As a continuation of her works, the Benedictine Fathers of Solesmes have edited also the 'Revelations' of Saint Mechtilde, her book on 'Special Grace,' and her 'Light of the Divinity' ; they are there on that shelf. . . ."

" Let me show you," said in his turn M. Bruno, " guides wisely marked out for the soul which escapes from itself, and will attempt to climb the eternal mountains," and he handed to Durtal the "Lucerna Mystica" of Lopez Ezquerra, the quartos of Scaramelli, the volumes of Schram, the "Christian Asceticism" of Ribet, the "Principles of Mystic Theology" of Father Seraphin.

" And do you know this ? " continued the oblate ; the volume he offered was called " On Prayer," was anonymous, and bore at the bottom of its first page " Solesmes, printed at the Abbey of Saint Cecilia," and above the printed date, 1886, Durtal made out the word written in ink, " Confidential."

" I have never seen this little book, which seems moreover to have never been brought into the market. Who is the author ? "

" The most extraordinary nun of our time, the abbess of the Benedictine nuns at Solesmes. I regret only that you are going so soon, for I should have been happy to let you read it.

" As far as the document is concerned, it is of a most extraordinary science, and it contains admirable quotations from Saint Hildegarde and Cassien : as far as Mysticism is concerned, Mother Saint Cecilia evidently only reproduces the works of her predecessors, and she tells us nothing very new. Nevertheless, I remember a passage which seems to me more special, more personal. Wait. . . . "

And the oblate turned over a few pages. " Here it is :

"' The spiritualized soul does not appear exposed to temptation properly so-called, but by a divine permission it is called upon to conflict with the Demon, spirit against spirit. . . . The contact with the Demon is then perceived on the surface of the soul, under the form of a burn at once spiritual and sensible. . . . If the soul hold good in its union with God, if it be strong, the pain, however sharp, is bearable ; but if the soul commit any slight imperfection, even inwardly, the Demon makes just so much way, and carries his horrible burning more forward, until by generous acts the soul can repulse him further."

"This touch of Satan, which produces an almost material effect on the most intangible parts of our being, is, you will admit, at least curious," concluded the oblate, as he closed the volume.

"Mother Saint Cecilia is a remarkable strategist of the soul," said the prior, "but . . . but . . . this work, which she edited for the daughters of her abbey, contains, I think, some rash propositions which have not been read without displeasure at Rome."

"To have done with our poor treasures," he continued, "we have only on this side," and he pointed out a portion of the book-cases which covered the room, "long-winded works, the 'Cistercian Menology,' 'Migné's Patrology,' dictionaries of the lives of the saints, manuals of sacred interpretation, canon law, Christian apology, Biblical exegesis, the complete works of Saint Thomas, tools of work which we rarely employ, for as you know we are a branch of the Benedictine trunk vowed to a life of bodily labour and penance ; we are men of sorrow for God, above all things. Here is M. Bruno, who uses these books ; so do I at times, for I have special charge of spiritual matters in this monastery," added the monk with a smile.

Durtal looked at him ; he handled the volumes with caressing hands, brooded over them with the blue lustre of his eye, laughed with the joy of a child as he turned their pages.

"What a difference between this monk who evidently adores his books, and the prior with his imperious profile and silent lips who heard his confession the second day ; " then thinking of all these Trappists, the severity of their countenances, the joy of their eyes, Durtal said to himself that these Cistercians were not at all as the world believed, solemn and funereal people, but that, quite the contrary, they were the gayest of men.

"Now," said Father Maximin, "the reverend Father abbot has charged me with a commission ; knowing that you will leave us to-morrow, he is anxious, now that he is better, to pass at least some minutes with you. He will be free this evening : will it trouble you to join him after Compline ? "

"Not at all ; I shall be glad to talk with Dom Anselm."

"That is understood, then."

They went downstairs. Durtal thanked the prior, who re-entered the enclosure of the corridors, and the oblate, who went up to his cell. He trifled about, and in spite of the torment of his departure, which haunted him, reached the evening without too much trouble.

The "Salve Regina," which he heard perhaps for the last time thus sung by male voices ; that airy chapel built of sound, and evaporating with the close of the antiphon, in the smoke of the tapers, stirred him to the bottom of his soul ; the Trappist monastery showed itself truly charming this evening. After the office, they said the Rosary, not as at Paris, where they recite a Pater, ten Aves, and a Gloria, and so over again ; here they said in Latin a Pater, an Ave, a Gloria, and began again till in that manner they had finished several decades.

This rosary was said on their knees, half by the prior, half by all the monks. It went at so rapid a pace that it was scarcely possible to distinguish the words, but as soon as it was ended, at a signal there was a great silence, and each one prayed with his head in his hands.

And Durtal took notice of the ingenious system of conventual prayers : after the prayers purely vocal like these, came mental prayer, personal petitions, stimulated and set a-going by the very machine of paternosters.

"Nothing is left to chance in religion ; every exercise which seems at first useless has a reason for its being," he said to himself, as he went out into the court. "And the fact is, that the rosary, which seems to be only a humming-top of sounds, fulfils an end. It reposes the soul wearied with the supplications which it has recited, applying itself to them, thinking of them ; it hinders it from babbling and reciting to God always the same petitions, the same complaints ; it allows it to take breath, to take rest, in prayers in which it can dispense with reflection, and, in fact, the rosary occupies in prayer, those hours of fatigue in which one would not pray. . . . Ah ! here is the Father abbot."

The Trappist expressed to him his regret at visiting him only thus for a few moments ; then after he had answered Durtal, who inquired after the state of his health, which he hoped was at last re-established, he proposed to

him to walk in the garden, and begged him not to incon-
venience himself by not smoking cigarettes if he had a mind
to do so.

And the conversation turned on Paris. Dom Anselm
asked for some information, and ended by saying with a smile,
" I see by scraps of newspapers which come to me, that society
just now is infected with socialism. Everyone wishes to
solve the famous social question. How does that get on ? "

" How does that get on ? Why, not at all ! Unless you
can change the souls of workmen and masters, and make
them disinterested and charitable between to-day and
to-morrow, in what can you expect these systems to end ? "

" Well," said the monk, enwrapping the monastery with a
gesture, " the question is solved here.

" As wages do not exist, all sources of conflicts are
suppressed.

" As every task is according to aptitudes and powers,
the fathers who are not strong-shouldered and big-armed
fold the packages of chocolate, or make out the bills, and
those who are robust dig the ground.

" I add that the equality in our cloisters is such that the
prior and the abbot have no advantage over the other monks.
At table the portions, and in the dormitory the paillasses, are
identical. The sole profits of the abbot consist on the whole
in the inevitable cares arising from the moral conduct and
the temporal administration of an abbey. There is therefore no reason why the workmen of a convent should go on
strike," concluded the abbot with a smile.

" Yes, but you are minimists, you suppress the family and
woman, you live on nothing, and expect the only real
recompense for your labours after death. How can you
make the people in the towns understand that ? "

" The social system may thus be summed up, as I think :
the masters wish to profit by the workmen, who in their
turn desire to be paid as much as possible for as little work
as possible. Well, then, there is no way out of that."

" Exactly, and there is the sad part of it, for socialism in
fact arises from kindly ideas, just ideas, and will always run
up against egotism and gain, against the inevitable breakers
of the sins of man.

" And your little chocolate factory gives you at least some
income ? "

" Yes ; that saves us."

The abbot was silent for a second ; then he went on,

" You know, sir, how a convent is founded. I take for
example our Order. A domain and the lands about it are
offered the Order on condition that it peoples them.
The Order takes a handful of its monks, and settles them
as a swarm on the soil given to it. There its task stops.
The grain must spring up of itself, or to put it differently,
the Trappists, severed from their mother-house, must gain
their livelihood, and suffice for themselves.

" So when we took possession of these buildings we were
so poor, that from bread to shoes everything was lacking ;
but we had no anxiety for the future, for there is no
example in monastic history that Providence has not
succoured abbeys who trusted in it. Little by little we
drew our food from the estate, and we learnt useful trades ;
now we make our habits and our shoes ; we reap our
wheat and make our bread ; our material existence is therefore assured, but the taxes crush us ; therefore we have
founded this factory, of which the report becomes better
from year to year.

" In a year or two the building which shelters us, and for
want of money we have been unable to repair, will tumble
down, but if God then allows generous souls to come to
our aid, perhaps we shall be in a condition to build a
monastery, which is the wish of all of us ; for indeed this
hovel with its rooms in confusion, and its rotunda-chapel,
is painful to us."

The abbot was silent again, then after a pause he said in
a low voice, speaking to himself,

" It cannot be denied, a convent which has not the look
of a cloister is an obstacle to vocations ; the postulant has
need—and this is quite natural—to mould himself in
surroundings which please him, to encourage himself in a
church which wraps him round, in a somewhat sombre
chapel ; and to obtain that result you want the Romanesque
or Gothic style."

" Ah, yes, indeed. And have you many novices ? "

" We have especially many subjects who desire to feel the
life of Trappists, but the greater part do not succeed in
supporting our way of life. Beside even the question of
knowing whether the vocation of the beginners is imaginary

or real, we are from the physical point of view clearly fixed
after a fortnight's trial."

" Eating vegetables only must crush the most robust
constitutions ; I do not even understand how, leading an
active life, you can bear it."

" The truth is that bodies obey where souls are resolute.
Our ancestors endured the life of the Trappists very well.
We want souls at the present day. I remember that when
I made my probation in a Cistercian cloister I had no health,
and yet had it been necessary I would have eaten stones !

" Moreover, the rule will soon be softened," pursued the
abbot ; " but in any case there is a country which, if there
should be scarcity, assures us a good number of recruits,
Holland."

And seeing Durtal's look of astonishment, the father
said,

" Yes, in that Protestant country mystic vegetation is
flourishing. Catholicism is all the more fervent that it is,
if not persecuted, at least despised, drowned in the mass of
Calvinists. Perhaps this belongs also to the nature of the
soil, to its solitary plains, its silent canals, to the very taste
of the Dutch for a regular and peaceable life ; but in that
little knot of Catholics the Cistercian vocation is always very
common."

Durtal looked at the Trappist as he walked majestic and
quiet, his head buried in his hood, his hands passed under
his cincture.

From time to time his eyes grew bright inside his hood,
and the amethyst which he wore on his finger sparkled in
brief flames.

No sound was heard ; at this hour the monastery was
asleep. Durtal and the abbot were walking on the banks
of the great pond, where the water was alive, it alone
wakeful in the slumber of the woods, for the moon, which
shone in a cloudless sky, sowed a myriad of goldfish, and
this luminous spawn, fallen from the planet, mounted,
descended, sparkled in a thousand little points of fire, of
which the wind as it blew increased the brightness.

The abbot spoke no longer, and Durtal, who was
thinking, intoxicated by the sweetness of the night, groaned
suddenly. He had just considered that at this same hour
the next day he would be at Paris, and seeing the monastery,

whose pale front appeared at the end of a walk as at the
end of a dark tunnel, he cried, thinking of all the monks who
inhabited it,

"Ah! they are happy!"

And the abbot answered, "Too happy."

Then gently, in a low voice,

"Yes, it is true we enter here to do penance, to mortify
ourselves, and we have hardly begun to suffer when God
consoles us. He is so good that He Himself wishes to
deceive Himself about our merits. If at certain moments He
allows the Demon to persecute us, He gives us in exchange
so much happiness that there is no proportion preserved
between the recompense and the sorrow. Sometimes when I
think of it, I ask myself how there still subsists that equilibrium that nuns and monks are charged to maintain, since
neither of us suffer enough to neutralize the repeated sins
of towns?"

The abbot stopped, and then went on pensively,

"The world does not even conceive that the austerity
of the abbeys can profit it. The doctrine of mystical
compensation escapes it entirely. It cannot represent to
itself that the substitution of the innocent for the guilty
is necessary when to suffer merited punishment is
concerned. Nor does it explain to itself any more that in
wishing to suffer for others, monks turn aside the wrath of
heaven, and establish a solidarity in the good which is a
counter-weight against the federation of evil. God knows,
moreover, with what cataclysms the unconscious world
would be menaced, if in consequence of a sudden dis-
appearance of all the cloisters, the equilibrium which saves
it were broken."

"The case has already presented itself," said Durtal, who
while listening to the Trappist thought of the Abbé
Gévresin, and remembered how that priest had expressed
himself on the same subject in nearly similar terms. "The
Revolution, in fact, suppressed all convents with one stroke
of a pen, but I think that the history of that time when so
many hucksters were busy is still to be written. Instead of
searching for documents on the acts, and even on the
persons of the Jacobins, the archives of the religious orders
which existed at that time should be ransacked.

"In working thus at the side of the Revolution, in sound-
ing its neighbourhood, its foundations will be exhumed.

Its causes will be brought to the surface, and it will certainly be discovered that in proportion to the suppression of convents, monstrous excesses had birth. Who knows if the demoniacal madness of Carrier or Marat do not accord with the death of an abbey whose sanctity preserved France for years."

"To be just," answered the abbot, "it is right to say that the Revolution destroyed ruins only. The rule of *in commendam* ended by giving the monasteries over to Satan. It was they, alas! that by the relaxation of their morals, inclined the balance, and drew down the lightning on the land.

"The Terror was only a consequence of their impiety. God, whom nothing longer withheld, let things take their course."

"Yes; but how can you now prove the necessity of compensations to a world which wanders out of the way in continued accesses of gain; how persuade it that it is an urgent need, as a preventive against new crises, to shelter towns behind the sacred bulwarks of cloisters?

"After the siege of 1870, Paris was wisely sheltered behind an immense net of impregnable forts; but is it not also indispensable to surround it with a cincture of prayers, to buttress its neighbourhood with conventual houses, to build everywhere in its suburbs convents of Poor Clares, Carmelites, Benedictine nuns of the Blessed Sacrament, monasteries which will be in some degree powerful citadels, destined to arrest the forward march of the armies of evil?

"Certainly the towns have great need of being guaranteed against infernal invasions by a sanitary defence of Orders. . . . But come, sir, I must not deprive you of necessary rest, I will join you to-morrow, before you quit our solitude. I have now but to say that you have only friends here, and that you will be always welcome. I hope that on your side you will keep no unfavourable memory of our poor hospitality, and that you will prove it in coming to see us again."

As they talked they had come in front of the guest-house.

The father pressed Durtal's hands, and slowly ascended the stairs, sweeping with his robe the silver dust of the steps, as he mounted, all white, in a ray of the moon.

CHAPTER IX.

Durtal wished immediately after Mass to visit for the last time that wood through which he had walked, in turn so languidly and so rapidly. He went at first to the old lime alley, whose pale emanations were verily for his spirit what an infusion of their leaves is for the body, a sort of very weak panacea, a kindly and soothing sedative.

Then he sat down in their shade on a stone bench. As he leant forward a little he could see through the moving spaces in the branches, the solemn front of the abbey, and opposite it, separated by the kitchen garden, the gigantic cross standing before that liquid plan of a church which the pond simulated.

He rose, and approached the watery cross, of which the sky turned the marble water blue, and he contemplated the great crucifix in white marble, which towered above the whole monastery, and seemed to rise opposite to it as a permanent reminder of the vows of suffering which he had accepted, and reserved to himself to change at length into joys.

"The fact is," said Durtal, who thought over again the contradictory declarations of the monks, confessing that they led at once the most attractive and the most atrocious life ; "the fact is that the good God deceives them. They attain here below Paradise, while they seek hell there. I have myself tasted how strange is existence in this cloister, for I have been here, almost at the same time, very unhappy and very happy ; and now I feel well the mirage which is already beginning : before two days are over the remembrance of the sorrows which then were, if I recall them with care, greatly above the joys, will have disappeared, and I shall only recall those interior emotions in the chapel, those delicious stolen moments in the morning in the pathways of the park.

" I shall regret the open-air prison of this convent. It is curious I find myself attached to it by obscure bonds ; when I am in my cell, there return to me all kinds of memories, like those of an ancient race. I find myself at once at home again, in a place I had never seen ; I recognize from the first moment a very special life, of which nevertheless I know nothing. It seems to me that something which interests me, which is indeed personal to me, passed here before I was born. Truly, if I believed in metempsychosis I might imagine I had been a monk in anterior existences ; a bad monk then," he said, smiling at his reflections, " since I should have been obliged to be reincarnate and to return to a cloister to expiate my sins."

While thus talking with himself, he had passed across a long alley which led to the end of the enclosure, and, cutting across the road, and through the thickets, he strayed into the wood of the great pond.

It was not in motion, as on certain days when the wind made hollows in it, and swelled it, made it flow and return on itself as soon as it touched its banks. It remained immovable, and was only stirred by the reflections of the moving clouds and of the trees. At moments a leaf fallen from the neighbouring poplars swam on the image of a cloud, at others bubbles of air came from the bottom and burst on the surface in the reflected blue of heaven.

Durtal looked for the otter, but it did not show itself ; he saw only the swallows which skimmed the water with their wing, the dragon-flies which sparkled like jewels, flashing like the blue flames of sulphur.

If he had suffered near the cross-pond, before the sheet of water of the other pond he could only call up the memory of healing hours, which he had passed lying on a bed of moss, or a couch of dry reeds, and he looked at it tenderly, trying to fix and carry it away in his memory to re-live again in Paris, shutting his eyes on the bank.

He pursued his walk, and stopped in an alley of chestnuts along the walls above the monastery ; thence he went into the court in front of the cloister, the outbuildings, the stables, the woodsheds, even the pig-styes. He tried to see Brother Simeon, but he was probably engaged in the stables, for he did not appear. The buildings were silent, the pigs were shut up ; only some lean cats prowled about in silence,

scarcely looking when they met each other, going each on
its own side, no doubt seeking some nourishing game which
would console them for the eternal meals of vegetable soup
served them at the monastery.

Time was getting on ; he prayed for the last time in the
chapel, and went to his cell to get his portmanteau ready.

While putting his things in order he thought of the
inutility of decorated rooms. He had spent all his money
at Paris in buying ornaments and books, for till now he had
detested bare walls.

But now, considering the blank walls of this room, he
admitted to himself that he had done better between these
four white-washed walls than in his room at Paris, hung
with stuffs.

Suddenly he recognized that La Trappe had weaned him
from his preferences, had in a few days completely upset
him. " The power of such an environment ! " he said to
himself, a little alarmed at feeling how he was transformed.
And he thought in buckling his portmanteau, " I must
however, go and find Father Etienne, for I must settle
my account ; I cannot be altogether a debtor to these good
people."

He went along the corridors, and ended by meeting the
father in the court.

He was a little confused how to open the question ; at
the first words the guest-master smiled.

" The rule of Saint Benedict is formal," he said ; " we must
receive our guests as we receive our Lord Jesus Himself,
that is to tell you that we cannot exchange our poor care for
money."

And when Durtal insisted, embarrassed,

" If it does not suit you to have partaken of our meagre
pittance without paying, do as you please ; only the sum
which you may give will be distributed in coins of ten or
twenty sous, to the poor who come each morning, often from
a great distance, to knock at our monastery gate."

Durtal bowed and handed the money, which he had
ready in his pocket, to the father, but he inquired if he
might not have a word with Father Maximin before his
departure.

" Certainly ; moreover, Father prior would not have let
you go without shaking hands with you. I will go and

make certain if he be free. Wait for me in the refectory."
And the monk disappeared, and came back a few minutes
afterwards, preceded by the prior.

" Ah, well," said he, " then you are going to plunge again
into the hurly-burly ? "

" Oh ! without any pleasure, Father."

" I understand that. It is so good, is it not, no longer to
hear anything and to be silent. However, take courage ;
we will pray for you."

And às Durtal thanked both of them for their kind
attentions,

" It is a pleasure to receive a retreatant such as you," cried
Father Etienne, " nothing repulses you, and you are so exact
that you are about before the hour : you rendered my task of
overseer easy. If all were as little exacting and as pliable."

And he admitted that he had given lodging to priests
sent by their bishops as a penance, ecclesiastics of ill-repute
whose complaints about food, lodging, the need of rising
early in the morning, never ceased.

" If, again," said the prior, " one could hope to recall them
to good, to send them back healed to their parishes ; but no,
they go away still more rebellious than before, the Devil
does not let them alone."

During this conversation a lay brother brought in some
dishes covered with plates and placed them on the table.

" We have changed the hour of your dinner, because or
the train," said Father Etienne.

" Good appetite, adieu, and may the Lord bless you,"
said the prior.

He raised his hand, and enwrapped Durtal, with a great
sign of the cross, who knelt surprised at the sudden emotion
in the monk's tone. But Father Maximin recovered himself
at once, and he bowed to him as M. Bruno entered.

The meal was silent ; the oblate was visibly distressed at
the departure of the companion whom he loved, and Durtal
looked with a swelling heart at the old man, who had so
charitably come out of his solitude to give him aid.

" Will you not come some day to see me in Paris ?" he said.

" No. I have quitted life without any mind to return to
it. I am dead to the world. I do not wish to see Paris
again. I have no wish to live again.

" But if God lend me still a few years of existence I hope

to see you here again, for it is not in vain that one has crossed the threshold of mystic asceticism, to verify by one's own experience the reality of the requirements which our Lord brings about. Now, as God does not proceed by chance, He will certainly finish His work by sifting you as wheat. I venture to recommend you to try not to give way, and attempt to die in some measure to yourself, in order not to run counter to His plans."

"I know well," said Durtal, "that all is displaced in me, that I am no longer the same, but what frightens me is that I am now sure that the works of the Teresan school are exact . . . then, then. . . . if one must pass through the cylinders of the rolling mill which Saint John of the Cross describes . . . ."

The noise of a carriage in the court interrupted him. M. Bruno went to the window and looked out.

"Your luggage is down."

"Yes."

They looked at each other.

"Listen ! I would wish indeed to say to you . . . ."

"No, no, do not thank me," cried the oblate. "See, I have never so thoroughly understood the misery of my being. Ah ! if I had been another man, I might, by praying better, have aided you more."

The door opened and Father Etienne declared,

"You have not a minute to lose, if you do not wish to miss the train."

Thus hurried, Durtal had only time to press the hand of his friend, who accompanied him to the court. He found waiting a sort of open wagon driven by a Trappist, who, below a bald head, and cheeks streaked with rose threads, had a great black beard.

Durtal pressed the hands of the guest-master and the oblate for the last time, when the Father abbot came in his turn to wish him a safe journey ; and at the end of the court Durtal perceived two eyes fixed on him, those of Brother Anacletus, who, at a distance, said adieu by a slight bow, but without other gesture.

Even this poor man, whose eloquent look told of a truly touching affection, had a saint's pity for the stranger whom he had seen so tumultuous and so sad in the desolate solitude of the wood !

Certainly the stiffness of the rule forbade all show of feeling to these monks, but Durtal felt thoroughly that for him they had gone to the limit of concessions allowed, and his affliction was great as he cast them in parting a last expression of thanks.

And the door of the monastery closed ; that door at which he had trembled in arriving, and at which he now looked with tears in his eyes.

"We. must get on fast," said the procurator, "for we are late," and the horse went at a great speed along the lanes.

Durtal recognized his companion, as having seen him in the chapel, singing in the choir during the Office.

He had an air at once good-natured and firm, and his little grey eye smiled as it glanced behind his branched spectacles.

"Well," said he, "how have you borne our regimen ? "

"I have had every chance ; I came here with my stomach out of order, my body ill, and the simple Trappist meals have cured me."

And when Durtal narrated briefly the stages of soul he had undergone, the monk murmured,

"That is nothing in regard to demoniacal attacks ; we have had here true cases of possession."

"And Brother Simeon discovered them ! "

"Ah! you know that . . . ." And he replied quite simply to Durtal, who spoke to him of his admiration for the poor lay brothers,

"You are right, sir ; if you could talk with these peasants and illiterate men, you would be surprised at the often profound answers which these people give you ; then they alone at the monastery are really courageous ; we, the Fathers, when we think ourselves too weak, accept willingly the authorized addition of an egg ; they never ; they pray more, and it must be admitted that our Lord listens to them, since they get well again, and indeed are never ill.'

And to a question of Durtal who asked him in what consisted the functions of procurator, the monk answered,

"They consist in keeping the accounts, in being the commercial agent, in travelling, in managing, alas ! everything which does not concern the life of the cloister ; but we are so few in number at Notre Dame de l'Atre, that we become necessarily Jacks-of-all-trades. For instance, Father Etienne is cellarer of the Abbey and guest-master, he is also sacristan and bell-ringer. I too, am first cantor and professor of plain song."

And while the carriage rolled along, shaken by the ruts, the procurator declared to Durtal, who told him how much the offices chanted at the monastery had delighted him,

" It is not with us that you ought to hear them ; our choirs are too restricted, too weak to be able to raise the giant mass of those chants. You ought to go to the black monks of Solesmes or Ligugé if you wish to find the Gregorian melodies executed as they were in the Middle Ages. By the way, do you know in Paris, the Benedictine nuns in the Rue Monsieur ? "

" Yes ; but do you not think they coo a little ? "

" I cannot say ; all the same their collection of tunes is authentic, but at the little seminary at Versailles, you have better still, since they chant there exactly as at Solesmes ; note this well, moreover, at Paris, when the churches decline to repudiate liturgical music, they use for the most part the false notation printed and spread in abundance in all the dioceses in France by the house of Pustet of Ratisbon."

" But the errors and frauds with which those editions abound are well known."

" The legend on which its partisans rely is incorrect. To assert, as they do, that this version is no other than that of Palestrina who was charged by Pope Paul V. to revive the musical liturgy of the Church, is an argument destitute of truth and void of force, for everyone knows that when Palestrina died, he had hardly begun the correction of the Gradual.

" I will add that even if that musician had finished his work, that would not prove that his interpretation ought to be preferred to that which has been recently constituted after patient researches by the Abbey of Solesmes, for the Benedictine texts are based on the copy preserved at the monastery of St. Gall of the antiphonary of Saint Gregory, which represents the most ancient and the most certain monument which the Church preserves of the true plain chant.

" This manuscript, of which photographic facsimiles exist, is the code of Gregorian melodies, and it ought to be, if I may use the expression, the neumatic Bible of choirs.

" The disciples of Saint Benedict are then absolutely right when they declare that their version alone is faithful, alone correct."

" How then comes it that so many churches get their music from Ratisbon ? "

" Alas, how comes it that Pustet has so long acquired the monopoly of liturgical books, and . . . but no, better hold one's peace . . . take this only for certain, that the German volumes are the absolute negation of the Gregorian tradition, the most complete heresy of plain chant."

" By the way, what time is it ? We must make haste," said the procurator, looking at the watch which Durtal held up to him. " Come up, my beauty," and he whipped up the mare.

" You drive with spirit," cried Durtal.

" It is true ; I forgot to say to you, that over and above my other functions, I also have, if need be, that of coachman."

Durtal thought all the same that these people were extraordinary who lived an interior life in God. As soon as they consented to redescend on earth they revealed themselves as the most sagacious and the boldest of business men. An abbot founded a factory with the few pence he succeeded in gathering ; he discerned the employment which suited each of his monks, and with them he improvised artisans, writing clerks, transformed a professor of plain chant into an agent, plunged into the tumult of purchases and sales, and little by little the house which scarcely was raised above the soil, grew, put forth shoots, and ended by nourishing with its fruit the abbey which had planted it.

Transported into another environment these people would have as easily created great manufactories and started banks. And it was the same with the women. When one thinks of the practical qualities of a man of business, and the coolness of an old diplomatist which a mother abbess ought to possess in order to rule her community, one is obliged to admit that the only women, truly intelligent, truly remarkable are, outside of drawing-rooms, outside of the world, at the head of cloisters.

And as he expressed his wonder aloud, that monks were so expert at setting up business,

"It must be so," sighed the father, "but if you believe that we do not regret the time necessarily spent in digging the ground ! then our spirit at least was free, then we could sanctify ourselves in silence which to a monk is as necessary as bread, for it is thanks to it, that he stifles vanity as it rises, that he represses disobedience as it murmurs, that he turns all his aspirations, all his thoughts towards God, and becomes at last attentive to His présence.

"Instead of that . . . but here we are at the station ; do not trouble yourself about your portmanteau, but go and take your ticket, for I hear the whistle of the train."

And in fact Durtal had only time to shake hands with the father, who put his luggage into the carriage.

There, when he was alone, seated, looking at the monk as he departed, he felt his heart swell, ready to break.

And in the clatter of the rails the train started.

Sharply, clearly, in a minute, Durtal took stock of the frightful disorder into which he had thrown the monastery.

"Ah ! and outside it, all is the same to me, and nothing matters to me," he cried. And he groaned, knowing that he should never more succeed in interesting himself in all that makes the joy of men. The uselessness of caring about any other thing than Mysticism and the liturgy, of thinking about aught else save God, implanted itself in him so firmly that he asked himself what would become of him at Paris with such ideas.

He saw himself submitting to the confusion of controversies, the cowardice of conventionality, the vanity of declarations, the inanity of proofs. He saw himself bruised and thrust aside by the reflections of everybody, obliged henceforward to advance or retire, dispute or hold his tongue ?

In any case peace was for ever lost. How in fact was he to rally and recover when he was obliged to dwell in a place of passage, in a soul open to all winds, visited by a crowd of public thoughts ?

His contempt for relations, his disgust for acquaintances grew on him. "No, everything rather than mix myself again with society," he declared to himself, and then he was silent in despair, for he was not ignorant that he could not, apart from the monastic zone, live in isolation. After a short time

would come weariness and a void, therefore why had he
reserved nothing for himself, why had he trusted all to the
cloister ?   He had not even known how to arrange the
pleasure of entering into himself, he had discovered how to
lose the amusement of bric-à-brac, how to extirpate that
last satisfaction in the white nakedness of a cell ! he no
longer held to anything, but lay dismantled, saying, " I have
renounced almost all the happiness which might fall to
me, and what am I going to put in its place ? "

And terrified, he perceived the disquiet of a conscience
ready to torment itself, the permanent reproaches of an
acquired lukewarmness, the apprehensions of doubts against
Faith, fear of furious clamours of the senses stirred by chance
meetings.

And he repeated to himself that the most difficult thing
would not be to master the emotions of his flesh, but indeed
to live Christianly, to confess, to communicate at Paris, in a
church.   He never could get so far as that, and he imagined
discussions with the Abbé Gévresin, his gaining time, his
refusal, foreseeing that their friendship would come to an end
in these disputes.

Then where should he fly ?   At the very recollection
of the Trappist monastery the theatrical representations
ot St. Sulpice made him jump.   St. Severin seemed to
him distracted and worn.   How could he live among stupid
people like the devout, how listen without gnashing his
teeth to the affected chants of the choirs ?   How, lastly, could
he seek again in the chapel of the Benedictine nuns, and
even at Notre Dame des Victoires, that dull heat
radiating from the souls of the monks, and thawing little by
little the ice of his poor being ?

And then it was not even that.   What was truly crushing,
truly dreadful, was to think that doubtless he would never
again feel that admirable joy which lifts you from the
ground, carries you, you know not where, nor how, above
sense.

Ah, those paths at the monastery wandered in at
daybreak, those paths where one day after a communion,
God had dilated his soul in such a fashion that it seemed
no longer his own, so much had Christ plunged him in the
sea of His divine infinity, swallowed him in the heavenly
firmament of His person.

How renew that state of grace without communion and outside a cloister ? " No ; it is all over," he concluded.

And he was seized with such an access of sadness, such an outburst of despair, that he thought of getting out at the first station, and returning to the monastery ; and he had to shrug his shoulders, for his character was not patient enough nor his will firm enough, nor his body strong enough to support the terrible trials of a noviciate. Moreover, the prospect of having no cell to himself, of sleeping dressed higgledy-piggledy in a dormitory, alarmed him.

But what then ? And sadly he took stock of himself.

" Ah ! " he thought, " I have lived twenty years in ten days in that convent, and I leave it, my brain relaxed, my heart in rags ; I am done for, for ever. Paris and Notre Dame de l'Atre have rejected me each in their turn like a waif, and here I am condemned to live apart, for I am still too much a man of letters to become a monk, and yet I am already too much a monk to remain among men of letters."

He leapt up and was silent, dazzled by jets of electric light which flooded him as the train stopped.

He had returned to Paris.

" If they," he said, thinking of those writers whom it would no doubt be difficult not to see again, " if they knew how inferior they are to the lowest of the lay brothers ! if they could imagine how the divine intoxication of a Trappist swine-herd interests me more than all their conversations and all their books ! Ah ! Lord, that I might live, live in the shadow of the prayers of humble Brother Simeon ! "

THE END.